D0963531

WILD ROSE

WINTER IS PAST

The Making of a Gentleman

RUTH AXTELL MORREN

Steeple Hill®

Published by Steeple Hill Books™

STEEPLE HILL BOOKS

Steeple
Hill®

ISBN-13: 978-0-373-78621-3
ISBN-10:   0-373-78621-2

THE MAKING OF A GENTLEMAN

Copyright © 2008 by Ruth Axtell

For Frances, a modern day "prison lady"
and
Thank you, Allison, for taking this ugly
duckling and helping turn it into a swan…

Let the sighing of the prisoner come before thee; according to the greatness of thy power preserve thou those that are appointed to die.
—*Psalms* 79:11

Chapter One

London, 1812

The hangman's noose swayed gently in the chill winter breeze, the pale Italian hemp stark in the murky light.

No matter how many hangings Florence had attended, the sight of a man—or woman—hanging from the noose caused her a sick feeling in the pit of her stomach. She shifted her gaze from it, although there was nothing to comfort the eye in the rest of the panorama facing her. Newgate Prison's classic stone facade, unrelieved by any windows, stared back at her, its walls as gray as the lowering skies above her.

The February wind bit at her. Shivering, she pulled her cape tighter. Despite the bodies around her, the cold penetrated through to her bones.

Perhaps because she'd eaten nothing since yesterday evening, preferring to spend the time in prayer and fasting for the condemned man.

The crowd pressed against her as new arrivals jockeyed for position. They had been drifting in since last evening when the portable gallows was wheeled in by the team of horses. Two crosslike structures supported a parallel set of bars between them. A lone noose hung from one of these bars, designed to support up to a dozen bodies. But on this rare occasion, only one man would be hanged.

A few guards stood below the platform, bearing pikes or muskets. Florence glanced over at the one nearest her. His unshaven face and slouched stance showed the effects of having stood watch all night.

Though the growing audience swelled, waist-high wooden barriers extending out along the walls of Newgate prevented anyone from getting closer than a few feet from the gallows.

Florence had been attending the hangings for six years now, ever since she'd begun ministering to the inmates of Newgate. She was determined to show them a last friendly face and let them know up to the end that there was somebody praying for their souls. She hoped a glimpse of her would remind them of the verse she'd shared with them at the end, *I am the resurrection, and the life: he that believeth in me, though he were dead, yet shall he live.*

"Last confessions of dying man! Tuppence. Get the true and final confessions of Jonah Quinn!" A man wending a horse with difficulty through the crowd waved a sheaf of printed broadsides, their ink no doubt still damp.

How she hated these executions, where a person's life was made a mockery and the proceedings a theatrical farce. She focused on the empty platform once again. The prisoner wouldn't be brought forth until half past seven. She knew the schedule well.

Lord, break his will. Soften his heart. Don't let him depart with that hardness of heart that prevents him from receiving Your mercy.

The prayer had become a litany to her since last night.

A prayer for Jonah Quinn, a man accused of forgery, one of the dozens of capital offenses codified in the "Bloody Code." It had been a shock to most sitting at the January Sessions that his sentence had not been respited. Nowadays, all but a few of the capital crimes were commuted to transportation. The Recorder of London, principal presiding judge at the Old Bailey, had stared hard under his dark brows so at odds with the white curling wig flowing over his shoulders at the accused as he pronounced the age-old words "hanged by the neck until dead."

The prisoner had remained as unmoving as the granite blocks before Florence now. He'd already stated his last words just prior to the judge's verdict. "God curse you all for hanging an innocent man!"

Florence had seen more than one man go to the gallows defiant, but many more were glad for the message of hope to take with them when all that was left to them was to face their Maker. She was reminded of the two criminals crucified alongside Jesus, the one unrepentant, the other humble and penitent before the Son of God.

Eyes closed, Florence shut her mind to the growing noise of the crowd as she took up her prayer once more. Only the Lord could break through to a man's heart.

"Quinn is an innocent man!" someone in the crowd yelled. A chorus of assent followed.

The shouts from the crowd intensified. The windows in the houses opposite the Old Bailey began filling up with the well-to-do. Many had paid several pounds to secure a seat above the crowd. Florence had heard rumors that even certain members of the House of Lords who had taken an interest in the case were in attendance, but she had no interest in scanning the windows behind her. Today, only one soul concerned her.

"Hats off! Hats off!" The shout of voices around her alerted her that the prisoner was being escorted out and those in the crowd didn't want their view impeded.

The Debtor's door opened and the sheriff came out, holding the prisoner by the arm. The condemned man took one look at the crowd. Instead of being intimidated by the sea of faces, he seemed to grow more defiant. His broad chest swelled out, and his bearded chin thrust forward before the sheriff jerked his arm.

They climbed the short flight of steps onto the gallows. The hangman followed behind them. The ordinary—or prison chaplain—brought up the rear.

It was the first time Florence was seeing Jonah Quinn in the light of day, the small iron grille of his cell door having afforded her few details of his face in the dark condemned man's cell.

Now, a white nightcap covered his shaggy black hair. His thick black beard was due no doubt to the six weeks he'd sat in his solitary cell since his sentencing. Weeks of deprivation in prison had not eroded his formidable build. The breadth of his shoulders reminded her of a prizefighter she'd once seen. As was customary, his wrists were bound in front of him and another rope was tied around his torso at his elbows, pinning his arms to his sides. The shackles had been removed from his ankles in the prison yard. The sheriff and the black-gowned ordinary looked puny beside him.

"A poor man gets no justice!" a second voice shouted from somewhere in the crowd. Others took up the chant, and soon there was a clamor of protests from the street. The guard beside Florence shifted his pike from one hand to the other, muttering curses under this breath.

The ordinary turned to the prisoner and indicated he could kneel to pray, but the prisoner shook his head, looking as unyielding as he had sounded at his trial. *Lord, save him!*

The sheriff signaled to the hangman, who took a step forward and pulled the nightcap down over the prisoner's face. Then he placed the noose around his neck.

A second passed, then at the sheriff's nod, the hangman stepped back and reached for the lever.

At that moment, a man plowed into Florence, throwing her against the wooden barrier and knocking the breath from her.

"For Jonah and for all the poor whose land has been stolen from 'em!" A sudden barrage of shouts came from all sides as men jumped the barrier and surged onto the platform like rats.

Time seemed to slow as Florence watched. Before the hangman could release the trapdoor beneath the prisoner's feet, a rough-looking man jumped him from behind and wrestled him to the ground. Others swarmed around the prisoner and cut him free.

The soldiers rallied, but the erupting mob blocked their attempts to reach the platform.

"Down with the king! Give us bread! Liberty for the people!"

Florence clung to the wooden barrier, terrified she would be crushed by the mob pressing against her.

The prisoner leaped from the platform and in one fluid motion jumped the barricade and landed beside Florence.

The guard raised his pike.

Florence stared at its sharp point, poised above her. The next instant, an arm grabbed her from behind and a cold blade of steel pushed against her neck.

"Anyone comes near and I'll slit 'er throat."

She didn't dare breathe. The guard's eyes flickered to hers. That second's hesitation saved her life. The pike was ripped from his arms by the mob.

Behind her, the crowd parted and the prisoner made his escape, dragging her along with him like a piece of flotsam, the press of bodies closing around them like the incoming tide.

"This way!" shouted a man.

They slipped down a narrow side alley, then along a wider road she recognized as Seacoal Lane. They came out onto Fleet Market, an area packed with vendors. Shouts and commotion followed them as stalls were overturned in their wake.

Quinn veered off the main thoroughfare, his hand clenching her arm in an unyielding grip. Through a covered courtyard and past derelict buildings, the area became grimmer and dirtier. They were going to the rookery of Saffron Hill north of Holborn. *God help her.*

"Come along!" the man—their guide—barked at them. Quinn yanked her forward and she stumbled in the pockmarked path. Here the roads were nothing but muddy tracks and the brick buildings full of boarded-up windows and decay. The stench of human waste was overwhelming.

Their guide seemed to know the area well. The two men leaped across the puddles and ditches while her smaller boots sank and skidded over the slimy ground. Quinn held her fast, giving her no option but to struggle to keep up.

Small secondhand stores and pawnshops lined the streets, fronts for stolen goods no doubt. Dirty children roamed the alleys, their ragged clothes offering little protection against the cold. Equally filthy adults squatted in doorways, often with a bottle in one hand, their stares dull and lifeless.

Though she was gasping for breath, the two men didn't slow their pace, but dashed from twisted alley to alley that bisected the toppling buildings like a rabbit warren. She soon lost track of whether they were headed north, south, east or west. Perspiration trickled down her back, despite the cold air stinging her face.

"Why—why...don't you...let me go...now," she panted.

Quinn threw her a scornful glance. "What, give up my surety? They catch me, you'll go down with me." He waved the knife at her, his teeth flashing an instant before facing forward again, urging her on with another painful jerk to her arm.

Her side hurt and her chest screamed with each breath. Just when she couldn't bear it anymore, he pulled her into a courtyard. She had only a glimpse before she was plunged into a dark stairwell. She stumbled down rickety steps riddled with gaps.

At the bottom, Quinn pushed her ahead of him into a low cellar. She leaned forward, her hands on her knees, panting like a hound after the hunt.

Only as her breathing slowed did she straighten and dare to look around. The two men conferred a few feet away from her. Relief trickled into her when they ignored her. Would she be able to escape them? Her glance went to the wooden door. It stood firmly bolted.

"Ye'll be safe here for now," the disreputable-looking guide told Quinn. "There's some kindling and victuals in the corner. Stay low. After I leave, ye're on yer own. The Boss doesn't want any more involvement." After a few more words, sprinkled liberally with oaths, and a slap on the back at their successful escape, the other man went to the door. He glanced back at Florence over his shoulder as Quinn unbolted it.

"Don't know what ye're going to do about 'er. Mayhap have some fun 'fore ye leave." His coarse laughter rang through the room as he climbed back up the stairs.

The sound of the bolt falling into place made Florence jump. She was truly alone now. She dared a look at her captor, a man who feared nothing and no one, and remembered the other man's words.

Lord, protect me. Show me what to do. Show me Your purpose in bringing me here. Only Scriptures could allay the terror that threatened to paralyze her.

She'd been face-to-face with many criminals

since her work at Newgate, but always there had been a guard within calling distance, or an iron grating separating her.

She was not alone, she reminded herself. The Angel of the Lord encamped round about her. If the Lord had allowed the events of the past hour, it must mean He had heard her prayer for mercy for this man's soul. The realization gave her courage.

Instead of approaching her, Quinn knelt down, his back to her. In the shadows, she heard him strike a flint and then saw a flash of light which soon grew into a flame as it caught the dry tinder.

Her glance strayed to the rest of the space. The cellar's stone walls dripped with dampness. Light from the outside showed through a small, boarded-up window at street level. Above them, wooden planks, dark with age, formed a low ceiling, with gaps here and there where the wood had rotted through. The floor beneath her feet was hard-packed dirt with moldy straw piled along the edges and a few rumpled blankets heaped in a corner, as if it had served as sleeping quarters before now. A rough-looking table and a few wooden chairs were the only articles of furniture. How many undesirables, running from the law, had hidden here before?

The fire that now burned steadily between a circle of stones was the only cheerful thing in the room. Florence drew near its warmth. The heat of her exertion had passed, leaving her more chilled than when she'd stood in front of the gallows.

How long before the guards would find this runaway convict? He continued tending the fire. Her eye fell on the knife, now stuck in his belt, its steel reflecting the glow of the fire. The memory of its cold blade pressed against her neck rose in her mind, and she experienced the horror of those moments once again.

She shook away the thought. She was alive and sure God had a purpose for her.

After several minutes, when the man continued to ignore her presence, Florence inched to the fire. But as soon as she drew near him, she wrinkled her nose, noticing the sour smell of his tattered garments. She sniffed at her cloak, smelling him even there.

He stood suddenly, and she flinched. His broad back muscles strained against his filthy coat. His presence seemed to fill the cellar. His attention continued fixed on the small fire.

"Don't think about leaving anytime soon." His voice was a near growl, low and gravelly, as if he hadn't used it for some time. "You just stay put till we see if those guards have lost our scent."

"You couldn't leave a trail more obvious than that one." As soon as the words were out of her mouth, she bit her lip. Why couldn't she be more like her brother, Damien, with his mild manners?

Quinn turned then. Dark eyes glittered at her from a swarthy face framed by an even darker beard. Thick black hair curled around his face, giving him a savage appearance, as she imagined Robinson Crusoe must have looked after his many years as a castaway.

She forced herself to hold her ground when he took a step toward her. He stopped so close to her, the heat of his brawny frame filled the space between them. "Think you're a clever one, do you?"

Her experience at Newgate had taught her that to show fear was fatal. She jutted her chin out. "Do you really think you can evade your pursuers?"

His lips curled in a sneer. "Those red-coated fools? They'll think twice 'fore venturing into this neighborhood. The Crown likely doesn't pay 'em enough to risk their miserable hides in 'ere." He fingered the knife's haft at his side. "Besides, what do I have to lose?"

His merciless tone sent a shiver through her.

Noticing it, he gestured toward the fire. "Best get yerself warm while ye can."

She blinked at the sudden change in tone. Was this the defiant brute who'd kidnapped her at knifepoint and now noticed she was cold? She rubbed the bruised spot on her arm where he had held it so tightly.

Keeping her movements careful and deliberate, Florence brought one of the chairs from the table toward the fire. The chair wobbled when she sat down. After assuring herself she wasn't going to lose her balance, she removed her gloves and stretched her hands toward the blaze.

She heard a scraping noise and turned to see

Quinn dragging the table closer. Then he placed the other chair in front of it and sat down. He opened a leather satchel thrown down by his companion and proceeded to remove its contents: a round loaf of bread, a few paper parcels and a bottle.

He unwrapped the first parcel, a wedge of cheese, and the second, a small joint of ham. With his knife, he hacked off a piece of cheese and immediately stuffed it into his mouth, even before proceeding to slice the bread and ham.

Those condemned to die were fed only bread and water for the last three days of their life, so he must have been famished. As he took the first bite of his rapidly made sandwich, his gaze fell on her. "Hungry?" he said through his full mouth.

She stared at his bulging cheeks, feeling a faint disgust, but surprised nonetheless that he had asked. "Yes."

"Help yourself." He cut off a few more pieces of bread and placed them on the paper holding the slices of ham and cheese.

"Thank you." She noticed he didn't leave the knife lying there, but stuck it back in his waistband after wiping it clean on his sleeve.

She moved her chair closer to the table and took a piece of bread, eyeing the dried-looking cheese. Quinn was halfway through his bread before she'd even finished arranging her meat and cheese atop hers. He reached across the table and took a swig from the bottle.

He caught her watching him. He lowered the bottle, setting it back with a thump before wiping his mouth with the same sleeve he'd used to clean the knife.

His eyes weren't dark as she'd first supposed. No, they were bottle-green like the one on the table, reflecting the flickering flames of the fire, beneath thick black brows and curly, brushlike lashes. For a split second, staring into those deep-fringed eyes, she thought she read vulnerability, a lost soul needing a message of hope. The next instant, he blinked, appearing once more savage and ferocious.

She looked away and took a bite of her bread and cheese, tugging as delicately as she could at the dry crust to tear it free. Although the stale food made her thirsty, she refused to drink from the bottle. No doubt it contained cheap gin. She noted he didn't offer her any but did leave the bottle within reach of them both. The chill in the cellar seeped to her very bones. What she wouldn't give for a hot cup of tea.

The Lord would provide in His time, she reminded herself, more certain than ever now that He had a purpose in bringing her here.

The edge of her hunger abated, she folded her hands on the rough tabletop and formulated what she should say. Above all else, she was the Lord's vessel. She licked dry lips. What would her brother do in her place? Damien was such a thoughtful man, so sweet of temperament. She slipped her watch out of the pocket of her dress.

Quinn was immediately alert, watching her movements.

Slowly, she lifted her hand. "It's my watch."

Relief darted through his hard expression and he looked back down at his food.

It was only half past eight. She found it hard to believe little over an hour had passed since she was standing at the gallows. She snapped the watch closed and stowed it away.

She cleared her throat. "How long do you plan to hold me here?"

He continued to chew. Finally he shrugged. "Until I figure out what to do with you."

"You won't get away, you know," she said, ignoring the fear his words had sent through her. Would he keep her here the entire day? What of Damien? Had he noticed her absence yet?

Quinn glanced up briefly from his food. "What d'ye know of anything?"

"Your only help now is Christ."

He swore.

She pursed her lips. "That certainly won't put you in His good graces."

When he said nothing, she continued. "They'll soon begin combing the neighborhoods. They'll flush you out like a partridge."

He snorted. "In this stew? They're scared o' stepping foot in here."

"Not if they're well armed."

He shrugged. "I'll keep moving. They'll never be

able to look in every hole of this rookery." He wiped his mouth again with the back of his hand. "The place is filled with Irish. They'll never give me away. They hate the English too much. Like as not, they'll send the soldiers on a wild-goose chase."

She pressed her lips together in consternation. His escape from the gallows certainly had done nothing to lessen his arrogance. "For a time, perhaps, but eventually the arm of the law is too strong. Where can you run?" Maybe if he were desperate enough, he'd listen to reason.

He swore at her. "Shut your bleedin' trap. It's none o' your concern."

"It is since you kidnapped me."

"That was to ensure me safety. As soon as it's nightfall, you'll be free to go. I won't be here, if you're thinking o' sending the constable looking for me," he added with a rude laugh.

The relief at his promise of her freedom was tempered by the fear of being left by herself in this rookery. "You needn't worry that I'll turn you in," she said with a studied indifference. "You'll have plenty to worry about on that score from the people in the neighborhood—or from your own companions, for that matter."

That last remark caught his attention. His eyes narrowed under his heavy brows. "You're the prison lady."

She acknowledged the name they called her at Newgate with a slight inclination of her head. "Yes."

He swore again. "I thought there was somethin' familiar looking about you. You're the one that offers the condemned false hope." He pushed the remains of the food away and belched. "As soon as you leave to your warm dwelling, they're left in the filth and cold of their prison walls, trusting their future to empty promises of a savior."

"The only One who can help you now is that Savior."

"Bah! I'll take my chances on me own."

"Where do you hope to go if you stay here? You may elude capture for a few days, maybe weeks, but eventually, they'll catch you. If you leave here, there'll be even a greater chance of detection. Someone will recognize you. Most people will fear you, the way you look now, like a great wild beast."

His eyes widened before they flickered away from her and back toward the fire.

She leaned forward. "You can stow away on a ship, but then what? Where will you go? France? We're at war with them. America? With the blockade?" She gave a doubtful laugh.

Quinn's large hands clenched on the tabletop, the only sign that her words were having any effect.

"You could always turn yourself in—"

"Never!"

"In a few hours, days at most, they'll have this place surrounded, mark my words—"

He stood, knocking his chair over backward. "They'll never take me alive."

She knew in those moments, as his green eyes stared into hers, that he spoke the truth.

Realizing the futility of arousing his ire further, she tried another tack. "You could petition to have your case retried. It's been done before."

"What do you know of my case?"

"I know enough to know you may be as innocent as you claim."

Her words caught his attention. Picking up the fallen chair, he retook his seat.

She leaned forward. "I've been around Newgate long enough to know that witnesses can be bought or sold."

He seemed to weigh her words a moment longer before shaking his head. "They'll never believe me if they didn't the first time."

"In any case, your innocence or guilt is not the most important issue. The fact is the Lord has given you a reprieve. You would have been condemned to a fate worse than mere death if you had swung on that gallows today."

His eyes registered surprise for a second. Then he threw back his head and laughed, a deep, rough guffaw. "Worse than mere death?" he mimicked her cultivated syllables. "I beg your pardon, madam, but it's easy for you to call it that since you haven't had a rope strung about your scrawny neck."

"I may not have stood where you stood today, but that doesn't mean I haven't watched enough souls go to their grave to understand the seriousness of their eternal destiny."

He leaned in close, his green eyes glittering with mockery. "Are you one of those who like to watch a man swing from the gallows? It shows how little fine manners separate the scum o' the Earth from those born to wealth."

She jerked back. How dare he accuse her of enjoying the sight of someone strangling at the end of the rope? Before she could think of a suitable retort, he had turned away from her as if tired of her conversation.

He swung out his knife again. She flinched, but relaxed when she saw he used it only to pick his teeth.

Florence shifted her attention to the fire, which had burned low. "May I replenish the fire?" she asked softly.

He grunted. Taking it for assent, she stood.

There were only a few sticks of wood left. She used one to stir up the remaining embers and laid what was left atop them.

Damien, I pray you don't worry about me. By now, he may have heard something about the escape. As far as she knew, no condemned person had ever slipped the noose.

"Did you know you would be rescued today?" she asked into the silence.

"No."

She drew in her breath. The enormity of his reprieve took her breath away. The Lord had indeed heard her prayer for mercy. "You were prepared to die today?"

He laid down his knife and looked at her. His expression was flat and unreadable. "As ready as a man ever is."

"You refused to kneel and pray."

He turned aside and spit on the ground. "What, kneel for the benefit of a jeering crowd and play into the hands of that cleric so he can use it as a lesson to hold over the other poor prisoners?" He clasped his hands together and closed his eyes. "Yes, dear people," he mocked the pious tones of the ordinary. "Witness here a dying man's repentance for a crime he never committed."

She had no words to reply to that. She knew the man he was referring to and could hardly refute what he was saying.

Not knowing what else to say and feeling stiff from kneeling by the fire, she stood and shook her skirt out. Although the chill had left her limbs, she felt exhausted. The night's vigil and the day's excitement were taking their toll. She sat back down and recommenced praying. The Lord surely had a plan, and she needed to know what He would have her do next.

Instead of showing signs of fatigue, Quinn seemed to grow restless. He stood and began to prowl about the low cellar. He investigated every corner of it. Then he checked the door. Finally, he came back, spread out a dirty blanket on the hard ground next to the small fire, and lay down.

"Remember, if you try anything, I have the knife right here." He patted the blade, which rested beneath his hands on his broad chest.

She sniffed. "It's not up to me to turn you in. The Lord spared your life for a reason."

He turned his back on her.

After a while, she heard the deep, even breathing that told her he was asleep. She began to recite Scripture. She felt her own lids grow heavy. Finally, able to fight the fatigue no more, she rested her head on the pillow of her arms and shut her eyes....

Chapter Two

Jonah opened his eyes. He tensed, as he'd done every morning in his solitary cell in Newgate. The fire pit in front of him brought reality back in a jumble of images.

The feel of the rough hemp about his neck. The cap over his face blocking out the sea of faces in front of him.

He was going to die, and he didn't know if he'd disgrace himself before the crowd. How they loved a good show. Would he suffocate quickly, his short, insignificant life snuffed out, or would the rope prove uncooperative and leave him swinging there for agonizing minutes?

Before he'd been isolated in the condemned man's cell, he'd heard richly detailed stories from other prisoners of how chancy a clean death was. Often the hangman would have to pull on a prisoner's legs so he'd die the quicker. A rare prisoner even survived the hanging, his throat raw and bruised, only to have to face the rope the next day.

Jonah didn't think he could go through such a proceeding twice.

Despite his bravado, he'd been terrified. He'd stared at the dank, stone ceiling of his cell as the hours ticked by, and contemplated his demise. What would the morrow bring? Where would his soul go after the rope cut off the breath from his body? Or would his life be ended for good?

He passed a hand in front of his eyes now, wiping away the last horrible memories. His shoulders ached from his position on the floor, though he was used to a hard surface from the wooden pallet in his cell. The fire had long since gone out. His feet felt numb.

Quiet breathing alerted him that he wasn't alone. The prison lady.

She—he didn't even know her name—still sat on the chair, but now her head rested on her arms and it was obvious she slept. She looked peaceful and harmless. He laughed inwardly, thinking how little the image reflected the reality. The woman's words were like barbs, pointed and skillfully aimed at a man's weaknesses.

They'll flush you out like a partridge. Her pale eyes had taunted him, her tone as self-assured as the presiding judge's at the Old Bailey. *You would have been condemned to a fate worse than mere death if you had swung on that gallows today.*

What did she know of his life? Who was she to

judge? Had she ever been accused of a crime she didn't commit? How would she have responded to a rope around her neck? Would all her preaching help her then? Not for a moment had she truly noticed the man in front of her.

He observed her in her sleep now, her back rising and falling in an even rhythm. A strange curl of something snaked through his gut. Something he hadn't felt in so long. Then her cutting words rose again and he saw her for what she was. His prisoner.

The tables were turned. He, the prisoner, with a prisoner of his own. He wasn't quite sure why he hadn't let her go once he was away from Newgate. Surety against the soldiers? Perhaps. Although he doubted the value of one woman's life to the soldiers. Especially such a scrawny one. He remembered how slight she'd felt when he'd half dragged, half carried her along the streets.

He shrugged. It no longer mattered. He'd let her go soon. She was of no use to him now. He'd have enough trouble keeping his own hide in safety. Two would be nigh on impossible.

He stood and listened but could discern no noises from the street. If the soldiers hadn't ferreted him out here, he might actually have a fighting chance. For the first time since his escape, he began to believe in his freedom. It had happened so quickly. One moment facing his death, the next offered a chance at liberty.

He didn't even know who had organized his

rescue. From the few words he'd exchanged with the cove who'd led him here, it sounded like an underworld boss. He certainly didn't have the kind of friends who'd risk their lives for him. If anything, circumstances had proved how quickly his acquaintances in the city would betray him.

Eventually they'll catch you. The prison woman's words came back to him…again. He threw an angry look at her sleeping form. How dare she invade his mind with her convictions? She was a nothing, a self-righteous little nothing.

And yet, her direct words, those clear gray eyes that cut through to a man's soul, haunted him, worsening his restlessness. He rose to his feet and paced, ignoring the pins and needles as his feet came back to life.

He thought of the many eyes in this rookery. Even when the streets appeared deserted, there were dozens of watchers from the broken and boarded-up windows. How long before someone turned him in? What if the Crown offered a reward for his capture?

He halted. Suddenly the walls seemed to be closing in on him, and he remembered the feeling of confinement in the dungeonlike cell at Newgate. He would *not* go back to that. They'd not catch him, he swore. They wouldn't! He'd die first.

The woman stirred and raised her head. Her hand went to her bonnet, half fallen off. Then she turned and her gaze met Jonah's.

"'Bout time you woke up."

"How long have I been asleep?" she asked, rubbing her eyes. The sight of her slim pale hands curled against her face gave her a vulnerability she'd lacked before, and Jonah felt an odd protectiveness sweep over him. What had she been thinking, exposing herself to prisoners and mobs? He remembered the other man's lewd words when he'd left him and they sickened him. This woman had a refinement that belonged to the drawing room, not hiding out in a hovel on Saffron Hill with a fugitive.

He remembered holding the knife to her delicate neck and guilt stabbed him. She smoothed back her hair while he watched. What was he going to *do* with her? He shrugged to hide his dismay. "You're the one with the watch."

She fumbled beneath her cloak and finally managed to extract the timepiece. "It's almost six o'clock."

"It'll be dark outside."

She pushed her hair away from her forehead and looked at the cold grate.

Her longing for a fire was clear. To distract her, he said, "I haven't heard any hoofbeats on the road above us so the search hasn't reached this quarter."

"*Yet.*"

He glared at her and turned back around. To think he'd felt a moment of pity for her.

She began to untie the ribbons of her bonnet and proceeded to remove it. She wore her light brown hair in a simple knot and her cloak was gray. Was she a Quaker? Despite her plain appearance, she had the air of a lady. It was more than her speech. It was something in her gestures and the cut of her clothes. Not that he'd ever had much contact with ladies in his life.

"You said you didn't know you were to be set free today, but did you know any of the men who stormed the gallows?" she asked.

"I had little time to see anything once the cap was removed from me eyes."

"Did you recognize any of them?" she persisted.

He frowned at her, wondering why the close questioning. Was she going to go to the authorities as soon as he released her? "I don't know nothing of any of 'em! And it's best you probably know as little as possible."

She arched a thin eyebrow at him.

He folded his arms across his chest. Did nothing cow her? "You're bound to be questioned once you return to your nice, cozy house."

She nodded slowly. "My reason in asking was to wonder if these men have made any provision for your escape. Will they take you somewhere else now?"

He turned and resumed his walk in the small space, not liking to be reminded of the future. "I wouldn't think they'd chance further involvement. It was dangerous enough what they did."

"Yes. If any were caught, they'd be up for treason." When he said nothing, she gave him that weighing look. "So, you are on your own now."

He shrugged as if the idea didn't bother him at all. "It's not the first time."

She chewed her lip a moment. "I have a suggestion."

He stilled but said nothing.

"My brother might be able to help you."

Was it possible? This sharp-tongued woman was offering him help? True, she had conceded he might be innocent, but to involve herself further, that entailed quite some risk. "Your brother?" was all he could think to say.

"Yes. He lives with me…I mean, I live with him. I…keep house for him." For the first time, she seemed nervous. Perhaps she realized the folly of dragging someone else into this mess and making him an accessory to a crime.

"How could he help a man in my shoes?"

"I d-don't know exactly, but he is very wise. He might know of somewhere you could go. He might be able to help you out of the country. I don't know… He's very levelheaded. He won't give you away."

"Who is he? Someone of importance?" Was she a wealthy nob and he hadn't realized it?

"Not in earthly terms. He's a curate."

He turned away, angry at himself for the spurt of hope he'd allowed her words to give him. "Ach! I can see the kind of help you have in mind."

"I was thinking in terms of material help in this case, not spiritual, although, you will need that as well. He is not rich, by any means, but I'm sure he'll help you in any way he can."

He refused to listen to any more. No doubt she was still only trying to save his soul, to make up for her failure with him in Newgate. Walking to the door, he pressed his ear to it. So far, silence. Carefully, he opened it, and stood listening a while longer. Nothing. He stepped out.

"Where are you going?"

"Wait here." Ignoring the note of worry in her voice, he proceeded up the stairs. Time to scout out the street and decide if the moment had come to move.

The street was dark. A few shadowy figures hurried along it. He could leave and skirt down the nearest alley. Best head toward Clerkenwell.

When he reentered the cellar, the woman had removed the pins from her hair until it fell loose about her shoulders. She was combing it through with her fingers. For a second his gut clenched, remembering his wife's similar motions with the tortoiseshell comb he had bought for her one time from a tinker.

When the woman noticed him watching her, she quickly gathered her hair in her hands and wound it back up in a tight knot.

"It's time to leave," he said.

She replaced the pins in her hair, then stood and straightened her cloak, her movements quick and efficient.

He came to the table and wrapped the food up.

Corking the bottle, he placed the things back into the satchel and flung it over his shoulder. Who knew when he'd have more?

He turned and found her standing near him. She was above medium height, the top of her bonnet reaching to his temple. Her pale gray eyes looked at him calmly. For a woman who had been abducted and kept hostage, she had shown an amazing amount of courage.

Suddenly, his conscience smote him. He couldn't very well leave her in this rookery. Despite his months in the brutal surroundings of Newgate, he remembered a time when he'd been among civilized people. Men who respected women.

He swallowed, remembering his own wife again. He'd never have left her to fend for herself in such a pit. He pushed open the door and gestured. "Either come with me and be quiet about it, or I'll leave you in this stew to find your own way out."

She followed silently behind him as he climbed the stairs once more. They stood in the doorway of the derelict building some time before he ventured out. Finally taking her by the arm in a sure, but not rough, grip and placing a finger to his lips, he stepped out of the overhang of the doorway.

Jonah had a fairly good knowledge of the layout of the neighborhood. He'd spent most of the past year since arriving in London in the surrounding areas, before they'd thrown him into Newgate. His eyes strained through the darkness, knowing that although no one was about, there was no telling how many people watched the street. It was an area where few lingered after dark and most had something they preferred hiding.

He reached an alley and walked down it, skirting the piles of litter. A cat let out an outraged meow and jumped up onto a jagged brick wall.

Their boots crunched over the thin layer of ice that now covered the puddles. He turned left and went down a narrower path. Another turn, then another, and they left the open area and were once more hidden by buildings.

He spared her a glance. "Where do you live?"

"Just outside Marylebone, beyond the Uxbridge Road tollhouse." She kept her words brief, as if understanding the need for quiet.

"I don't know that part of town. I'll leave you where you can get a hack."

They skirted another building then went down another alley. Soon the streets widened and more pedestrians and carriages were to be seen. He made a wide circle around Gray's Inn. He knew he was taking a grave risk entering this neighborhood, especially so early in the evening, but he'd made up his mind he wouldn't leave this innocent woman alone in the stews of London.

Suddenly a crowd of uniformed men turned the corner just as he was ready to emerge from an alleyway onto a main street. Horse guards, by the jingle of their spurs against the cobblestones. Jonah jerked to a stop, pulling the woman by her middle against him. He didn't have a chance to unsheathe his knife to hold to her throat or cover her mouth with his hand. He didn't dare move, didn't dare breathe, nor make the slightest sound to draw the men's attention as they passed in front of him.

One of them slipped and clutched at his companion's arm.

"By George, Harry, have a care," the other admonished, giving him a shove that sent him dangerously close to where Jonah was standing. "If you can't hold your liquor, you belong with the Grenadiers!" Laughter rang out all around them.

By their tone, they were likely leaving a tavern and not on a manhunt. Even so, if one so much as turned in his direction, they'd see him where he stood only a few feet away in the shadows. His attention slid to the woman in front of him. Her bonnet hid half his face. He could feel her slim frame beneath his grip. All she had to do was call out and he'd be finished.

As the seconds ticked by, he realized his entire future hung on this woman's whim. The sweat broke out on his forehead and armpits. His heart pumped in deafening thuds as he relived those last moments on the gallows.

Then the soldiers were gone. Their laughter faded, as did their footfalls on the cobbles. The ensuing silence was only broken by his heartbeat. Slowly, he loosened his hold on the woman's midriff. She stepped a few inches away from him, as if awaiting his next move.

She hadn't given him away. He swallowed, still scarcely believing his good fortune. He took a large gulp of the frigid air, breathing in the taste of freedom.

He mustn't risk another near encounter with the law. Taking her arm once again, he crossed the street after a quick look up and down it. He led her at a rapid pace a few more blocks on a less-traveled side street. Finally he stopped.

"If you walk in that direction," he said, gesturing, "you'll come to Red Lion Square. Continue a little farther and you'll reach Holborn. You shouldn't have any trouble finding a hack there to take you where you live." He thought of something. "Do have any blunt to pay your fare?" He certainly had nothing to give her.

She nodded. "I'll manage."

"All right. I'll leave you here." He swallowed, finding it hard to say the next words. It had been a long time since he'd felt gratitude to anyone for anything. "And…uh…thanks for holding your tongue back there."

"I told you I wouldn't give you away." Through the darkness, he could feel her straightforward look. "Don't forget my offer. If you find nowhere to go, come to my brother. St. George's Chapel on St. George's Row just above Hyde Park. You'll not be turned away by the Reverend Damien Hathaway."

He shifted on his feet. "I don't expect you'll be

seeing the likes o' me unless it's at the end o' the noose. I'll be long gone from London ere you wake up tomorrow."

She shook her head. "You're a fool. Look at you. You don't even have a greatcoat. How long are you going to survive in this cold?"

"I survived this long. I'll manage."

They stood eyeing each other for another few seconds. Would he ever see her again? Strange how the thought gave him pause. Even now, she was berating him, and yet he felt she meant him good and not harm.

Without another word, she pulled the hood of her cloak over her bonnet and turned away from him. His hand almost reached out to stop her, but then he dropped it back to his side. What had he meant by the gesture? What could he say to her?

In a certain sense, he owed her his life.

Her footsteps took her rapidly in the direction he'd pointed and she disappeared into the night.

He stood a second longer before hurrying back into a side street and toward the East End of London.

Florence stumbled from the hackney after a long ride across London. Her stiff fingers fumbled with her purse. Finally, she paid her fare and turned toward her house.

She breathed in the fresh, cold air. Her neighborhood seemed more like a village than a part of London. Beyond the parsonage lay orchards and fields. She walked up the steps to the large brick house where she and her brother lived since he'd been given the curacy of the small chapel.

She tried hard to forget the image of Mr. Quinn with his dirty clothes that offered so little protection from the elements. If he returned to the cellar, there was no wood left for a fire. Or would he head out of London on the Great North Road and hope to sleep under cover of a forest?

It would be harder to hide in a village.

She shut the front door behind her as the rattle of the coach faded in the distance. Familiar warmth enveloped her.

"Florence! I thought I heard someone come in. Thank God, you're alive!" Damien hurried toward her, his arms outstretched, his pace fast in spite of his wooden leg.

They were not a generally demonstrative family, but it felt good right then to be held in a warm embrace. He smelled good, too, his cravat freshly starched, a great contrast to the stink of the other man and his surroundings.

Damien pulled away from her. His blue eyes searched her face. "Tell me what happened, where you've been, I heard so many stories."

"I hoped you wouldn't be worried." She slipped out of his embrace and began to undo the clasp of her cloak. "First, let me get near the fire. It's a raw night."

"Of course, forgive me for keeping you standing here." He took her cloak and bonnet and hung them on the hook. "I must also let Albert and Elizabeth know you are back. They were most concerned."

"Yes, let me go to the kitchen at once."

She spent the next several minutes assuring their two old retainers that she indeed was safe and sound. Finally she was able to sit with her brother in his study, her feet on the fender, a hot cup of tea in her hands.

"I've been praying for you since this morning, Florrie." Damien used the nickname she hadn't heard since they'd been children. "I heard there'd been a storming of the gallows and you'd disappeared in the fray. Some said you were abducted, others that you'd been crushed by the mob. It took a troop of guards quite some time to subdue the crowds."

She shuddered, remembering the violent mob. "That explains how Quinn was able to get away. I can still scarcely believe what happened. The hangman was ready to release the drop, when all of a sudden a dozen men besieged the gallows and cut down the prisoner a second before his feet would have dangled in the air." She put a hand to her cheek, picturing it all again. "The next thing I knew Quinn had grabbed me and was holding a knife to my throat."

Damien drew in a sharp breath.

She raised her eyes to meet his gaze. "I'm sure he thought to use me as a shield." She refrained from telling him how close she had come to having the guard's pike embedded in her.

"How cowardly to grab a woman. Did he hurt you?"

"No." She pictured the events as she stared into the fire. "I think he reacted out of pure fear—fear of being recaptured," she added, remembering the man's fierce look when she'd mentioned the authorities closing in. "As soon as he made his way through the mob, most of whom sympathized with the prisoner, I must say, he just kept going." She shook her head. "I wonder if he even intended to take me at all. It almost seemed as if he simply forgot to let go of me." Her arm was still tender from his bruising grip.

Damien reached across and covered her hand with his. "How terrifying for you."

She smiled. "I know. Oddly enough, after a while, I was no longer afraid. I was too stunned by how the Lord was answering prayer." She leaned forward. "The man was set to die. The Lord has given him a stay of execution. Jonah Quinn was not ready to face his Maker, in the state he was in."

Damien nodded, a small smile curving his lips. "It certainly seems like the hand of the Lord when I see it was you out of all the crowd who was taken."

Florence went on to describe where they had hidden out all day.

Damien shook his head in wonder. "And he didn't hurt you."

"No. I think he was more bluster than real threat." For such a fierce-looking man, he'd behaved almost…gallantly, even to bringing her at great risk to himself to a place where she could get a hackney. She recalled their near brush with the soldiers.

What would her fate have been in the hands of another sort, like the fellow who had led them to the hideout? She shivered.

"Did they search for him very long?" she asked her brother.

"They spent more time subduing the mob, from what I heard. It has certainly caused an uproar. I think it's the first time, in memory at least, that someone has escaped the gallows. The Crown will be nervous with the unrest there's been since the war. They're already saying it's the Jacobins who are responsible."

"The prisoner claimed ignorance of his rescuers."

"He could be speaking the truth." Damien cleared his throat. "They're sure to question you once they know you're back."

She frowned into her tea. "There's little I can tell them, or wish to."

"Did you get any sense of its having been planned?"

She looked at her brother, her heart heavy. "No. I don't think there is even a plan for Quinn to hide out or be smuggled abroad. It's only a matter of time before the authorities find him."

Damien nodded thoughtfully, his own glance straying to the fire. "So many poor unfortunates housed in Newgate. They won't have any mercy on this man if they catch him."

"He insisted on his innocence right up to the end." A wave of desolation swept through her when she remembered how alone he'd looked when she'd left him. She'd been so sure the Lord had called her for a special purpose in the man's life.

She looked at her brother sadly. "I wasn't able to get through to Mr. Quinn at all. He remained deaf to any of my admonitions to seek the help of the Lord. He disappeared into the night where he left me and I doubt I shall ever see him again." She paused and hesitated on the next words. "I even told him he could come here, that you would be able to help him in some way. I felt sure…" She stared unseeing into her teacup.

"Don't fret. You were obedient in going where the Lord led you and witnessing to this unfortunate soul. You have nothing to reproach yourself with. You must trust the Lord now to finish the work begun in Mr. Jonah Quinn."

His swarthy face came to her mind. Underneath the filth and foul language, she'd sensed a man of substance. A soul worth saving.

Lord, help him find You, she prayed silently. The streets of London could be cold and inhospitable.

Jonah spent the next few days moving from one abandoned cellar to another, searching through the refuse around Westfield Market by night for a scrap of food. When he was able to find some fuel, he hazarded a fire in the various hovels, but he dared not risk detection. He trusted no one around him. He had no contact with those who had rescued him and gave up hoping for more. He was on his own, the way he'd been since his wife and children had perished.

It had been their doom the day they'd come to London. But what else could he have done once the open fields around his village had been enclosed? They'd been left with no land to graze their few cows or grow any wheat. With the war lasting so long, the price of wheat kept going up, so they could hardly buy bread anymore.

Jonah pushed the memories from his mind. It did no good to go over the same thoughts. What was done was done. He couldn't change a single fact of his miserable destiny.

He had no funds, precious little food, not even a coat he could huddle under.

He was beyond help.

It was only a matter of time before he'd die of exposure or the authorities would catch him. Already he'd felt a burning in his throat that had grown worse each day until he could hardly swallow. The gin was long since gone, so there was nothing to relieve the pain.

He scratched his itchy scalp then folded his arms once more over his chest, tucking his fingers under his armpits. How had he gone from a life of hard work but basic satisfaction at the end of the day to the life of a virtual beggar in the city?

He'd never wanted much. Life had been good the way it was. He'd come home to Judy and the two babes, eat his plate of potatoes or bread and butter, sometimes with a piece of bacon, stretch out his legs before the fire, then retire for the night in their small cottage. That life seemed one of a king now.

The decline had come fast, starting when he could find no work in the city because he was an "unskilled laborer." He'd learned the meaning of that term quickly on. His wife had been more fortunate at first, finding piecemeal work, picking over silk for a family in Spitalfields. But with the difficulties in that industry, the employment had soon dried up.

He'd only managed to find work for a few days at a time, mainly digging ditches. The day he was forced to snitch a piece of fruit off a market stand to bring something home to the wee ones, he thought he'd sunk as low as a fellow could.

For a while Judy had taken in laundry, but it left her exhausted, her hands worn, and when the cold weather set it, she'd gotten sickly spending so much time wet. One by one, the little ones had also succumbed to the fever until Jonah had been the only one left.

That's when he'd met a cove by the name of Stevens. He'd seemed an upright gentleman with an honest trade. He'd promised Jonah employment in his shop. The wages were low, but Jonah was desperate enough to take anything.

The job had been humble enough. Sweeping the shop, unloading the wares from the delivery wagons, all used goods, sorting through the dirty clothing and odd assortment of wares. Gradually, Jonah had grown to wonder at the steady supply of merchandise, especially when he'd seen the number of pocket watches and rings. When he'd begun to ask questions, his boss had laughed and told him to mind his own business.

Then came that fateful day when Mr. Stevens had asked him, with that cherubic smile on his face, to take the banknote to one of his suppliers.

The next day, he'd been accused by the man of passing a false bill.

It was only during the long months sitting in Newgate awaiting his trial that Jonah had pieced it all together. Stevens's shop had been nothing more than a front for stolen goods. When Jonah had begun to question things, Stevens had seen that it was time to get rid of him. No one had believed Jonah's simple denials in the face of the evidence of the forged note. The evidence was ir-refutable. The trial had lasted no more than five minutes before he was declared guilty and sentenced to hang.

Jonah bowed his head on his folded arms. Why did he fight against the inevitable any longer? Why not give up the ghost and be done with it?

A woman's sharp words pushed past the despair engulfing him. *If you find nowhere to go, come to my brother.... You'll not be turned away by the Reverend Damien Hathaway.*

She'd not given him away when she'd had the chance.

Despite her snappish tongue, she'd proved to be a true and stalwart ally.

Was she his only hope?

Chapter Three

Florence walked from the chapel through the dark orchard to the rear of the parsonage. The rain fell in cold hard drops and she was glad of her hood. She had just finished arranging things on the altar for tomorrow's service.

She quickened her step while trying to avoid the muddy puddles, but it was impossible to see them all in the dark. Ahead, the lights of the house windows beckoned with their golden glow. She fumbled with the latch of the door to the walled kitchen garden. The box hedge brushed its stubby wet branches against her, sending forth its pungent odor. They'd have to trim it back come spring.

A sudden rustling made her heart jump. She froze.

"Who's there?" her voice rapped out. A vagrant or Gypsy seeking a roof over his head for the night?

A large figure moved from the shadows. "You said I could come to you."

More than his voice, she recognized his size. "Mr. Quinn!"

"Shh! I'm a wanted man, if you haven't forgotten." He stepped closer.

His face was filthy and haggard. Dark circles ringed his eyes. She wasted no more time on questions. "Come along. You'll freeze out here." Without a backward glance, she quickened her step along the stone path. How long had he been standing there in the freezing rain?

"Oh!" She felt her foot slip on a slick stone. Before she could land on her backside, a strong grip stopped her fall. She well remembered that iron hold.

He let her go as soon as she regained her balance. "Watch your step."

"Tha-thank you." She straightened. "Come along," she said, her tone firmer than she felt inside.

Where had he been since she'd last seen him? It had been, she calculated, five days. She'd prayed for him each one and thanked the Lord that he was still free—if alive—since her visits to Newgate had told her he hadn't been apprehended.

They'd only questioned her minimally. Few people had even been aware she'd been grabbed by the prisoner. The warden let the matter drop when she gave him the scant details of her abduction. She was thankful she hadn't had to lie. She'd merely told them Jonah Quinn had let her go once he'd found a hiding place. She had told them nothing of the location of the cellar. In truth, she would have no idea how to find it again herself.

They reached the back door to the parsonage. Quinn closed it behind them and she turned to look at him in the lamplight. The warm glow only emphasized his drawn cheeks and rough beard, all dripping from the rain.

"My goodness, you must be frozen." He wore the same jacket and breeches she remembered, everything soaked through. "Come along to the fire."

She gestured to the bench in front of the hearth. "Sit down, while I fetch my brother and some dry things for you."

He looked as if he wanted to say something, but she hurried from the room. It was a miracle if the man didn't catch his death.

She rushed to her brother's study first. "Damien, you must come immediately."

"What is it, Flo?" he asked, half rising from his desk chair.

"It's him. He's come."

"Who?"

"The escaped prisoner, Jonah Quinn."

He dropped his pen. "Where is he?"

"I've brought him to the kitchen. He's chilled to the bone. Who knows how long he's been standing in the garden."

Damien was already heading for the door. "I'll talk to him."

"Yes. Let him know he's safe here, for now. I

must get some dry things for him." She eyed her brother's slim frame. "May I rummage about in your clothespress? I doubt anything of yours will fit him, but he can't stay in those wet garments."

"Rummage away, even if it's only for a nightshirt."

Jonah turned at the sound of the door. A young man—a gentleman by the look of his refined features, neatly trimmed hair and dark clerical clothing—stared at him. Of above average height and slim, his resemblance to his sister was obvious. Jonah remembered she'd said he was a curate.

The curate stepped forward, a pale hand outstretched. A distinct limp brought Jonah's eye to a wooden leg, just below the knee. *Pity.*

"Welcome." The word held genuine warmth. "I'm Reverend Damien Hathaway. You met my sister, Florence, the other day during your…adventure," he added when Jonah said nothing.

After a second's hesitation, Jonah stood and held out his own grimy hand. The other's shake was firm, despite its more fragile, neat appearance.

"Jonah Quinn," was all he said.

"Please, sit down, Mr. Quinn. Welcome to our home." Hathaway smiled, and Jonah was struck by the friendly goodwill in the man's clear blue eyes.

"Goodness, Florence was right. You're soaked through. She has gone to get some dry things. You'd better get out of those as soon as possible. Let me help you with your jacket."

Before he could comply, another door opened. He tensed, wondering if he must flee again. A gray-haired woman peered in.

She gave Jonah a sharp look and it was all he could do not to look away.

"Ah, Mrs. Nichols," the curate said, as if Jonah's appearance was the most natural thing in the world. "As you see, we have a visitor with us on this inhospitable evening. I was just going to fetch a blanket for him. Florence has gone for some dry clothes. I suggest some tea and perhaps a hot bath?"

"Of course, sir, I'll have Albert fetch the tub. Dear me, it's an awful night to be about. Come, let me take your coat." She gave Jonah a quick curtsy. "Elizabeth Nichols, at your service."

Jonah gave a quick bow of his head then stopped. He couldn't give his real name. He hadn't thought of that wrinkle. All he'd thought about was getting to somewhere warm and dry.

He looked across at Reverend Hathaway and read understanding in his eyes. "Kendall," Jonah finally said. That was his mother's family name. "William." No one would think to connect Jonah Quinn with his brother's name. "William Kendall, at your service," he said, and held out his hand.

"Very good, Mr. Kendall," the servant said.

Hathaway stepped forward. "Mr. Kendall has come to stay with us a while."

"Of course, sir." She turned away and went to

hang up his coat, as if she were used to having ragged guests appear at all hours of the night.

The next moments were filled with bustle and confusion as Jonah sat on the bench by the fire, unable to stop the shivers racking his body. Mrs. Nichols came up to him with a large blanket. "Here you go, sir. If you'll remove your wet things, you can just wrap yourself up in this till your bath is ready."

"Yes, madam," he answered, suddenly overwhelmed. He'd never been waited on in his life, except by his wife, who'd served him his supper when he'd come in from the fields and cleared it away from him when he was done.

When the others had left the room, he slowly began to remove his boots. Both were split at the soles, hardly affording protection against the wet streets. His stockings, full of holes, were soaked through. After removing them, he hesitated, wondering where to set them. The flagstones looked clean enough to eat off and the Dutch tiles along the wide-open range shone.

Just as he laid the dirty socks in a sodden heap on the floor, the door opened. The prison lady, Miss Hathaway, reappeared carrying a bundle of things in her arms.

She seemed startled to find him alone. "Where did everyone go?"

"To fetch me a bath," he answered, pulling the blanket tighter around his shoulders.

She laid the armful on the table. "I've brought

some of my brother's things, though you are larger than he is. It's mostly nightclothes once you've had a bath." She spoke quickly as if she, too, were nervous. She wasn't still afraid of him, was she?

An older man entered the kitchen, carrying a tin tub in one hand and a bucket in the other. "Evening, Miss Hathaway." He gave Jonah a quick bob of his head before going to the range to pour the bucket of water into a large black kettle.

When the man had left again, Miss Hathaway indicated the rest of the things she'd brought. "Here are towels, a bar of soap, a hairbrush and, as I said, some nightclothes and a dressing gown from my brother. I shall leave you now and prepare your room." She turned to go.

Before she reached the door, he said, "Those others—" He cleared his throat. "They won't, uh, give away who I am?"

"Mr. and Mrs. Nichols? Oh, no. They're used to seeing strangers come and go from here. As I told you, my brother never turns anyone away from his doors. You'll find refuge here."

"You don't think they recognized me?" He remembered the odd look the woman had given him.

Miss Hathaway fingered the white lace at her collar, her only sign of hesitation. "I…cannot be certain. They know I was…abducted by you five days ago, but with scant details." She looked away from him. "I thought it better to say little of the matter to anyone save my brother. I was questioned by the authorities of Newgate. Again, I gave few details, as I didn't wish…to lie. I—I was glad then I knew little myself. I wanted to give you a chance to be gone from London…as you said you were planning."

He could feel his face heat. Fine job he had made of his chance at freedom. He thought on her words. It didn't bode well. Perhaps he shouldn't have come here, the very place the authorities might look.

As if reading his thoughts, she said, her voice regaining its self-assurance, "I shouldn't worry too much. My part that day has been all but forgotten and the Nicholses are trustworthy."

Alone again, he sat wrapped in the large blanket, sipping a cup of tea before the fire and pondering where he'd ended up. From huddling in the freezing cold for five days to being treated like an honored guest. The open warmth and acceptance with which the curate and his sister had received him left him uneasy. Could he trust such kindness?

And Miss Hathaway. Jonah shook his head in further amazement. She'd not only held her tongue, but seemed to have forgotten how he'd held her at knifepoint and kept her hostage an entire day.

The old manservant returned and poured the heated water into the tub. When he'd gone, Jonah rose, feeling the full weariness of all those days on the run.

With an effort, he shed his torn breeches and eased into the hot water. He couldn't remember the last time he'd had a bath, not even a pitcher of water and cake of soap. Even though he couldn't stretch out his legs in it, he wished he didn't have to leave the water. His body couldn't seem to get warm despite the steaming water and blazing fire in front of him.

He grabbed up the bar of soap. As it hit the water, it released a fragrance. He put it up to his nostrils. Despite his stuffy nose, he got a whiff of lavender and saw the little purple buds embedded in the bar. They reminded him of life in the country and the herbs his wife used to hang upside down from the rafters to dry.

He dunked his head in the water and began to scrub the months of filth from his scalp and beard, working his way down to his neck and chest.

His bathwater soon turned gray. With a sigh of regret he took the pitcher full of water left for him and let the clean water run from his head down the length of his body, feeling cleaner than he'd felt since arriving in London.

By the time he'd toweled dry, he was shivering again. He put on the nightshirt. It was long enough, but a trifle tight around the shoulders. The dressing gown was the same. He sat in front of the fire and rubbed his hair dry, hoping to get warm again. A voice called through the door, "May I come in, sir?" The older man, Nichols, peered into the room.

"Aye, come in."

"Good, I see you finished your bath. Mistress says to come up to your bed as soon as you're ready and we'll bring you a bowl of soup, if you'd like."

Soup. His very gut rumbled at the word. "I could

use something hot." He rose and followed Mr. Nichols up a carpeted stairs, the plush material blissful under his bare feet. He wondered if he could ask for a shot of gin. That would further warm his bones.

He entered a neat bedroom. A full-size bed filled most of the space. A fire burned in the grate.

"There you go, sir. Just make yourself comfortable. I'll bring your soup up in a trifle."

"Tha-thank you," Jonah found himself stumbling over the simple words, words he'd rarely used of late. Suddenly he sneezed.

"Coming down with something?" Mr. Nichols tut-tutted. "Here, let me get you a handkerchief." He rummaged about in a chest of drawers and handed him a white square.

Like everything in the house, it appeared clean. Jonah brought it to his nose. It also smelled clean.

As soon as he was alone, he climbed into the bed. He felt the full exhaustion of days on the run, of being afraid to sleep, of running from place to place…

He was roused with the arrival of the older woman who was carrying a tray. "Here you go, sir, some hot soup and a hot toddy to help put you to sleep. Albert said you sounded a bit congested."

Jonah sat up as the tray was placed on his lap. In a split second he'd downed the tumbler of sweetened hot water and rum that stood beside the bowl. He smacked his lips before picking up the spoon and going to work on the soup. The woman adjusted the pillows behind him.

The soup was tasty, thick and savory, with chunks of beef and barley through it. So much like his wife's cooking, back in the days when life had been kinder, except this contained a lot more meat.

He'd just finished it, and was almost wishing for a second dish, when Miss Hathaway reentered with her brother. The curate smiled at Jonah. "How is everything?"

"Good," he answered, his attention still on his food. He was debating whether to ask for some more soup, or just collapse into sleep, when Miss Hathaway approached his bed. Like the other woman, she arranged the pillows behind him. He could smell the scent of lavender on her gown's sleeve as she reached past him.

Suddenly she stepped back. "Look, Damien, he's full of vermin."

Jonah turned to her, a hunk of bread halfway to his mouth, not liking the alarm in her tone.

Her brother came round to her side of the bed and touched his scalp. "Excuse me, Mr. Quinn, for taking such liberties."

Jonah sat still as the man began to probe his scalp.

Finally the man stood back, his brow furrowed. "A little bad news, I'm afraid. Lice."

Jonah's hand immediately went up to his scalp and rubbed it. As usual it itched.

"It's not unusual to become infested, most probably while you were at Newgate. The thing is, it's catching, and we don't want it to spread."

Miss Hathaway addressed her brother. "He'll have to be shorn. I shall fetch the shears and a cloth to catch the hair. We'll have to shave him as well. Pity we didn't see this below stairs."

She spoke of him as if he wasn't there, but before he could raise any objections, she had left the room.

"Why don't you finish your meal," Mr. Hathaway said in a gentle tone.

Jonah turned back to the remaining bread and butter, which no longer held any appeal. Before he could take it up, he sneezed.

"It sounds like you've caught a chill," the curate said, sympathy in his tone.

"Aye." Jonah picked up the piece of bread and forced himself to eat it. As soon as he'd swallowed the last bite, he lay back against the heaped-up pillows.

Hathaway, immediately at his side, picked up the tray. He stood a moment and cleared his throat. "I'm glad you came to our house. It gives me a chance to thank you for not harming my sister the other day."

Jonah's face heated at the memory of abducting an innocent woman. "I—"

"She's the only family I have left, and she's very precious to me." The curate's face was so open and sincere that Jonah felt doubly ashamed.

He'd once cared for his family like that. Only he'd lost them. He felt his throat swell up and something sting his eyes.

Relieved to hear the sound of the door opening, he turned away from the curate.

Miss Hathaway entered, equipped with a pair of shears, shaving blade and strop, followed by the old man carrying a steaming bowl of water and more towels.

For a moment, Jonah's gaze locked with Miss Hathaway's. Only his wife had ever shorn him.

"Good, he's finished," she said, addressing her brother. She proceeded to wrap the large cloth tightly about Jonah's neck and secure it behind him. Her touch was deft and sure. "Come, Albert, you may shave him. As soon as you're finished, I shall cut his hair."

Before he could react, she stepped away from him, and Mr. Nichols took her place. He laid a steamy hot towel against his beard and then proceeded to lather it. Slowly, Jonah eased himself back, enjoying the feeling of the hot, soapy water against his skin. Maybe this wasn't such a bad idea….

In a few efficient strokes, his beard was nearly gone. He brought a hand up to his cheek, hardly remembering what clean-shaven skin felt like.

"Just a few more strokes, sir, and I'll be done."

Jonah removed his hand.

"There you go, sir, if you want to rinse your face off."

Jonah did so, then was handed a towel to dry himself off.

Miss Hathaway stepped up to him, brandishing her shears. Without so much as a by-your-leave, she was clipping at his hair with quick movements. The sheet around his neck was soon covered in thick, black curls. He wondered if he had any hair left.

"That's as close as I can cut," she told her brother. "I shall continue with the razor."

Razor? He shifted away from her. "What do you mean, razor?"

She looked down at him. "It means I intend to shave your head. Now, sit still so I don't nick you."

He turned to her brother. "Reverend, I—"

"It's the best way to ensure no vermin remains in your scalp," Mr. Hathaway told him, his expression apologetic.

Jonah brought a hand up to his hair. It felt short and spiky. "It seems most o' my hair's been cut away already."

"It will soon grow back, and with the proper—" he coughed "—hygiene, you should remain lice-free."

The next he knew, small but firm hands were working up a lather in his remaining locks. She really meant to shave his scalp. He pulled away from her.

Miss Hathaway's hand clamped down on his shoulder. "Sit still."

But he'd have no more of her treating him as if he were a half-wit. He threw the blankets off himself and swung his legs over the side of the bed. "No one's touching my scalp," he said, standing to his full height.

She glared up at him. "Now see here, we'll not have the house infested by vermin because of your stubbornness." She pushed down on his shoulder, but he shoved her hand aside.

"It is just a temporary measure," her brother said, coming between them and laying a hand gently on Jonah's arm. "You'll see how quickly it grows back."

"It's my scalp you're talking about."

"You're perfectly right. Permit me to apologize. You see, it's probably our own fear of getting the lice that caused our overzealous reaction. Please forgive us for discussing your condition as if you weren't present."

Jonah sneezed.

Hathaway offered him another clean handkerchief. He looked at it a second, then slowly took it. Why was the curate being so generous after the fuss Jonah had raised? He blew his nose. "Well, I suppose if it's the only way…"

Hathaway eased him back against the pillows. "It's the quickest and most effective treatment. Your hair will grow back in no time."

Jonah pulled the covers back over himself. "At least I won't have to bother with a comb."

"That's the spirit."

His sister moved to take away his pillows. "I shall have to change the casings. They're likely infested already." Disgust edged her words.

He glared at her. Who did this stick of a woman think she was? "If you don't want me here, just say the word and I'll take my leave." He shoved away from the brother's hand and launched himself from the bed. Not two steps and his legs gave out, forcing him to clutch the bedpost. If he'd felt humiliated coming to this house before, standing now in his nightshirt, wobbling like a babe, was too much. "Where are my clothes?"

Before he could take another step, a wave of dizziness swept through him. His hand slipped from the bedpost. His body hit the floor with a large thud.

"Mr. Quinn! Oh, dear!" Miss Hathaway knelt at his side. He felt her touch on his shoulder. "Damien, we must get him into bed."

Hathaway crouched down at his other side. "Are you all right, Mr. Quinn?"

Miss Hathaway's soft hand went to his forehead. "He's feverish. It's no wonder, the way he was standing out in the rain. Mr. Quinn, can you stand if we help you?" Finally she was looking directly at him, her pale gray eyes showing real concern.

He attempted to rise, feeling their assistance on either side of him, but he couldn't stop shivering, so he just knelt there, teeth chattering, limbs trembling, sight blurring….

Florence looked at her brother in alarm. "He's very ill."

Damien felt his forehead and nodded. "Let me get Albert and see if we can get him back in bed."

"I think between the two of us we can manage."

Damien frowned. "I don't know, he's a large man."

The two of them put their arms under Quinn's and began to hoist him up, but her brother was right. He was large and too heavy for the two of them to move.

Quinn began to stir. His thick eyelashes fluttered upward and his green eyes looked into hers. "Wh-what—where am I?"

"You're here with us," she said in a soothing tone. "You must have gotten light-headed. Do you think you can stand so we can help you back to bed?"

Quinn blinked a few times as if focusing and finally shook his head as if to clear it. He reminded Florence of a great beast, except this time he no longer had shaggy locks to shake.

With a deep breath, he strained his torso upward. Both Florence and Damien aided him at each side. His legs buckled under him when they finally got him upright.

"Careful, there," she murmured, feeling his weight fall upon her as she draped one of his arms over her shoulder. "You're almost to the bed. Just a few more steps…"

He collapsed against the headboard.

Florence replaced the pillows she had removed earlier, deciding not to attempt to shave his scalp until he fell asleep, which by the looks of things, would be in a matter of minutes.

"Just lie back, Mr. Quinn."

"I believe he will go by Mr. Kendall from now on," Damien said quietly.

She looked across at her brother, who had walked to the other side of the bed and was tucking the blankets around the sleeping man.

"It's the name he gave Albert and Elizabeth."

"I see," she said, adjusting the blankets on her side. She hadn't thought of that issue. Her glance strayed to Quinn, who had closed his eyes, his thick lashes resting against the flushed cheeks. Although they'd helped many people who came to them, they'd never had a fugitive from the law under their roof. Of course he couldn't use his own name. She chewed her lip, beginning to understand the full implications of offering Quinn refuge.

Subterfuge, deception…it all came down to the same thing. They'd have to lie.

She noticed Quinn still shivering despite the heavy blankets and placed a palm gently on his forehead again. It was quite warm to the touch. "Should we call Mr. Hershey?" she whispered to Damien.

Before he could answer, Quinn's eyelids shot up. "Who's that?"

"Our apothecary," Damien said before she could answer.

Quinn grabbed his arm. "Don't tell a soul I'm here."

"It's all right," Damien soothed him. "You're safe here."

"Swear to me, don't…tell anybody…"

"All right," Damien agreed. Only then would Quinn release him. Florence tucked the blankets up closer to his chin. His jaw was clenched tight, as if to keep his teeth from chattering.

"I'll bring him some hot tea," she said, and bent to turn down the lamp. Then she retrieved the supper tray. Once they got him quiet, she'd bring more hot water and finish her job with the razor.

Chapter Four

Florence wrung out a cloth and spread it across Quinn's forehead, as she'd been doing over the past four days. It was now a fight for his life as fever racked his body. The man had not proved easy to nurse. His large, muscular frame thrashed about every time they tried to remove his wet nightshirt or move him the slightest to change the linens underneath him.

She regarded him now. He slept peacefully at the moment, his face at rest. Gone were any traces of the savage-looking man who'd abducted her. In his place was an individual with strong, handsome features. His jaw was square. Either she or Albert had been shaving him to ensure he remained free of vermin. She'd grown to know the feel of every plane of his face. She knew the curve of the cleft of his chin to the small dimple placed in the center of it. Her eyes traveled over his smooth skull. She'd managed to shave it while he slept. His head was nicely shaped, as well as his ears, she noted, which didn't stick out, but lay flat against the sides of his head.

Her brother's entry interrupted her contemplation. "How is he?" Damien asked in a low tone, approaching the opposite side of the bed.

She sighed and sat back. "More or less the same. One moment the fever breaks, then a few hours later it's back. I don't like the sound of his cough either."

Damien nodded and bent over Quinn, feeling his cheek with the back of his hand. "Yes."

"He continues delirious."

"Yes, I've heard him. He seems most disquieted over several things. Probably due to his recent experience on the gallows and daring escape. It's understandable."

"Yes. He mentions a Judy and Mary and…a Joshua," she said, recalling the names. "I wonder if they are his family." She refrained from voicing the obvious—his wife and children. Strangely, she could not picture him as a husband and father, when she'd seen him only as alone and on the run.

"Likely. Why don't you let me sit with him a while?"

Why did she feel loath to leave Quinn's bedside? Florence glanced at the clock on the mantelpiece. Almost half past ten in the evening. "You need your rest. You are preaching tomorrow."

"I won't stay up long. It will give me an opportunity to go over my sermon."

In truth, her neck and shoulders ached with fatigue. "If you're sure," she said slowly. At his nod, she rose from her chair and took up her needlework from the table.

When Damien had seated himself in her vacated chair, she lingered at the foot of the bed. "You haven't decided yet what to do about Mr. Qui—Kendall?"

"I don't think there is much we can decide until the fever passes."

"And if it…shouldn't?" It was the first time she'd allowed herself to voice the thought she'd fought to keep at bay. She couldn't believe this man's life was to be for naught.

Damien adjusted the blankets on that side of Quinn. "I don't think the Lord saved this soul from the gallows to take him so quickly. We must wait and see what He would have us do."

Her brother's words reassured her. "Of course."

With a murmured good-night, she departed the room. If Damien felt as she did, it must be more than her own personal desire to wish to see Quinn well and strong. All she desired was for the Lord to have His perfect way in this man's life.

Jonah felt alternately as if he were being beaten with a rod or his body was once more huddled outside in the icy cold. At those times, he couldn't get warm, and his body shook so his teeth rattled. The pounding between his temples wouldn't go away.

He'd fall asleep only to find himself back in the dungeon of Newgate, lying against the dark stone walls of his cell. Or worse, feeling the rope around his neck and knowing in a few seconds it would be jerked against him with bruising strength. In those moments, he couldn't move, no matter how much he thrashed about. His body felt trussed like a bird's, helpless to do anything but swing in the air as he gasped for air.

He'd wake up shivering to brief moments of light. His surroundings seemed warm but he couldn't get any of that warmth into his bones. Different faces hovered over his, pressing cold compresses against his skin, chilling him even more, or thrusting spoonfuls of warm broth or foul-tasting liquids into his mouth. He welcomed the former as the heat soothed his sore throat and struggled against swallowing the latter.

Strong arms would hold him back and a stern voice would scold him. "Come, Mr. Quinn, you must drink this if you hope to be well."

He knew that voice. Firm, uncompromising. It belonged to that woman, the prison lady with the spare frame and pale features. Once he'd opened his eyes and stared straight into her light-colored ones—either washed-out blue or gray.

"You aren't going to die on us now, Mr. Quinn. You haven't put us to all this trouble to give up the ghost now." With that she'd placed another ice-cold cloth on his forehead.

Sometimes she called him Kendall, sometimes Quinn, which confused him. He hadn't the strength to argue with her. His body needed all its force to fight against the chills racking it.

Other times he'd awaken to see a pretty young woman hovering over him. She reminded him of his Judy. Plump, dark haired and rosy cheeked. This one, though, looked scared most of the time. Was he that frightening to look at? Once he'd been considered not a bad-looking sort, back in his youth. He could have had his pick of the lasses, but he'd chosen Judy for her saucy smile and curvy figure.

He remembered calling for Judy and little Mary and Joshua more than once. He kept hoping they'd answer, but only soft murmurs greeted his words.

Then finally came that night when he felt drenched. The linens clung to him. He didn't think he could sweat so much.

"God be praised. The fever has broken." The woman's voice again.

"Hallelujah." Her brother's lower, gentler one responded. Jonah struggled to open his eyes as strong arms helped him sit up. "Come, sir, let me help you with this nightshirt. It's soaking."

It was lifted off him and another, dry, one was put over him, enveloping him in its clean warmth.

"We must remove the sheets as well." The woman's hand gripped him lightly by one shoulder, helping to keep him upright.

Before he could move, they had stripped the sheet from under him and were smoothing a dry one in its place. Then the covers were removed and a dry sheet placed over him, the blankets replaced and the pillows plumped up behind him.

"Here, drink this." Miss Hathaway's hand came up under his neck and helped prop him forward to take a sip from a glass. Cool liquid slipped down his throat, which no longer hurt to swallow, he discovered. He began to gulp down the liquid, a watery, slightly sweetened drink, bringing his hand up to the cup to lift it farther.

"There now, careful or you'll spill it." He could already feel it dribbling down his chin. Miss Hathaway removed the cup and brought a cloth up to wipe him. "Would you care for some more?"

He nodded, not sure if his vocal cords were going to respond properly. She raised the glass to his mouth and this time he drank more carefully.

"There. Mustn't overdo on the first day." She placed the glass on the table and patted his mouth once more before helping him to lie back against the pillows.

She smelled the same as the cake of soap he'd used the first night here. The lavender scent brought back the evening of his first bath and decent meal. "How—" He stopped, his voice raspy beyond recognition.

"What's that?" She had leaned closer to him and peered at him. He had the sense those gray eyes missed little. After nursing him through this bout, she'd probably seen more of his hide than most people.

He attempted to clear his throat and instead erupted in a paroxysm of coughing.

"Easy there, Mr. Qu—" She handed him a handkerchief. "Your fever has broken, but your lungs are still quite congested."

When his coughing had subsided, he began again. "How long've I been lying here?"

"Nearly a fortnight. You came to us on a Saturday eve, and it is now Wednesday, the fifth of March."

He laid his head back and shut his eyes. February had gone by without his recollection, except for blurred images.

No sooner had his head touched the pillowcase than he sensed the difference. His fingers touched his scalp. It felt the way his chin did when he hadn't shaved in a few days.

His eyelids opened and he stared at the woman standing over him. She'd had her way after all.

"No lice, I suppose," he muttered.

Although she didn't smile, he thought he detected something like humor in those gray eyes. "You are lice-free, I'm happy to report."

He hadn't the energy to feel angry. Lying back, looking at Miss Hathaway, he suddenly realized the great debt he owed her for nursing him through. If he'd been sick nearly a fortnight…

If he hadn't found his way to this house, where would he be now? Long dead in some gutter, his body picked over by stray dogs.

Quinn's condition improved rapidly after that day. His appetite grew in like measure, and Florence had to struggle to get him to satisfy himself with light custards and broths until she judged him sufficiently improved to digest more solid food.

"Is it back at Newgate I am?" he asked three days later, looking with disdain at the poached egg lying in a bowl, its only accompaniment a thin sliver of dry toast.

"Your stomach has held nothing down but teas and broths for over a week. If you don't want to suffer severe abdominal pains, you will satisfy yourself with what Mrs. Nichols prepares for you."

"You want to keep me weak as a kitten and at your mercy in this bed, is what I think," he said, picking up the spoon and shoveling it into the watery egg. "First you shave my head while I'm lying out of my wits, and now you starve me."

She folded her arms to keep from boxing his ear. Ever since he'd regained consciousness, he seemed to do nothing but complain to her. To the others, he behaved with more politeness than she'd expect from a Newgate convict. But to her he seemed to do nothing but find fault. Was he still angry that she'd shaved his head?

"On the contrary, Mr.…Kendall," she told him

now, "I'd have you strong and well so you no longer grumble. Honestly, what have the reverend and I brought upon ourselves opening our doors to you?"

For a second, she read a stunned hurt in his eyes. But it was gone immediately as he focused on wiping out the remains of the egg in his bowl with his toast. A man of his brutish strength and rude ways wouldn't be bothered by her words. Still, her conscience smote her for her unkind remark. What would Damien say if he'd heard her?

After she'd left the room, Jonah sat on the edge of the bed and swung the covers off, his arm feeling like jelly in the process. He needed to use the chamber pot and didn't want to ring for either the curate or Albert. Not after Miss Hathaway's remark.

Her comment rankled. No less because it was true. What had he brought on these innocent people? If he should be discovered hiding in the parsonage, what would happen to them?

He scratched his jaw, his whiskers feeling itchy, although not nearly as bad as his face and scalp had felt for months now. Once again, he passed a hand over his head, unused to the smooth feel of it. Although it didn't feel so smooth now. Rough stubble grazed his fingertips.

He took a deep breath and tried to stand. A wave of dizziness passed over him and he reached out for a bedpost, but he was too far away. He fell back down on the soft bed.

He twisted around as a knock sounded on the door. It couldn't be one of the women—they never knocked as they came in with some potion to administer or to take the very sheets from beneath him and make up his bed.

"Come in."

The Reverend Hathaway poked his head in the doorway. "Good morning, Mr. Kendall," he said with a smile. "I hope I'm not disturbing you. My sister said you were awake."

"No, you're not disturbing me." He quirked his lips. "I was just about to use the chamber pot—" His words broke off as the reverend came in followed by his sister.

Her clear gray gaze locked with his. Any softness he'd sensed in them during his fever had long since gone.

"Of course. If you'll excuse us, Florence." Hathaway turned to his sister. For a second she seemed to hesitate—goodness knows, she probably thought she owned him body and soul after nursing him the way she had—then with a nod, she retreated and shut the door behind her.

Hathaway helped Jonah to his feet. "I'm sure you're feeling as weak as a kitten. It's understandable. You'll quickly regain your strength." As he spoke he led Jonah to the screen in the corner of the room. "There you go. Need any more help?"

"No, I'll manage." He'd been helped on and off a bedpan enough already by Albert.

"Very well, I'll leave you and return in a few minutes."

After Jonah had finished, he managed to make it to the dressing table and splash water on his face and hands. As he took up a facecloth, he noticed a hand mirror lying facedown on the table. Gingerly he took it up and turned it over.

An unrecognizable face stared back at him. A skull covered over with a light layer of black fuzz, gaunt cheeks shadowed by a layer of bristly whiskers. He passed a hand over his jaw once again, feeling the hollow cheeks, which made his cheekbones look wider. His face had always been full, his neck corded with muscle. Now, he looked like a caricature of that man.

He fingered the cleft in his chin. At least a few recognizable markings still remained. The eyes, too, were familiar. Their dark green irises, framed by black lashes and covered by heavy black eyebrows, stared back at him.

He scowled as his gaze traveled upward to his skull. His forehead seemed way too high now with no black curls to frame it. At least the hair was growing back although it looked shorter than his beard at this point.

He looked like a wrestler or prizefighter, except he no longer had the girth required.

A knock sounded once again on the door. He quickly put down the mirror and began making his way back to the bed, calling out "Come in" as he did so.

Mr. Hathaway returned with his sister. The curate hurried forward and took Jonah by the arm. With a defiant look at Miss Hathaway, Jonah shook the other man off. "That's all right, Reverend. I'm getting me legs back."

"That's good." Hathaway helped tuck the blankets around him once Jonah was in bed, then pulled up a chair for his sister and one for himself.

Again, Jonah glanced at the woman. She perched in that ramrod straight way of hers. So prim she was, with the tongue of a harpy. Pity, the brother seemed to have gotten all the looks in the family. Whereas the curate was blue eyed with wavy, light brown hair, his sister was a pale likeness. Her cheeks, although smooth, had no color in them. Her hair, covered with a lacy cap, was also light brown, but straight and of a shade with no golden tints in it like her brother's. Her eyes were a washed-out imitation of his, neither gray nor blue. And yet, there was something compelling in them. Something that challenged a man, the way they could stare him down.

He looked away suddenly, ashamed of his critical appraisal. This was the only person who'd opened her doors to him and who'd nursed him for the past fortnight.

Hathaway folded his hands on his lap. "I wanted to have a talk with you now that the fever has broken. I realize you still need some time to recover your strength, but I thought it a good time to discuss what we ought to do in the coming weeks."

Hathaway's blue eyes searched his. "You are still a wanted man. Although the commotion died down in the time you were ill, your name remains among the wanted and there have been posters with your picture placed around Newgate according to Florence."

Jonah's eyes went to Miss Hathaway. "You've been back there?"

"It's my work."

He frowned, imagining it wouldn't be long before the constable came around.

As if reading his thoughts, she said, "You may rest easy, Mr. Kendall. They know nothing about my abduction except that I was held for a few hours in a place on Saffron Hill I would never be able to find again."

The news didn't ease his worry. Jonah went to rake a hand through his hair. His fingers met stubble and he made a fist.

"Nothing has been posted around here or in Mayfair," the curate added in a hasty tone. "I'm sure the magistrates believe you are hiding somewhere in the East End, indeed, if you even remain in London."

Only somewhat relieved, Jonah took a deep breath and unclenched his hand. "I don't suppose anyone'd ever imagine me holed up in the West End."

The reverend returned the smile. "That does

make things a lot easier. You must remain in hiding for the foreseeable future. If you were discovered now, it would mean a prompt hanging with doubled security. From the newspaper accounts, the Crown has been made a fool of. The band rescuing you seems to have been led by a competing receiver of stolen goods. A question of revenge and encroachment of one another's territory. Perhaps they thought they could use you against your former employer."

Jonah shook his head. "And I was the ignorant gull caught in the middle."

"It seems so. Though I doubt that will make the authorities any more sympathetic to your case." The curate paused. "Florence and I have been discussing your choices."

Jonah glanced from one to the other. Miss Hathaway hadn't spoken yet and her serious face made him question whether he had any choice but the noose. "Do I have any?"

Hathaway smiled faintly. "A few. You can leave our house once you feel fully recovered, if you choose. I wouldn't recommend that path unless you have some friends or family who are willing to help you out."

Jonah shook his head. He had no one to run the risk of hiding him…other than this man and his sister.

Miss Hathaway leaned toward him. "Have you *any* family at all?" When he said nothing, she added, "You mentioned a…Judy…and Mary and… Joshua in your fever."

He turned away from her gently probing look

and picked at the threads of his coverlet. He felt his neck flush as he pictured himself ranting out the most personal details of his life in his delirium. "I…had a wife and two bairns."

Her soft voice broke into his thoughts. "What happened to them?"

He kept his eyes fixed on the blanket beneath his hands, its pattern blurring. "Brought 'em—" He cleared his throat. "Brought 'em with me when I came to London." After a few minutes he was able to continue. "All three died last winter from fever."

"I'm sorry," both of them said.

He wiped the corner of his eyes with the back of his hand, despising himself for his loss of control. When he finally looked at the Hathaways again, he read only compassion in their eyes.

"You've nothin' to be sorry for. It was the fault of a city that doesn't let a man defend himself nor earn the bread to feed his family."

"Do you have any other family?" the curate asked.

"My kin is scattered across Bedfordshire. I lost touch with 'em once we came to London. I wouldn't want to involve them in my misfortune. They have little eno' as it is. They're likely facing terrible times themselves."

Hathaway nodded. "Another option is to flee the country. We could provide you with some money, but I know little enough of getting you aboard a ship heading to lands beyond. You'd need false papers for one thing. France, the closest, would be difficult as we're at war. With the blockade, seas are danger-ous if you should choose to venture farther."

Jonah could not imagine leaving England. Just leaving his native village and coming to London had proved disastrous.

Miss Hathaway spoke. "There is one other pos-sibility."

Slowly, Jonah raised his head as she continued. "I would say 'impossibility,' except that my brother would remind me we serve a God of the impossible."

Jonah waited, his body tensing.

"Commutation of your sentence."

The words meant nothing to him. "I…don't ken the expression."

The curate explained. "If we appeal to the home secretary for clemency—that is to say, mercy—there is a possibility that your sentence could be commuted to life or to transportation to the colony."

"You mean I'd either have to rot in that stinkin' Newgate cell, or be stuffed into the hold of one of those prison hulks—"

"Most likely it would mean transport," Miss Hathaway said.

"Which means death on the seas."

"It *is* a harrowing journey, I'll grant you, but for those who arrive, there is the chance for a fresh start."

"Living like a slave out there for the years of me sentence."

The young curate leaned forward. "There is also the possibility of a royal pardon."

Pardon. The word rang in the stillness. Then Jonah remembered he wasn't guilty in the first place. "For something I never done?"

"Something you did *unwittingly,*" the curate corrected gently. "If we could get the home secretary to consider the innocence of your action, there is a chance for a full pardon."

Miss Hathaway cleared her throat. "Do not let my brother's words get your hopes up, Mr. Kendall. There is *very* little likelihood of a pardon. Your best hope lies in transport to the colony. However—" her slim fingers formed pleats in her skirt as she spoke "—my brother has a scheme, and I am willing to consider it, however little chance it has of succeeding."

"Don't let my sister's words frighten you."

Jonah looked from brother to sister and back again, his worry only growing. What did they mean, "scheme"?

Miss Hathaway folded her hands in her lap. "There would be no hope for clemency unless you showed yourself a thoroughly reformed individual."

Jonah frowned at her. "Reformed from what?"

"Reformed from the defiant individual who stood on the gallows refusing to kneel in prayer and who later flaunted all authorities when he fled the gallows."

In contrast to the grim picture his sister painted,

Mr. Hathaway's tone was gentle. "Pardons are not as uncommon as you may think. Many a man—and woman—has been issued a full pardon when they've shown themselves repentant of their deed."

His uneasiness grew. "But I'm not guilty of anything."

"Unfortunately, the fact that you were rescued from the gallows and a riot ensued will not go over well with the home secretary," the curate reminded him. "However, Miss Hathaway has achieved a good reputation working among the prisoners of Newgate. If she vouches for your character, that will guarantee you an audience at least."

Jonah looked at Miss Hathaway. He knew little of her work as the prison lady.

The curate continued. "That is only the beginning, however. We must also prove to the home secretary and to the lord chancellor, and ultimately to the prince regent himself, that you are a reformed individual—a man who looks and sounds respectable, a man as far from the one who escaped the gallows as day from night."

"The first step, therefore, Mr. Kendall, is to transform you into a gentleman," Miss Hathaway finished for her brother.

Jonah stared at her as if she'd told him he must fly to the moon. "A what?"

"A gentleman. A man the home secretary can understand. He knows nothing of the plight of a poor farmer from East Anglia whose cattle has lost its grazing rights through the system of enclosures, but a man who is presentable, can speak his language, and is an upright member of society, exercising a trade and living an exemplary life—that man *might* just win the secretary's sympathy."

Jonah gave a bark of laughter. "A gentleman! Who would ever believe Jonah Quinn as a gentleman?"

Mr. Hathaway tapped his knee, a light of optimism in his eyes. "If you allow Miss Hathaway and myself have a go at your, er, education, you might be surprised at the results." He turned to his sister. "Miss Hathaway can coach you in the finer points of etiquette, manners and dress, and I can help you refine your speech a bit. By the way, can you read?"

Jonah grunted. "Well enough."

"That's very good. Did you receive some schooling as a child?"

He shrugged. "Taught meself to read once I arrived in London. Never had no need of it back home."

They both looked at him, eyes wide.

He stared right back at them. Didn't they believe him?

"That's remarkable," Miss Hathaway said. "How did you do that?"

Did she think he was as brutish as he looked? "I found an old schoolbook in the rubbish. It must have been a child's primer, all beat up and dirty." He shook his head at the memory of hours spent in the dim light of evenings, bent over the torn pages. "I studied it and studied it until I figured out the pictures." He smiled, remembering the drawings. "*A* is for apple, *B* for boy, *C*...cat. If I close my eyes, I can still see those pictures. The letters and their sounds began to make sense and soon I could put together the letters I saw on street signs and make out whole words. 'Course I can't read a whole lot, but enough to get by."

"And no one had ever taught you before?" Her tone remained dubious.

"No." He folded his arms across his chest. "And I had no need of it neither, farming the land." Bitterness crept into his voice. "When I still had some land to farm."

Hathaway sat back with a satisfied air. "This is wonderful. If you'll permit me, I can help fill in the gaps, perhaps teach you some arithmetic as well."

"I don't mind. I suppose I'll have to while away my time somehow till I'm fit again. I'm as weak as a fish right now."

"That will pass. Now, to more practical matters. You took the name William Kendall the first night you arrived. Does anyone know you by that name?"

He shook his head. "It was the first thing that popped into my head. William is me brother's name and Kendall me mother's family name."

"Very clever. It will do, don't you think?" The curate turned to Miss Hathaway.

"Yes," she answered more slowly. "My brother and I don't believe in telling falsehoods," she said. "However, in this case, we see the necessity of concealing your identity. And since they are family names, they are not wholly untrue."

"So, from today forward, we will only refer to you as Mr. Kendall."

Jonah thought of something else. "Where are me clothes? I think I'd like to get out of this bed. Seems I've been here months."

He turned to his sister. "His clothes?"

"I'm afraid they've been disposed of."

"What do you mean, disposed of?" Quinn asked, feeling a sudden terror.

"Burned."

"Burned?" He swore then stopped in midsentence at Miss Hathaway's stern frown.

"The vermin," she said. "We had to ensure there would be no spread of it through the household."

He stared at her, panic growing in him. "I had some…things…" Once again, his face felt hot at having to confess these things to this lady.

"You had a lock of hair and a small square of cloth in one pocket," she said in a softer tone. "I saved them for you, supposing they were sentimental keepsakes." She rose and went to the bedside table. From the drawer she extracted a ragged square of dirty calico and the dark curl. She handed them to him. "Is this what you meant?"

He took them without a word, enclosing them in his fist, ashamed and comforted at the same time. These were the only keepsakes he had of his former life, the lock of Judy's hair and the bit of cloth from one of little Mary's frocks. He swallowed the lump in his throat. Nothing remained of his Joshua. He cleared his throat and glared at the woman standing over him.

"So, what am I supposed to walk around in? My nightshirt?"

"We'll procure some new clothes for you." She turned to her brother. "We can send for Mr. Bourke, my brother's tailor," she added, sparing Jonah a glance. She continued addressing her brother. "He can measure Mr. Kendall and have some things made up for him. Mrs. Nichols and I can begin immediately on some shirts and neckcloths."

Again she was treating him as if he wasn't in the room. "In the meantime what am I supposed to do?" he said to her back.

She turned to him. "In the meantime, you'll have to satisfy yourself with a nightshirt and dressing gown of my brother's."

"I haven't much choice, I suppose?" His glance went slowly from sister to brother, and he saw the understanding in their eyes. He was not just referring to the state of his wardrobe.

"I'm afraid not," Hathaway said, an apologetic note in his tone. "Which brings me to the most important question."

Jonah stared into the young man's eyes.

"Are you willing to trust us to do what is best for you for however long you remain under our roof?"

The curate smiled as he ended, softening the solemnity of his words.

Miss Hathaway's expression was not so encouraging. Her gray eyes measured him. "My brother believes this is your best chance. I am willing to do whatever I can to ensure you are presentable." She paused. "My brother has asked for your trust. But my question to you is, can we trust you? Will you do your part, Mr. Kendall? It will be no easy task to change the habits of a lifetime."

Her steady gray eyes looked skeptical and her words left him with no doubt that he would have to earn her approval.

Was he up to it?

Did he have a choice?

The young curate held out his hand. After a moment, Jonah stretched out his own. The two clasped hands, sealing their bargain. Although he didn't shake Miss Hathaway's hand, somehow he knew the biggest hurdle would be to prove himself to her.

Chapter Five

Florence sat on the striped settee in the upstairs morning room and watched Mr. Bourke wrap his tape measure about Mr. Quinn's neck. "Sixteen and a half. A thick neck," he mumbled, jotting on his notepad.

Quinn stood in his nightshirt, a stoic look on his face. His hair was starting to grow in, showing a black shadow all over his head. Florence frowned. The shadow continued down the front of his cheeks. The man hadn't shaved again this morning. She gave a mental shake of her head. It would take more than her brother imagined to change this man's personal habits and bring about any semblance of gentleman.

The tailor whipped the tape measure off. "Arms apart." Quinn spread his arms out. "Wider, please." The little man reached around Quinn's torso with the tape, resembling a squirrel trying to embrace a mighty oak. To his credit, Quinn remained patient.

He hadn't said anything since greeting the tailor with, "Come to dress me at last?"

He whistled. "Forty-five and a quarter…a broad chest that," he muttered. He proceeded to his waist. "Thirty-three and a quarter." The tape went around his hips. "Thirty-eight."

He clicked his tongue, looking at the numbers on his pad. "Not a classic build. The shoulders are too broad, though at least the waist is trim. He certainly won't require a corset."

Florence cleared her throat. "All we need, as I explained earlier, are good suits of clothes proper for a gentleman of, er, Mr. Kendall's stature." The tailor wrapped the tape around a bicep.

"Fourteen and a quarter. Make a fist please… sixteen and a quarter," he noted of the expanded bicep.

Again, he tsk-tsked. "This man's dimensions are quite disproportionate, more suitable for a prize-fighter than for a gentleman."

Quinn cocked an eyebrow at the smaller man. "I have fought in the ring a time or two."

The tailor stepped back. "Indeed, sir? Where was that? Maybe I've see you fight."

"I rather doubt it. They were local fights during country fairs, and suchlike, up in Bedfordshire."

"Pray, let us continue with the fitting." Florence eyed Jonah with a frown. So, they not only had a convict on their hands, but also a prizefighter.

"Yes, of course, Miss Hathaway." Bourke

glanced down at his notepad, continuing to talk to himself. This time the words no longer sounded critical, but were beginning to reflect awe. "The shoulder span wide, the waist narrow, the hips—" he nodded his head, his lips pursed "—the same. Now for the back." He stepped behind Quinn and spread the tape across the breadth of his shoulders. "Eighteen and a half. Nice and wide…will require more cloth than usual."

The tailor peered around at Florence, the tape measure dangling from his neck. "I see a navy-blue, double-breasted tailcoat with square tails…let us say…to the knee, not farther, a bit of gathering at the shoulder, a narrow collar with a long roll to here…" he said, waving his hand to illustrate the point. "Velvet perhaps on one? A waistcoat of the same material and one of a contrasting color? Red satin?"

She pressed her lips together in disapproval. The last thing she needed was his turning Quinn into a macaroni. Before she could contradict him, the tailor took a few steps away from Quinn and eyed him. "As for materials, a fine broadcloth, one in navy, another in black? Or perhaps bottle-green?" He turned to Florence again.

"Green," she found herself saying and only then realized she was thinking of the color of his eyes. She glanced up at them and quickly away.

"Excellent choice, Miss Hathaway." The tailor wrote down the color. "And the waistcoats? A half a dozen? Cashmere, lutestring, a satin for Sunday wear," he rattled off, answering his own question. "I have a lovely embroidered silk in pink and blue…"

"Nothing to call attention," she said at once. "Sober colors, cream or ivory and some dark to match the coat."

He looked down his thin nose at her. "Miss Hathaway, everything Bourke & Sons of Bond Street does is in the utmost taste." He turned his back to her and surveyed Quinn, the measuring tape stretched taut between his hands. "Now for the length. Excuse me, sir." He bent over and held the tape down the outside of Quinn's leg to his bare ankle. "Very good." Then he proceeded to measure the inward length.

Florence averted her gaze but not before it crossed Quinn's. Was that amusement she read in their black-fringed depths? Or were they merely sardonic?

She pressed her lips together and looked away from him. If he thought to discompose her, he had another think coming. She'd seen enough of the man during his fever that the sight of a tailor measuring his leg could hardly put her to the blush. Without conscious thought, she remembered the broad planes of his muscular chest and ropelike biceps when she'd bathed him.

She rocked her leg back and forth across her knee and fixed her eyes on the fireplace across the room. She must really polish the candlesticks on the mantel. The silver bases were showing signs of tarnish. Soon it would be time for the spring cleaning—

"And the thighs…" Mr. Bourke whipped the tape measure around one. "Twenty-five. No padding needed there."

"I should hope not," Florence said, unable to keep her gaze from flickering back to the outline of Quinn's leg. The tailor moved the tape measure around the circumference of one calf then down to his ankle. She swallowed, noting how well proportioned his legs were.

The tailor flipped his notebook shut and began to roll up his tape measure. "I think that will do for now. I shall have a pair of trousers and a coat and waistcoat ready to be fitted in—" he pursed his lips "—shall we say, three days?"

"Three days I'm to be without clothes?"

The tailor blinked at Quinn's tone of outrage. Florence stood at once. "What he means is that he really needs the first outfit as soon as possible. His others were, er, damaged beyond repair."

"Oh, rest assured, we shall have a few good outfits ready in no time."

"Very well, we shall make do with what he has for the present." She gave Quinn a stern look so he wouldn't commit any more slips, before turning back to Bourke. "Mr. Kendall only needs some presentable suits, nothing too fancy. Shall we expect you Thursday morning then for the first fitting?"

"Nine o'clock, Miss Hathaway, if that is not too early for you?"

"Certainly not. Nine o'clock it is then." She

escorted the tailor to the door. "Why don't you have a cup of coffee before you go?"

"That would be lovely…."

Their voices faded down the hall. "That would be lovely," mimicked Jonah in a simpering tone. "In the meantime I continue flitting about in a nightshirt. I'm almost as much a prisoner in these fancy surroundings as I was back at Newgate."

"What's that about Newgate?"

Jonah jumped, but relaxed at the curate's smiling face in the open doorway.

"Oh…just mumbling to myself."

"I saw Mr. Bourke leaving. I trust your fitting went well."

"If getting every inch of meself measured means a pair of trousers and shirt, then it went splendidly."

Hathaway chuckled. "You'll soon be walking around like a fine gentleman."

Jonah harrumphed and marched back into his bed. "I'd as soon have a pair of trousers and a plain shirt o' Albert's if it meant going about clothed today."

"Well, why not? I'll talk to him straightaway. I'm sure he wouldn't mind lending you something."

Jonah's eyes widened at the man's ready assent. "You will?"

"Certainly. Why wouldn't I? You must be tired of hanging about up here all day. I apologize for ignoring you most of yesterday. Sundays are busy days for us."

"You had guests," he began, thinking of the fancy coach he'd seen parked in front of the house as he'd whiled away the lonely hours upstairs.

He smiled. "Yes, the rector of the parish. Reverend Doyle. He's a most learned man." With a lift of his brows, he indicated the chair, and Jonah quickly nodded, realizing the man was asking his permission to sit down. It was his house, after all, his room, his bl— furniture, for goodness' sake.

"He's your boss, is he?"

Hathaway settled down in the straight-back chair. "Yes, you could say that. But more than that he's a mentor and advisor. He's taught me a lot over the years." He rubbed the cloth of his knee breeches just above the wooden leg. "He's the one who made it possible for me to attend university."

"Is that so?"

"Yes. His high recommendation to a local lord gave me favor with the gentleman, who paid for my studies there."

"Your own kin didn't have the blunt?"

"No. My father was a clockmaker, you see."

"He wasn't a gentleman?" He looked at the fine cut of the man's coat. "But I thought you were a—"

Hathaway quirked an eyebrow, humor lighting his blue eyes. "A gentleman? No, I'm an artisan's son. It shows how much a man can achieve with the proper education."

Quinn shook his head. "But you've got to have a head for letters."

"Yes. But there's a lot the average person's head is capable of if given half the chance."

Quinn scratched at the stubble of his jaw. "You think so?"

"I know so. My sister and I teach children at the local orphanage in Marylebone. These children come from all levels of society, and yet they are like sponges." The curate's long fingers moved in animation. "You should see how quickly they learn their letters and numbers and are clamoring for more."

"But they're young. Their minds are, like you say, sponges."

"Yes, that is so. An older person may be more set in his thinking, but that doesn't mean his brain is less capable of learning if he sets his mind to it."

Jonah merely shook his head.

"You'll see, by week's end, you shall be dressed like a gentleman and soon my sister shall have you speaking and behaving like one, too."

He remembered Miss Hathaway's exactitude during the fitting. "Miss Hathaway and Mr. Bourke seemed mighty particular about the sort of clothes I'm to wear. I never realized there was so much involved in dressing like a gentleman."

Hathaway chuckled. "Don't let it rattle you. I let Florence take over the selection of my wardrobe long ago, realizing she had a much better eye for such things than I did. Left to my own devices I'd probably wear the wrong waistcoat with the wrong coat, or a different colored pair of stockings—"

Jonah started to laugh until he glanced down and realized the man's error. The wooden leg seemed to grow larger between the two of them. He coughed. "How did you, uh, lose the leg?"

Hathaway touched the leather strap holding the wooden peg in place. "A wagon ran over me as a child."

Jonah widened his eyes at the calm tone.

"I was eight. I was in charge of herding a flock of ducks back to our pond and I ran after one, heedless of the traffic on the road."

"I'm sorry, sir."

"I was fortunate not to be killed altogether. But the Lord was merciful. He spared my life for my parents' sake. They only had Florence and myself," he explained.

Jonah shook his head at the young man's lack of self-pity. He himself couldn't get over the fact the curate wasn't even the son of a gentleman. He'd never have guessed it. He made a very fine-looking gent from his golden brown hair to his aristocratic features. "Pity about the leg, though," he said.

A flush was the only indication that the words might have caused him any discomfort. "Perhaps it was a blessing in disguise."

Jonah cocked an eyebrow. "How do you figure that?"

"I think my, er, impediment has made me more readily submit to God with my whole heart." His lips curved upward. "I can identify with Jacob in the

Old Testament when he wrestled with the Angel of the Lord one night. Are you familiar with the story?"

Here it came. Was Hathaway going to evangelize him the way his sister did those at Newgate? "No...I never heard much o' the Bible."

"Pity. Well, Jacob wrestled an entire night with a stranger."

Jonah leaned forward. A wrestling story, that sounded interesting.

"Jacob was going to meet his brother, whom he had wronged many years before."

"Hmm. And he got into a fight?"

He grinned. "God met with him one night."

Jonah raised an eyebrow.

"Jacob was all alone. God appeared in the form of a man and wrestled silently with him. It wasn't until Jacob found it impossible to best him that he realized this was more than a mere mortal."

"It was God?"

"The Bible says it was 'the Angel of the Lord.' Jacob was a shrewd fellow. When he perceived it was a divine being, he wouldn't let go until he received a blessing."

Jonah rubbed his bare head, still expecting to find thick hair there. "Can a man fight with God and come out alive?"

"If God has a purpose with that individual and must first wrestle with him to put to death the 'old man.'"

"The old man?"

"The man in the flesh," Hathaway explained. "He will always contend with the man of the spirit."

"So, how do you figure all this in your own case?"

Hathaway smiled. "Well, to break the stalemate, the Angel eventually touched the hollow of Jacob's thigh and it immediately became dislocated. Jacob walked with a limp for the rest of his life."

"Ah." He was beginning to see the connection. "So, would you say God fought with you and you lived through it but lost your leg?"

Hathaway's eyes twinkled. "I would say, rather, I came out of that accident with a realization, earlier in life than most people, of how much I must depend on God."

Jonah rubbed an earlobe. "You weren't railing at God for such a misfortune?"

The curate shook his head, a far-off look in his blue eyes, as if he were seeing himself again. "I was only a lad of eight. My parents had raised me to know a God of love, not one of vengeance. After the terrible physical pain of the accident was over, I was faced with a different situation."

Jonah waited.

"Being viewed with pity by my elders or with ridicule by my peers."

"Aye."

"I had to get used to people staring at the absence of a leg first thing, before they even looked at my face. I needed desperately to be able to hold my head up in public." Hathaway continued more slowly, his long, lean fingers rubbing the cloth of his pant leg above the wooden peg. "I think this need made it easier for me, in a way, to submit to God. It made me understand more quickly God's love for me."

He gazed keenly at Jonah. "No matter how human beings were to treat me, I could be sure God did not look at the exterior man, this man of flesh with its glaring imperfection, but He looked deep into the interior of me, and saw the real man I was, whole and sound."

Jonah shifted uncomfortably as he remembered the scorn he'd endured when he'd been shackled like a murderer and heard the clank of the iron-barred door closing behind him. He wasn't one of those criminals, he'd wanted to rail at the turnkey, but all he'd seen was ridicule and derision on the grimy face.

"When I lost my leg, I learned the truth of the Scripture verse which says 'my strength is made perfect in weakness.' It might have taken me many more years to understand and submit to that teaching if it hadn't been for the accident. I probably wouldn't have achieved all that I did for a mere clockmaker's son—gone to Oxford, been ordained as a clergyman, and now at the age of six-and-twenty gotten a curacy in the greatest city in the world." He sat up and smiled. "I would probably be a simple watchmaker, working alongside my father in his small shop and content with that."

Jonah cleared his throat. "Would that have been so bad? You had a roof over your head, a fair income, I'll wager, and your family around you." So many had far less.

Hathaway looked at him with understanding. "No, I'm sure I would have been content...but would the Lord have been?"

Chapter Six

Was it just four days ago, I was still simply a man and not a confounded gentleman? Jonah tried to hide his grimace, but every time he moved it seemed something pinched or dug into him.

His neck felt as if it was encased in swathing an inch thick and a foot high. He could hardly bend his chin down enough to see his food. His new "pantaloons," as they were called, chafed him they were so fitted. His coat and waistcoat, similarly close-tailored, made him feel he had to ask the sleeves their leave before he could maneuver his arms. He didn't think he could lift them much above his shoulders.

What wouldn't he give now to be back taking his meals in the kitchen with the Nicholses, dressed in Albert's comfortable work clothes? Apart from a couple of hours each morning with Hathaway in his study, Jonah had spent most of his days helping Albert with any chores that needed doing.

He was momentarily distracted from the discomfort of his new clothes by the sight of the serving dishes set on the table by the young girl, Betsy, the Nicholses' daughter, the one who always reminded him of his Judy when she'd been that age, before illness and poverty had worn her down to a shadow of herself.

Jonah winked at the girl as she moved away, and she blushed and began to giggle, but stifled it quickly at Miss Hathaway's frown.

Mr. Hathaway bowed his head. A quick glance showed his sister following suit. Jonah did the same, having become accustomed that each meal began with a blessing.

The curate's soft tones broke the silence. "Dear Heavenly Father, we thank You for the food before us. We ask You to bless it for our bodies' use. In Your Son's name, Amen."

Good. Short, sweet and to the point.

Soon a heaped plate was passed to him and he gave a sigh of satisfaction, breathing in the savory scents wafting from it. Each day brought a new variety of food. He wondered if he'd ever get used to having such a tasty array set before him. Today's plate held a joint of chicken leg and thigh, some boiled potatoes covered in a creamy sauce, some mashed turnips—good, filling food. He picked up the thick folded napkin at the side of his plate and unfolded it as he saw Miss Hathaway do. Then he tucked it into his cravat, though there was precious little space in which to do so.

Jonah leaned forward and picked up the chicken leg and brought it to his mouth. It was as succulent as it smelled. He took another healthy bite.

The sound of Miss Hathaway clearing her throat made him look up.

Both Mr. and Miss Hathaway sat looking at him as he held the chicken leg a few inches from his lips. Mr. Hathaway quickly focused back on his own plate. His silverware clinked on the surface of the china as he cut into his chicken.

Miss Hathaway rested her knife and fork at an angle against the edges of her plate, her lips pursed as she continued studying Jonah without saying a word.

He slowly stopped chewing, the remaining bit of chicken feeling like a wad of wool when it finally went down his throat.

"In this household, Mr. Kendall, we do not eat our meats with our hands." She fixed her gaze on the chicken leg still held between his fingers as if it were a rat the cat had carried in. "We use the two implements at either side of your plate. They are set there for a purpose." In illustration, she lifted her knife and fork upright, suspending them between her thumbs and forefingers above the snowy-white tablecloth.

Jonah's glance flickered to Mr. Hathaway's, but he found no succor in that quarter. The curate didn't even look up from his food but continued to eat as if unaware of the silent battle being fought between his sister and Jonah.

Jonah took an instant decision. So far, he'd behaved with amazing patience and forbearance— allowing himself to be shaved bald like a plucked chicken, then standing half-naked while a foppish tailor wrapped him in a tape measure, all the while under Miss Hathaway's ever-critical eye.

He brought the chicken leg back to his mouth. And though it no longer tasted as it had a moment before, he took a good healthy bite and began to chew, loudly.

Only when he'd swallowed did he put down the offending leg. He looked at his fingertips. They were shiny with chicken grease. He proceeded to lick them off one by one, reminding himself with each appendage, that this was what he'd always done in his own cottage.

The sound of his mouth against his fingers was the only one in that large dining room with its heavy dark furniture and spotless tablecloth covered with crystal vases and shining silver bowls. So much silver could have paid his rent for a few years.

Lastly, he took his hand and swiped the back of it against his mouth to remove any lingering chicken juices. All the while he returned Miss Hathaway's icy stare with a steady one of his own.

"You realize, *Mr.* Kendall, do you not, that where you spend your future, your very life, depends upon your manners." She cleared her throat. "A *gentle-man*—" she placed only a slight stress on the word "—holds his silverware thus." She replaced her knife and fork on the table and picked them up again, poising them over her plate as if in preparation to cutting her own chicken.

"And if they be as ignorant as I am?" he asked blandly, ignoring the throb of a pulse at his temple.

He heard a choked sound from Mr. Hathaway, but when he turned to look at him, he found him once again with his head studiously bent over his plate, his napkin held to his mouth.

"They shan't be."

"What makes you so sure o' the fact?"

"They'll have been trained, unlike you, to the office of gentleman since the time they were in short pants. Eating properly will have become second nature to them by the time they are out of the nursery." She paused. "How old did you say you were, Mr. Kendall?"

Before answering her question, he lifted the crystal goblet beside his plate and took a long swallow. He smacked his lips before setting it down. "I didn't say."

"And how old, precisely, are you, Mr. Kendall?"

"Four-and-thirty November last." He drummed his fingers on the tablecloth. "Let's see…sitting in an overcrowded cell, awaiting trial, as I recall. With no money to buy extra victuals, I was enjoying the standard fare of hard biscuits and watery soup."

He had the satisfaction of seeing Miss Hathaway look back down at her plate.

"Thirty-four is a fine age for a man." Mr. Hathaway broke the awkward silence. He sat back in his chair at the head of the table and toyed with the stem of his glass. "You're over the folly of youth yet haven't yet entered into the infirmity of old age. Our Lord was in his early thirties when He began His ministry on this earth."

"Is that so?" Jonah asked, his mind still on his silent battle with Miss Hathaway. She had taken her first bite of food—a small, dainty bite, he noticed—and now chewed, her prim mouth firmly closed, making no sound.

He looked back down at his own plate, which no longer looked as appetizing as when it had been served him.

"Your first real test," Mr. Hathaway said in a gentle tone, "will be when you sit at table in company." He glanced down the length of the table at his sister. "We have frequent guests here at the parish. Florence has her ladies' group, and we often have dinner guests. The rector dines with us most Sundays, or we go to St. Marylebone and dine at the vicarage. He will probably be the first one to meet Mr. Kendall, don't you think, Flo?"

She nodded, her face returning to him, her look measuring. Jonah studied the delicate movements of her throat as she swallowed. Only then did she speak. "That is likely."

Mr. Hathaway turned back to Jonah. "The rector is a personal friend as well and frequently stops to call. If he doesn't question your presence in our household, others will accept you. He is the only one of our parish even aware of my sister's abduction that day at Newgate."

"It is thankful the craze over Lord Byron has eclipsed your escape from the public's memory," Miss Hathaway added drily.

Jonah looked from her to her brother. "And if I don't pass the good rector's inspection in spite of all Miss Hathaway's instruction?" It was *his* neck at most risk, after all.

Hathaway fingered his napkin holder. "I'm afraid then the safest course would be for you to remain indoors, in hiding. You'd only be trading one prison for another, and I don't believe that would be acceptable to you."

Jonah took another swallow from his goblet and set it down with a thump. "I'd prefer a hanging to that."

"Just so." The curate sat back. "That is why it is so crucial that you follow Miss Hathaway's instructions."

Jonah glanced to the other end of the table, expecting to see smug triumph on her thin face. Instead, her gray eyes were...assessing. With a heartfelt sigh of capitulation, he picked up his knife and fork and proceeded to cut into the piece of now-cold chicken.

He was stopped by Miss Hathaway's soft but implacable voice. "The knife and fork is held in this manner."

He looked up and, without a word, copied her example. It felt awkward to hold them as she indicated. He watched her cut a morsel hardly big enough to tuck behind a molar, spear it neatly with the tines of her fork and hold it aloft. "A gentleman never takes a piece larger than the size of a large marble." So, saying, she popped it into her mouth and chewed. A few seconds later, she spoke again.

"You must endeavor to make as little sound as possible with your mouth while you chew. Mouth closed, of course. No smacking of your lips, no matter how tasty you find the food. And absolutely no picking at your teeth in public. You have been furnished with a toothbrush and powder in your room and you are to use those after a meal if you are at home, and before you retire at night, and in the morning before you appear in company."

"Yes, madam."

"Miss."

"Yes, miss." He sawed into his drumstick, hitting the bone. The leg slid across his plate. He pierced a piece of meat once more with his fork, holding it in place while he attempted to cut if off from the bone again. His tongue was between his teeth and he could feel a slight sweat break out on his forehead. But it would probably not be permissible to wipe his forehead with his napkin.

Finally, he got the blasted chunk of meat on the fork. It looked larger than a large marble. He glared at Miss Hathaway, but her head was bowed as she cut a piece of her own food. He brought the chunk to his mouth and began chewing. With his mouth closed.

By the time his drumstick was absent of most of its meat, it almost seemed more trouble than it had been worth to satisfy his hunger. He looked at the strands of meat still clinging to the bone. If he'd been back at his home, he'd have taken it up in hands and cleaned every last fiber off. In recent years it had been a rare occasion when they'd had any chicken.

He sighed and sat back. Well, he was living a new life now.

He'd have to adapt to it.

Even if it killed him.

Florence pushed open the kitchen door later in the afternoon to see if the chicken soup she had asked Elizabeth to prepare and properly pack in jars was ready to take to the prison.

She stopped short at the sound of Betsy's laughter. Quinn sat at the table, his legs stretched out in front of him. Although he still wore his new outfit, he'd removed the jacket, which lay in a careless heap on a chair beside him. His cravat hung on either side of his neck, his shirt collar open at the neck.

The sight of him in such a relaxed pose filled her with both annoyance and understanding. He looked so at home in the Nicholses' surroundings. Couldn't Damien understand that it would take more than a change of clothes to transform this field farmer into a gentleman?

A pile of walnuts lay in front of him on the table. He held one between his two large palms.

"You don't believe me, lass?" he asked Betsy.

Betsy leaned over his side. "I can't see how you can shell that nut without a cracker."

Albert, seated across from Quinn, chuckled. "You'd best not challenge him, lass." Two tankards stood between the men.

Without another word, Quinn pressed the base of his palms together. His face grew red with the exertion. Or, with the ale he'd drunk, Florence thought.

A few seconds later, Quinn held his hands out to Betsy, the walnut shell in a few pieces.

"Oh, my! I'd never have believed it possible if I hadn't a seen it with me own eyes."

Quinn carefully extracted some of the nut meat with his fingers and held it out to her. "Here, have a morsel, lass. It'll put some color in your cheeks, though I can't say you need any. Must be Mrs. Nichols's good cooking what does it." He glanced at the older lady with a wink.

"Thank you, sir," Betsy said, her fingers touching his as she took the nut meat from him.

Florence let the door shut behind her with a bang, bringing all eyes her way as she entered the room. "Good afternoon," she said, sparing Quinn only a glance before heading toward Elizabeth. "I came to see about the soup."

"Yes, Miss Hathaway. I have everything set out

here." She led the way to the other end of the kitchen to a table along one wall.

Betsy's shrill laugh rang out. Florence's glance veered abruptly to the center of the room. "You must remind Betsy not to be so free around gentlemen," she said in a low tone.

Elizabeth glanced with concern at her daughter. "Oh, Miss Hathaway, I thought with Mr. Kendall residing under your roof, he was...well..." She peered into Florence's eyes and her voice lowered to a whisper. "He is all right, isn't he?"

"Yes, of course, he's all right. Mr. Hathaway wouldn't have invited him otherwise..." Her voice slowed, hoping what she said was the absolute truth. If anything happened to those in their care, she'd never forgive herself. "But it is unseemly for Betsy to be so free in her ways. A gentleman who doesn't know her might misinterpret her behavior."

"Oh, I'm sure Betsy doesn't mean anything by her manner. You know she's always been a lively girl."

"Yes..." Florence had known Betsy since she'd been a little girl of five and Florence a young lady of fifteen. At eighteen, Betsy had turned into a well-endowed girl. Her gown, though modest, with her white chemise buttoned properly up to her neck, did not hide her generous proportions. Betsy's plump arms were encased in long sleeves that strained against the fabric. Dark curls peeped around her ruffled white mobcap. She was poking Quinn in the arm at something he was saying to her.

The girl's lively ways, as her mother called them, had never bothered Florence before. She didn't know why the sound of her animated chatter should irritate her so now.

"Besides, Mr. Kendall is a much older man," Elizabeth added. "I shouldn't think he'd take our Betsy's behavior amiss."

Florence pressed her lips together. "I've seen too much unacceptable behavior from men to trust them with any young woman of virtue."

"Yes, miss, I appreciate your looking out for Betsy. She is young. I'll speak to her."

After packing up the jars of chicken soup in a lined basket, Florence turned to leave the room. At another burst of laughter from Betsy, she stopped midway to the door. She stepped toward the table and cleared her throat. "Mr. Kendall, you will be joining us for evening prayers after supper, I trust." She made it a statement not a question. Since he was dressed in his new clothes, she decided it was time for him to begin participating as a full member of their household.

He looked at her in surprise, and she had to suppress the spurt of annoyance that flared up in her at his complete disregard of her presence in the kitchen. "What's that you say, madam?"

How old did she appear to him for him to address her as "madam"? She repeated what she had said.

"Evening prayers? I never attended such a thing. It's not in church?"

"No, right upstairs in the drawing room. Mr. Hathaway usually reads from the Scriptures and discusses the passage."

His deep green eyes seemed to be laughing at her. "In that case, I guess I'll be present." He ended with a wink at Betsy, whose giggle erupted from her rosy lips. "You'll have to stick your elbow in my ribs if I nod off."

Betsy's eyes rounded. "Oh, Mr. Kendall, no one falls asleep when Mr. Hathaway preaches."

He raised his dark eyebrows. "Is that so? Well, I must hear him for myself."

He was behaving like a schoolboy. "You shall, this Sunday," Florence informed him.

He eyed her again, and she felt his look travel the length of her from the top of her cap down to her flat chest. She swiveled away from him, impatient with herself that she should care what this…this… *fugitive* thought of her endowments.

"Until this evening at eight o'clock then."

Quinn's ringing laughter—no doubt at another of Betsy's saucy witticisms—followed her from the kitchen.

Later that afternoon, bearing her provisions, Florence descended the hackney cab at the Old Bailey Lane in front of Newgate.

"Good day t' ye," the keeper greeted her as she stepped through the large stone archway. She tipped one of the prison guards to take her bags.

She followed the turnkey down a dark stone corridor. Shrieks and shouts echoed off its high vaulted ceiling, making her feel, as usual, that she was passing from London into another world. The closer they got to the women's block, the louder grew the shrieks.

"I don't know how you dare come back here after your abduction," the turnkey said, as they entered the southernmost quadrangle of the building. He shuffled in front of her, the ring of keys jangling at his side, and shook his head. "They haven't yet caught that fellow."

She eyed him sidelong, keeping her face expressionless as she'd schooled herself to do. "They have no new information?"

"Nary a one, s'far as I've heard." He scratched his thinning circle of gray hair. "It's as if the man disappeared off the face o' the Earth." He chuckled. "'Course that's impossible. 'E has to be hiding himself somewhere. I say 'e's gone over the Channel. Probably fightin' for Boney now, curse 'is soul."

She didn't answer, deciding the less said the better. The large key grated against the lock and the heavy oaken door was opened for her.

The prison's fetid smells assaulted her as she approached the women's cellblock.

"Careful, they're restless today. A transport is scheduled for this week."

"Yes, I see, thank you."

"What ye come to bring us, Miss Florence?"

Dirty arms reached for her through the bars. "What's in your satchel? Did you bring me some bedding?"

"Mistress Hathaway, come to save our souls?" A straggly-haired woman, her arms hanging through the iron bars, called out to her as she passed.

"Jesus is the way, the truth and the light, you know that very well, Estelle," she replied with a glance in her direction. "I'll come visit you directly."

"Miss Hathaway, can you give me a few pence for a meat pasty? No one's come to visit me, and I've 'ad nothing to eat."

"I've brought some victuals if you come around to me."

She greeted those she was familiar with, but there were many new faces. Women awaiting trial. Those who'd been there longer were the ones already sentenced and languishing in their cell until their ship left for Botany Bay.

The turnkey let her into the first cell and took his place at a chair in the corridor to await her return.

She pushed her way through the women who crowded around her.

"You must let me through. How is Millie?" she asked of an inmate who had been sick on her previous visit. They allowed her passage until she reached a row of bedding three tiers high along one wall. On the ground were smelly pallets, above were two rows of hammocks.

She knelt over a woman lying on the cold ground and felt her forehead. She was still feverish.

"There now, Millie, I've come back with some fresh straw for your bed," Florence told her, keeping her tone cheerful.

She opened the large sack she'd carried in one hand. Another woman began to help her clear away the damp and smelly straw under the woman's blanket. "Thank you, Sally, you're a dear. Would you take that to the doorway? I'll have the turnkey remove it for me when I leave."

"He'll charge a farthing for that."

"Yes, no doubt. Come, Millie, you're going to have to sit up a moment. I've brought you a clean nightgown." They helped the woman dress. After they'd changed her bedding, Florence propped her up against the wall. "Now, let me help you swallow down some of this soup just off the fire."

The woman looked at her and smiled wanly. "You're too good, Miss Florence," she said in a hoarse whisper. "You needn't bother. I'm not long for this world."

"Not if you don't have some of this good soup. Now, let's have a spoonful." Florence poured out a cupful from the jar in her other satchel. "It should still be warm."

After the woman had taken a few spoonfuls, she said, "I remember what you told me last time you was here."

"Do you now?" she murmured, spooning in another quantity of soup. "About Jesus?"

"Yes. The story about Him and the children."

She gave a faraway smile. "I used to have children. Don't know where they've all gone now."

"Jesus knows."

The woman's bloodshot eyes looked at her with a glimmer of hope. "D'ye think so?"

"I know so. He says He knows every hair of our heads. He knows where they are. Even if they've passed from this world, He'll have charge over them."

"Will He bless them the way He did those in the story?"

Florence dabbed at the woman's chin with a handkerchief. "Yes. There's another story I shall tell you today, but first let me have you lie back down so you won't tire yourself. Here, one more spoonful and you'll finish the bowl."

The woman swallowed the spoonful then rested her head against the stone wall as if exhausted with the effort.

Florence laid aside the cup and spoon and gently guided Millie's form back down onto the fresh ticking.

She glanced at the women standing and kneeling beside her. "Here, I've brought a bag of scones, freshly baked by Mrs. Nichols. Pass it around so everyone may have one, and sit around us so you may hear the story."

There began a silent scuffle as several women reached for the bag held out by Florence. She waited until they quieted and then handed it to a woman who was meeker than the rest. "There you go, Livvie. Why don't you take one and pass it

around to the others? You are in charge of the bag."
She gave her a smile.

The women grew silent and made room for one
another around Florence and Millie. There were
many more women in the room, and some came
around to sit on the outskirts of their circle. Others
continued their card games and drinking. Others
leaned out through the bars to yell at the turnkey.

Florence folded her hands on her lap and began
to speak. "There once lived a very rich man. He
wore only velvets and fine linen. His clothes were
rich purple…"

She was forced to stop every few minutes as the
women interrupted her with questions and
comments, relating the details of the story with their
own lives on the streets. By the time she arrived at
the place where the rich man was burning in the
flames, the women had fallen silent, their eyes riveted
on her, their mouths agape with wonder and horror.

"The rich man could look across and see Lazarus
at Abraham's bosom. He probably saw how well-
off the beggar was now. Who knows if he ever acknowledged Lazarus when he used to see him
outside his gates, but in the Bible, it was clear he
knew the beggar's name, for he called out to
Abraham and asked for him by name. It says he
asked Abraham to send Lazarus to him to dip his
finger in water in order to cool his tongue."

Florence took advantage of the absolute quiet in
the circle around her to say, "Can you imagine being

so thirsty that even a drop of water from someone's fingertip would help you? Do you remember that Lazarus only hoped for a crumb from the rich man's table, and now here was the rich man, hoping for only a drop of water from Lazarus's fingertip."

A collective ooh sounded around her.

"Abraham told him he could not send Lazarus to him because there was a great gulf fixed between them, and no one could pass from the one side to the other."

"Served the rich man right!" a woman said, her arms crossed tightly in front of her.

"He got 'is comeuppance!"

"Would he never have water to drink?" a woman asked fearfully. "Would he always be burning up?"

Florence looked at her. "He could have saved himself. Now, all he could think of were his five brothers, still alive on Earth. He wanted Abraham to send Lazarus to them to warn them of their fate if they didn't change their ways.

"But Abraham said they had Moses and the prophets. He was talking of the Scriptures. If they didn't heed what was written in the Holy Scriptures, why would they listen to Lazarus?

"And then, the rich man thought of something marvelous. Wouldn't his brothers listen if someone came up from the dead and warned them?"

A murmur arose from them.

"But Abraham told him that even if someone arose from the dead, they still wouldn't believe him." She looked into each face staring back at her. "One *has* arisen from the dead not only to warn us, but to promise us all the blessings enjoyed by Lazarus. All we have to do is accept and believe His word. Jesus said, 'I am the resurrection and the life. He that believeth in me, though he were dead, yet shall he live.'

"Do you want to accept that promise today? Do you?" She smiled at each woman, praying in her heart for each one.

"I do," came a whisper from the ground at her side. She started, and turned down to look at Millie, whose flushed face was now radiant. "May I?"

Florence took her warm hand in hers. "Of course you may. You need only believe that Jesus was sent from God the Father, and that He came to die in our place for our sins. He came to give us His life, so that you might have eternal life. Do you believe that, Millie?"

The woman nodded her head.

"Then you need only ask for forgiveness and receive Jesus as your Lord and Savior. Do you want to pray along with me?"

"Yes…"

Florence squeezed her hand and bowed her head and began to pray.

"Lord, I come to you a sinner…"

By the time the two had finished praying, other women were crouched around Florence asking her to pray with them, too.

* * *

Florence offered up prayers of thanksgiving on the ride home. This was what she lived for. No matter the filth and degradation she must submit to. The beauty of one soul saved was worth any sacrifice, any price.

Tonight not one, but six—six!—women had received Jesus Christ as their Lord and Savior.

When she entered the parsonage, she felt exhausted but elated. Five of the women were scheduled to be transported that week. Florence was deeply thankful to the Lord for the work He'd wrought in each heart.

She knew they faced a long and brutal voyage. Rarely did anyone hear of the fate that befell those who were shipped to New South Wales. Florence had promised to bring them some provisions before they departed for the ship.

She removed her cloak and hung it up on the hook. Tomorrow she would begin making up the packets. Over the years she had devised a list of necessities for the women to take on the long sea voyage: a pair of petticoats and chemises, half a dozen handkerchiefs and caps, several pairs of stockings, a sewing kit, and large squares of muslin, some bed linens and a blanket. She worked with a group of ladies from the church. In a few days they could have several kits made up.

She made her way to the kitchen, looking forward to a strong cup of tea before she shed her clothes and put them to soak. The kitchen would be quiet, since the Nicholses had gone to a Bible study.

Florence pushed open the door to the kitchen and stopped short when she saw Quinn.

He sat in his shirtsleeves on the bench in front of the fire. Beside him stood a bottle of gin and a glass, which he brought up to his lips.

Chapter Seven

At the sound of the door, he swiveled around. "Oh, it's you." He didn't sound particularly glad to see her. "Good evening." He lifted his glass in a salute and took another sip.

A pulse began to beat in Florence's temple. So, this soused heathen was what her brother was sacrificing his ministry, his reputation, his very life for! She let her breath out slowly, trying to calm the fury that rose swift and hot in her at the sight of Quinn taking his ease at her brother's expense.

He lowered the glass and plunked it on the bench beside him. His lips glistened in the firelight from the foul drink.

How dare he!

She marched over to him and yanked the tumbler from his unresisting fingers. "We do not indulge in spirits in this house. Do you understand?" She turned to the fire and flung the remains of the drink over it.

A flame flared up for an instant, reaching high up the chimney and causing them both to draw back.

The initial shock in Quinn's eyes slowly disappeared as he turned his attention back to her. His eyes narrowed and his square jaw hardened, the dark stubble covering it telling her once again he'd neglected to shave.

Like a slumbering animal awakened, he rose to his feet. Keeping his eyes on her, he lifted the bottle from the bench and brought it to his mouth. She watched his throat work as he took a good, long swallow.

He withdrew the bottle from his lips and wiped his mouth with his sleeve. "What's put you in such a cheerful mood? A church meeting?"

She felt herself tremble inside but would not show it. "As a matter of fact, I've been to your old quarters."

At the lifting of a heavy black eyebrow, she uttered the single word, "Newgate."

He gave a short bark of laughter. Not the fearful response she'd aimed for. "What've you been doing there, saving more souls?"

She thrust her chin up. "Six women gave their hearts and souls into the Lord's keeping this afternoon."

He snorted. "What, by telling them some pretty stories so they'll be satisfied with their sorry lot here on Earth?"

"They are *not* 'pretty stories.'" She grabbed the bottle from him and marched to the soapstone sink. "They are truth."

"What are you doing?" For the first time she heard a note of alarm in his voice.

"Ridding this house of an evil." She raised her arm and began tipping the bottle sideways.

She didn't think such brawn could move so quickly, but before more than a thin trickle had begun to pour out of the bottle's mouth, his large hand clamped about her wrist, causing her to think how easily he could snap it.

The two stared at each other, the air between them crackling with anger.

Then, he took the bottle from her. "You can tell me how to hold me spoon and you can shave me head to rid it of vermin, but you ain't going to tell me what I can drink."

She folded her arms against her chest and faced him. "I most certainly have the right and will exert it as long as you are under this roof. Is that clear?"

His green eyes glittered. "Is that the tone you use with those hapless men and women in Newgate? Were those conversions tonight freely won? Mayhap they'd agree to anything if only to rid themselves of your sharp tongue."

His words stung but she only lifted her chin. "What would you know of anything? Have you ever listened to the truth of the gospel? If you had, you'd probably not have found yourself at the mercy of that man who so ill-used you. You'd probably not have found yourself with a noose around your thick neck."

He took another swig of the bottle. "Truth? The truth is they're sitting in their own filth. Anything is better than what they have. They'll listen to you for a few minutes or an hour if you'll give them a few raisin buns and a pint of ale."

"You ungrateful brute." She reached for the bottle, but he lifted it out of her reach. "Give me that! We will not have a drunken lout living under this roof. Drink will not solve your problems."

"What do you know of my problems? You've never had any demons chasing at your heels. Your brother provides for all your needs so you can lord it over the unfortunates at Newgate. I'll drink when I've a mind to and not have some old maid telling me what I can and can't do."

Old maid! Florence gasped, no longer knowing what angered her more, his drinking or his cruel taunts. As he brought the bottle to his lips again, she wrapped both her hands around its base.

"What the—" Gin spilled over his chin and down the front of his shirt as she gave it a fierce tug. "Give me that, you sorry excuse for a woman—"

He tightened his grip on the neck of the bottle, but it was too late. Florence hung on like a starving cur with a bit of bone. Gin splashed them both.

"Let go of it, you wench!" He yanked hard, and though she resisted, the bottle slipped from her hands and back into his possession. Gin soaked the front of his shirt, plastering parts of it to his chest.

Quinn stared at the near empty bottle, then at her,

his face growing red. "Why, you—" A long string of oaths followed.

She nearly slipped on the puddle of gin on the floor between them, so quickly did she thrust her finger at him. "You listen to me, you ignorant lout. There will be no spirits in this house but the simple ale or cider you have at mealtimes. Furthermore, there will be no such language as has just erupted from your foul mouth. If I ever hear such vile words again, I'll—I'll—I'll wash that mouth of yours out with soap," she finished, latching on to the first thing she could think of.

Quinn stepped back from her, his expression dark. At least she had his full attention. She wasn't finished with him.

"You'd better get one thing clear this evening. You are here under my brother's good graces. He's risking all for you—his good name, his home, his livelihood. And you did naught to deserve it but show you were in need. Is that understood? All it will take is one word, and you'll find yourself back in Newgate so fast you won't have time to utter a blasphemy. You are one swing away from the rope, do you hear me?"

She jabbed her finger at him, missing his stubbled chin by a hairbreadth. "If you find yourself back on the gallows, I will feel no pity this time, but I can tell you with certainty you will burn for all eternity, and you will have deserved it for your blasphemous words!"

Quinn stared at her a long moment. Then, without a word, he grabbed up his coat from the bench and headed for the door, the near empty bottle still clutched in one hand.

"Where are you going?" Sudden fear filled her. What if he risked showing himself in his condition and appearance?

He gave a harsh laugh. "To perdition, if you have anything to say about it!" He flung open the door and slammed it shut behind him so hard the walls shook.

She stood in its echo as the reality of what had happened sank in. Then she ran to the door and watched his long stride quickly take him out of sight.

She turned back to the kitchen, unsure what to do. *Oh, Lord, guard him. Don't let him be seen. Don't let him be caught.* What foolishness would his anger lead him to commit?

She raced up to her room to see if she could catch sight of him from her upstairs window, but by the time she arrived there, he was nowhere to be seen. Her anger at Quinn evaporated as quickly as it had arisen, and she was left with horror at her own conduct.

Where had he gone? Would he be back? Had she driven him away? She remembered her words. She'd all but condemned him to eternal damnation.

Where was the Christian charity in her? She'd behaved like a coldhearted shrew. How could she have lost control like that? She'd never behaved in such a way, not even with the worst inmate at Newgate.

She tossed and turned that night, remembering

the words of Jesus that what came out of one's mouth was worse than what one put in it.

She remembered her disgust not only with Quinn's drinking, but with other, minor, details like his unshaven cheeks, the way he wiped his mouth with his hand. She, who hated when people saw only her brother's disability, was judging a man by his external appearance and habits. Where was the Lord's love and forbearance in her when it came to Quinn?

His words came back to her, making it sound as if she did her charitable deeds only so she could feel good about herself. No. It wasn't like that! The Lord knew her heart.

But the accusations persisted until she finally fell into a restless sleep. Several times she woke with a start and strained her ear, listening for the sound of someone coming in, but the house remained as still as a tomb. Where had Quinn gone? The night was cold. What if he'd had a relapse of his fever? If anything happened to him, it would be on her conscience.

What would Damien say? This last thought was worse than all the others. Her brother exhibited a patience and good humor with their houseguest no matter what the man did or said. Why did Christ's love come so easily to Damien? Was it because his handicap had made him more sensitive and tolerant to the failings of others?

But while she might not be handicapped, Florence knew what it was to lack. She was painfully aware of her failings as a woman, possessing not beauty, charm or a pleasing manner. She knew what it was to be judged inferior because of what a person saw, before taking the trouble to discover what lay beneath the surface.

Quinn's angry accusations swirled once more through her mind. *Old maid...sorry excuse for a woman...* He'd seen right through to her deepest flaws and flung them at her, proving how worthless she was in all aspects that mattered. She covered her face with her hands, reliving her humiliation.

Jonah didn't look back. He kept walking, his breath puffing out of his nostrils. Every curse he knew erupted out of his lips. He'd rot in...before staying another minute in that...house where his every...move was watched and measured. Judged and condemned. He'd never felt so unworthy. Even in prison, he'd felt himself better than the others around him.

Here, he was made to feel like something wiped off someone's shoe.

"Whoa there, young man, where are you off to as if the hounds of heaven are pursuin' ye?"

Albert's voice brought him up short. The older man stepped in front of him just as Jonah reached the orchard behind the parsonage.

"I'm leaving, that's what I'm doing."

Albert's eyes held a glint of humor. "For the evening or for good?"

Jonah resisted the urge to swear some more. "For good. You can tell Miss Too-Good-for-this-Earth Hathaway that I don't need her Christian charity. Who does she think she is, treating a man like he's dirt?"

Albert chuckled. "What d'ya do to rile her?"

Jonah kicked at the flagstone at his feet and his glance fell on the bottle still in his hand. When he looked back at Albert, he noticed the man's attention on it as well.

"You mustn't mind her manner," said the older man. "She can be a bit strict, but it's for yer own good."

"Well, I've had enough of her tongue-lashings. I'll be finding myself a place where a man can be himself." He moved past Albert.

"Why don't you come over first and have a glass of ale with me and tell me what she said that was so awful."

The kindness in the other man's tones halted him. "I thank ye kindly, but I feel too angered inside to be good company at the moment, so I won't upset your household with my unruly tongue."

"Why don't you walk your anger off for a spell? Then come to my kitchen for that glass. I'll be here and the invitation still stands."

Jonah nodded. Not as acceptance of the invitation but to placate Albert. He'd be long gone from this place ere his anger was spent. "Thanks. Well, I'm off." He took a deep breath and forced himself to leave.

The night was cold, but he ignored the chill that soon invaded his body after the warmth of the kitchen. He headed north, away from the houses, not sure where he was going, knowing only that he wanted to get away. After about a mile, hardly noticing anything around him, his pace slowed. He saw only empty fields not yet tilled.

He continued walking, his shoulders hunched over with the deepening cold. The sky grew darker and he wondered where he would spend the night.

Miss Hathaway was the most unreasonable woman he'd ever come across. His Judy had never objected to his taking a bit o' the gin, she'd even joined him in a glass or two. It was the only thing to dull the hunger and make one forget the dismal prospects of the city. Miss Ramrod-Spined Hathaway in her warm cozy house could never possibly understand that.

He'd never drunk anything but ale back in his village. But in London, gin was cheap and plentiful and the only thing to enable a man to live without hope.

He kicked at the dirt in his path, cursing Miss Hathaway anew. What did she know of his life? He'd drown in gin if it helped block out the wails of his babes for food when he'd been unable to provide for them. What did she know of the cries he heard in his head? Cries only the drink could silence?

For a moment, he'd wanted to tell her that, of the grief that ate at him, but doubtless all she'd care about was the fact he drank. Her type were all the same—devoid of any true humanity aside from the good deeds they felt would save their own souls on the judgment day.

His breathing grew more ragged as the images rose. He realized he still carried the bottle in his hand. He went to take a swig and swore. There was little left to do any good.

He drained the last drop and flung the bottle away with an oath. The sip he'd taken burned in his throat, hardly enough to warm him against the frigid night air.

When he began to approach Maida Vale, he hesitated. He faced the prospect of sleeping under a hedgerow or being seen and questioned in the next village. He didn't relish either one. For a long time he stared at the lights of the few houses, weighing his choices.

His anger was spent. Left only was cold, loneliness and hunger. He stood huddled against the icy wind that whistled through his thin coat. He'd left in such a hurry, he'd forgotten his greatcoat and hat. His shorn hair offered little shield against the gusts.

He remembered Albert's invitation. Slowly he turned and viewed the road back.

He'd visit the old man. He wouldn't stay longer than that. Then he'd decide his next course.

The soft glow of firelight was visible through the window of Albert's small cottage next to the parsonage. Jonah hesitated a few more seconds, but another biting gust assaulted his naked scalp and numb ears. Following the path that led to the door, he approached the caretaker's house and knocked against the windowpane.

Several moments passed and no one came. Blast it. He'd waited too long. He had turned around, bracing himself for a night in the cold, when he heard footsteps inside.

The door opened, and Albert welcomed him with a smile. "Come in, William."

"I know it's late," he began. The inside warmth tingled against his frozen cheeks.

Albert stood aside and gestured. "Don't stand there and get the kitchen cold, come in. I was about to retire but I'm glad you've come." After shutting the door behind him, Albert stared hard at him a moment under his iron-gray eyebrows. "I think a cup o' hot tea'll suit you better now than that tankard o' ale."

Jonah merely nodded, rubbing his hands against his arms to warm them.

Albert gestured him to a place by the fire and went about fixing the tea. He turned to offer him the mug. "There, that'll warm your insides."

Jonah cupped the thick, warm mug between his hands. A fire had never felt better in his life.

His host sat quietly, sipping his tea, as if giving Jonah time. Jonah breathed in the steam rising from the cup. Gradually he was warm again and calm enough to speak. "Miss Hathaway found me drinking some gin in her kitchen."

Albert chuckled. "I guess that didn't set too well with her."

"She got angry enough to pour most of it down the sink."

"She's probably seen enough of the dangers of gin not to want it in her household."

"Yes." He understood that part of it. He'd certainly seen the dangers of it on the streets of London.

"Don't take it to heart. She's just lookin' out for you."

Jonah snorted.

Albert chuckled again and took another sip. After a moment he asked, "Think you'll go back?"

"Not as if I had anyplace else to go." He sat staring at the tea, unsure when he'd made the decision to return.

"You could stay here the night."

His mug froze halfway to his lips. "You'd let me stay here?" Of course, Albert didn't know that Jonah was really an escaped convict.

"'Course, why ever not? Ye'll see, by tomorrow morn, things'll look different. You and Miss Hathaway will see eye-to-eye again."

Jonah said nothing. After his exchange with Miss Hathaway, he didn't think it too likely.

They finished their tea and Albert stood. "It's best we turn in. I can make you up a pallet here in front o' the fire if you'd like."

Jonah cleared his throat and looked down, feeling unworthy of this man's kindness. "I'd... uh...be grateful."

When he was left alone, Jonah stretched out in front of the embers. The floor felt hard, despite the blankets under him. His body had grown soft in the past weeks of sleeping on a feather mattress. He'd best not get used to such luxuries. There was no telling when such comforts would be snatched away from him and he'd be on the run again. He'd almost lost them tonight.

He rested his head on his arm and stared up at the shadows flickering on the ceiling.

Would Miss Hathaway admit him back? She'd made it clear it was the curate who'd taken him in in the first place, not she. Would she tell Hathaway about Jonah's drinking?

Would Jonah have to go crawling back to Miss Hathaway and promise never to touch another drop again? His throat stuck at the thought of having to beg her pardon. She'd like that. He imagined himself kneeling in front of her, his hands clasped before him, while her merciless gray eyes stared at him in utter scorn, her lips pressed downward in an uncompromising line, and her arms crossed over her bony chest.

He remembered her stinging words and sighed. She'd been right. All it would take would be one word from either her or the curate, and he'd be facing the hangman's noose again.

When would they realize they'd taken on too much and want to be rid of him? His presence in their household was a daily risk, not to mention an embarrassment—leastways for Miss Hathaway.

He rubbed his heavy beard stubble, remembering the look of disgust on Miss Hathaway's face as she'd eyed him. As if she was such a sight for the eyes. It was true she was always neat and clean, even after several hours at Newgate.

But she was as cold as the stone walls of the prison. Those gray eyes of hers could chill a man's bones. Funny thing was, the occasional moments he'd caught her smiling with her brother, they'd actually been pretty, softening her face. He shook away the thought.

Any softness she seemed to possess was made hard by the judgmental heart within. A man would never find comfort in the arms of such a woman.

He stopped short at the direction of his thoughts and shuddered. Where had such a notion come from?

Damien, Damien! He's gone. What have I done? Florence could barely see Damien through her tears. She fell on her knees, fists clenched. The poor man was probably in the constable's cart, heading back to Newgate.

Quinn's dirty face, haggard and worn, assaulted her mind. His head had fallen to one side, eyes closed. The thick rope around his neck had drained his life—

Florence awoke with a gasp, the only sound in

her bedroom the thudding of her heart. It took her a few more seconds to realize the nightmare vision had only been a dream. Then she glanced at her clock. Half past eight! How late she'd slept! It was because she'd been awake half the night worrying about that no-good, ungrateful—

Shoving away the covers, she sat up quickly. She had to get downstairs before Damien sat down to breakfast. What would she say when he asked about Quinn's empty place at the table?

Mrs. Nichols and Betsy were already in the kitchen when she entered some moments later, hastily washed and dressed.

"Good morning, Miss Hathaway. How are you this fine day?"

"I—I'm well. I'm sorry I'm late."

"Oh, that's quite all right. Betsy and I have everything under control, don't we, Betsy?"

"Yes, Mum," her daughter said as she brought out a tray of buns from the oven.

Florence grabbed the basket lined with a linen napkin. "Here, let me remove those."

"Yes, miss."

"Where is Albert?" she asked over her shoulder.

"Oh, he already breakfasted. I 'spect he's in the yard. That man can't wait till spring." The older woman glanced out the window. "With the sunshine today, it do feel like it. He'll probably begin some plowing."

"Has my brother breakfasted already?"

"No. He's been in his study until a moment ago."

She wanted to ask if they'd seen Quinn at all, but bit down on her tongue. If he had left, so be it. If he came back, he'd have to show himself to her or her brother.

But there was no sign of Quinn in the kitchen or at the dining table when Florence sat down with Damien.

Mrs. Nichols hadn't even set him a place, and Florence wondered how word had traveled so quickly of his departure.

"Good morning, Flo," Damien said, unfolding his napkin and smiling at her down the length of the table. "How are you this morning?"

"I have felt better—"

"Oh, I am sorry to hear that. What's the matter?" He frowned, his glance straying to Quinn's place. "Where is Mr. Kendall, by the way? And why isn't his place set? Did he breakfast with Albert earlier?"

"No, I don't believe so." She took a deep breath. "I'm sorry I interrupted you before. You said you weren't feeling well."

"No, I didn't mean I was ill. I just…didn't sleep very well last night."

Damien's glance went from her to the empty place. "This doesn't have anything to do with Mr. Kendall's absence, does it?" he asked softly.

He always seemed to be able to discern when something was troubling her. She met his eyes. "I'm afraid it does."

Just then the door opened and Florence dropped her napkin. Quinn stood in the doorway. Florence swallowed at the sight of him, in one of his new suits, a fine dark blue jacket and yellow waistcoat. His jaw was clean shaven and he had the scrubbed look of someone who'd just had an invigorating wash.

With a quick glance at her, he focused his attention on Damien. "Good morning, sir. I hope I'm not too late."

She bent down from her chair to pick up her fallen napkin and mumbled, "Good morning" as she did so.

Damien smiled. "Good morning, Kendall. You're not late at all. We've only just sat down ourselves. Come and join us. Oh, I'm sorry, I don't know why your place is not set this morning."

Florence stood at once and headed for the sideboard. "Let me get some cutlery," she said hurriedly, not looking in Quinn's direction. She felt unaccountably flustered and rushed about getting fork, knife and napkin together.

Quinn coughed. "I believe it's because I had something to eat earlier. Mrs. Nichols probably thought I wouldn't have any more." He gave a nervous laugh. "She don't…doesn't…know my appetite."

Florence brought the utensils to his place. She could smell the soap on him as she set the things down. He remained standing by his chair until she finished. She felt his focus on her all the while.

"Thank you," he murmured.

She glanced at him, her own voice lost somewhere in her windpipe, as she tried to read his expression. Was he repentant of his behavior yesterday? Or was he still enraged? She could read no anger in his green eyes. Was there cocky amusement in them? She didn't think so. Was it the same uncertainty she felt herself?

Before she could decide, she bowed her head and whispered, "You're welcome," and hurried back to her own place.

Thankfully, her brother kept Quinn occupied with conversation for several minutes as they served themselves. Since theirs was a small household, they didn't keep the breakfast food on the sideboard, but on the table in front of them.

Knowing his preferences by now, Florence poured Quinn a cup of coffee from the urn at her side. As she reached to pass it to him, he anticipated her and stretched out his arm to take the cup and saucer from her.

"Thank you, miss."

"You're welcome." What else was she going to say to him once the courtesies of the meal were over?

Was he going to beg her pardon?

Another thought struck her. Did she owe him an apology? No! Her mind rebelled at the notion. He had to know that he must submit to the rules of this house.

She felt a gentle rebuke of God's Spirit. This man was under their protection, and her duty was to witness God's love and mercy to him.

Even if it stuck in her craw to apologize to him.

"Florence, I wanted to discuss something with you," Damien said in the silence. Her head snapped up, but he was already looking in Quinn's direction. "With both of you, in fact."

Quinn laid down his fork, a look of worry creasing his forehead.

Damien brought his napkin to his mouth and patted it before setting it down. Then he cleared his throat. "The rector of our parish, Reverend Doyle, will be dining with us this Sunday after services." When Quinn said nothing, Damien continued. "I'd like you to join us."

Quinn blinked. "Me, sir?"

"Yes. You're to be part of this family for some time to come. I believe with your new garments and your, uh, shorn hair, you resemble nothing of the man who stood at the gallows. Moreover, very few, if any, members of the congregation, much less Reverend Doyle, would have attended the hanging, or have any idea of what you look like. Any drawings of you posted about look nothing like your actual self."

A dozen thoughts ran through Florence's mind, none of them good. "Can you…risk it?" she asked. Her nightmare was too real. What if Quinn said or did something that would show him for what he was? Not only a common laborer, but a fugitive from the law.

Damien regarded her. "It's been my experience

that what a person doesn't expect to see, he won't. No one who comes here will expect to see a condemned man who escaped the gallows. Much less will they suspect anything when they meet a well-dressed, presentable gentleman who—" here his mouth curved upward "—knows how to hold his knife and fork."

"And if I blunder and do something I'm not supposed to?" he asked.

Florence could detect no sarcasm in his tone, and she realized he was as concerned as she was, if for a different reason. For him, it meant the gallows. As she had so summarily reminded him the evening before. Had that been the reason he'd come back? Because she and Damien were his only hope? Instead of giving her any sense of satisfaction, the sense of responsibility weighed more heavily on her.

Damien glanced from him to Florence and back again. "I think if you pay strict attention to us in the coming few days, and heed all my sister's instructions, even when they seem to make no sense from your point of view, you will be fine. On the day of the dinner, just follow our lead if you have any doubts, and—" here he grinned outright "—if you are unsure of how to answer something, just remain silent, and have one of us fill in for you. We are…more accustomed to dealing with the rector than you are."

Florence said nothing more. She would have a word with Damien later, when Quinn wasn't present. No need to worry him with how concerned she really was over her brother's plans. As a man, he couldn't possibly see the subtleties involved in training someone to act like a gentleman.

She eyed Quinn now, taking care not to be noticed by him. He clutched the scone in this large hand and brought it up to his mouth and took a healthy bite, much larger than a gentleman would.

Quinn's cheek bulged with his portion. A few crumbs had fallen on his shirtfront and vest. He grabbed his napkin and bunched it in his fist, bringing it up to this face and swiping it across his mouth.

She turned away, thinking of the rector's neat, precise manners. Did Damien expect her to perform miracles by Sunday afternoon? Especially now, after the words they'd exchanged the evening before?

"I'd also like you to attend Sunday morning services with Florence and me."

Florence stared at her brother. Wasn't it too soon to show Quinn in public? Another peek at Quinn showed her that he, too, did not welcome the news.

"We also attend a prayer service Sunday evenings, but I wouldn't require you to attend that, unless you wished to, of course."

Jonah coughed. "Are you sure you want me seen in front of people?" He held the half-eaten scone in his hand.

Damien took a sip from his cup and set it down quietly. "Yes. I think the only way we are going to pull this off is to treat you as the person whose identity you've assumed. You are an acquaintance of ours from the north who has come to stay with us and explore his prospects in the metropolis. The sooner you are introduced by us into our admittedly small society, the more quickly people will accept you.

"Soon, they'll take your presence among us for granted. If you'd like, I can teach you the trade of clock repairer, or we can search around for some other skill you might be more inclined to learn."

Quinn's look went from Damien back to his scone. Slowly, he lowered his hand, as if he hadn't realized it had been suspended. "If you're sure I won't shame you at your table…or among your acquaintances…"

"I'm sure." Damien rubbed his hands together. "So, if that's settled, perhaps you'd care to sit with my sister after breakfast and go over a few simple table manners. Then, if you'd join me in my workshop, we can begin your first lesson in clock repair. Afterward, we can resume your reading. Then you are on your own until supper. I have several calls I must pay on parishioners."

Quinn had a slightly dazed look. "Yes, uh, sir."

"One other thing." Damien took up his knife and fork. "If you are to assume the role of a gentleman, you must desist in calling me 'sir.' I am your equal. You may address me simply as Damien, when we are together as now, or Hathaway or Reverend Hathaway when we are in public, and I shall do the same for you, William." He smiled as he pronounced the assumed name.

"Yes, si—" A flush crept over his shaved cheeks. "Reverend."

"Damien." Her brother resumed eating, as if he had said nothing out of the ordinary.

Florence suppressed a sigh. How like her brother. To think about something for days and then suddenly make an announcement as if it were the most natural thing in the world.

And the bulk of the responsibility would fall on her shoulders. It already had, actually. She thought of the scene last night again. If Damien had an inkling…

She glanced from their guest to Damien. She would have to protect her brother from his most high-flown and altruistic impulses. He was an idealist, always expecting the best from people.

And Quinn? She looked at him again. He was struggling to get his large fingers through the loop handle of his delicate teacup. A bit of tea splashed onto the saucer. If last night's episode wasn't so fresh in her mind, she would have found the sight amusing and oddly…touching. He was undoubtedly as frightened as she. After all, it was his life at stake.

Could she pull off this transformation? More importantly, could he?

Chapter Eight

"Please remain seated, Mr. Kendall," Miss Hathaway told Jonah when Hathaway had left the dining room.

Jonah stiffened. What was she about now? Another tongue-lashing over spilling some tea on his saucer? Not his fault these bl— He stopped himself in time. *Blasted,* he amended, teacups weren't made for large hands like his.

Betsy cleared the plate in front of him and wiped the crumbs from the tablecloth. He looked down at the empty place, feeling like a schoolboy summoned to the headmaster's office. He still hadn't figured out how to ask—beg—her pardon for last night.

Before he could decide what to do, Miss Hathaway brought a clean plate and set of silverware from the sideboard. Without saying a word, she placed them before him.

He waited, wondering if she was going to mention their set-to with the gin bottle. But she turned from him and set a clean place for herself before seating herself catty-corner to him. Her movements held the same purpose and determination with which she'd fought him for the bottle.

"Now, I shall show you a few differences in the way you eat from the way a gentleman eats and I want you to make a note of them."

She took up her knife and fork and brought them to the empty plate. "I noticed this morning that this is how you hold your silverware." She pretended to cut something on her plate then brought the fork up to her mouth.

"Now, notice the difference with how my brother eats." She moved the position of her hand on the fork from clutching it upright like a stake to holding it at an elegant downward angle to the plate. Once again she imitated cutting something on her plate.

"It does look more dainty," he said, amazed at how closely she must have been observing him. Every time he'd turned her way, she'd been looking somewhere else.

"Indeed. And when you cut, you must cut a small enough portion of food so that you can chew and swallow before you respond to someone who might choose to address you at that moment. Let's find an example. Ah, Betsy has not removed the bread basket." Miss Hathaway reached out and took two slices from it. "Let us pretend these are two portions of meat." She placed one on his plate, and one on hers. "Note how small the piece I cut is." He watched her cut and spear a tiny morsel with her knife and fork.

"That's not enough to satisfy a child."

"Nevertheless, each forkful you take should not exceed it. I want you to ask me a question as soon as I put it in my mouth." She lifted the fork with the small square of bread and brought it to her mouth.

As soon as her lips had closed around it, she began chewing in a way that hardly moved her jaw muscles. His gaze moved to her lips, soft and pink, like a pale rose, with nary a crumb. He pulled his attention from her mouth and looked into her eyes. "Were you sorry to see me show up again this morning?"

Her eyes flew to his and she stopped chewing. She swallowed what remained in her mouth. "You can see the advantage of having cut off only a small piece of food."

"I beg your pardon—" There he went again, blurting out the wrong thing.

She set down her utensils and cleared her throat. "If someone asks you an unexpected question and you are at a loss as to how to answer, you will be in no danger of choking on your mouthful."

"I can see that." He bit back a smile. If she was going to pretend they hadn't had a blow-up quarrel last evening, well, then, so would he. As he waited for her next instruction, he couldn't help letting his eyes travel over her. As usual, she looked perfectly neat and clean in a light blue gown and white chemise, every hair tucked into the cap she wore as if she was a married lady instead of a maiden. He felt himself flush as he remembered the insult he'd flung at her in the heat of anger. Calling her an old maid. She wasn't that. She certainly didn't look old enough to be so. He wondered how old she was…

He started, realizing she'd been saying something. "You place your fork and knife so, when you want to take a sip from your glass or wipe your mouth with your napkin." She demonstrated both procedures as she spoke. "This morning, you wiped your mouth so. A gentleman would merely pat his lips."

She removed the napkin from her mouth after touching it briefly. Her lips were slim and pink with a nice bow at the top. Her nose was narrow with a slight bump, the nostrils flared in a dainty sort of way. Her eyes were turned downward and he noted the lashes. They were tinted gold at the roots and grew darker at the tips. Her eyebrows matched them in color. Her skin was evenly pale like alabaster.

She raised her eyes and looked at him as if waiting for him to say something. "You…uh…certainly notice a lot of how a fellow eats."

"My brother may think you are ready to face society, but I want to ensure you won't disgrace him."

He remembered more of her words last night and realized her primary concern had been her brother—not herself. Perhaps he'd misjudged her somewhat. Before he could say anything, she added, "I *was* somewhat surprised to see you walk in this morning as I knew not what to expect after last night."

He'd almost forgotten his earlier question to her and now her reply took him by surprise. Her gray eyes seemed to be weighing him, and he wondered for those seconds what it would take to measure up to a lady like her. She cleared her throat softly. "I thought you might have decided to leave us permanently."

He said nothing, not yet ready to admit he had crawled back, his tail between his legs, when in fact that's exactly what he'd done.

She fingered her napkin. "I take your coming back to mean that you are ready to accept my brother's— *our*—conditions for your residence in this household?"

Not a whit of yielding in those deceptively soft eyes. The woman was as rigid as a tree trunk. He blew out a breath, knowing when he was beaten. Curious thing was, at the moment, he didn't seem to mind. Instead of anger, he felt a certain security, the way he had when she hadn't turned him in to the soldiers. This woman's standards might be impossibly high, yet her word was good.

"Yes, miss." When she said nothing in reply, he

wondered what more she wanted. Was she expecting him to beg her forgiveness?

She picked up her knife and fork once again. "All right. Now you try with this slice of bread."

He did his best to imitate her, holding his fork and knife poised above the piece of bread on his plate.

"Yes, that is perfect." She was actually smiling at him, her tone encouraging, so different from the one she'd used on him last night.

The gleaming, cream-colored porcelain plate with its delicate chain of flowers circling its edge stared back at him. He pretended the slice of bread was a joint of roast. He brought his knife and fork over it, the way Miss Hathaway had demonstrated from the plate set before her. Not too quickly and small, penny-size bites of meat.

"Never show people that you are hungry even if you have gone without food for hours."

The knife sank into the soft bread then squeaked against the plate as he made a sawing motion back and forth.

"That's it. Now bring it up to your mouth."

He did as he was told, making sure to keep the fork tines turned downward, the way Miss Hathaway held hers. He chewed with his mouth closed as he brought the fork back to the plate and set it down carefully against the edge. Then he brought the napkin and tapped it against his lips, resisting the natural impulse to rub it against his mouth.

"That's much better. Now, you must practice that until it becomes second nature to you."

He felt like asking if that's what she'd done—practiced wiping away any softness from her nature until she appeared as hard as a seasoned piece of wood, its sap long since dried out of it?

On the next breath he wondered what it would take to discover if anything soft and vibrant still lay within. He could feel himself flush. He bet a gentleman didn't think such thoughts about a lady.

Jonah stood over the large kitchen garden and breathed in the damp morning air. Give him the soil any day to a formal dining room and a blasted neckcloth. He took up a rake and began smoothing over the earth he and Albert had just finished spading. He'd removed his jacket in the morning sunshine and rolled up his sleeves.

"We'll have some fine peas by June," Albert said from his end of the garden.

"We will, indeed," he agreed, and took up a hoe. With it he formed a long furrow down the length of the garden patch.

He knelt down beside the row. In went the hard little dried pea. With his forefinger he pushed it into the soft earth and placed the next little pea an inch beside it. On down the row he went.

When he'd finished his row, he sat back and removed his cap to wipe his forehead with the back of his arm. The sky was a beautiful blue with soft, scudding clouds in the distance. Birds twittered from their leafless perches all around him. He could almost imagine himself back on his small holding, setting out the first seeds in spring…instead of a wanted man, hiding out from society until he could be presented as a new bird in fine plumage with manners to match.

He shook his head, thinking of his lessons in "deportment," as Miss Hathaway called them. If he managed to get through another one without feeling like a great, bumbling oaf—either that or succeeding in reining in his impulse to shout and bellow at her—it would be a miracle of self-control on his part, maybe the true test of a gentleman. It seemed he couldn't say a sentence without her stopping to correct some word he'd said wrong—a word he'd been using his whole life.

And not to mention the other words—the ones that were second nature to him, but which Miss Hathaway glared and called profanities of the vilest sort. It got so he hardly dared open his mouth for fear he'd say something wrong.

He glanced across the garden. "Tell me, Albert, how long have you worked for the Hathaways?"

Albert stopped working and leaned against his hoe. "My mum and da worked for their parents before the Reverend and Miss Hathaway were so much as a thought. I've seen them both grow up. Mrs. Nichols fed them so they'd grow strong and stout."

"I wouldn't say she succeeded in that last one," he said, picturing Miss Hathaway's slender figure.

Albert shook his head and smiled. "No, they both shot up like young tree limbs, straight and thin, like they was reaching for the sky."

"Oh?"

Albert nodded. "In a way, they were. Always looking upward, heavenward."

"Ah, religious."

"Not religious, exactly." Albert removed his own cap and scratched his gray head. "Lookin' out for others, more like. Not that their parents didn't help people, but not like them. Mr. and Miss Hathaway seem consumed with living for the 'least o' them.' It's like they're never as happy as when they're serving in some capacity."

"D'you think it had anything to do with Mr. Hathaway's losing his leg?"

Albert replaced his cap. "Mebbe. Hadn't really thought on it. Nothing like misfortune to make you see others in trouble. But he was always a sensitive tyke. Takin' in birds with broken wings, coming to me to ask me if I could fix 'em up. Field mice the cat was toying with. He'd rescue them before all the life was out o' 'em and bring 'em to me, and I'd have to tell 'im it were too late, better to let the poor thing die. Then he'd dig a little hole and bury the critters and say a little prayer over their graves."

Jonah marveled at the image. When he'd been a boy, all he could remember was trying to get enough to eat and thinking of animals as things to hunt. If it was too small to eat, it could be toyed with. He and the cat had had that in common. Since when was an animal something to be rescued and cared for, much less prayed over? He shook his head and turned his attention to the next row.

"What about Miss Hathaway?" he asked after several minutes. "Why didn't she marry and set up her own household?" He remembered the way she'd blanched when he'd called her an old maid. Every time he thought of it, he felt ashamed of himself.

Albert straightened and stuck his hoe in the damp earth. "You have to understand Miss Hathaway. She had to shoulder a lot of responsibility when their parents passed away. Her brother was still away to school and she had to keep things going for him. Since he's been ordained a clergyman, she runs everything the way her mother did before her. As I said, she's very protective o' young Hathaway."

Jonah nodded his head, having begun to suspect as much. "She sure seems to think the sun rises and sets on him."

"That she does."

"Was she always so—" How could he put it? Demanding? Bad tempered?

Albert chuckled. "Exacting?"

"Aye, that's the word."

"Well, I remember Miss Hathaway as a young thing, like our Betsy is now. 'Cept she was always so serious, too serious, Mrs. Nichols and I always thought, but it was understandable after their folks died. Miss Hathaway took care o' them in their illness and then felt responsible, you see."

"Responsible? What, for their deaths?"

"No, nothing like that, although I know she took it hard. No, she felt responsible for young Damien. He's always been her special charge, ever since he lost the leg, you know." He chuckled. "She used to defend him at school if she heard he'd been picked on by the other boys. She weren't afraid of any boy, no, not her."

Jonah pictured a slim young girl beating her fists against a youth's chest. He smiled, remembering the way she had wrestled the gin bottle away from him.

Albert looked off in the distance. "I do recall a young gentleman calling a few times. That was when Miss Hathaway was, let's see, not quite twenty." He squinted one eye as if to calculate when it had been. "Nice young lad. Mrs. Nichols paid more attention to the goings-on than I did and used to tell me there'd be a wedding 'fore autumn that year."

"What happened?" Jonah crouched over the row, feeling the sun warm his back. He tried to imagine a young Miss Hathaway with a gentleman courting her.

"Don't rightly know. Her parents both fell ill and she had to nurse them. A few months later the parson was marrying the young gent to another miss in church. Mrs. Nichols was stunned, I can tell you."

So the cove had jilted Miss Hathaway? Worthless scoundrel. She might be an exasperating woman at times, but she didn't deserve that.

Jonah turned his attention to the next row, wondering why he was so bent on Miss Hathaway's courting days. She was his teacher, a hard taskmaster whose compliments were rare.

Why was it, when she did bestow one, it warmed him more than a tumbler of gin and a meat pie hot out of the oven?

Where was Quinn?

Florence glanced at the long case clock in the entry hall. They needed to be at the chapel in a few minutes. On Sundays, they barely had time to dress and down a hurried breakfast of bread and tea in the kitchen, then head over to the chapel before the first parishioners arrived.

She looked anxiously at Damien, who sat on an ottoman, his Bible opened on his lap. As usual, he seemed unperturbed, though he was often quiet before delivering his Sunday morning sermon.

Her own nerves were another story. Where was that man? Still struggling with his new clothes? She whirled around at the sound of footsteps coming down the stairs. It would be Quinn's first public appearance, and she had grave misgivings. She had prayed long and hard about it last night and early this morning as she lay in bed awake.

Damien looked up with a smile. "There you are, William. Well, Florence? He's here. Let's be off."

She said nothing, too busy scrutinizing Quinn from head to toe. His rugged jaw was clenched, as if he, too, realized the risk they were all running. At least it was freshly shaved, she thought, noting the nicks here and there.

He'd chosen one of the new suits the tailor had delivered just yesterday, this one a deep-plum-colored jacket with matching cloth-covered buttons. The buff-colored waistcoat blended seamlessly with his knee breeches of the same shade. She nodded her approval at the subdued color. White stockings and black shoes with small buckles finished the outfit. Her gaze traveled up a bit and she frowned at the wrinkles in the white material.

"I say, William, you do look a proper gentleman," Damien said.

"Thankee, si—I mean, Reverend Dami—Hathaway." By the time he'd finished, his face was red. "You look like a regular minister."

"Thank you, I think," Damien replied with an amused glance down at his own familiar attire of knee-length black coat, white preaching bands at his collar, black vest and knee breeches. He turned to her. "Well, what do you think?"

She frowned at Quinn, continuing her inspection. "Your stockings need smoothing and the cravat needs to be redone." She clucked her tongue. They were running out of time. "Damien, you must remind him of how to tie a proper cravat."

"I rather think you are better at that since my clerical collars are mere stocks."

"Come along to the parlor. We haven't much time," she said to Quinn. "Please remove your neckcloth."

The two men trooped after her into the sunny front room. "Here," she said, "stand by the mirror so you can see how it's done." She pulled over a low stool and climbed onto it in front of Quinn, leaving him enough room to look over her shoulder into the wall mirror behind her. She was now at eye level to him. He stood obediently, holding out his neckcloth to her, his shirt unfastened at the collar.

Trying to ignore his sudden proximity, she took the white linen square from him and shook it out. "It's already wrinkled, but it will have to do." She stopped and frowned. "What's this?" She showed him the reddish-brown stain.

"Must be blood." He rubbed his jaw. "I nicked myself shaving. Not used to shaving every bless—'scuse me, every day."

She noticed the small cut on his jaw and heaved a sigh. "We'll need a clean neckcloth." Her eyes met his inches from hers. The bright sunlight turned his irises a startling green. "Ahem. Please—uh—fetch a fresh one from your room."

His fingertips touched hers as he took the linen back from her. "Yes, miss."

She stepped down from the stool, dismissing her silly reaction as merely nerves over the whole morning. As Quinn left the room, she called after him.

"You'll have to take that one to the kitchen. Ask Bet—Mrs. Nichols to put it to soak."

In the silence following his departure, she noted the ticking wall clock.

"Don't fret. We've still time," her brother said softly.

She looked across at him. "Perhaps you should go on over. We'll be there directly."

He took out his pocket watch and snapped it open. "I've a few minutes yet."

She continued looking at him.

"What is it?" he asked.

Florence pressed her lips together, her earlier misgivings returning. "Are you sure you know what you're about?"

"You mean taking William to church?"

She nodded. "Yes. Everything…dinner today with the rector. Are you sure he's ready?"

"We must trust the Lord to guide us through."

She wrung her hands together. "I know. Yet one slip. You saw how clumsily tied his cravat was. And his stockings, as wrinkled as a farmer's. You may put him in finely tailored clothes, but he's still nothing but a laborer beneath them."

"You can't make a silk purse out of a sow's ear, you mean?" Damien replied with a slight smile.

"Something like…"

He came up to her and placed his hand on her shoulder. "Isn't that what our Lord does to us?"

Trust Damien to have a suitable spiritual reply.

"Yes, but in His case, it's an unfathomable miracle. And He takes a lifetime to accomplish it."

Damien nodded. "Ah, there you are, William. Just in time."

Florence whirled around, not having heard him come in. How much of their conversation had he overheard? He walked over to her and handed her the neatly folded linen. "Here you go. Truss me up like a dandy."

"That I'll not do," she said, stepping back onto the stool. "I shall merely tie a respectable knot so your neckcloth doesn't shame the rest of your fine suit of clothes."

"The little man outdid himself, didn't he, making a suit to fit the likes o' me?" he said, glancing down at himself.

"Mr. Bourke is a fine tailor." She shook out the long strip of linen and proceeded to fold it. "Please lift your collar completely so it comes up above your ears."

She found herself staring at the wisps of dark hair visible at his parted collar. "Please tuck your shirt closed."

He did as she said, hiding the slice of his chest from view.

She helped him fold his collar in place, her fingertips inadvertently brushing the smoothly shaven skin of his jaw in the process. The contact was barely a whisper yet sent a shivery streak down her arms.

"We bring the neckcloth around like so," she said as she wrapped the linen around his neck from front to back, then brought it back to the front. She had to reach her arms past his neck in order to do this. She leaned in closer, working the cloth snug about him, so close to his face she could hear his breathing.

Her heartbeat quickened and heat flushed her face. She fumbled with the length of material, wanting to rush and break the close contact but knowing she would ruin the starched cloth if she did so. She concentrated on the linen in her hands, careful not to look at Quinn. She had never performed this task on anyone but her father and brother.

As if sensing her thoughts, he asked, "How did you ever learn how to tie a man's neckcloth?"

"I needed to teach my brother." Flicking her gaze upward, she was startled to see how closely he was observing her. "I told…you to, uh, look in the mirror to see what…I'm…doing."

Damien stepped over to them. "Yes, when I went up to Oxford for the first time, I was a hopeless ignoramus."

Florence concentrated on forming the three pleats on one side of the cravat. "I didn't want him shamed before all those gentlemen's sons, so I taught him how to tie a proper cravat."

"And how did you know how to do it if he didn't?"

Despite directing him to look in the glass, she could feel Quinn watching her as she carefully folded the material.

"I studied it in the illustrated fashion magazines and asked the tailor. I practiced on Damien until I got it right."

Damien laughed. "She'd have a whole pile of linens crumpled at my feet before she pronounced herself satisfied."

She allowed herself a brief smile. "Now, then, I am doing a 'Mathematical' on you, one of the simpler styles. Take care not to crease the material except in these three places, here by your ear—" she pointed out to him, holding one end of the cravat in place with the other hand "—and here in the middle of the cloth, and lastly, here below it. Then the other side," she murmured, following suit. "Then we make a knot in the front like so." She straightened slightly, maneuvering the stiff material into place. Finally, she patted the knot down. "That should do it. You need to tuck these ends into your waistcoat."

His hands came up to take the two ends of the linen from her. His fingers brushed against her knuckles, and for a second she felt a tingling all the way to her toes. She dropped her hands immediately. "You may, uh, button up your waistcoat, too."

While he finished doing as she bade, she stepped down from the stool, but not before his hand came up to her elbow to help her down. She stepped away as soon as she was back on solid ground, feeling a need for some distance from him.

"Excellent," Damien said.

Florence walked a few paces away and tilted her

head, surveying her work. Quinn's hair had grown out a little more, appearing fuller and darker. What was more, his natural broad-shouldered posture lent him an air of dignity she hadn't quite noticed before.

He glanced at her then and she felt the heat rise in her cheeks.

"Do I pass inspection?"

Slowly she nodded. "Indeed, you appear a gentleman."

Damien rubbed his hands together. "Shall we go to the chapel then?"

"Oh, yes, let's not be late." Florence hurried toward the door. Here she'd been standing admiring Quinn, when the service would soon be starting. What had she been thinking? She was no longer a foolish young girl of nineteen, but a mature spinster of eight-and-twenty. She mustn't forget that. One mistake was enough for a lifetime.

Chapter Nine

"Amen," Jonah echoed the others around the dining table after the Reverend Hathaway's grace. He opened his eyes.

The table was laden with all kinds of tempting dishes. After the long church service, Jonah would have done such a fine dinner justice if it hadn't been for the presence of the Hathaways' guests. He looked at the rector seated directly across from him. His elderly mother, her gray hair arranged in a profusion of ringlets around her wrinkled face, sat at the rector's side.

Jonah had been introduced to them after the service. For a few seconds, beneath the rector's assessing look, Jonah had been certain the man saw him for who he truly was. But after a curt nod, Doyle had given his attention to Miss Hathaway.

Jonah had forgotten his own fears as he observed the two chatting together. The rector's manner went from autocratic to charming in a matter of seconds as he bent his tall, austere body to listen to Miss Hathaway. What had amazed Jonah more than the rector was the transformation in Miss Hathaway. Suddenly, she was no longer the strict, serious task-master, but a shy, blushing lady who looked more like a schoolgirl. Jonah had stood riveted, not realizing his mouth hung open, until someone had bumped into him and he'd snapped it shut and turned away.

Now, in the dining room, Jonah forced his attention from them and turned to Damien, who sat at the head of the table carving the joint of lamb. The sight of it should have made his mouth water, but now all he could focus on was not committing any blunders.

Betsy brought in more covered serving dishes, giving him a saucy wink as she turned his way, but which he was too nervous to return.

"Here, William, let me serve you some of this succulent lamb." Jonah handed the curate his plate. Hathaway handed it back to him piled high with slices of the rosy meat.

"Would you care for some gravy or preserves?" Miss Hathaway's voice startled him.

He stared at her, trying to glean from her expression which he was supposed to accept, but her face gave him no clues. "Gravy—er—both," he finally answered.

She merely filled his plate, her attention no longer on him as she answered something the rector said. Jonah frowned at the man who seemed to be the only one to bring out a gentler side to Miss Hathaway, and wondered why the notion should bother him so much.

As the conversation flowed around him, he looked down at his plate but could hardly bring himself to take a bite, too afraid was he of picking up his knife and fork. He couldn't remember anything Miss Hathaway had taught him over the past week.

This morning in church, he'd been the object of many curious stares as he'd sat beside Miss Hathaway in the exposed chancel reserved for the curate's family. Now, looking up, he saw old Mrs. Doyle observing him, but when he smiled uncertainly, she merely smiled back and returned her attention to her plate.

He gulped down a mouthful from the heavy crystal goblet at one side of his plate then almost choked when his glance met the rector's.

Although dressed in the same clerical black as Hathaway, Doyle had a stately, dignified air far different from Hathaway's simple, friendlier manner. His full head of salt-and-pepper hair contrasted with his still unlined face. His eyebrows were dark, like his eyes, his nose aquiline. Right then, his glance seemed to slide straight down its narrow length to Jonah, looking past the fancy cravat to the fugitive who lay beneath.

"And what is it you do, Mr. Kendall?" Doyle proceeded to take a small bite of lamb—a part of

Jonah's mind registered the fact that its size was exactly what Miss Hathaway had recommended—and chew as his dark eyes rested on Jonah.

There was a momentary lull in the conversation around the table, and he felt all attention directed his way.

Jonah coughed and quickly brought the goblet back to his mouth. Easy now, he told himself. They had rehearsed this beforehand. He swiped the napkin across his mouth, remembering too late to "pat" it across his lips. He turned his eyes back to the rector. "I was…uh…a farmer in Bedfordshire." Oh, no, he was supposed to be from up north.

"Yes, he had a small holding in Bedfordshire," added Hathaway quietly.

Jonah laid his napkin down on the table, irritation rising at his own timidity. He imagined the rector, like most, owned some substantial estates, in addition to drawing the earnings from several parish livings. How much did he get from Hathaway's chapel? he wondered.

Forgetting his earlier fear, Jonah pushed his plate back and stuck his elbows on the table. "I farmed till I lost my land."

The man chewed thoughtfully. "And just how did you lose your land?"

Before Jonah could reply, Miss Hathaway said, "Through an unfortunate series of events." With a slight frown at Jonah, she set down her fork and knife and folded her hands. "Mr. Kendall is staying with us until the Lord opens a new door for him. He is thinking of setting up in business."

"Indeed?" The man's gaze flickered back to Jonah. "What business is that?"

Miss Hathaway gave Jonah no chance to reply. She smiled at the rector. "As you know, Damien needs someone to take over the clock business. He will be training Mr. Kendall to see if it suits him." She sighed. "It was Papa's dear wish for Damien to follow in his footsteps, but clearly that is not to be." She looked down the length of the table to her brother. "He makes a fine curate, don't you think so?"

Jonah stared at Miss Hathaway, amazed at the way she was making everything sound as natural as could be. It almost made him believe in the future she described for him.

"Yes, indeed I do. Apropos of that, Damien, I meant to mention today's sermon to you." The rector frowned, taking up his glass of claret.

"Yes, I wanted to ask your opinion," Damien said, his voice eager.

Jonah breathed a sigh of relief that the focus was off him.

"You must use caution in the topics you select. You might set a dangerous precedent in telling people it is all right to break the rules. The next thing you know, you'll have chaos on your hands as each one goes out and does whatever he wants."

Jonah clutched his silverware more tightly in his

fists. Who did the old windbag think he was? He'd thought Hathaway's preaching fine.

Damien widened his eyes. "I certainly hope they didn't take the sermon in that light. I think I was pretty clear that religion is not about a legalistic set of codes, but it is about following the Lord Jesus, emulating His mercy and compassion to our fellow man."

"Nevertheless, you are preaching to many an ignorant person who needs little encouragement to flaunt the rules of the church." The rector dabbed at his mouth with his napkin and set it down. "Now, may I suggest you do a series on something like the seven deadly sins. Or, you may read the series I did on the Beatitudes. Come to my library and borrow a copy."

"Yes, sir, I recall the series you preached."

"You have done remarkably well in your first few years at St. George's. I commend you, my boy. You must be thinking of a helpmate one of these days."

"A helpmate? You mean a deacon?"

The rector chuckled. "No, dear boy. A wife."

Damien's cheeks reddened.

It was as plain as day to Jonah that the fellow didn't want to discuss the subject of a wife.

Doyle continued, as if unaware of Damien's discomfort. "Someone like the late Mrs. Doyle was to me. She was an exemplary woman, meek and docile, a perfect clergyman's wife, a most worthy woman."

"Yes, your wife was a lovely lady," Damien said in a heartfelt voice. "She was always very kind to me—" he looked at his sister "—and to Miss Hathaway."

"A clergyman's wife must be modest in appearance, quiet spoken, chaste, above reproach…" The rector's glance strayed to Miss Hathaway. "Miss Hathaway embodies all I mean, a credit to her gender. It will be hard to find her equal."

Jonah looked at Miss Hathaway. Her normally pale cheeks had reddened and she fiddled with the brooch at her neck. "Reverend Doyle, you pay me too much honor."

Her shy smile made Jonah's gut tighten, and not from the food on his plate. So it was like that, was it? Wasn't the rector too old for her? His glance swung from the rector to Miss Hathaway and back again. The man could easily be her father.

"Nonsense, my dear lady. Someday you will wish to set up your own household and I'm sure you desire to see your brother nicely settled with the right wife."

"Yes—yes, of course, but there is no haste. I'm here for as long as Damien needs me."

The rector turned back to Damien. "Still, your parishioners expect a minister to have a wife."

"Yes, Reverend Doyle." For the first time, the twinkle of humor had faded from Hathaway's eyes. The young man looked down at his plate, although he did not proceed to eat.

Jonah cleared his throat. "I expect people don't much care one way or n'ther about whether the parson has a mate or not, as long as he's available to them when they need something."

All eyes turned to look at him again. What had he said now? He'd only tried to get the attention off the poor boy. Whether Hathaway wed or not was no one's business but his own.

"On the contrary, Mr. Kendall," the rector said in the kind of tone that made Jonah feel as inferior as if the man knew exactly his humble origins, "the members of a congregation expect the shepherd of the flock to be 'husband to one wife, vigilant, sober, of good behavior…' to quote First Timothy. Of course, here Paul is talking about the office of bishop, but he says much the same of the office of deacon. I believe we can safely say that a curate falls somewhere between the two." He chuckled at his own humor and the Hathaways immediately joined with him.

"Yes, sir," Damien said. "Well, I shall certainly take your words under advisement."

"Do so. You may be sure Mrs. Doyle—" the rector looked at his mother fondly "—and I shall be glad to offer any advice and counsel once you have your eye on a particular young lady."

"Yes, dear boy." Mrs. Doyle smiled at him. "You know we move about in society quite a bit. We'd be happy to introduce you to a young lady out for her season."

"Thank you," the young curate murmured, his attention fixed once more on the plate in front of him.

The rector began questioning Damien on the affairs of the church, and finally Jonah began to relax enough to remember his appetite. After all, he'd only had a piece of toast and cup of tea early this morning.

He listened with only half an ear as the conversation went on around him. Miss Hathaway was just as informed as her brother on everything that went on in the parish. Having taken the edge off his hunger, Jonah eased back in his chair. The rector paid no more attention to him as he and Damien entered into a theological discussion.

Jonah found himself wanting to stretch his legs and wondered how much longer they'd be sitting at table.

His glance kept returning to Miss Hathaway. She was quite pretty today in her church getup, a light-colored gown sprinkled with violets. She also wore her hair differently, with matching violet ribbons threaded through it. He found himself remembering how she had tied his cravat.

Her ever-nimble fingers had deftly folded the cloth. He'd stood studying her face, wondering about her. How old was she? Her skin was quite smooth. Her attention had been fixed on his cravat, as if completely unaware of the human body that stood in front of her.

He'd noted the pink tip of her tongue just visible between her lips as she'd concentrated on the knot. His glance had strayed lower, taking in the high lace collar she wore. She'd had to remove her lacy gloves in order to tie his neckcloth.

Her glance crossed his now as she spoke to the rector. She averted her eyes, not pausing in her speech.

Jonah twirled the stem of his glass in his hand and eased his legs out in front of him. For a moment, he wished he were still taking his meals in the kitchen with the Nicholses. If this long, drawn-out affair was what was expected of a gentleman, then he had second thoughts about being included in the Hathaways' circle. He stifled a yawn behind his hand, finding himself growing sleepy after the strain of the morning. He hadn't gotten much sleep the previous evening, too worried about today's appearance. He found himself tempted to smile as his focus drifted to the rector, realizing how easy it had been to fool people. And all because of a well-cut suit of clothes. What would the toff do if he knew he sat eating with a condemned man? The man had probably never come within a mile of Newgate. Unlike Miss Hathaway…

His attention reverted to her and he looked at her with new admiration. She, at least, practiced what she preached. Jonah thought of her history as related by Albert. If she'd always been burdened by the care of her brother, had she ever had the chance to be a woman in her own right?

Had her young suitor broken her heart for good?

"My dear Miss Hathaway, you are too observant," Doyle said with another one of the low chuckles that were beginning to grate on Jonah's nerves.

She smiled, casting her eyes downward. "You flatter me."

So, the old goat saw some tender green shoots to

devour. Jonah clamped his mouth shut before he said something he might regret.

Just because he'd fooled the old clergyman today didn't mean he could go about pretending his life was anything but that of a fugitive hiding from the law.

Jonah Quinn had outdone himself. Not only had Reverend Doyle accepted Quinn's presence in their household, but Quinn had actually appeared and behaved himself as quite a gentleman.

Florence hummed to herself as she made her way to the kitchen that evening, carrying a bundle of clothes in her arms. Although it was late, she needed to put the garments she'd worn to the prison to soak.

A small smile played around the corners of her mouth. She hadn't been able to erase it since the rector and his mother had bidden them farewell this afternoon.

Florence crossed the threshold and stepped into the quiet kitchen.

"Oh!" She hadn't expected to find anyone still up. Quinn sat hunched before the fire just as the last time she'd come upon him. Her hands tightened on the bundle of clothes as she wondered if he'd been drinking again.

"What are you doing sitting in the dark?" she asked, her voice sounding sharper than she'd intended.

He craned his neck around. "Just thinking. Isn't it allowed?"

"Of course. I—you just startled me. I didn't expect to see anyone here at this time of night."

"Don't worry, I don't have a bottle of gin at me side."

"I see that." She took a step toward him to assure herself of the fact. But there was nothing visible anywhere. "The thought hadn't occurred to me."

"Tell me another good story."

"After all you've gone through today, it would be…understandable…if you…"

"Downed a few pints?" He gave a short laugh. "Why, thankee kindly, miss," he said with what sounded like mock humility.

She drew herself up, wondering why he was in such a morose mood. "You needn't take offense. It was a nerve-racking day for everyone."

He swung around on the bench to face her fully. "What are you doing creeping into the kitchen after everyone's retired for the night?" His regard traveled down the length of her.

She remembered her outfit and clutched the collar of her dressing gown together with her free hand. Even though she'd seen Quinn in his night-shirt for most of the first fortnight he'd stayed with them, she'd never appeared in anything but her daytime wear before him.

"I just came down to…uh…put my things to soak." She indicated the bundle in her hands. "I didn't have a chance to yesterday when I returned from Newgate."

"Don't want to catch any vermin."

She peered at his face, but the dark shadows cast by the flickering firelight behind him prevented her from seeing if he was making sport of her. "The place is filled with the worst filth imaginable."

"I know."

"Yes, of course."

He sat in his shirtsleeves. Even though he was alone, a gentleman never sat in his shirtsleeves. He'd removed his cravat to boot. She must speak to him about that.

"Do I pass inspection?" Now, the mockery was clearly unmistakable.

"What have you done with your neckcloth?"

He dug into the pocket of his knee breeches and held it up. "I haven't lost it, if that's what you're afraid of." He looked at it. "Though I'm afraid I've wrinkled it up quite a bit."

She remembered tying it for him in the morning…the feel of his eyes on her…the breadth of his neck…

She took a step back and cleared her throat. "Well, at least it lasted you through the day."

"Think I passed your rector friend's inspection?"

She didn't like his tone of voice in saying "rector friend." "Reverend Doyle seemed to accept you as a houseguest of ours. You…did very well."

He seemed to hesitate a second, then narrowed his eyes. "You certainly were quick with your answers to him about me."

She felt her face grow warm. She still wasn't comfortable with the fact that she'd so readily spoken such half-truths so glibly to anyone, much less to a man she greatly admired and respected. "The rector is a very astute man. If we'd shown the least hesitation where you were concerned, he would have detected it at once."

"The rector seems plenty interested in what goes on with you and your brother."

"Reverend Doyle has done a lot to promote my brother within his profession. It is only right that he should show an interest in our lives."

"One thing is interest, another is poking his nose where it don't belong."

"*Doesn't* belong," she corrected automatically. "I…I meant to thank you for coming to Damien's aid during dinner. He…wasn't prepared for the rector's suggestions about finding a wife." She plucked at her collar, uncomfortable with the topic. "Especially after his remarks on his sermon topic." Even though Quinn had risked calling attention to himself with his remark, his willingness to intervene on Damien's behalf had earned her admiration and gratitude.

"The way I see it, your brother's life is his own. Whether he chooses to take a wife or not is his business."

"You are correct. However, the rector only takes an interest because he cares about Damien." She moved away from Quinn, uncomfortable with the scrutiny under his thick, dark brows. "In any case, while I appreciate your defense of my brother, it was unnecessary. It only served to draw attention to yourself. Your presence here is already unusual enough without adding to it."

"I thought you said your brother never turned anyone away from his door."

"He doesn't. I was referring to vagrants and others who come to the back and beg a piece of bread. But we've never had—" she looked down at the bundle in her hands, suddenly awkward with the words she sought to say "—more than an overnight guest or someone who might seek shelter for the night in the barn when the weather is inclement and be on his way the next morning."

The mockery in Quinn's eyes faded and he looked away. "Aye. You needn't remind me of the risks you're taking. Don't think I'm not aware o' them."

She kept her eyes fixed on her bundle of clothes. "All I meant was you need to be discreet in everything you do or say. You owe my brother a great deal."

"And you'll exact a price for your charity, no doubt."

Her backbone stiffened. "What's that supposed to mean?"

"Nothing. Don't mind me. I guess I just need a shot of gin and don't have it available."

Was he sitting there feeling sorry for himself? After all she and Damien were doing for him? She had no time for such antics. She made a move toward the scullery. "It's late. I'd better get these in water."

She stepped into the stone-floored room. She'd set the clothes in water and wash them out tomorrow.

Just as she reached for the tin tub on the wall, Quinn appeared behind her and stretched his arm past her. She caught her breath, her heart pounding. How had he sneaked up behind her so silently? His arm was only inches from her temple. The awareness of his muscular frame so close left her dizzy.

He took the tub off its hook on the wall and stepped back. "Where do you want it?" His voice was low and gruff.

"I—" What was happening to her? She had to exercise some control over herself. "Here on the floor. I'll fetch some water from the cistern." She scurried on ahead of him.

He did as she bade. Before she could collect the water, he took the pitcher from her hand and began to fill it.

It left her nothing to do but crouch beside the tub and put in her garments, aware of her petticoat, shift and chemise, stark white against the gray of her gown. He stood over her and poured the water over them. "Th-thank you."

"Aye."

She dipped her hands into the water, pushing the garments down so they'd saturate, vibrantly aware that Quinn remained where he was. Why didn't he move?

She stood, tightening the sash on her dressing gown. If it weren't so late—and if she were alone—she'd fix herself a cup of tea.

"Care for a cup o' tea?"

She jumped. "What? Oh—" Again, he seemed to have read her mind. It was uncanny at times. She moistened her lips. "All right. A cup of tea would be lovely." Why had she said that? It was late. She should go on up to her room. But she remained standing there until he moved first.

She followed him back into the kitchen.

"Have a seat," he said. "I'll take care of it."

She perched obediently on the bench and watched him. He checked the kettle and, assuring himself there was hot water, proceeded to open the tin of tea. He spooned the tea leaves into the pot and poured the steaming water over them. His white shirt was open at the collar and his waistcoat hung unbuttoned, but still there was something elegant in his appearance.

The clink of the top onto the teapot startled her from her furtive observation. To hide her discomposure, she fetched a tea cozy and placed it over the pot.

Quinn seemed untroubled by their silence. It irked her that he seemed at peace when she felt so jumpy inside. What was wrong with her lately? She was used to being in the company of men, both the foul-mouthed drunkards in the prison and the gently spoken types in the drawing room. What was it about Jonah Quinn, that he fit neither camp? No longer was he the image of the rough convict or laborer. Yet, in spite of the tailored clothes and schooling in etiquette he'd received, he was by no means the refined gentleman. Rough one moment, yet when quiet, watching her with discerning eyes, too familiar by far for a gentleman.

He poured the tea into their two cups. Heartbeat rising again, she scooted over to make room for him beside her on the bench. He set down her cup beside her and sat down with his own. As before in the scullery, his brawny frame filled the space, and she had to resist the urge to move herself an inch or two away from him.

He glanced sidelong at her. "So, you really think it's going to work, turning me into a gentleman?"

She fiddled with her teaspoon, trying to think how to answer. She didn't want to discourage him, and yet she didn't want to give him false hopes. "I pray it will for your sake…and my brother's."

"You're afraid if I get caught, they'll blame your brother. What can they do to a clergyman?"

She closed the opening of her dressing gown tighter about her neck. "That shows how little you know. Can you imagine what it will do to his reputation if it is discovered he harbored an escaped convict? Why, I'm sure it's considered breaking the law, if not worse—perhaps even treason. His clerical collar would probably not prevent his being locked up."

"Imagine that. You'd be visiting your own brother at Newgate," he said with a chuckle.

She glared at him, finding nothing amusing in the scenario. "I hardly think that's something to joke about."

His eyes, looking dark and reflecting the firelight, studied her. "Sometimes I make jokes when things are too serious."

"I'd probably end up sitting alongside of him in his cell for that matter." Suddenly, she had to smile at the incongruous image of the two of them locked up together.

"Except you'd probably wind up in the women's cell, and there's no telling whether you'd be able to see him or not."

They fell silent again. Then he said, "You two care a great deal for each other."

She shrugged, uncomfortable with the topic. Others had called her overprotective. "We're all we have left of our family."

"He said the same thing to me."

"Did he?" When had Damien discussed their relationship with him? "You know what it's like to lose those you love."

"Yes."

"You have no family left up in…Bedfordshire?"

He glanced away from her and back toward the fire. "Yes, some kin, but I've lost touch with them. I'm sure no one would want to acknowledge a convict, much less a runaway one, now."

"Yes. It could be dangerous for them."

"So, you're stuck with me for the present. Which

brings me back to my question. You think this playacting will work?"

"It depends partially on you."

His eyebrows rose. "How so? I've felt I really have very little to do with any decisions these days."

"But only you can decide whether you want to carry out our suggestions about your—er—conduct."

He shook his head, his eyes filled with amusement. "I think I've been behaving with a vast deal of restraint." He ran his hand over his head. "Having my head shaved off to start with."

"But it's growing back." She frowned. "That reminds me, you must do your best to shave every morning." She peered in the glowing light from the fire at his shadowy jawline. "Perhaps even in the afternoon if we are going out in the evening or expecting guests."

He rubbed the same hand over his jaw, and she swallowed at the raspy sound, her throat dry. "Not used to shaving so often. Twice a day? How can a man find the time for so much grooming?"

"Gentleman implies a man with ample leisure on his hands," she answered, trying to ignore the sensation that the sight of his forefinger continuing to rub across his cheek caused her.

"So you'll be willing to show me off in company?"

"Of course. We must be able to pass you off in company to ensure that no one recognizes you."

"No new converts at Newgate yesterday?"

She lowered her cup, wondering at the sudden

change of topic. "My ministry is to sow seed. I shall not always be there to see the harvest."

"A farmer's hope is to bring in the harvest."

"A Christian learns to think in terms of eternity, not merely season to season."

"For a farmer, the end of the harvest season brings either a full belly in winter or starvation."

"Yes, I realize you are bound by temporal considerations, serious ones. That is why those who have are commanded to help those in need."

He blew on his tea and took a sip.

"You must endeavor to sip without making a sound."

He gave her a sidelong glance but took another, quieter sip. "Better?"

"Yes."

"What about you, Miss Hathaway? No plans to set up your own household, like the good rector advised you?"

His voice was soft. Again, she became aware of how close he sat next to her and how she was dressed. He was too big and broad. "You mustn't… ask…impertinent questions."

Instead of looking contrite, he said, "Just how old are you? Seven-and-twenty? Eight-and-twenty?" He leaned back, his glance skimming over her. "You can't yet be thirty."

How dare he eye her like a mare about to foal. Thirty, indeed! "A gentleman never asks a lady her age," she said through stiff lips.

"Don't get your dander up. I can't imagine you've reached thirty yet."

"I'm eight-and-twenty, if you must know."

He nodded. "You don't look bad for a woman of eight-and-twenty. You'll probably have another one o' them fellows from the church courting you soon."

She turned away from him, surprised at the anger that rose up in her at the remark. How could he joke about something so personal? The next second she felt the blood drain from her face. *Another one of them fellows?* How could he possibly know about…?

When she said nothing, he added. "You'd better hope so, if you don't want the rector sniffing around your heels."

She whipped around and stared at him, her dismay forgotten. "What did you say?"

"You heard me."

She would not stand for such unseemly suggestions. How dare he imply such a—a—lewd thing? She banged the teacup down on its saucer and stood up. "You are being deliberately rude and impolite. Reverend Doyle is the noblest gentleman of our acquaintance. Such a thing would never…why, it doesn't bear thinking on!"

She belted her sash more tightly around her waist. "Furthermore, it is no business of yours when and whom I marry, *if* I do. Your role in this house is to follow our example and be careful no one suspects who you really are. Is that understood, Mr. Kendall?"

"Follow your orders. Aye, that's clear enough."

He looked away from her and picked up his cup. His sip was as silent as Damien's.

Suddenly she felt ashamed of herself. Perhaps she was more tired than she thought. The strain of introducing Quinn to society. That must be the reason. Yes, that was it.

She cleared her throat. "I apologize if I seemed rude to you just now. It's just that you must learn that there are certain things you don't ask a lady."

"Oh, I understand fully and I shall endeavor to carry out all your orders." His tone of voice mimicked hers and he continued looking straight ahead at the glowing fire.

She took a step back. "Well, I shall leave you to your ruminations. It has been a tiring day."

"Aye, that it has."

She picked up her teacup and took it to the sink.

"Good night, Mr. Kendall," she said at the door.

He didn't turn around. "Good night, Miss Hathaway."

Jonah sat before the fire, too tired to move. He felt weary in his soul. This was a different tiredness from that after a hard day's labor in the fields when he'd come home, eat his supper and fall asleep almost immediately, a deep sleep that would only be interrupted by the sound of the cock crowing before sunrise.

This was a weariness that made him question whether it was worth getting up tomorrow and continuing the masquerade they'd begun. Wouldn't it be simpler to just give himself up? After all, what was his life worth? Who cared whether he lived or died?

Miss Hathaway had the ability to look down her slim nose at him and make him feel worth less than a ha'penny. She was right. Who would ever believe him to be a gentleman?

Now that fine rector, there was a gentleman. From the man's satin-lined coat to his tapering white fingers, he reflected generations of quality. When he bothered to focus his cool gaze on Jonah, Jonah felt the full extent of the gap between the two of them.

Jonah shook his head. Reverend Hathaway had a soft heart and perhaps believed he could save Jonah with a little polish and a few changes of clothes. Quality like that worn by Doyle went much deeper. It wasn't something one could put on and take off in the evening.

The Hathaways had risked their lives and reputations for him. Was he worth it? Did he have a right to continue exposing them to all the dangers his presence in their household represented?

Yet, where could he go? What could he do for them in return? He looked around the shadowy kitchen. He wasn't used to a life of inactivity. He felt sufficiently recuperated from his illness and ready to take on something. But all he knew was manual labor. All he'd been able to do was offer Albert some help around the yard. The man was getting on in years and seemed to carry out all the heavy work at the parsonage.

Miss Hathaway had said her brother would train him in clock repair, but so far, Mr. Hathaway had seemed more interested in improving his reading skills and teaching him the Scriptures.

Jonah rubbed a hand over his face. Life was too difficult a conundrum to work it all out in one night.

He couldn't figure Miss Hathaway out either. One moment she snapped at him, the next she seemed as nervous as a wren around him.

He thought she'd freeze him with a look when he'd asked her age. He chuckled. Eight-and-twenty. Not so old. Yet not so young. Now that he'd had a chance to study her up close a time or two, he'd begun to realize how superior her looks were. Not the kind he'd ever have paid any notice to before. But she did have a pair of fine gray eyes. Her lashes were golden, as were the softly curving eyebrows above them. Her nose was narrow, her lips finely chiseled, not full like he preferred on a woman, but slender and a delicate pink.

What he'd judged as pale and washed-out at first glance now struck him as refined and of superior quality.

He shook his head. What was he sitting there thinking of Miss Hathaway's looks for? She was a lady and he was a coarse laborer, a condemned man to boot.

The hour was late, and here he was becoming fanciful.

Chapter Ten

"How nice of you to stop by for a visit," Florence told the rector and his mother. She shifted in her seat and wondered where Quinn was. Would he notice the carriage in the drive? She hoped he wasn't out helping Albert somewhere in the fields. He knew those tasks were better reserved for the mornings when there was little likelihood of unexpected visitors.

She wished Damien were here, but he was at the orphanage. To hide her anxiety, Florence busied herself with ringing for tea.

Quinn could be unpredictable in his behavior, one moment looking as elegant as a gentleman, the next, letting out an oath fit for a sailor.

Unfortunately, the rector's mother could be a stickler for proper behavior. Would they ask for Quinn?

Thankfully, the rector had other things on his

mind. "Damien has begun literacy classes at the workhouse." His tone held disapproval.

"Yes," she replied. "He has been thinking of it for some time."

The rector frowned. "He had mentioned an idea he had. I had not encouraged him to pursue it. Teach them to read and they'll no longer be satisfied with their lot."

Florence formed pleats in her gown. "I assure you, he is using the Scriptures as his basis, so I don't think you'll see a bunch of Jacobins coming out of his classes." She hesitated. "I was thinking of offering a similar class to some of the women at the prison."

The old lady's eyes rounded. "The prisoners? What do they need to read for?"

"Those that are being transported—both men and women—for instance," she began, "could use the skill once they arrive in the colony."

The rector leaned toward her. "My dear Miss Hathaway, you must consider this decision carefully. You don't want to take on too much. I find you looking a bit peaked, don't you, Mother?"

The old lady scanned her through her lorgnette, and Florence had to make an effort to remain still. If she was looking tired, it wasn't from her prison work. Sleep had been eluding her at night ever since…her evening visit with Quinn.

She began swinging her foot back and forth and brought it to an abrupt halt. She turned with relief at the sound of the door. Betsy came through with the tea cart.

As Florence busied herself with serving the tea and handing the cups to Betsy, she took advantage of the moment to mouth to the girl, "Quinn?"

"What's that, miss?" Betsy asked.

Florence bit her tongue in annoyance. "Nothing. Here, please take these to Mrs. Doyle," she said, giving her a plate of cakes.

"By the by, where is your houseguest?" the rector asked.

"He is out, I believe." Florence sipped her tea, hoping he wouldn't ask for any details.

"He is a singular-looking gentleman," Mrs. Doyle remarked. "Most arresting features."

"Ye…es." Florence's hand faltered on her cup.

"How did the two of you meet him?" the rector asked.

"We…well, it was unexpected." She set down her cup. "You know how Damien is always hearing of people needing help."

"Yes. A true altruist, your brother." The rector smiled. "I'm always advising him to have a care. People can take advantage, you know."

"Yes." Florence glanced toward the window facing west. "There's a bit too much sun, isn't there? I don't want it getting in your eyes, Mrs. Doyle." She stood and went over to adjust the blind from the afternoon rays.

"You're most considerate, Miss Hathaway," the

elderly lady said. "This is delicious cake. You must tell Mrs. Nichols."

"I shall, indeed."

"So, you say this fellow Kendall was recommended to your brother?" the rector persisted, setting down his empty cake plate.

"Yes…in a manner of speaking." Well, it was on the Lord's recommendation they had taken him in. As Florence took the cord in her hand, her gaze roamed over the grounds. She could see Albert had finished planting much of the kitchen garden. Today, she'd heard him mention he'd be pruning some of the trees in the orchard. She looked toward the bare branches of the apple orchard.

Two men were there. Albert stood below one gnarled tree, speaking to the man in the tree.

Quinn. He was high in the tree, a pruning saw in his hands. Florence frowned, recognizing the rich plum color of one of his new coats. The dun-colored breeches and white stockings and black shoes…all part of his new wardrobe.

What was the man thinking?

Her fingers tightened on the thin rope. She glanced back into the room. What if the rector were to see him out there? Wouldn't he find it odd to see their houseguest—a gentleman farmer—behaving like a hired hand?

She bit her lip, glancing back outside. She couldn't very well leave at that moment and march out to the orchard.

Stifling her annoyance, she let the cord swing free and made her way back to the settee.

"I'm sure Mrs. Nichols would share her cake recipe with your cook, if you'd like," she said, making an effort to smile in the woman's direction.

"Yes, I should like that," Mrs. Doyle said, taking a sip of tea.

"Mrs. Nichols has a wonderful recipe for apricot compote. It makes a lovely accompaniment with the cake," she said, her leg swinging back and forth. She stilled it.

The rector smoothed down his white stock. "The Duke of Winchester is planning a dinner party."

"Indeed?" The Duke of Winchester was the most important man in Marylebone.

"I had thought to ask him to invite you and Damien."

He had Florence's full attention now. Neither she nor Damien had ever been privileged to meet the duke.

Doyle's spoon clinked against his cup. "I could include your houseguest, if you should so wish it."

Florence's cup rattled against the saucer as she brought it down a little too forcefully.

The rector continued. "I've been telling the duke of your brother's sermons and how your congregation has grown in the last few years. He is most interested in meeting him."

"I...see." How would she reply about Quinn? Would she have to give the rector an answer this afternoon? How would Quinn ever pass the duke's inspection? A man whose mansion took up most of Portman Square?

Yet…if Damien caught His Grace's attention… Florence's thoughts began to race, her worry about Quinn momentarily pushed aside. It could be just the sort of patronage her brother needed. His work was too important to be relegated to an out-of-the-way corner of London. With the proper backing, there was so much more Damien could accomplish in his work with the poor.

She leaned toward the rector. "Tell me more about the duke…"

"Why don't you trim that one there?" Albert pointed to the branch a few feet away from Jonah.

"This one?"

"Yes, that's the one."

Dutifully, Jonah made his way toward the tree limb, gripping the apple branches before him and creeping forward on his knees. When he was close enough, he leaned forward and began to saw through the branch. Movement was restricted in a gentleman's coat and cravat, but he hadn't wanted to take the time or trouble to change his garments when he'd spotted Albert out in the orchard. The man was too old to be scaling trees. Besides, Jonah had never been able to back down from the challenge of a stubborn tree.

"I wasn't able to prune the orchard last spring," Albert said from below. "I'd taken a fall and my back wasn't right. And this spring, with the women-folk telling me to have a care with this and have a care with that, I can hardly take a step that one o' them's not after me."

Jonah chuckled. "We used to have to trim the fruit trees on the lord's estate. Never got to enjoy any of it, though."

"You'll get to enjoy these. The best Cox Pippins in all London. My Elizabeth makes a tart that'll make your mouth water."

It was on the tip of Jonah's tongue to say he might not be around come autumn. He didn't know how much Albert knew or suspected of his identity, but since the Hathaways hadn't given him leave to confide in Albert or his wife, he thought it best to keep his mouth shut.

The limb fell to the ground with a thud. As Albert collected it, Jonah shimmied back to the center trunk. "What about this one?" he asked, pointing with his saw to another branch.

"You've got the eye," Albert said with a nod, beginning to cut the fallen branch into smaller pieces.

Jonah proceeded to the branch in question, but not before noticing the streak of dirt he'd gotten on his light-colored breeches with his last maneuver.

He ignored the stain as he set to work. "How does it look now?" he asked the older man when he'd lopped off a few more branches.

"Like you did when you had your head shorn."

Jonah chuckled, removing his hat and wiping his

handkerchief over his forehead. He ran a hand over his scalp. His hair now covered it in a thick layer, though it was hardly half an inch thick. "I felt like a new-laid egg."

"You sure looked like one," Albert said, chortling.

Jonah joined him in laughter and waved his saw. "If I hadn't been so sick, no one would have been able to get that close to me with a razor."

"I'm sure you're right. But it did the trick. You look like a proper gentleman these days."

Jonah made his way back down the tree. His stockings snagged on the thin branches sticking out from the main limbs and the lichen stuck to the knees of his breeches. He brushed himself off when he reached the wet ground. He'd have to change before presenting himself to Miss Hathaway; otherwise, she'd give him one of those looks that was enough to make him turn tail like a dog.

Thankfully, she was probably out on one of her parish visits. He accompanied Albert to the next tree and surveyed it a moment before he grabbed the V-shaped lower branches and heaved himself up to begin the next pruning job.

An hour later, the sun sat lower in the sky, its rays casting long shadows across the orchard. Jonah had only progressed through a few more trees. Large piles of branches lay under each one. He lifted his arm to wipe his forehead but stopped himself in time and used his large handkerchief instead. His throat was parched and he could just taste the pint of ale when this job was done.

Glancing toward the house, he spotted Miss Hathaway making her way across the yard. "Your mistress is coming this way," he told Albert, as he noted her purposeful stride.

Albert followed his gaze. "So she is."

Jonah turned his attention back to his work. When he'd finished sawing through the thick branch and it gave a final crack before giving way, he noticed Miss Hathaway standing beneath the tree. He paused to wipe his forehead with his handkerchief.

She frowned up at him through the bare branches before turning to address Albert. Irritation creased Jonah's forehead at her ability to ignore him when it pleased her. What had he done now?

"Be so good as to tell Mr. Kendall to change into his old clothes if he decides to climb trees."

"I'm sorry, miss," Albert began, his ruddy face showing a deeper red. "It's my fault. I should be up there meself—"

She put a hand on his arm, her tone softening. "No, indeed, Albert. It's too much for you. We shall have to see about hiring an assistant for you. You did right in asking Mr. Kendall's help in the meantime. But Mr. Kendall knows he must take care of the things others provide for him," she said, with another pointed look upward.

Jonah could feel his temper heat. If Miss

Hathaway thought he was an ungrateful wretch, he'd tell her a thing or two. He scaled down the tree limb and swung from the nearest branch. Just as his feet hit the ground he felt his sleeve pull away from the body of his jacket with a ripping sound.

By the time he turned to her, Miss Hathaway was already heading back to the house.

"I guess she's a bit put-out," Albert remarked.

"When isn't she?"

Albert chuckled. "She may seem harsh at times, but her heart's in the right place."

Jonah snorted as he bent to pick up the saw he'd dropped. He felt the gap in his shoulder immediately. He pulled himself straight, wondering how much damage he'd done to his jacket. He wriggled his shoulder in a circle but couldn't determine anything except that something had come loose.

Albert didn't seem to notice anything. "Why don't we call it a day? I'm thinking a mug of cider will taste good."

Jonah nodded, though the thought of quaffing down a pint no longer held the appeal it had a few moments ago.

After washing up in the scullery, Jonah and Albert entered the kitchen. Mrs. Nichols turned from the stove. "You two look chilled. How about some mulled cider? I have it heating here."

"Just what I was telling William we needed," Albert said to his wife.

Betsy stood at the table, kneading a large lump

of dough. Jonah ambled over and poked his finger into it. "Are we to have fresh rolls for our supper?"

She swatted his hand away. "Don't be daft. This be for tomorrow's bread."

"So, what'll we have with our cider?" he demanded in mock outrage. The girl never failed to remind him of former, easier times with his Judy. She was the youngest of the Nicholses' many children, the only one still at home, so she was the spoiled baby of the family.

"It's nothing you'll be havin' if ye don't watch your tongue. You know I feed you good," Mrs. Nichols called over her shoulder from her place by the stove.

"That I do," he said. The two men sat down at the other end of the table from Betsy. Mrs. Nichols soon had a mug of steaming cider in front of each.

"Now, there, what do you say to that, eh?" she asked, setting a plate of gingerbread in front of them.

"More like it, is what I say," Jonah said, taking a square of the warm cake. The coziness of the Nicholses' kitchen and their simple acceptance of him helped him forget the uncertainty of his life for a few minutes and pretend he was still the man he used to be back in his village.

Mrs. Nichols swatted him across the back. "You'd better teach him to mind his manners," she told her husband.

Albert chuckled. "Don't be too hard on him. He's already managed to earn Miss Hathaway's disapproval once today."

Mention of her name reminded Jonah of his torn jacket. He brought the tankard of cider slowly down from his lips. He'd removed the jacket as soon as he'd entered the house, and now it sat rolled up beside him on the bench.

The two women laughed as Albert recounted Miss Hathaway's words upon seeing Jonah up in the apple tree in his good clothes.

He pondered what he was going to do about the big gap between the sleeve and body of the jacket as he continued sipping his cider and eating the cake in front of him.

"Poor Miss Hathaway trying to make William into a gentleman and he thwarting her at every turn," Albert said with a laugh.

Even though the elderly couple never asked him anything about his past, they knew from the state of him the night he'd arrived that he was no gentleman, and they'd seen how the Hathaways were busy reforming him.

He swallowed the last of his cider and rose from the table. Betsy was busy shaping the dough into rounds. Her hands and half her forearms were covered in flour.

"I bet you're just as able with the needle as you are with shaping bread," he said with a smile.

The girl's cheeks turned redder and she looked down with a smile. "Me mum scolds me for not being able to sew a straight seam. She says I'll never have anything ready before my wedding day comes."

He drew back, his eyebrows raised in mock surprise. "And when is that great day to be?"

She giggled and shook her head, refusing to meet his eyes. "I haven't e'en a beau yet!"

"That's a situation that'll soon be remedied. 'Fore you know it, they'll come swarming round yer mum's kitchen here, and they won't be in search of sweet buns."

Her dark curls danced around her mobcap as her laughter increased.

"Careful now, or you'll ruin those nice breads you've shaped so nicely."

Her hands stopped immediately and she looked up, worried. He had an inclination to pinch her round red cheeks as if she'd been a little girl she so reminded him of his Judy when he'd first noticed her. "Now, are ye sure you don't know how to stitch a little?"

"What've ye need of stitchin', Mr. Kendall?" Mrs. Nichols came round to inspect the bread loaves.

"Oh, just a little thing."

"Our Betsy can scrub a floor to shine and make bread to melt in your mouth, but she can't even sew up a decent pocket handkerchief."

"You sure those plump fingers, so deft with the bread dough, can't sew up a stitch?" Jonah asked with exaggerated disbelief.

Her mother smiled. "If you don't mind a crooked stitch."

Betsy giggled.

Jonah heard the sound of a throat clearing. His

laughter died at the sight of Miss Hathaway standing in the doorway. She was looking so disapproving, he wondered if she'd come to scold him some more over his clothes.

The sudden silence at her appearance annoyed Jonah. Why should their moment of fun be dampened by someone just because she was a lady? He turned his back on her and marched back to his tankard, forgetting that he'd already emptied it.

Miss Hathaway walked straight to Mrs. Nichols. "Could you please come with me to the stillroom? I want to see how much spirit of lavender we have left. There's a woman who is recovering from a fever at the prison. And also, I want to check our supply of arrowroot jelly."

Mrs. Nichols wiped her hands on a cloth. "Yes, miss. I think there's plenty o' both and also some extract of chamomile."

As the two women left the kitchen, Albert cleared his throat. Betsy giggled. Jonah drained the last drop from his tankard then carried it over to the scullery, wondering why Miss Hathaway had succeeded in breaking up the mood of the group. Blister her!

"I hear Bill the Bull is boxing this Saturday in the field behind the reservoir," Albert said in a jovial voice.

Jonah turned to him, his irritation forgotten. "Who's he fighting?"

"I heard he's challenging anyone who dares fight

him. There's a twenty-guinea purse for anyone who beats him."

Jonah stared at him. Twenty guineas represented a fortune to him. "Twenty guineas, you say?"

Mrs. Nichols and Miss Hathaway reentered the kitchen. "What's this about twenty guineas?" the older woman asked.

"I was just telling William of a boxing match," her husband answered.

Mrs. Nichols set down some jars on the table. "Is that the fight you mentioned to me?"

"The very one. Bill the Bull against anyone who cares to challenge him."

Miss Hathaway frowned. "If it's a fight you're talking about, there'll be betting and drinking. It's something to steer clear of."

Jonah couldn't let that one pass. "A boxing match is a contest of strength between two men. It takes a good deal more than brawn to beat an opponent."

The others looked at him with respect. All but Miss Hathaway.

"You've fought in the ring, haven't ye?" Albert's voice held awe.

Jonah shrugged, pleased despite himself. "A time or two."

"Did you ever fight Molyneux?"

"No, I never got the chance, but I would've liked to, I can tell you," he said.

Albert nodded at Miss Hathaway. "You know, boxing is a gentleman's sport as well."

"Perhaps as a sport. But any fight in the open air is bound to be a fixed fight. There'll be brawling and all sorts of gambling going on," she said.

Albert said nothing more.

"What are you dawdling for?" Mrs. Nichols asked her daughter. "Get those loaves in their tins."

Betsy jumped. "Yes, Mum."

Miss Hathaway placed the bottles and jars in a basket. "Thank you," she told Mrs. Nichols. "I shall take them with me on tomorrow's visit." She left the kitchen without giving Jonah so much as a glance. For some reason, that annoyed him even more.

After she'd left the kitchen, Mrs. Nichols went back to the stove. Suddenly, she turned to Jonah. "You know, if you need something mended, Miss Hathaway is the one for the job. She sews a very fine stitch."

Jonah shifted in his seat. "Uh, that's all right, Mrs. Nichols. It was nothing I needed right away."

"Well, she's always at her mending in the evenings. She wouldn't mind."

Albert chuckled.

"What are you laughing about?" she asked her husband sharply.

"Oh, nothing, nothing at all."

At supper later that evening, Florence noted Quinn had changed into another coat. She frowned. Had he soiled the plum one so badly in the orchard that he could no longer wear it?

After saying grace, Damien unfolded his napkin

and turned to Quinn with a smile. "How was your afternoon?"

"Fine," he said, then stopped, his gaze crossing Miss Florence's. "I—that is, Albert and me begun—"

"Albert and *I began*," Florence corrected him.

He glanced at her again, then away. "That's right. Albert and I began to prune the orchard."

"Oh, wonderful. I know Albert is getting a little old to be up in the trees." Damien turned to his sister. "We really need to see about hiring him an assistant. It would be a shame to let the orchard go."

Before she could answer, Quinn replied, "That's all right, I can help him. I'm used to pruning."

"You are?" Damien nodded in relief. He smiled at Florence. "You see what a blessing having Mr. Kendall here has become to us?"

She looked pointedly at her brother. "He missed Reverend Doyle's visit this afternoon."

Damien had the grace to look abashed. "Oh, I see." He gave Quinn an embarrassed smile. "Well, I did as well."

Florence didn't give Quinn a chance to reply. "That is neither here nor there. The rector knows you are at the orphanage on Tuesday afternoons."

Quinn set down his utensils with a loud clatter and gave her a defiant look. "The way I see it, the less I rub shoulders with that fancy cleric, the less danger I'll put us all in."

She laid down her own cutlery without a sound. "Although I appreciate your consideration, Mr.

Kendall, what would have happened if the rector or Mrs. Doyle had chanced to see you in the orchard? After all, in your plum-colored coat, among the bare branches, you were not hard to spot. Must I remind you that you are to confine your menial activities to the hours before noon? Any visitors will generally pay their calls in the afternoon. Only tradespeople come in the mornings."

She saw the flush creeping into his face and felt only somewhat mollified. But it didn't do away with her ill humor completely. As they continued their meal in silence, it brought her no joy to have had to reprimand Quinn before Damien. Her brother never seemed to find fault with anything Quinn did or didn't do, leaving the burden of correcting him to fall fully on her shoulders.

As she toyed with the food on her plate, she pictured Quinn in the kitchen that afternoon, standing so close to Betsy. Flirting! Why, he was almost old enough to be her father.

"I been thinking o' what you told me at our last lesson," Quinn said to Damien.

Her brother looked up from his plate with a smile. "Oh, what was that?"

"When God sent Hagar away. Seemed kind o' hard."

Damien set down his utensils. "It illustrates a point. Only the child born to his wife, Sarah, was to be the child of promise."

As Quinn asked another question, Damien

pushed his plate aside and began a detailed explanation. Florence turned to watch Quinn's face as he puzzled things out. She was half-envious of his interest and at other times would have easily entered the discussion, but this evening she felt out of sorts.

When she saw Quinn take up his fish cake in his hand, she said without thinking, "Mr. Kendall, you must use your fork and knife so, to eat this with." She demonstrated with her own.

He looked at her a few seconds, during which time she could feel the skin of her cheeks grow warm. Without a word, he put the fish cake down and picked up his fork and knife and imitated her method of holding them. She proceeded to cut a small piece of the breaded cake and bring it to her mouth.

Damien cleared his throat. "God provided for this other child of Abraham's, quite generously, in fact, but he made it clear his inheritance would only pass through the line of Isaac."

Quinn nodded and picked up his cup. He took a healthy swallow of ale. Then he belched.

Florence stared, hardly believing what she'd heard. She turned to Damien. He, too, was staring at Quinn, but he quickly recovered and glanced away. Quinn, however, had caught both their looks.

He lifted the napkin from around his neck and brought it to his mouth and wiped with an exaggerated motion. "Pardon me. Where I come from a good belch shows one's compliments to the cook."

Florence put down her fork and knife. "A belch

may be customary at Newgate but not in this dining room."

The color seemed to drain from his face and she could hardly believe the words that had come out of her mouth.

He pulled the napkin from around his neck and threw it onto the table. Then he stood and, with exaggerated neatness, tucked his chair in and bowed to both of them.

"In that case, I won't inflict my filthy Newgate manners on you anymore." He turned on his heel and left the dining room.

Florence turned to meet her brother's look.

"A lifetime of habits is not easily broken."

His gentle tone only increased her irritation. "And what if his very life depends upon forming new habits?"

"I know…" He sighed. "I'll speak to him later."

She turned to fold up her napkin, her own appetite at an end. "Don't bother. I think he does these things deliberately."

"I notice you lose patience quite readily with him. Is something the matter? Has he said or done something to you?"

Her fingers stopped their motion. "No, of course not."

"If it's his coarse manners, I know you are used to much worse at Newgate, or even at the workhouse. Is it the fact that he's under your own roof day in and day out?" Damien's quiet tone probed her.

She stood from the table. "No, I told you." She gripped the back of her chair and tried to calm her voice. "I'm sorry. I didn't realize I was being impatient with him. I thought it was my duty to improve his manners, so that no one suspects his real identity."

"Yes, of course, and I didn't mean to interfere with that. It's just that…sometimes one must use a voice of encouragement with a person."

"Just as sometimes one must be tough with those one most cares about." She remembered having to exhort her brother as a young lad to learn to use his wooden leg and not be afraid to go out and be seen, not to limit himself or hide in his room as his sensitive nature would have inclined him to do.

He seemed to understand her words. With a long sigh, he turned away from her. "So be it."

Jonah sat on the edge of his bed, his ripped jacket bunched in his hands. There was no help for it. He'd have to go to Miss Hathaway and beg a needle and thread from her. He'd die before he'd ask her to sew it for him. He ground his teeth. No, it couldn't be so hard to sew a few stitches. He spread out the area where the seam had come apart. Torn threads hung from each side. He tried bringing the edges back together as they should be, but they fell right apart as soon as he removed his fingers.

Only thread would hold them in place.

He'd never actually paid attention when he'd seen Judy sew a garment. In and out would go her needle.

He might be an ignorant lout, but he was no coward. If he could face the hangman's noose without quaking, surely he could face one high-minded lady.

Resolved, he stood and marched to the door.

Chapter Eleven

By the time Jonah reached the sitting room, he wished he'd never climbed a tree that afternoon. He entered the softly lit room, where normally he would feel welcome. As usual, Damien sat reading aloud to his sister, and Miss Hathaway sat…stitching.

With a nod in Damien's direction, Jonah crossed the room, feeling like a beggar having to face someone who held all the riches. The remark Miss Hathaway had made at dinner in her quiet, cultured tones about Newgate still burned like a branding iron. He wished he could shout at her, but he knew he was in a different world here, where no one shouted, least of all a gentleman at a lady.

When he reached her chair, she didn't look up. She sat in a large armchair, like a queen on her throne. Jonah stared at the crown of her head. Her light brown hair, parted in the middle, was visible in front from the thin lace cap that covered the back of her head.

Finally, as if aware of his gaze on her, she lifted her head. He wasn't sure what he read in her gray eyes. Scorn? Or was there something else? Confusion?

"Yes?"

He must have been mistaken. Her tone sounded dry and emotionless.

"I was wondering—" He cleared his throat and began again. "I was wondering if I might borrow a needle and thread."

Her arched eyebrows rose a fraction. "Needle and thread? Why?"

He could feel his irritation growing. "What d'ya mean 'why'? Why would a body borrow needle and thread but to sew."

Her fine eyebrows drew together in puzzlement. "Do you need something mended? Bring it to me."

"That's all right. I can do it meself."

"Myself," she corrected. "Nonsense. Bring it to me and I'll put it in my workbasket." With the toe of her slipper she indicated the pile of linens in the wicker basket at her side.

"No…no, I don't want to trouble you with unnecessary work."

She looked back up at him. "Do you know how to sew?"

He could feel the flush spreading from his neck. Would that he still had his thick beard to hide behind. "Not exactly…but I can manage. It's only a bit o' stitching needs doing."

Her brother had stopped reading as soon as Jonah

had begun speaking, and probably heard every word of their exchange.

"Very well," she said, her tone sounding reluctant. She bent down, reaching for her sewing box on the floor beside her workbasket. He moved to bring it closer toward her.

"Thank you," she murmured. She lifted the lid, which was worked in some kind of colored thread, pink and white roses against a white background. Was every detail in a gentry's household made to depict beauty in some form?

She glanced up at him. "What color thread do you need?"

He stared. He hadn't thought about that. "Uh, dark."

"Dark? What color 'dark'?"

"Purplish-like. Like my coat."

Her eyes narrowed. "Is this thread for your new plum-colored coat?"

He looked down at his feet. His black leather shoes looked scuffed and had bits of mud sticking to them from today's venture in the orchard. "Aye, 'tis." He lifted his chin and stared back at her.

"The one you chose to wear to prune the orchard today?" Her voice had resumed its frosty tone.

He lifted his chin a notch higher. "The same."

She turned back to her collection of threads and rummaged among them. "You'd think if a person is being fed and clothed, the least he can do is keep his clothes in one piece."

She could have slugged him and it wouldn't have hurt as much as those words. Before he could recover himself, she had found a spool and held it up to him. "Is this the shade you were looking for?"

He stared at it, momentarily forgetting her cruel gibe. The thread looked to him the exact shade of his coat. He shook his head in amazement.

He was about to reach for the thread, but she was now taking a needle out of the pincushion and stuck it sidelong into the spool of thread.

He held out his hand. Instead of giving him the spool, she said, "Bring me your coat, Mr. Kendall."

Hathaway cleared his throat. "Uh, Jonah, my sister does an excellent job of mending." Humor underscored his quiet words. Jonah turned slowly to face him.

"I would be in rags otherwise. I seem to come in every day with some damage to my clothes." His face took on a more serious look. "There's another reason we need your clothes in tip-top condition."

Jonah cocked an eyebrow.

"The wealthiest man of the parish, the Duke of Winchester, will be issuing an invitation to us to dine at his house." Hathaway paused, seeming to assess Jonah, in a gentler manner than his sister's yet in no way less thorough. Jonah felt he was being weighed and judged. "Reverend Doyle asked us if we wanted you included in the invitation. I told him that, yes, we would naturally want you included."

Jonah's eyes widened. To be invited to a duke's

table? A man so high and mighty he could be the king. Never in his wildest imaginings in his village could he have envisioned sitting down to Lord Aston's table on his estate and he'd only been a baronet. Jonah had never even stepped into the man's kitchen.

Mr. Hathaway looked down at the book in his hands. "There is certainly a risk involved in having you there. Someone might recognize you, although I think there is little danger of that. The kind of people to frequent His Grace's establishment would not be the kind to be present at a Newgate hanging. But, any less than gentlemanly behavior or language would certainly be noted among this set."

"Why should I even want to be among those kind of folks?" he began. He had enough difficulty as it was satisfying the high-and-mighty Miss Hathaway.

"That's a good question," Hathaway said, surprising Jonah by taking his question seriously. "The main reason would be because you are a guest in our house, and we want you to be treated as one of us." He coughed before Jonah could say anything to this astounding phrase. "The second reason is that it will be the first time Miss Hathaway and I are to go to this man's residence. I've only met him a handful of times at Marylebone Church. He is a very powerful man, a member of the House of Lords. Reverend Doyle has told him about me, and the duke is desirous of making my acquaintance." Hathaway's eyes fixed on him. "The Duke would be a very powerful ally if ever we would be in need of help."

Jonah stared back at him, gradually understanding. He wasn't so thick he didn't know the danger he was in every day that he stayed in the Hathaway house. "You mean if ever I'm discovered?"

Hathaway nodded slowly. "In any event, it would look strange now that the rector knows of your presence here if we didn't want you invited. He would begin to wonder why."

Jonah shifted on his feet. The mere notion of going to this lord's house already made his stomach knot up. "I don't know. I can't even dine at your own table without doing or saying something that's not right." He looked back at Miss Hathaway, but she shifted her focus away as soon as he did. Was she sorry for the remark she'd made?

"That's why it's so important to follow Miss Hathaway's instructions and emulate her manners. She doesn't mean to scold. She is just concerned that you not do or say anything that would lead people to suspect you are anything but Mr. William Kendall, gentleman farmer from the north."

Jonah rubbed the back of his neck. "I still don't like it."

Miss Hathaway spoke up for the first time. "Mr. Kendall may be right. He might very well do or say something to disgrace himself. If he feels he's not ready to be seen in civilized company…" She left the sentence dangling.

He locked gazes with her again. This time she did not look away and he swore there was a challenge in those clear gray eyes of hers. "Afraid I might belch if the inclination so took me?"

She pursed her lips, as if seriously considering his suggestion. "Perhaps. If you think I'm particular, you have seen nothing of polite society. You shall be seated at a great table with upward of twenty guests. You will have to make conversation with the lady at your side. You will be faced with countless covers of food. You will need to know enough to take a few bites from each but by no means wolf down everything in front of you. The same with the goblets of wine constantly being replenished before you." Her slim hands began to gesture as she spoke.

"On no account can you permit yourself to become inebriated. An intoxicated man is not a discreet man. Do you understand me?" Her look was uncompromising.

"Oh, I understand you fully." He swung back to Hathaway before his sister could see the distress her little description had caused him. "I'll leave it up to you, sir. But I can't promise you anything. I'm a countryman born and bred. My ways aren't the ways of the gentry. You can try to fill me with all the niceties you can in a fortnight, but my head is thick and sometimes it doesn't make sense why a man must hold his fork so and not so."

Damien laughed out loud. "I would say not to

worry your head about the details overmuch. Just follow my sister's lead as much as possible. We'll endeavor to have you seated beside her at the table. In the meantime, why not bring her your jacket, which I conclude must have undergone some wear and tear this afternoon?" His blue eyes twinkled.

Somewhat reassured, Jonah turned to leave. Only at the last second did he remember to nod to Miss Hathaway before leaving.

A gentleman did that.

By the next day, Jonah had made up his mind that things were going to change. After that last remark of Miss Hathaway's reminding him how they were feeding and clothing him, he decided he'd had enough.

He might have lost everything else, but he still had a shred of pride left. He left the parsonage right after his morning lesson with the curate. He would show Miss Hathaway he wasn't the worthless man she thought he was. Sometime in the night the resolve had formed and by dawn had hardened. He may not be able to act like a gentleman among the titled folks, but there were a few things he could do to prove he wasn't a complete sponger.

One of them was boxing.

He remembered the competition Albert had mentioned a few days ago. Now, he stood at the corner of Hyde Park and studied the announcement nailed to the thick trunk of an elm tree.

Bill "The Bull" Elliston Challenges Any and
All Comers to the Ring.
Purse of Twenty Guineas to the Winner!
Saturday, 25th of March, behind the Reservoir, Paddington

Jonah's resolve strengthened as he read the announcement. He'd not only step up to the challenge, but he'd beat every man there and win the purse!

He pictured himself throwing down the money at Miss Hathaway's feet. Even she couldn't scoff at the sum of twenty guineas. He'd never been beholden to any man. He would certainly not be to a woman. He kicked at the dirt at his feet, and in doing so, noticed the dust covering the toe of his new leather boots. They were softer and more comfortable than any shoes he'd ever possessed. Warmer, too, against the cold March wind.

He'd be able to pay for them and more with the prize money.

He'd have to ask Albert to be his second. He knew of no one else he could trust. A man usually needed two assistants, a knee man and a bottle man. Maybe Albert knew of someone who'd come with them. Would Albert even agree? They'd have to keep it secret from Miss Hathaway. He remembered her disapproval the day Albert had first mentioned the fight.

There was also the risk of appearing at a public fight. Would he be recognized? The kind of people attracted to a fight were the same as would have been at Newgate that day.

Jonah looked around him now. It was one of the few times he'd stirred from the parsonage. It didn't escape him that where he stood was the old site of Tyburn Tree where many a man had been hanged.

He'd only crossed the street to Hyde Park, and already he felt exposed. But no one seemed to pay any attention to him. A few people strolled far away on the grounds of the park. Occasional carriage traffic passed through the tollgate on their way out of the city. But for the most part, he was alone at the outskirts of the city, the vast park to the south of him and mostly fields to the north. He could almost fool himself into thinking he was living in the country again. The air even smelled fresh here, unlike the neighborhood he'd known during his sojourn in London.

Would his appearance in the ring be sufficiently different from the man who'd stood on the gallows almost two months ago?

"Albert, what would you say to being my second? I've been thinking about that fight you mentioned the other day."

Jonah had waited until he and Albert were on their way to do the evening milking to broach the subject of the boxing match.

Albert turned to him with a twinkle in his eye. "Think you can beat The Bull?"

"There was a time I was known as a bit of a champion."

Albert shook his head. "The reverend probably wouldn't approve. Miss Hathaway certainly won't," he added, concern deepening the lines around his mouth.

Jonah looked away. "She doesn't approve of anything a man would take pleasure in."

Albert rubbed his chin. "She would probably say that when a man discovers the pleasures to be had in the Spirit, he'll no longer find pleasure in worldly pastimes."

Jonah spit in the grass. "Well, d'ye think ye can be my second?"

"Let me think on it. I'll have to talk it over with Mrs. Nichols, that's for sure." He chuckled. "She'll likely want to come watch you fight, anyway."

Jonah peered at the older man as they entered the barn. "You don't disapprove yourself? You're a religious man."

"I'm a believing man, if that's what you mean." He eyed Jonah from under his gray eyebrows. "I'm thinking you've got something to prove and I'd rather be at your side than let you go it alone."

Jonah looked away, suddenly uncomfortable. "I wouldn't want Miss Hathaway to be angry at you."

"A man can't make his peace with God until he faces his demons."

"I don't go boxing to face any demons. I go to face a flesh-and-blood man and prove I'm stronger and cleverer than he is, so I can bring home a pot o' money."

Albert laughed as he brought up a stool to the cow waiting in her stall. "Well, maybe you'd better begin training before the match. It's only a few days away."

By the Saturday of the fight, the temperatures had risen, and the morning felt balmy. Jonah was sure it was a favorable omen.

He'd been working out in back of the barn for the past few afternoons, whenever the curate and Miss Hathaway had gone away on their different rounds. Albert had filled a burlap sack with sand and hung it from an oak tree.

Albert had said they'd have to tell the Hathaways about the fight come Saturday, but Jonah had been adamant.

"You know she'll forbid it," he had argued.

Albert's face had been troubled. "But you can't keep it from the Hathaways."

"I'll just say I'm out working in the back fields on Saturday. I aim to win that prize money." His look had hardened. "I *need* to win it."

He flexed his muscles, feeling in prime shape. The good food he'd been enjoying at the Hathaways' was showing its effect in his regained weight. With all the work in the garden and orchard, his muscles had toughened.

Now, he and Albert stood along the sides of the roped-off area of the field designated as the ring.

People had been arriving for the past hour and crowded around the ring. Four wooden stakes held the rope in place. The bag with the prize money dangled from one corner.

Jonah nodded at the bag. "That's going to be mine come the end of the day."

Albert eyed Jonah's opponent. The Bull stood with his legs planted apart, his arms folded, at one end of the ring. "You may have a good fight before it's yours."

Jonah scoffed. "More fat than brawn is what I see."

Albert shook his head. "You sure you want to go through with this?"

The sack of prize money hung heavy on its rope. "I'm sure."

The crowd spread out across the field. There were few women present, none of whom looked any too respectable. Jonah could see side bets being negotiated by individuals standing at the edges of the ring.

A few carriages had driven across the fields and parked behind the multitude, bringing fashionable young nobs to view the fight. Jonah watched a gentleman jump off his high-perched phaeton and throw the reins to his tiger. He hailed an acquaintance across the yard and the two met up with a slap on the back. A silver flask was passed from one to the other.

There'd be more drinking before the matches were through, Jonah knew, as he surveyed the crowd.

The referee stepped to the center of the ring and clanged his bell, signaling the beginning of the challenge. "Who will face our champion, Bill "The Bull" Elliston? Who is daring enough to stand up to this giant weighing fourteen stone?"

Elliston swaggered to the center of the ring and took in everyone with an insolent look. Murmurs of awe rippled through the gathering.

Jonah sized him up once more. The referee was right to call him a giant. His fists were the size of hams in a butcher's window, his biceps and chest rippled. He topped Jonah by a few inches and was broader all around.

Albert's low tone reached his ear. "You know there are other ways to get twenty guineas, if it's the prize money you're after."

"With that girth, he's probably slower than a cow in pattens."

Albert chuckled. "I hope you're right." The older man sobered. "You don't have to do this, you know."

Jonah lifted his fists up to his face and jabbed the air. "I'm ready to take him on."

A couple of other men had stepped up by then. They looked scrawny against the champion.

"I'll let The Bull dispatch them before I go in," he decided.

After agreeing to the few rules, the first fighter stripped off his coat, waistcoat and shirt. The referee bent down and made a long mark with chalk in the middle of the ring, dividing it in half. The two contenders positioned themselves toe-to-toe at the line.

The crowd hooted and whistled.

As Jonah had predicted, the fight didn't last long. After only three rounds, the champion had knocked the first fighter down, and the man was unable to get back on his feet before the count of thirty was up. He was dragged off the field by his two seconds.

The next fighter lasted only one round. Bruised, his lips bleeding, he limped off the ring, supported on either side by his men.

"All right. Anyone else taking on The Bull? Or is he to remain our champion?" The referee shouted to the crowd.

"This is it," Jonah muttered in an aside to Albert. "Send up a prayer for me," he added with a wink.

"That I shall…never you fear."

Jonah stepped up to the ring. "I'll challenge The Bull," he said quietly to the referee, his eye traveling to the champion, who sneered back. He was missing one of his front teeth.

"Knock him flat, Bull! One round will finish him!" came the jeers.

The referee ignored them. "All right, who are your seconds?"

Jonah introduced them. Albert had brought along a friend.

"All right, strip and step into the ring," the referee instructed Jonah, eyeing him. "How much do you weigh?"

"Twelve stone, last time I knew," he replied.

"Ye'll need every bit of it against The Bull!" a man near the ropes shouted and everyone laughed.

Albert helped him off with his good coat and waistcoat. Jonah grimaced, thinking what Miss Hathaway would say if she could see the garments now. Never fear, he would take care the clothes she and her brother had paid for didn't get soiled. He untied his cravat and pulled the fine lawn shirt over his head and handed them to Albert.

Despite the sun, the air felt cool on his bare skin. He'd soon be wiping the sweat off his brow, he knew. If he lasted that long, he reminded himself, with another look at his opponent.

He'd just have to be quicker and nimbler. If the man succeeded in wrestling him to the ground, he'd be overpowered. Jonah drew in a deep breath and walked toward the center of the ring. The Bull loomed before him like a brick tower. Jonah came to a standstill, the toe of his shoe lined up with the chalk in the dirt. His opponent placed his dusty shoe opposite his.

At the referee's word, the two men brought their fists high in the air in front of them. At the clang of the bell the first round began.

Jonah felt the familiar rush of adrenaline that he hadn't experienced in some time. It was the excitement of being in control of a situation—not knowing how it would turn out, whether for or against him, but having a good shot at victory if he kept his head.

He danced around The Bull, feinting and retreating, then blocked a left jab with his arm and immediately brought his right fist up to the man's stomach. His fist hit a wall of iron. The man recovered and swung his fist up to Jonah's face. Jonah stepped back just in time.

The two continued circling and jabbing at each other but no hit was made.

"What's the matter, Bull," a voice shouted, "Kendall too quick for you?"

The Bull roared and charged at Jonah, who swerved away just in time, sending his opponent running all the way into the ropes. The crowd hooted and whistled.

The Bull bounced back and righted himself. When he turned around, Jonah read hatred and a desire for revenge in his bloodshot eyes. If the man's temper was hot, it could work to Jonah's advantage, as long as he himself remained cool and in control. He knew he'd have to wear his opponent out—and stay out of his way until he succeeded.

Once more, they danced around each other, jabbing, sometimes connecting, more often not. Jonah landed a punch to the man's jaw. He felt the impact all the way up to his elbow. The Bull staggered backward but didn't fall. He brought his right fist and struck Jonah in the ribs. Jonah bent over double, the breath knocked out of him.

Before Jonah could right himself, The Bull grabbed him around the waist with his two arms and squeezed. Jonah locked his arms around The Bull's thick neck, remaining in their clinch for what seemed forever.

The crowd chanted their names in a fever pitch of excitement. "Throw him down! Throw Kendall down!" they yelled.

Jonah could feel his hold weakening against the other man's superior strength. He had to find a way to break loose and not fall. Gritting his teeth, he pushed his head hard upward. He heard the "ooph" of the man's expelled breath as his head connected with The Bull's chin. Jonah took advantage of his loosened hold to break away. He brought a hard right to the man's temple, then a rapid left hook to his jaw. Giving the man no time to recover, Jonah swung another punch into his neck. The Bull staggered backward.

Jonah put his hands together and brought his arms down hard against the man's neck again, felling him completely.

Deafening roars exploded from the crowd. "The Bull is down!"

The referee stood over him. "One!…two!…three!"

The large man gripped the dusty ground and slowly lifted himself to his hands and knees.

"Seven!…eight!…nine!"

Jonah didn't wait to see more as Albert hustled him over to his side of the ring. The two men sponged him off and gave him an orange to suck on for energy.

"You're doing good. Just keep it up. You were right, the man's slower than a three-legged troll," Albert told him.

Jonah grunted, saving his breath for the ring.

"Twenty-two!…twenty-three!…" the referee's count echoed in the air.

"You'd better get back up to the mark," Albert advised him.

He nodded and returned to the center of the ring.

The second-round bell clanged. Jonah noticed a distinct slowing in The Bull's movements but knew he could be tricking him. They jabbed at each other some more, each one managing to land a punch here and there. Once again his opponent locked his arms around Jonah, knocking the wind out of him. This time giving Jonah no chance to butt his head into him, The Bull swung him down to the ground. Jonah landed with a heavy thud, his bare back scraping the dirt.

He heard the counting begin above him. He had to stand although every bone in his back felt jolted. He twisted himself around and managed to get on all fours.

"He's down! Kendall's down!" came all around him.

They thought he was finished. With a deep, shuddering breath, Jonah stood to his knees.

"Come on, William!" Albert shouted from behind him. "Come on, you can do it! Stand up, man!"

He finally dragged himself up. He could feel blood running down one side of his face. Once again, Albert led him off to his corner to sponge him off quickly.

"Up to the mark!" the referee shouted, pointing to the new line he'd drawn in the dirt.

The two men squared off once again. "Had enough, little man?" The Bull jeered at him, his broad face mottled with dirt and sweat.

Jonah bared his teeth. "Come on and find out, unless you're as slow-witted as you are slow-footed."

"You're finished," The Bull spit.

"We'll see about that." Jonah brought his fists up to his face in preparation for the next round.

Florence looked up from her sewing as Mrs. Nichols approached her chair. "Yes?" she said with a smile.

The older woman knotted her hands in her apron.

Florence laid her mending on her lap. "Elizabeth, is something the matter?"

"No, miss. Not precisely, that is. I just…well, I thought you should know, that is, before Betsy and I left, you see."

"Leave? Where are you going?"

"Oh, I've left everything tidy in the kitchen. I'll be back before supper."

"That's all right." Florence smiled. "Is there something special you've arranged, an outing on this fine day?"

"Not precisely," she repeated. "You see, Albert has taken Mr. Kendall…to the fields yonder…by the Basin." Her voice ended in a mumble.

Florence began to feel a twinge of alarm. "What

are you talking about? I thought they were going to the market over in Wembley."

Mrs. Nichols looked down at her hands, visibly uncomfortable. "I told Albert to tell you the truth."

Florence set aside her sewing on the table beside her and sat straight. "You'd better tell me all." Quinn must be at the bottom of some mischief, she was sure of it.

"It's the fight, you see. Mr. Nichols has agreed to be Mr. Kendall's second today on the field…" Her voice dwindled off.

"A fight?" She thought back, trying to remember when she'd heard of a fight.

The other woman bit her lip and nodded. "Oh, dear, I knew it was wrong to keep it from you."

Florence waited, her lips pinched.

Mrs. Nichols wrung her hands harder in her apron. "I told Albert he should be no part of it. But he thought he'd better accompany Mr. Kendall, keep an eye on him, you know, rather than have him go off on his own. He was determined to go, you see… Anyway, I was getting ready to go, Betsy and me both, to see how things have turned out." She shook her head. "I sure hope he hasn't hurt himself."

"What sort of a fight?" She couldn't believe how steady her voice sounded when inwardly she was seething.

"A boxing match," she said, looking down and speaking in a low tone as if saying the words quietly would soften their significance.

"A prizefight." She felt her anger grow into a cold, hard knot in her chest. "You'd better come with me to Mr. Damien and tell him everything."

"Well, I would, but I'm afraid we haven't much time…if we're to see the match."

She stood, her alarm growing. What if Quinn were recognized? "Let us inform Damien and then be on our way. You said the Basin? That's about a mile up the road. You can explain on the way."

She knocked on the door to her brother's workshop. At his voice, she entered. "I believe Mr. Kendall has decided to oppose a champion in a prizefight this afternoon."

Damien looked up from the dismantled clock in front of him. "What's that?"

She spread out the wrinkled notice Mrs. Nichols had taken out of her apron pocket. "Albert is acting as his second."

Damien frowned. "It looks dangerous."

She nodded. "In more ways than one," she added with a significant look. If Quinn had his hide beaten, it would serve him right. If someone among the riffraff recognized him, he'd get more than his hide beaten. She'd wring his neck before he'd ever have a chance to have the noose do it for him.

Damien rose from the table. "We'd better see what it's all about. Thankfully, it's in a field just up the road."

Chapter Twelve

Florence could hear the shouts of the crowd long before they arrived at the wide field. She picked up her skirts to quicken her pace, then glanced at her brother, hoping he was able to keep up with them.

As if reading her mind, he shook his head and continued on, using his walking stick to maneuver through the trampled grass.

"Do you think he'll win?" Betsy asked her mother. "William's so strong. I can't imagine he'll get knocked down once."

Florence stared at her. *William?* The chit was calling Quinn by his first name? The news deepened her exasperation at the man.

Damien turned to the girl. "He's up against a pretty fierce opponent if the poster is to be believed. The Bull sounds like an undefeated champion."

"Oh, I hope he's not hurt, not our William. He's so jolly and nice."

Jolly and nice? Florence had seen precious little of that side of Quinn. But she remembered the times she'd come upon the foursome, laughing and talking. Those were the only times she'd been made to feel out of place in her own kitchen. She'd always felt completely at ease with Mr. and Mrs. Nichols, even Betsy, whom she'd taken in hand and taught many things, including reading and sewing. Just because she was hopeless at finer embroidery, it hadn't been for lack of teaching.

When had she started to feel unsure of herself each time Quinn sat with the Nicholses in the kitchen?

Florence forgot her annoyance at Betsy as soon as they reached the fringes of the noisy crowd. She craned her neck but could see nothing over the people's heads. A sudden chorus of shouts told her something had just happened in the ring.

Without waiting for Damien to make a way for her, she began squeezing through the wall of bodies in front of her. "Excuse me, please. Make way, please."

A burly man glared at her. "Hey, what d'ye think ye'r doin', pushin' yer way through, like ye own the place!" His breath reeked of liquor, his cheeks were covered with thick stubble.

She stared right back at him. "I'm with a clergyman. If you don't want us to summon the constable, you'd better make way for us."

With an oath, he moved enough to let her pass. She elbowed and pushed her way through the press. Angry looks and words followed in their wake, until people, seeing Damien's wooden leg, grudgingly let them through.

Florence was gasping for air when they finally emerged at the edge of the roped-off ring, the smell of unwashed bodies almost as bad as those at Newgate.

At the sight in front of her, everything else faded. How could one of these men be Quinn? Rivulets of blood and sweat ran down their battered faces and chests.

Florence had never before witnessed a boxing match. The reality was more gruesome than she'd imagined. She covered her mouth with her hands as the man called The Bull, who looked half a head taller than Quinn and broader in the shoulder, landed a punch to Quinn's jaw. The thud resounded over the cheers. Florence bit her lip to keep from crying out as Quinn staggered backward a few paces but she could see he was barely standing.

How long had they been at it?

By now, both men looked like bloodied beasts as they lunged at each other with incoherent grunts. They held their fists up high, their knuckles visibly raw.

"What round are they on?" Damien had the presence of mind to ask a bystander.

The man turned incredulous eyes on them. "It's the eighth round! Can you believe it?"

"Impossible!" her brother said, the concern in his eyes deepening.

The man chortled. "They're as stubborn as bears.

Neither one wants to give in though they've both fallen to the ground so we thought they'd never be up again." He shook his head in disbelief. "But they keep getting up."

Florence could hardly bear to watch yet was helpless to look away. She sucked in her breath each time a fist connected with flesh. How could men do something so barbaric? They roared like animals on a charge, and Florence was reminded of Quinn as the defiant prisoner on the gallows. Had he learned nothing of more civilized behavior while living with them?

Tearing her gaze from Quinn, she scanned the area until she spotted Albert at the opposite end of the ring. He didn't see them, too intent on encouraging Quinn with his shouts. How could dear Albert have agreed to this madness?

At the gasp from the crowd, her attention swung back to the center of the ring. The Bull had knocked Quinn flat. She wanted to cover her eyes. Quinn looked lifeless. Had the other man killed him? *Oh, Lord, no!* Would his life be ended this day? Her heart seemed to stop as she waited to see if he would rise.

The referee stood over him. "One!…two!…" He flung down his hand with each count.

A collective gasp burst from the audience when Quinn finally moved. Like a leviathan in his death throes, he rolled over. Florence cowered beside her brother, hearing Quinn's groans. Biting her fist, she watched him rise in stages, first to his hands and knees and finally to his feet. His back was black with dirt and covered with lacerations.

"Fifteen!…sixteen!…"

Quinn lurched over to Albert's end of the ring and collapsed onto the other man's knee. Immediately, Albert squeezed a sponge of water over Quinn's head and took a bottle of water and poured it down his throat. Quinn's throat muscles worked up and down, drinking greedily of the liquid.

"Nineteen!…twenty!…"

Assisted by the two men, Jonah stood back on his feet.

How could he think about returning to the fight?

But he shook the men off and staggered to the center of the ring where his opponent awaited him.

The two men squared off, setting their toes to the freshly drawn line, standing with elbows bent, fists curled tight, right legs drawn forward. Florence could see them muttering things to each other and watched the bloodlust rise in their eyes.

She could see they were both near their end. Like two drunken louts, their movements erratic, they danced around each other, their fists flailing in and out, in and out, over and over until one or the other managed to knock a punch at the other, almost as if by accident.

Florence prayed, her lips moving silently. *Oh, Father, make it end soon. Make it end soon. Protect Quinn. Forgive him for his sheer stupidity.* How could he expose himself—them all—like this? She was going to beat some sense into him if it was the last thing she did.

Would anyone recognize him? Her eyes darted through the crowd then back to the ring. Although his hair was short now, and he was minus a beard, and he was more heavy than he had been when he stood on the gallows, in other respects, Quinn once again resembled the filthy man who'd taken her hostage that fateful day.

Had it been…a mere two months ago that not only his, but her own, life had changed so dramatically? Never had she found herself so angry with one individual at the same time she felt such anguish for him.

Florence bit her lip, cringing as a punch connected with Quinn's jaw, sending him reeling back a few paces, though he managed to remain upright. Slowly, she released her breath.

The next moment she resumed her tirade. How could Quinn have done such a thing? Had he so little regard for his own safety, much less that of those who'd harbored him these weeks? Had he no gratitude for all her brother had done for him?

She craned her neck forward as the shouts rose anew.

"Darken 'is lights, Kendall! Land 'im yer fives! That's the way!"

Somehow Quinn had managed to connect with the other man's jaw. The Bull's head snapped back and before he recovered, Quinn was raining punches on either side of him, at his neck and face. He didn't let up, but kept at it until the other man stumbled back several steps.

She cringed as Quinn bent his head down and rammed it against the man's stomach. The man's breath was knocked out of him and like a giant tree, he tumbled onto the ground, sending up a cloud of dust.

The shouts around the ring rose to a frenetic roar. The referee stepped over to the fallen man and began his count.

"The Bull is down! The Bull is down! Kendall has taken down the champ!" The cries deafened Florence so she couldn't hear the referee's count. She prayed the man would stay out cold if only it meant the end of this madness.

The Bull didn't move. By the time the count reached twenty, the man had only managed to move his head.

"Thirty!" The referee swung both arms out, signaling an end to the fight. "We have a new champion!" he shouted, taking Quinn by the arm and raising it up. "William Kendall. Quick-footed Kendall!"

The crowd took up the chant. Albert and his friend rushed to Quinn and draped his arms around their shoulders, helping him back to his corner. Florence could see no more as the crowd rushed onto the ring like floodwaters breaking down a dam.

Damien reached out a hand to her. "Come on. Let's try to make our way around."

This proved more difficult than they'd bargained for. Everyone pressed forward, eager to congratulate the new champion.

When they finally managed to reach the other side of the ring, Albert noticed them first. He looked up from sponging Quinn's face. "Reverend Hathaway!" His eyes widened. "Miss Hathaway!" His glance went past Florence. "Elizabeth! What do you mean bringin 'em 'ere?"

"Hello, Albert," Damien replied for them all. "How soon do you think you can bring him home?"

Quinn turned. At the sight of them, his mouth split open in a wide grin, his lip dripping blood at one corner.

Florence gasped. How dare he grin like an ape as if he had no cares in the world? She forgot her worries over the fact that a few moments ago he'd almost been killed.

In that second his gaze crossed hers, his eyes brilliant green in the sunlight. "You're looking at the new champion."

"Was it worth it?" she said, through stiff lips.

He leaned his neck back as Albert wiped away more of the blood from his face. "Every lick," he replied, his smile saucy despite the bloody lip. His eyes shifted to Damien. "Hullo there, Reverend. Did you see how I leveled 'im?"

"I did, indeed. Think you can walk?"

"I reckon so, why?"

Damien's glance flickered over the crowd, his voice lowering. "It's best you get away as soon as possible. You've achieved a certain amount of notoriety today. We don't want you taking any chances."

Quinn's smile disappeared as he took in the rest of their party. He looked back at Damien with a frown. "Think there's any danger here?" he asked, his own tone barely above a whisper. "It's a far cry from where I was."

"It's better to err on the side of caution," Damien said. "Can you stand?"

Albert put an arm around Quinn as he attempted to stand. "Guess I'll manage," he said.

"That's a good man." Damien turned to Albert. "Why don't you get his shirt on, and we'll wait to clean him up and bandage him when he's back?" His gaze flickered over Quinn's bloody torso. "Think you can wait that long?"

"I think I gave better than I got, what d'ye think, Reverend?"

"I think you're right," Damien said with his first smile.

Florence pressed her lips together. Hopefully, Damien would not succumb to Quinn's charm and weaken over this serious matter.

Betsy's voice bubbled over her shoulder. "Oh, William, you were wonderful."

Florence glared at her as the girl shoved past her to Quinn's side. Mrs. Nichols followed close behind her, the two women smiling like silly schoolgirls.

As they offered Quinn their congratulations on a fight well fought, Florence turned on her heel.

She'd had enough of this spectacle. If he was going to expose himself to the awful danger of discovery, she wouldn't be a part of it. She started pushing through the crowd.

"Excuse me, make way here, please!"

Florence was ready with water and washcloths when she heard the sound of celebration outside the kitchen door.

Quinn and the rest trooped in, everyone still laughing and talking as if they'd been to the races.

"I'm going to break open a cask of ale to celebrate your victory," Albert said.

"Let me get the glasses," Mrs. Nichols said, coming in after him and untying the knot of her cloak. "Oh, Miss Hathaway, we wondered where you had got to."

"I thought someone had better put something on those cuts and bruises before they fester."

At that, they sobered and went about their tasks. Damien entered last, closing the door behind him. He joined Florence at the table. "I don't think anyone remarked particularly on our departure. Certainly, no one followed us all the way here. I think everything will turn out all right." He squeezed her shoulder and gave her a small smile, which she tried to return without much success. While she had waited for their return, her mind had kept going

over the fight and all the possible negative consequences, not least of which were the wounds in-
flicted on Quinn's body. If they didn't fester, it
would be a miracle.

Her glance strayed to the victor, and she winced
inwardly at the sight of his battered face.

As if sensing her observation, Quinn's eyes met
hers. "Ready to bandage me up?" he said with an
irrepressible smile.

She turned back to the basin of water without a
word. How could he make light of this?

Damien gave her shoulder another squeeze and
turned to Quinn. "Why don't you come here and
have Miss Hathaway doctor you up a bit? You do
look a bit the worse for wear."

"I do feel a bit beat-up. Haven't been in a good
fight for some time."

Damien helped Quinn off with his outer garments.
Florence frowned at the plum-colored coat. It was
probably stained with blood by now and reeked of
sweat. Later, she'd have to see if it was salvageable.
She turned to the pile of clean lint she'd brought
from the pantry.

Quinn was struggling to bring his shirt up over
his head, since Damien had gone to hang up his
coat. Before Florence could step closer to help him,
Betsy rushed to his aid.

"Let me get that for you, William."

The name on Betsy's lips stung Florence afresh.

"Your arms must be sore from wrestling the other

man." Betsy bent over his hand. "Ooh, look at your poor knuckles, they're raw!"

"A mite." Quinn lifted his arms with a groan as the girl gently tugged at the soiled and rumpled white shirt and lifted it over his head.

He smiled down at her. "Thank ye, lass."

"Sit here," Florence said in clipped tones, forgetting her anger for the moment at the knife-thrust of pain the sight of Betsy's familiarity with Quinn caused her.

She bent over the basin of warm water and wrung out a washcloth then approached Quinn's broad bare back, trying to decide where to begin. Gingerly, she touched a bruised and scraped shoulder blade.

"Ouch! Have a care, woman. What do you think I am, a bag o' meal?"

"An ignorant animal from what I saw on the field." Giving him no chance to reply, she plunged another washcloth into a basin of cold water. "Here, put this against your eye if you don't want it to swell the size of an egg tomorrow."

She continued sponging down his back.

Betsy sat down across from Quinn at the table. "I wish I could'a watched the fight from the beginning but Da didn't let me come."

Florence indicated the basin on the table. "Betsy, fetch me some more warm water."

Betsy blinked, looking chastened. "Yes, miss."

When Florence had finished sponging the dirt off his back, she said in clipped tones, "Turn around."

He moved slowly. It was no wonder, thought Florence, eyeing the cuts and scrapes on every inch of his torso.

She squeezed water out of the washcloth then approached him once more. He sat back with his elbows on the table, his broad chest laid bare to her.

Swallowing against the sudden tightness in her throat, she stepped closer. She placed the hot cloth against his upper chest and wiped the dirt away gently.

He let out a satisfied sigh. "That feels good."

"You're filthy." Her sharp tone contrasted with her quavering insides. As she continued sponging off his chest, she reminded herself of all the times she'd sponged him off when he'd been feverish. Then he'd been a stranger, a fugitive at their mercy, unconscious most of the time. Now, she could feel his eyes following her every move.

She swiped at the streaks of dirt, watching the water flatten the sprinkling of dark hair on his chest. Blowing out a breath, Florence straightened. With the back of her hand, she wiped the perspiration from her forehead then braced herself to continue her task, hoping her hand would remain steady.

He flinched as her cloth touched his rib cage. "Have a care there."

"It's not my fault you're bruised. If you'd acted like the gentleman you're supposed to be, you wouldn't find yourself in this state now." The thought fueled her anger and propelled her on with her task.

Quinn sucked in his breath as she touched a

bruise then swore as the cloth rubbed against an abrasion. "What d'ye think I am!"

She dunked the cloth back in the water and watched it color immediately with blood and dirt. "Watch your language. You certainly didn't mind acting like an animal in the ring."

"Well, now I'm outta it and don't need more of a beating."

She worked her way up to his grimy neck. "Ouch! Careful there." He brought his hand up and swatted at her.

"I wouldn't have to rub so hard if the dirt weren't so ground in. Bring me another basin of water," she snapped at Betsy when she came over to ogle Quinn's wounds. "Make it hot this time."

Quinn twisted around to glare at her. "You want to scald me on top of everything else?"

"It wasn't my doing you're in the shape you're in now. In case you've forgotten, you're supposed to look like a gentleman in a fortnight."

The two fell silent as she began with his face. Albert filled a tankard and brought it to Quinn. At Albert's look of inquiry her way, Florence shook her head. She would *not* toast to his foolhardy victory. There was no telling what it would cost them.

"Here's to the new champion!" Albert said, lifting his tankard in the air.

"Hurrah!" shouted the others, following suit.

Florence watched Quinn tip back his head and quaff down a generous portion. His Adam's apple moved up and down as the liquid went down his throat. He smacked his lips and brought the tankard down with a thud. Had she taught him nothing?

She wrung out the washcloth. How could he be so callous about putting everyone at risk by his public exhibition?

"Need any help, miss?" Mrs. Nichols asked, approaching them.

She handed Mrs. Nichols the washcloth. "Yes. You can help me wash him off so I can put something on these cuts." Her hand was beginning to shake, whether with anger or another emotion, she wasn't about to ask herself.

Florence bent over her medicine box and removed a jar of basilicum ointment for the cuts. "Betsy, prepare me some bread crumbs, with the dried elder flowers and chamomile flowers hanging in the pantry for a poultice."

"Yes, miss."

The girl scurried off to get the ingredients. Soon the kitchen filled with the smell of boiling vinegar water mixed with the herbs.

"You look as if someone has stepped on you," Florence said to Quinn as she dabbed ointment on the cut at the edge of his lips.

"It certainly feels like it."

"There, now you're all cleaned up," Mrs. Nichols declared, stepping back with a satisfied look.

"Thank ye kindly, Mrs. Nichols."

Quinn's jaw was prickly under her fingertips

from the feel of his beard. Florence hurried to another cut, this one on his temple. He could have been killed. She bit her lip as she pictured his opponent's fist smashing into Quinn's temple.

She frowned, looking more closely at his dark hair, which was now curling around her fingers. "You've got cuts in your scalp as well." Once more she took the washcloth and went to work on his scalp. His hair felt silky to the touch. The smell of soap reached her nostrils as she dabbed at the wounds.

"Did you see me fight?" Quinn's voice startled her as he craned his neck to address her.

"Why would you think I saw you fight when you didn't deign to inform either Mr. Hathaway or myself that you proposed to exhibit yourself in public this way?"

The amusement in his green eyes died as he saw the coldness in hers.

"I figured I'd surprise you when I won."

"What made you so certain of victory?"

He shrugged, wincing immediately afterward. "I just made up my mind about it."

"So, are you satisfied now that you've exposed yourself to a crowd of people?"

"No one recognized me there. Besides, the result was worth it." He turned to Albert. "Where're my winnings?"

Albert hurried over with a dirty pouch.

Quinn hefted it with a satisfied smile. Florence

heard the clink of coins from the bulging sack. "This is the reason I went into the ring."

Before she could say anything, he untied the sack and upended it onto the table. A pile of coins fell out.

"Twenty guineas," he announced in a triumphant tone.

Florence's mouth went dry. "You did this for money?"

He nodded, a wide grin splitting his face. "Take it, it's yours."

Her glance went from his face to the pile of money and back again. "What do you mean?"

"I won it for you."

Damien approached him. "Oh, William, you didn't have to—"

If she had thought she was angry before, her ire knew no bounds now. "How dare you expose us all to danger and then offer us your filthy lucre!"

His smile faded. An ugly look came into his eyes.

She could feel the heat growing in her face. "It's not enough my brother has risked his reputation, all those of this household, his very life for the sake of your worthless hide but you have to go out and publicly expose yourself—for what?" She pointed at the pile of money with her washcloth. "For a pile of gold! How dare you? *How dare you?*" She glared at him. "You, Mr. Kendall, are indeed despicable!"

Quinn rose and stepped toward her, his bare body towering over her. "You want to know why I done it?" He jabbed a finger at her chest so she flinched.

"I'm fed up with your making me feel like a beggar. I been eatin' and drinkin' 'ere without a penny o' me own to spare. A man gets tired o' people lording it over 'im." He picked up a fistful of the coins and he shook them at her. "So you can take the bl—" The rest of the sentence was filled with oaths as he flung the money at her feet.

Her mouth widened in outrage. He was blaming her! Without thinking, she took up the soapy wash-cloth and shoved it in his mouth while he was still swearing. Ignoring his cut, she began rubbing with all her might.

He struck her hand away so hard she reeled backward. The next second he bent over, gagging.

Albert was at his side immediately. "Here, man, take a swig o' this to rinse out your mouth." He put the tankard into his hands. Quinn grabbed it and staggered to the sink, coughing and spitting as he went.

"I've had enough of your filthy mouth," Florence said to his back. "I've told you not to blaspheme in this house."

With a last mouthful of ale spit in the sink, he turned, the look in his eyes sending a wave of fear down her spine. As he stalked toward her, she noted his lip was bleeding afresh.

The kitchen had grown silent. As she looked away from Quinn, she noticed the others staring at her with disbelief. Even Damien's eyes held wonder.

She had the sudden urge to hide. She'd not felt

so exposed since…not since she'd had to face a church full of people at Eugene's wedding.

She picked up the washcloth that had fallen on the floor. "You may finish with him, Elizabeth," she said in her most dignified tone. Then she turned and began walking out of the kitchen, keeping her steps evenly paced, when all she wanted to do was pick up her skirts and flee.

By the time she reached the sanctuary of her bedroom, tears were running down her face.

How could she have lost control like that in front of everyone? She who prided herself on her ladylike behavior and self-control? What kind of virago had she turned into since Jonah Quinn had come to their house? Who was she? She no longer knew herself.

In the wake of her departure, the kitchen was silent except for the sound of the fire in the range. Quinn looked around, but everyone's gaze dropped as soon as it met his. He suddenly felt like a strange animal. What was wrong with everyone?

Damien was the only one to speak. He cleared his throat and approached Jonah. "I'm sorry. I mean, please don't take Miss Hathaway's actions…her words…to heart. She was…she was…I mean—" The normally eloquent man was at a loss for words. "She was hurt that you would think we wanted to be repaid for anything we've given you. Please forgive her. She's clearly overset by the sight of seeing you in the boxing ring."

Jonah shoved past him and began to collect the coins from the table. All the pride he'd taken in bringing home something of substance had evaporated, leaving him with the same feeling of shame he always got around Miss Hathaway. Well, if she didn't want his twenty guineas, he certainly wasn't going to let it go to waste. He hadn't had his body beaten and battered for nothing. It was clear his welcome at this household was at an end. He'd need the coin to see him on this way.

Damien reached out, staying his hand. "Why don't you come with me into the study where we can discuss things a little more?"

The significance of the words was not lost on Quinn. Miss Hathaway's accusations had been made in front of everyone. His eyes roamed the room before returning to the reverend. "I don't see that any more words are necessary," he said in a sullen tone.

"Please."

Jonah shook off his hand but didn't have the heart to deny him this last request. For it would be his last. "Very well," he said, and continued picking up his money.

Then as if a spell had broken, everyone began to move about. Albert knelt down and picked up the fallen coins from the floor. Mrs. Nichols and Betsy began clearing up the basins of water. Everyone talked of everything but Miss Hathaway's behavior.

Jonah fumed in silence, his anger growing cold and hard with each passing minute.

* * *

Jonah awoke disoriented. His room had grown dark. He squinted at the clocking ticking on the mantelpiece. Eight o'clock. Had he slept so long? He'd just lain down after his chat with Damien. The poor boy had tried everything to convince him to stay, but all Jonah had promised was to sleep a night on it.

Jonah sat up and immediately winced. His ribs, his shoulders, his abdomen, every muscle of his body groaned as he sat up. "I'm getting too old for fisticuffs," he muttered, sitting for a few minutes before attempting to move farther.

He'd missed supper, his growling stomach reminded him. He yawned and scratched his head until coming against a tender bump. He didn't dare attempt a stretch. Feeling like a rheumatic old man, he stood gingerly and shoved his feet into his slippers. He had fallen asleep in a clean shirt and breeches. He remembered too late he'd left the other things in the kitchen. Well, he'd go down there now and see if he could find something to eat. He worked his jaw, hoping it wouldn't be too painful to chew.

He left his room, closing the door softly behind him. The upstairs hallway was silent. He imagined the Hathaways in their sitting room with their dignified evening tasks. His lips turned down in derision.

Before he'd taken more than two steps, the door opposite his opened and Miss Hathaway stepped out. She seemed as surprised to see him as he was to see her.

Her face looked paler than usual, as if she, too, had just awakened from sleep. She put a hand to her hair then jerked it back. "You missed supper."

He shrugged, although his stomach didn't feel so casual about the fact.

"If you're thinking of troubling Mrs. Nichols, don't. She's gone to her home for the evening."

Her clipped words rekindled his anger. She had humiliated him for the last time. Her slim silhouette against the gathering dusk showed him suddenly how powerless she really was. What was she but a woman? He'd let her demean him once too often.

She had no right to belittle his prize winnings. He'd won the twenty guineas fair and square and would take them with him on the morrow. But not before he'd given her a piece of his mind. He took a step toward her.

As he advanced, she took a step back but could move no farther, her back against the door. He smiled with grim satisfaction. Let her be the one to cower for a change. He'd acted the gentleman long enough.

Then she stopped, as if reading his mind, and straightened her shoulders a fraction, lifted her chin a notch, and stared him straight in the eye as she waited for him to approach.

He admired her courage, but it didn't stop his advance.

Part of him told him to go back. But it was too late. He wanted it out with her now, for once and for all.

He didn't stop until he was inches from her,

close enough to detect the rise and fall of her chest. "You're angry because you think I put everyone's life in danger? You can blame yourself if that's the case." At her widened eyes, he continued. "Yes, yourself. If you hadn't continued lording it over me every minute o' the day that every stitch on my back I owe to you—"

He swatted away the hand she brought up as if to defend herself. "I'm not finished with you yet." He leaned down to her. She edged her face away from his until it bumped against the door panels. "You know what I think? I think you're afraid o' me."

"That's nonsense."

He ignored her words. "Aye, afraid o' me." Why hadn't he realized it before? She was a woman. Beneath that prim and proper act, she was a woman. Why had he felt he had to cower before her?

"You're afraid maybe I'll see who you really are behind that disapproving look o' yours." He read outrage in her eyes, and this time, instead of thinking of the anger she held back, he thought of the passion.

He brought up his hand and touched her cheek. Her skin felt as soft as a babe's under his fingertip as he began to stroke it.

For a moment he forgot his anger as he stared in wonder at her cheek then at her lips, which had parted slightly. He swallowed, suddenly conscious of how long it had been since he'd known a woman's comfort.

His fingers traveled downward and he anchored her chin between them. As soon as he did so, she began to struggle, but he only tightened his hold on her and brought her chin up so her lips were only inches from his. "You give your life to your brother and your religious causes so you don't have to look at yourself." He gave a mirthless laugh. "You probably scared any man that ever came close to you, and hid behind those pious pinched lips o' yours." His breath fanned her lips. "When all along, what you needed was a man strong enough to crack that prim pose o' yours."

Her eyes widened and he read the panic in them. At the same time, a pulse began to throb in his temple and he could not remember what he was angry about.

She had stopped struggling and her eyes were no longer looking into his, but had dropped down to his lips.

That finished it for him. The next second he closed the gap between them and covered her mouth with his. He almost jerked back at the jolt of pain in his lip. He'd forgotten the cut. But he shut out the pain, a greater need ruling him.

He ground his lips against hers, using no gentleness, his desire to humiliate her quickly disappearing into his own need for her. He forced her mouth open and felt her shock.

The heels of her hands came up to push against his chest, but they were nothing against his superior size. He pinned her against the door, taking pride in his greater strength. Just as he'd defeated a man larger and broader today, he would defeat this slip of a woman who'd lorded it over him too long. He'd prove to her that beneath her self-controlled front beat the heart of a woman.

He bent her body to his, determined to break her will. She whimpered against his mouth. The sound, like that of a wounded bird, penetrated the haze of passion clouding his brain. Suddenly he realized what he was doing. *Forcing himself upon a lady.* He dropped his hands as if she were a live coal and stepped away, horror overwhelming him and extinguishing the ardor of the instant before.

Her eyes reflected his horror. Two bright spots of color stained her usually pale cheeks. Her pink lips had deepened in color as well. His heart smote him when he saw the stain of blood at one corner of her mouth, until he realized it was his own blood. He brought up a hand and wiped the back of it across his bleeding lip.

At the same time she covered her mouth with a hand. "Go," she whispered. "Please go." The voice was low and pleading.

He felt a wave of self-disgust so strong he staggered back. What had he done? Attacked not just a lady, but Miss Hathaway, the only one to offer him help when he'd been on the run.

Never had he assaulted a woman. He'd not do it to the lowest tart. But a *lady*. The enormity of what he'd done choked him.

Before he could move, Miss Hathaway dropped her head and leaned against the door, looking more than ever like an injured creature.

What had he done? He reeled away from her like a great lumbering beast with nowhere to hide.

Florence heard Quinn's steps retreat along the hallway and down the stairs. In the distance she heard a door open and shut. Not until complete silence reigned did she dare move. Slowly, her hand came down and she observed its tremble as if it belonged to someone else.

Her first kiss.

Long ago, she'd dreamed about it, but in her deepest imaginings, she'd never conceived of anything so brutal. She'd imagined a soft peck or a gentle joining of two mouths. A tenderness that surpassed all. Instead she'd been assaulted, left at the mercy of a man's brute force. She felt a stickiness and tasted a salty substance on her lips. Had he ripped her lips apart? It had certainly felt so. But as she explored the edge of her mouth, she discovered no cut.

She stilled. The blood was his. He'd broken open his wound in his attack on her. More than the joining of their mouths, his blood seemed to brand her and fuse her to him in some strange, indelible way.

Would her lips show the evidence of his kiss tomorrow? Would others look at her and know what had happened to her? Would they see the change in her? For she knew she was changed forever.

She shuddered and covered her face. She should feel outraged. She should run to Damien and demand that Quinn quit the premises this very night.

But she knew she would do neither. She would remain silent.

For the shame she felt was principally directed at herself.

Because a part of her craved more.

The realization stunned her and broke open the seal of all her deepest and darkest yearnings. How could she ever look Quinn in the face again and know what she knew now?

You're afraid maybe I'll see who you really are. His words came back to her.

Only he had seen her secret longings and guessed how much she'd wanted him.

Chapter Thirteen

"Good morning, Flo."

Florence whipped her head up, her heart pounding. But it was only Damien entering the dining room. "Good morning."

Damien seated himself and unfolded his napkin. "Sleep well?"

She read only sympathy in his gaze. "Why do you ask?" She looked down at her place, hoping he hadn't noticed the circles under her eyes. She could feel her cheeks warm, thinking of her greater fear—that he not remark anything out of the ordinary about her mouth.

She'd scrutinized it this morning in the harsh light of day in her hand mirror but could find no evidence of Quinn's kiss. Same lips, no bruising, gone all traces of blood. She'd spent a good while examining her entire face, but other than signs of fatigue, there was nothing to mark the profound change in her.

"Morning, Reverend, Miss Hathaway."

Florence jumped at Albert's voice as he peered around the door frame. "Beggin' your pardon, but Mr. Kendall sent me over to tell you he'd be spending a few days over at the cottage." The old man cast an apologetic look Florence's way and then continued addressing Damien. "Said he wasn't too presentable."

"Is he all right?" Damien asked. "Should we summon the apothecary?"

Albert shook his head. "Oh, nothing a few days won't mend." He chuckled. "Got a lip that's pretty swollen and one eye kind o' shut up and colorful."

"Doesn't he need nursing?" Florence couldn't stop herself from asking then bit her lip as Albert's eyes turned on her. He, too, was looking at her with sympathy.

"Oh, Elizabeth and Betsy'll take good care o' him, don't you worry yourself none, miss."

Of course. Her concern turned bitter in her throat as she pictured Betsy hovering over Quinn, her ample bosom thrust under his face. "Thank you for informing us, Albert," she said.

Albert tipped his head and left the room.

As soon as he'd said grace, Damien cleared his throat. "I, uh, had a talk with Kendall yesterday afternoon."

"What—oh?" She looked up and suddenly stilled. Did her brother know? Her hand went to her heart.

"I think I convinced him not to leave."

When she said nothing, Damien continued. "His pride took a bit of a beating."

She looked down, heat burning her cheeks. She fisted her napkin. "I...I...don't understand what happened."

"I think having the Nicholses witness the whole thing just took away from the joy of his win."

She stared at her brother. What was he talking about? Then she remembered. The scene in the kitchen. She sagged back from the force of relief.

"Are you all right, Flo?"

She nodded and bent over her plate. The kiss last night had overshadowed her entire memory of everything else yesterday. She collected herself with a sip of tea before addressing her brother.

"Quinn shouldn't have taken the risk of appearing in a boxing match. You saw the crowds there."

Damien sighed. "It was a foolish thing he did, going out in public in that way. I explained it to him. Perhaps that's another reason he's keeping out of sight. Maybe he needs a chance to think on things. Florence?"

She lifted her eyes to meet Damien's kindly gaze. "He was intent on leaving, you know."

It was her turn to look away, embarrassed as she recalled her behavior in the kitchen. "I didn't mean to lose my temper—"

"I know you didn't. I explained to him that you were overwrought from the fight."

Overwrought? Florence touched her lips. How could she explain how she felt now?

"Are you all right with Quinn's staying on here?"

How could she answer that? No one must ever know what had transpired above stairs…yet, how was she ever going to face him?

Four days later, when Jonah awakened at dawn, he realized he had imposed on the Nicholses' hospitality long enough. He rose from the narrow cot and eyed himself in the mirror, as he had each morning. Each morning it had been the same. Anticipation warred with dread—anticipation at seeing Miss Hathaway again…and dread at the prospect.

This morning was no exception. As he picked up the mirror, he almost hoped to see the monstrous swelling of his face still there. But his face looked almost normal. Even the cut on his lip was healing nicely.

How could a man feel so twisted up about one person?

As he entered their small kitchen, Albert came in from the barn. "You look fit as a fiddle this morning."

"I feel about as tightly strung," he said. He sat down to his dish of porridge and picked up his spoon. "I think I'll go up to the house today."

The old man observed him then nodded. "I suppose that's a good idea."

"Get back into my gent's togs."

The older man chuckled. Mrs. Nichols placed a dish of porridge and cup of tea in front of her husband. "Thank ye, my dear." Albert bowed his head and said a quick prayer, then picked up his spoon. After a few mouthfuls, he paused and looked at Jonah.

"What's the matter, my face still bad?"

Albert shook his head. "I...uh...saw some posters in town day 'fore yesterday. Forgot to mention them till now."

"Posters? What sort of posters? Another fight?" The last thing he was interested in was another boxing match.

"No. Wanted posters. Of that fellow who escaped the noose a while back. Jonah Quinn."

The porridge Jonah had just swallowed suddenly felt like a lump in his throat. "Where did you see these posters?"

"Oh, a ways from here. Down by Piccadilly."

Jonah studied the man before him. How much did Albert suspect?

"They were glued over the old ones, like they'd just been put there. I figured they'd given up on ever finding him. But now...who knows." Albert shrugged and continued with his porridge.

Was Albert trying to warn him?

After breakfast Jonah pushed the disturbing news from his mind and headed over to the parsonage. He had enough of a challenge for one morning. Besides, Piccadilly was far from this edge of London. He'd just lie low for a while. That is, if Miss Hathaway permitted him to stay on at the parsonage.

He had waited until he knew she had finished her breakfast and closeted herself in the sitting room to do her accounts before he sneaked up the back stairs to his room. He didn't want to face her without looking as presentable as possible.

He stared at the array in his wardrobe. The fine coats and waistcoats mocked him. Did he propose to cover his sin with a gentleman's attire?

All these days Jonah had done nothing but chastise himself. Although the Bible talked about forgiveness, he knew it was too late for him. The damage was done. He'd proved himself as low an individual as Miss Hathaway had always viewed him. If he'd felt himself deep in the mire while he was sitting at Newgate, the night after the fight he'd sunk about as low as a man could. Forcing himself on a woman. During his time in Newgate, he'd been able to rail at fate, how unjust life had been against him, wrongly accused of a crime he hadn't committed.

After what he'd done to Miss Hathaway—he couldn't even whitewash his attack with the word *kiss*—there was no one to blame but himself. He'd abused the trust and goodwill of two individuals who'd taken him in off the streets, fed and clothed him, and offered him his only chance at a new life.

Despite his words to Miss Hathaway, and his own sincere intention of leaving forthwith with his bag of prize money, Jonah realized that he didn't want to leave this household.

There was goodness in this place, the first real goodness he'd found in London.

He thought of his own home back in the country.

It had been rough and base in comparison, he now saw. They were like two animals in many ways, he and Judy. They had taken no thought beyond each day. But now that his eyes were opened to another mode of living, he saw how hard it would be to go back.

When he finished dressing, he gave himself a final inspection in the long glass. He wore the dark green coat, gold waistcoat and buff breeches. His cravat looked presentable, his short hair had been brushed till it shone, his stockings were straight, his black shoes polished.

He marched resolutely down the stairs to the sitting room, but stopped at the sound of voices through the door. He hadn't expected visitors this early. Well, it was too late to back out now. Heaving a deep breath, he turned the knob and pushed it open.

As he stood framed in the doorway, two pairs of eyes turned his way, including those of Reverend Doyle.

Jonah fought the urge to turn tail and run. His eyes sought Miss Hathaway's. It seemed he couldn't manage anything right these days, including an apology. "I…I'm sorry, I didn't know you had visitors."

Florence—Miss Hathaway—sat straight and dignified in a dark blue gown. But as soon as he looked at her, she bowed her head, not meeting his eyes.

The rector rose. "Ah, Mr. Kendall, good afternoon."

Jonah took a tentative step into the room. "Good afternoon, Reverend."

Doyle peered at his face. "You look as if you've been in a fight."

Knowing it was best to bluff it out, Jonah gave him a disarming smile even as his knees trembled, Albert's words about the wanted poster coming back to him. "You have the right of it. A boxing match."

The rector arched a dark eyebrow. "Indeed?"

Jonah rocked back on his heels. "Yes. Excellent sport, boxing, don't you agree?"

The rector rubbed his chin with a slim hand, his gold signet ring glinting on his pinky. "I believe it has achieved some merit as a sport with the opening of Gentleman Jackson's school."

"I don't know too much about that. All I know is that it pits two men against each other in a contest of strength and wits." He stared at the rector's bony chest, wondering how quickly it would take to dispatch the man—half a round?

The rector raised his chin a fraction. "Wits?"

Jonah folded his arms over his chest and nodded. "That's right. You have to be quicker than your opponent and you have to anticipate his punch before he strikes, in time to block it."

All the while, he was conscious of Miss Hathaway. How would she receive him? Would she even speak to him? Instead he was forced to brazen it out in front of this popinjay.

When the rector resumed his seat, Jonah dared turn to her. "I don't mean to…uh…intrude on your company."

Her navy gown was edged with a white ruffled collar that reached all the way up to her chin. Long sleeves in tight gathered puffs covered her arms from her shoulders to midway down her hands. As usual, a white, lacy cap covered most of her hair.

"Good afternoon, Mr. Kendall," she said in a low voice, her eyes not quite meeting his. "Please…have a seat. The rector was paying us a call."

"I take it you bested your opponent, Mr. Kendall," Doyle said from his seat.

Jonah nodded. "Speed and nimble feet are more valuable than size, I'll tell you that."

"Mr. Kendall proved that the other day."

Jonah looked with surprise at Miss Hathaway, but her attention was now directed at the rector. "His opponent was both taller and had a greater girth than Mr. Kendall."

"You witnessed the match?" Doyle's tone registered amazement and disapproval.

She fiddled with the ruffle at her neck. "I…only came at the very end…to accompany my brother. He was concerned about Mr. Kendall's welfare."

"Yes, quite. Well." Doyle turned back to Jonah. "I can see you are no worse for wear. A bit bruised but no serious injuries, eh?"

"No." Jonah fingered his jaw, glad the swelling was down and that the color around his eye had faded to a light green and yellow. "The referee made sure we abided by the rules. No hitting below the waist or wrestling an opponent once he was down."

"Yes, ahem," Doyle said. "I'm sure Miss Hathaway needn't hear the particulars." He turned to her with a gentle smile.

"No, indeed, sir." She smiled and looked downward, smoothing down her skirt. Jonah felt a punch in his gut. He'd never know that kind of gentle smile from her now. "Please have a seat, Mr. Kendall," she repeated, and he jumped to realize she'd noticed he still stood.

Betsy entered at that moment with the tea cart. Instead of finding a seat, Jonah walked over to the girl and took the handles from her. "Oh, thank you, sir," she said, her mouth curving in a grateful smile.

"Nothing gives me greater pleasure than helping a pretty maiden," he replied automatically, glad to have something to do with his hands. He pushed the cart in front of Miss Hathaway. "Here you are."

Instead of looking pleased, she immediately busied herself with the tea service without even a thank-you. His heart sank. Could he ever do anything right around this lady? What had happened to him? Ever since they'd met, he seemed to be nothing but a brute. And now that he'd gone too far she'd be right in never speaking to him again.

Before he could decide what to do, she held out a cup and saucer to him. "Would you please take this to Reverend Doyle?"

Wordlessly, Jonah took them from her, noting she only raised her face to the height of the cup and saucer. She removed her hand from the cup and saucer and he retreated.

The rector indicated the small table beside him with a slight wave of his elongated hand. "Thank you," he murmured as Jonah set it down.

Too restless to take a seat himself, Jonah walked toward the window embrasure.

"Would you care for a cup of tea, Mr. Kendall?"

He swiveled around, startled to hear her address him so politely…so normally. He stared at her a second. Her gaze, still averted, was focused somewhere slightly below his face, around his neckcloth. Was something wrong with it? He'd practiced all morning. Now he realized why no gentlemen could do without a valet.

"Uh, yes…that would be lovely," he replied. *Lovely? That would be lovely?* Those words had just come out of his mouth? He was starting to sound like the good rector.

Jonah glanced his way. The man was calmly sipping from the delicate-looking china cup, the saucer held in one hand, the cup in the other with just three of his fingers barely holding on to the small, slim handle.

Why hadn't Damien asked Jonah to leave the house since that evening? Could it be Miss Hathaway had said nothing to her brother? Was she too ashamed? He studied her as she poured his tea. She looked particularly fetching this afternoon in the dark blue. But also unapproachable. A suit of armor couldn't have covered her more thoroughly than her gown. It only underscored how grievous his conduct had been.

He narrowed his eyes at her. Was she terrified of him? He wouldn't be able to stand it if that were the case. He knew her courage. Did she now fear him more than the worst criminal in Newgate? He wasn't that kind of man, he wanted to tell her.

But all he could do was stand like a dumb ox and watch Miss Hathaway's movements and try to figure out what thoughts were going through her head. He noticed her slim fingers around the teapot handle and curled his own thick fingers into his palm. She added nothing to his tea, knowing how he took it. They'd never had sugar in the house for him to learn to take his tea sweet. They'd rarely been able to afford tea, for that matter.

Then she held the cup and saucer out to him.

Jonah stepped forward hastily and took it from her. The tentative smile on his lips died as he noticed she still didn't direct her gaze upward to his. This time it was fixed on the flower-patterned cup and saucer between them. The cup rattled slightly as it exchanged hands. "Th…thank you," he said, his voice sounding shaky to his ears.

When she made no reply, he finally turned and stepped away from the tea cart. His glance darted about, wondering where to go now. He didn't like the rector—he wasn't sure why—and the last thing he wanted was to sit here between the two of them, listening to the cleric fawn over Miss Hathaway in his overpolite speech.

He finally made his way across the room to an alcove by the window as the other two resumed their conversation. He rested the cup and saucer against one of his knees, knowing when he took a sip he'd have to remember not to slurp.

"Returning to our discussion, Miss Hathaway," Jonah heard the rector say, "I fear that it would be impossible to use any of the church's funds for your endeavor. The parishioners wouldn't understand your good intentions. They have their charities in the local workhouse and orphanage. There is the upkeep of the sanctuary and grounds, as well as the parsonage, you know."

"Yes, I realize that. I just thought perhaps to purchase a few books and writing utensils…" Miss Hathaway's voice dwindled off.

Jonah had missed their previous conversation but gathered now that it had something to do with helping the women at Newgate. "I imagine the church treasury is quite fat," he said.

Both Miss Hathaway and the rector turned to him and stared. No doubt he'd done it again, but at least he finally had her full attention.

Miss Hathaway snapped her mouth shut and looked away again immediately. Her long slim hands smoothed down her skirt and he remembered them tending to the cuts on his face. "It may appear that way to an outsider," she said quietly, "but

Reverend Doyle is quite right. There are many expenses we don't see."

The rector set down his cup in its saucer with scarcely a sound. "The good citizens of London are at the mercy of the criminal element. The streets are worse every year. Cutpurses threaten pedestrians at every corner. Loose women hang about the squares, so brazen as to even inhabit the better neighborhoods now. Children come to beg and end up picking an honest citizen's pocket." He shook his head sadly. "No, my good man, the citizens would find it hard to sympathize with Miss Hathaway's good intentions of spending their tithes upon those in our prisons. Good money after bad, they would say, and in many cases, they would right. Let the riffraff be transported to Botany Bay."

Jonah opened his mouth to argue, but a quick shake of Miss Hathaway's head stopped him. What was she afraid of?

The rector knew precious little about those sitting in Newgate. There he sat in his black coat and be-jeweled shoes and he had the nerve to condemn those who had had the misfortune to be caught on the wrong side of the law only because they could find no honest work. Of course, there *were* bad elements in Newgate, but many had been made bad through their circumstances, caught, like himself, in the wrong place at the wrong time with no one to defend them.

In spite of his righteous anger, he held his tongue. For Miss Hathaway.

He owed her more than he could ever repay.

Although it took two cups of tea and a tedious while doing nothing but sitting and looking gentlemanly, Jonah remained in the drawing room until the rector finally got up and said his farewells. At times, it seemed as if the rector was waiting for Jonah to get up and leave the room first. That only strengthened Jonah's resolve to stay put till the old windbag left. Even if he was dreading the moment of truth alone with Miss Hathaway.

When the door finally shut behind the rector, Jonah panicked. How was he going to broach the subject uppermost on his mind with Miss Hathaway? He wasn't a man to mince words. He knew she'd probably reject any words of apology he offered, but he must make amends somehow.

As soon as Miss Hathaway turned from closing the door of the sitting room behind her, Jonah cleared his throat.

Miss Hathaway looked at him then quickly away. The color of her gown made her smooth skin look paler. He was sure it made her eyes look bluer, if he could ever catch a glimpse of them. It made him realize he'd wanted to do so ever since that night. He'd wanted to get a good look into those gray eyes to see what he'd read there. Icy disdain? Hatred? Rage? Offended modesty?

As the seconds ticked by, he realized he could delay no longer. He pulled his coat straight. "About the other evening—"

That got her attention. She held up a hand as if to fend him off. He took an immediate step back, distressed to think she believed he might attack her again.

She turned away. "Pray do not speak of it. Consider it forgotten."

He clamped his mouth shut, not expecting that. Cold resentment or angry accusations, but not this…this dismissal of his unspeakable behavior. Was she so terrified she wanted to forget it completely? If only he could.

He tried again. "What I did was—"

"You were undoubtedly intoxicated…too much celebrating your victory. I am disposed to forget it and…and suggest you do the same." She spoke so low he had to strain to hear the words. But her back was rigidly straight and there was no mistaking the fact that she did not want to discuss the topic.

She thought he was intoxicated? He'd had nothing to drink. He'd just gotten up from a few hours' sleep.

"I didn't hurt you—"

"No!" She finally turned to face him, her hands clasped in front of her. "Nothing to signify," she said more calmly before clearing her throat. "As I said, I do not wish to speak of this…unfortunate… incident ever again." There was a ring of finality to her words.

Jonah could only stare at her, his mind struggling to adjust to the notion that his brutal kiss had been relegated by Miss Hathaway to an "unfortunate incident." He tensed, sure there would be more. Undoubtedly, her next move would be to ask him to leave her home.

She took a deep breath. "What we need to do now, Mr. Kendall…"

He braced himself.

"…is concentrate on continuing to transform you into a gentleman." Her tone was brisk, businesslike as usual.

Had he heard her correctly?

She walked over to the sofa and stood behind it, supporting her hands on its back. "What I propose—that is, if you agree—is that we continue with my instructing you in the manners of a…a gentleman. You may recall, we have received an invitation to dine at the Duke of Winchester's."

He could only nod dumbly, hardly believing she wasn't asking him to leave. Instead, she was talking of a duke's dinner party.

"You took a grave risk in appearing before such a crowd at the boxing match. Apart from the obvious physical dangers, when you dressed the part of a fighter, you resembled too closely the old Jonah Quinn who stood before Newgate."

He looked down at his feet, thinking of the new wanted poster. It was a foolish thing he'd done, entering that contest for a sum of money. What had he been trying to prove?

She sighed. "However, I trust that, as Damien says, no one will have recognized you in the ring. In future, you must endeavor to continue this…masquerade. I needn't tell you that your very future depends upon it."

Slowly, he raised his eyes and finally was able to meet hers. It was straight and uncompromising, the way it had always been. It also proved his earlier supposition. Her irises looked more blue than gray this morning against the dark blue gown.

Was it possible she truly cared about his welfare? "I understand. No one knows it better than me—myself."

She cleared her throat, her fingers rubbing at the satin upholstery of the couch. "You did…very well at tea today with the Reverend Doyle. I can see you have made progress. You replied to his queries in a self-assured yet civil way. You knew enough to remain silent the majority of the time, so there was little he could find fault with. Despite your bruises…you looked the part of a gentleman."

"I looked the part?" If ever he'd felt less like a gentleman, it was now.

"Yes. You appeared the perfect gentleman. The suit…the color green becomes you." Her gaze slid away from his. "Mr. Bourke certainly knows how to cut a suit."

He looked down at himself. This was the first

time she had paid him a compliment on his appearance. He rubbed at the broadcloth of his jacket absently, his thoughts too jumbled at the moment to make any sense of the past five minutes.

He coughed into his hand. "Very well," he said finally, hoping to live up to her expectations. "I trust your judgment." If she chose to believe he had been the worse for drink and was disposed to overlook his behavior on those grounds, Jonah would never again bring up the topic that caused her so much distress she preferred to block it from her memory. And he swore to himself he'd never do anything to dishonor her again.

During the course of the next few days, Florence resumed her morning sessions with Quinn over the dining table, this time reviewing what he could expect at a fancy dinner party. Once again, they practiced holding utensils, cups and goblets, increasing the number by several and demonstrating how many courses he might have to sit through.

She'd had to strengthen her resolve each morning as she sat down with him, to forget what had happened that night and concentrate solely on their goal: to make Quinn into a presentable gentleman before the Duke of Winchester and his circle.

She turned to Quinn now as they paused after a lengthy lecture on the order of rank among the titled. "You will be assigned a lady for the procession into the dining room. Endeavor to remember her name when the hostess introduces her to you. Hopefully, she will be some half-deaf dowager and you can content yourself with merely taking her arm and following those in front of you."

He seemed to hang on her every word, his green eyes fixed on her so intently that it was an effort for her to breathe, let alone think straight.

She struggled to maintain her train of thought. "However, if she is a young matron or, worse, a debutante, try to curb any inclination to flirt."

His brow furrowed. "Flirt? Why ever would I do a thing like that?"

"You do have that tendency."

"If you're talking about what happened the other night—"

She drew away from him, shocked that he'd dare to refer to that incident. "Certainly not!"

He immediately leaned back himself as if aware of his proximity to her. "Forgive me," he mumbled.

She smoothed down the tablecloth before her and endeavored to speak calmly. "I was referring to the way you behave around young Betsy."

Now he was the one to look amazed. "Betsy? Barely out of pigtails, that one. What in the world does she have to do with flirting?"

She waved a hand, annoyed at having to explain something so obvious. "You are too free in your compliments with her."

He made a sound in his throat. "What are you

talking about? She's a pretty, young lass. I mean nothing by telling her so."

What would it be like to have a man shower one with compliments as easily as he did to Betsy? "It may be innocent banter and perfectly acceptable to a woman of Betsy's class." She heard her own voice, sounding as stuffy as an embittered spinster's. "However, in higher society, you must have a care with how you behave around a young, unmarried lady. Anyone just out in society will be extremely innocent and not used to the ways of men. Anyone older—and married—will be a practiced flirt, and you must be even more cautious with your words around this type of lady, if you don't want to find yourself with more than you bargained for. Is that understood?"

He planted his fists on the tablecloth. "Let me make something clear before anything else. I've never 'flirted' with Miss Betsy. By G—, the lass is young enough to be my daughter."

He stopped, and the two stared at each other. Florence could feel her cheeks grow hot at the recollection of the last time Quinn had taken the Lord's name in vain.

Before she could react, he looked away from her. "Beg pardon."

She sighed, realizing his apology was sincere.

At the sound, he met her gaze once more, his deep-fringed eyes sorrowful. "If only that soap of yours would do my filthy mouth any good, I'd have you wash it out a dozen more times."

Before she could think what to say—too astounded by his simple admission—he shook his head. "I'm afraid I've been swearing and cussing since I was a tyke. It's a habit I just can't seem to break. I'll try my best to watch myself around you because you're a lady—"

She leaned forward, unaware she'd placed a hand on his forearm until she saw his gaze travel to it. She whipped it away at once. She had made sure not to touch him since…that evening. "It's not because I'm a lady that you should watch yourself. It's because—" How could she explain? She began again. "You are right, it will take more than soap and water to break that vile habit."

His green eyes looked puzzled. "Are you saying I need something stronger?"

"In a manner of speaking." Her earlier discomfort forgotten, she strove to make him understand. It seemed as if suddenly the real reason Quinn was among them was revealing itself. This was the moment she'd been praying for since the morning she'd stood below the gallows.

"You have been made a temple of God," she said, choosing her words with care. Oh, how she wanted him to understand. "It's because He dwells inside of you that your language should reflect the new man you are."

He stared at her. "I always thought it was because you wanted to turn me into a gentleman."

"But don't you see? That's what a true gentleman is. He is a man of principle, of honor, of chivalry. He is not a man who is careless with his speech, or who goes about flirting with young girls, or who behaves in a manner unmindful of the consequences to others."

"I told you I never flirted with Betsy. She's a mere lass."

She sat back, remembering how they had gotten on the subject. "Hardly."

"In any case, that's the way I regard her. She re—" He stopped abruptly. His face was flushed and he was no longer looking at her directly.

"She what?" Florence asked, her curiosity aroused.

He rubbed his forefinger against the tablecloth, as if embarrassed. Her heart began to thump, wondering what hidden thought he would reveal about Betsy. Could she bear to hear it?

"She reminds me of my Judy…when she was that age. Not in the way you seem to think," he added hastily. "More like seeing her takes me back to that time when I was that age, beginnin' to court Judy." He sighed deeply.

Florence's chest constricted with a sense of his bereavement. She'd known the loss of her two parents so quickly one after the other…and the pain of rejection from a suitor whose feelings hadn't been as deep for her as hers for him.

But to lose one's wife and two young children to illness and virtual starvation. To feel helpless against the grating poverty…

"I see," she said softly. She had to curl her hand against the tabletop to keep from reaching out and covering his. "I'm sorry." The words seemed inadequate to express what she was feeling for him and the depth of her longing to comfort him at that moment.

Before she could say anything more, he leaned back in his chair and pinned her with a stern look. "And another thing I want you to get clear, I may be a gentleman in name only, but I don't trifle with a woman's feelings. I was married to one woman and never was unfaithful to her. I'll probably be too tongue-tied around these great ladies at this dinner to do much more than open my mouth to say how d'ye do."

She looked away, thankful that he was too indignant to notice how his words were affecting her.

If he never flirted or trifled with a woman's feelings, how was she to interpret his kiss? Anger and hurt pride? She'd told herself that over and over— every night as she lay in bed awake reliving it.

Quinn had been intent on punishing her that evening. That's all the kiss had meant to him.

Would it have made it any better if he had been trifling with her emotions?

And if there were any other reason?

And why did she keep torturing herself over it?

Chapter Fourteen

"The Reverend Damien and Miss Hathaway. Mr. William Kendall." The footman's stentorian tones sounded above the noisy drawing room.

Jonah stood with the Hathaways at the entry of the immense room aglow with the light of two chandeliers and dozens of wall sconces. He had never seen such splendor. Only now did he realize how simple the Hathaways' parsonage was. What he'd viewed as luxuries beyond his reach were merely comfortable furnishings in comparison with the duke's living quarters. Gilt frames around massive paintings filled every available wall space, whose paper was like brocade. The high ceiling was sculpted in elaborate swirls.

Jonah wiped his sweaty palm down the length of his knee breeches then quickly followed the curate and Miss Hathaway as they entered the room.

It was already filled with people, who had

scarcely turned at the announcement of their names. He expelled a silent breath of relief. The first hurdle of having to pass the line of footmen below and climb the red carpeted stairway to the drawing room was past. Now, for the dinner itself.

"So, what do we do now?" he asked Miss Hathaway in an undertone as they stood among the richly dressed guests. She was his anchor in this mad storm.

She turned toward him. "We await our hostess to tell us whom we are to escort into dinner."

"Where's the duke?" he asked, rubbing a hand against his jaw, then stopping at the frown on Miss Hathaway's face. A gentleman wouldn't do that in public, he supposed. At least his jaw felt smooth. He'd heeded Miss Hathaway's advice and shaved just before dressing this evening.

"I don't see His Grace…oh, there he is," Damien said.

Jonah turned enough to follow Damien's focus.

"All these gents look alike to me."

"Well, you shall not be in doubt much longer, as I see the rector approaching him."

Jonah watched Doyle engage a gentleman in conversation, noting the easy way he smiled at something the man said.

So, that was the mighty duke. A stately man in this late thirties, Jonah would guess, with dark hair. He turned back to the Hathaways.

"How much longer do we have to wait here?" he asked Miss Hathaway in an undertone.

"Until our hostess assigns us our dinner partners."

"Oh…uh…that's right." All her meticulous instructions and now his mind was as blank as a washed slate. He'd be lucky if he remembered his assumed name this evening. How was he ever going to fool all these elegant people around him into thinking he was one of them?

His eyes sought Miss Hathaway again, but she was looking away from him, surveying the company. It gave him a chance to observe her for a few minutes the way he'd been wanting to do since they had assembled at the parsonage that evening.

He had never seen Miss Hathaway looking so… He searched for a word. *Ladylike.* No, that wasn't quite right. She always appeared ladylike. *Feminine?* Yes, maybe that was more accurate. Was it the lower cut of her gown? For the first time she wasn't wearing anything to cover the neckline.

His glance strayed over this area. It was creamy smooth. Her gown was tied just under her bosom with a silver braided cord. She hadn't much in that department, it was true, but somehow it suited her. Her build was slim and sort of statuesque. The new word came to mind as he thought of the marble statues they had walked past down the long corridor of the duke's palace.

Miss Hathaway's gown, a sky-blue, offset her pale complexion to perfection. She wasn't wearing a cap this evening, either, and her sandy hair was drawn up in a knot with a few tendrils allowed to fall against her temples.

She wore long white gloves that went beyond her elbows. But the upper part of her arms were bare with only little caps of sleeves covering the very tops, leaving most of her shoulders bare. She had a slender neck, adding to her graceful appearance.

Just then she turned to him and he could feel his face redden at being caught staring at her. "Ahem…I hope I haven't forgotten everything you taught me."

Her eyelids fluttered downward. "I'm sure you will do fine. Remember, if you have any doubts about which fork or spoon to use, just look to Damien or myself and copy our movements."

Jonah sighed, wishing once again the evening were already behind them. He observed all the gentlemen around him. He certainly looked like them, in his new black evening coat and black knee breeches. He felt as trussed up as a fowl in the white silk waistcoat, but he had to admit it was very elegant. He patted the cravat, feeling a bit proud of himself for being able to execute the Waterfall with no help from anyone.

The curate clicked open his watch. "I shouldn't think it would be too much longer until dinner is announced. It is now a quarter of an hour over the time stated on the invitation." Their low tones could scarcely be heard above the growing buzz of voices around them.

"Ah, Damien," the rector's voice drifted over Jonah's shoulder, sending a new chill down his spine. "I'm so glad you could come this evening. May I present, His Grace, the Duke of Winchester?"

Damien bowed. "Your Grace."

Jonah turned slowly. The moment of truth had arrived.

"My sister, Miss Florence Hathaway," Damien said, a hand to her elbow, "and our friend, Mr. William Kendall of Bedfordshire."

Our friend. The title resounded deep within Jonah and he felt a sudden swelling in his throat so he could hardly say, "Your Grace," when the duke turned his way.

The man's dark eyes seemed to pierce his very soul and for an instant Jonah felt sure the duke would burst out with, *Jonah Quinn, the man wanted by the law!*

But he did nothing of the sort. With a slight nod, he turned his attention back to Hathaway. "I have heard more and more of late of your sermons at St. George's."

Jonah let his breathing return to somewhere near normal as the two men began discussing church. But his peace was short-lived as he noticed the rector engage Miss Hathaway in conversation. The room was too noisy for him to catch much of their conversation, but Jonah could feel his blood begin to heat at the familiar way the rector touched Miss Hathaway's forearm as he related something amusing.

And the look in Miss Hathaway's eyes…as if she worshipped the man. The cleric could probably do no wrong in her eyes. How could any man ever compete with a saint like that?

In a few moments, the duke left them. Jonah frowned at the rector, wishing he would make his excuses as well.

Only a few more minutes went by before their hostess approached them, a haughty woman with a profusion of feathers on her head and diamonds about her neck. The dowager duchess, Miss Hathaway had told him beforehand, the duke's mother.

She indicated the young lady Hathaway would lead in. Jonah's heart sank when she turned to Doyle and informed him that Miss Hathaway would be his partner.

Then she fixed Jonah with her cold blue eyes. "You will escort Mrs. Woburn." With that pronouncement, she left him.

He turned to Miss Hathaway. "Who the blazes is she?"

"A footman will bring her to you when dinner is announced."

They hadn't much longer to wait. As soon as a footman announced they were to make their way to the dining room, there was a general movement as couples paired off. The duke left the drawing room first, a beautiful woman on his arm, followed by the dowager, with an elegant, white-haired gentleman taking her arm.

"Mrs. Woburn, sir." A footman approached Jonah, an overweight, middle-aged woman at his side.

Jonah was suddenly tongue-tied. What was he supposed to say? He remembered Miss Hathaway's strict warnings not to flirt with any lady. At least this was no spring chicken. He glanced at Miss Hathaway and she gave him a slight inclination of her head as if to reassure him.

He bowed to Mrs. Woburn. "Good evening."

The lady favored him with a going-over. He hid his shock, thinking ladies didn't behave as forward as lowborn women. Nor that they wore rouge and lip color as this lady did, as bright red as a cherry's. "Good evening, Mr. Kendall, I'm much obliged to your company tonight." She held out her hand and he extended his arm the way he saw the rector do with Miss Hathaway.

Mrs. Woburn looped her hand through the crook of Jonah's arm. With a final, panicked look Miss Hathaway's way, Jonah took his first step into the fashionable world without his able teacher.

Miss Hathaway looked as stricken as he over his dinner partner, but it was too late for either of them.

Jonah bent forward to help himself to another mouthful of the roast peacock. He had never eaten so much meat in his life. Roast lamb, hare, a haunch of beef, chicken pie, turbot in cream, quail in pastry. No poor man's fare, not a piece of bacon or an oyster in sight.

And the fruit! He'd never seen such a variety— oranges and apples spilling across the white cloth,

merely there for decoration, it seemed. And candied
fruits arranged on tiered platters in the middle of the
tables, grapes, cherries, strawberries, no thought to
season of the year. Did they all come from hothouses?

He hadn't dared reach for half of the dishes in
front of him, too mindful of all Miss Hathaway's
warnings in the days leading up to the dinner party.

But Mrs. Woburn, seated on his right, had not
seemed hampered by any scruples, as she asked
him time and again to pass her a dish.

Miss Hathaway sat across from him, between
her brother and the rector. It was too far away to
carry on a comfortable conversation, there was such
a din, with waiters moving around them and platters
passed hither and thither. But every once in a while
he'd catch her approving nod, or he'd look to make
sure he was holding his fork and knife the right way.
There had been a soup course earlier and he hadn't
taken up his spoon until he'd seen her take hers.
He'd remembered her instructions for how to slip it
into the shallow soup bowl away from him and then
to bring it up to his mouth without slurping it.

After those first tense moments in the drawing
room, the evening had proceeded without disaster,
although Mrs. Woburn seemed a trifle too interested
in him and he had to deflect any personal questions
with a smile and murmured reply. He was usually
able to distract her with one of the dishes a waiter
brought along.

At least Miss Hathaway could be happy he had

no young debutante to flirt with. The observation about Betsy still rankled. How could she think he'd ever flirted with the young maid? Not only was the girl a child, as he'd told her, but he'd never treat a daughter of people he esteemed as much as he did the Nicholses with that kind of disrespect.

Had he lost all estimation in her eyes after his unforgivable behavior that night? Did Miss Hathaway think him the most depraved man on the face of the Earth?

He glanced across at her now. She leaned over to take a spoonful of the refreshing sorbet placed before them by the waiters. Even that she did with utter grace, taking only a small portion on her long-handled silver spoon. At that moment she looked up and their eyes met.

She immediately looked away when she saw that he wasn't going to ask her anything.

It had been the same way ever since he'd kissed her. Her eyes never quite met his, and when they did, they quickly skittered away like a frightened kitten's. Had he horrified her so much with his behavior?

He, for his part, found it impossible to forget that evening the way she'd asked him to. Would that he had been intoxicated. By now, the details would have faded into a fuzzy recollection. Instead, each day, he dwelled all too often, and in too much detail, on the memory of her mouth, the scent of her cheeks, the fragile feel of her in his arms.

"Did I tell you the duke is my third cousin on my papa's side?" Mrs. Woburn asked him.

He dragged his attention away from Miss Hathaway and turned to his dinner partner. "Yes, yes, you did, madam," he replied as politely as he could.

"My papa and the old duke would hunt together every autumn on the duke's estate up in Cheltenham. Ah, the pheasant and grouse. Nothing like it. Although, what we were served tonight was quite savory, didn't you find?" she inquired, batting her brown eyes at him.

He nodded his head and turned back to his sorbet. It was tart, lemon, he decided, letting it melt on his tongue. He looked down the length of the table. Towers of pineapple and palm fronds hindered his view of many of the guests, but he could just distinguish the duke himself at the far end. The man had been engaged the entire evening with those guests seated nearest to him. Jonah could only make out an elaborate ostrich feather of one lady.

The duke's glance crossed his and stopped. For several seconds his eyes rested on Jonah even as he continued to speak to a guest seated at his side. Jonah's heart hammered in his chest. He felt like a rabbit caught in a poacher's snare. Then, the moment passed as the duke looked away to another dinner companion.

What seemed hours later, after sitting with the men over their port, Jonah was able to locate Miss

Hathaway. Why was he so anxious to be by her side again? She had told him she was uncomfortable in such crowds. He still could scarcely believe it, for a woman who didn't quail being taken at knifepoint by an escaped prisoner.

He spotted her seated by herself on a settee in the large drawing room. When she finally noticed him coming toward her, her eyes briefly gave him a welcoming look and her mouth broke into a tentative smile before she looked away from him again.

He wished there was some way he could put her at her ease around him and prove to her he was capable of behaving like a gentleman, that he'd never again take such liberties.

"May I?" he asked, standing before her.

"Of course, please have a seat." She scooted over to the far end of the settee, however. "Did everything go well?"

"I survived the session having said nothing to excite attention, having said very little at all," he told her with amusement. "Most of the gentlemen seemed more interested in their port, so I doubt I could have made much of an impression no matter what I'd said." He refrained from repeating the coarse language many of the men had used—again, reminding him of a much lower class of people than what he would have expected of such exalted company.

"Where is Damien?" she asked, concern coloring her voice.

"Not to fear. He was coming to look for you as

well, but some old lady accosted him and wanted to discuss last Sunday's sermon."

She relaxed visibly. "That is a frequent occurrence. People enjoy his sermons and always want to ask him something about them afterward. He is accustomed to it."

"And how has your evening been?" He glanced sidelong at her, wishing he could stretch his legs out and lean his head back against the sofa. He wondered how much longer until they were free to leave.

"It has been uneventful, which is a blessing. You have done very well. No one seems to find you an oddity at all."

He observed her closely, wondering whether there was any mockery in her words. Finally, as if feeling his regard on her face, her eyelids rose and her gray eyes met his. He did, indeed, find a hint of humor in them.

"You've done your job well, in that case," he said softly.

Before she could reply, they heard a rustle of skirts and a stir in front of them.

Miss Hathaway immediately looked up, her attention wholly consumed by the party standing before them. "Your Grace," she said, sounding flustered.

The tall, dark-haired Duke of Winchester bowed over her hand. Now, there was a stylish-looking gent, observed Jonah. He wore a black evening coat like Jonah himself. But somehow, this man's seemed to be a second skin, whereas Jonah felt himself to be the complete counterfeit he was. And Jonah admired the cravat when the man straightened and turned his way. After countless attempts at tying a simple Mathematical, Jonah knew how deceptively easy this one looked. It was probably impossible to achieve without a first-rate valet.

Jonah stood, wondering whether to extend his hand to a duke. Probably not. He merely bowed his head. "Your Grace," he repeated Miss Hathaway's words. He nodded to the others in the duke's party, a beautiful woman who looked down her nose at him, and a middle-aged gentleman trailing beside the couple, eyeing Jonah through an eyeglass that magnified his one eye to almost twice the size of the other.

The duke narrowed his dark eyes at Jonah. "I've seen you before." His clipped words startled Jonah. "Who did you say you were?"

"Kendall," he managed to answer without stumbling over the syllables. "William Kendall, at your service. Your Grace," he hastened to add and bowed his head again, then wondered if that made him appear too much like who he really was, a mere laborer, bowing and scraping before the high-and-mighty lord of the manor. He straightened and looked the duke square in the eye.

Before Jonah could think how to answer the duke, Miss Hathaway spoke up. "You may very well have seen Mr. Kendall at some point, but I'm certain if he had met you, he would not have forgotten the meeting."

The duke's dark eyes finally left Jonah and turned Miss Hathaway's way. Jonah had to admire the smooth way she had drawn the duke's attention off him.

"You are the lady Reverend Doyle has been telling me about, the one who works with the prisoners."

She inclined her head. Again, Jonah stood in awe of her calm when all he wanted to do was flee to some dark place and hide.

To his astonishment, the duke held out his arm. The lady beside him stared, aghast. "Come, I should like to hear more of your work."

Miss Hathaway rose, obeying the imperial command.

Jonah watched them walk off, his own breath slowly releasing. The duke's abrupt statement came back to him. *I've seen you before.*

Could the duke have seen him somewhere before? The fight? He struggled to recollect the toffs present that day, but his attention had been too much taken with the upcoming contest and his opponent on the other side of the ring. Surely, he would have noticed someone with so commanding a presence as the duke.

He remembered Albert's words about the wanted poster. Could the duke have seen it and recognized Jonah from it? Jonah fingered his chin. Would the absence of a beard be enough to transform his features?

The duke looked as shrewd as a weasel…and as

cunning. If he thought Jonah looked familiar, would he try to discover why?

Dear Lord, he found himself praying for the first time. *What do You intend? Will my life be a constant looking over my shoulder, living in fear of discovery? And what of the Hathaways? They've done nothing but help me. Will You protect me from discovery, at least for their sakes? They are about Your business, after all.*

Jonah couldn't rest easy after that, but found himself walking the perimeters of the large room, visibly controlling his pace so that it would appear he was merely taking a turn like some of the other couples he saw around him.

He felt a keen sense of relief when he saw Miss Hathaway return from her own stroll with the duke. She came back to the settee and remained standing as she looked about her. He hurried to her side.

"Well, what did he say?" he asked, studying her features for any signs of discomposure.

But she smiled at him—the first real smile she'd given him. "Oh, Mr. Kendall, he wants to help me with the project of reading materials for the women at Newgate! Come, let us sit down and not draw attention to ourselves." She sobered. "That was an unsettling moment when he thought he recognized you."

"Yes…" He sat down more slowly beside her. She didn't seem to notice his proximity this time. "What do you think about it?"

She waved a hand in dismissal. "I admit, I felt my

heart in my throat the moment he pierced you with
his eyes. But I'm sure it was a case of mistaken
identity. We're always thinking we recognize
someone. In any case, I think he has fully forgotten
the moment. He was most interested in the project
at Newgate." Once again, her countenance radiated
excitement the way it did when she came back from
the prison to tell him that someone had been saved.
"He is willing to cover the costs of some materials—
books, paper, pencils, some chalk and slates. No one
else believes it can work, but they haven't seen the
desire of these women to improve themselves."

Jonah made the appropriate sounds of interest,
but he was more interested in watching her facial
expressions. Her eyes shone, and her pale complexion glowed. How little he knew this side of her.

"I realize not all of them will participate. Many
are hardened to their situation and scoff at me. But
there are a surprising number who, if not for themselves, then for the sake of their children, are willing
to strive for something better. Oh, and, yes, I even
dared to mention some sewing materials, and he
agreed most readily—" Suddenly, she stopped
speaking. "What's the matter?"

"Nothing. What do you mean?"

"The way you're looking at me..." Her voice
faltered, and she lowered her eyelids. "I thought...
something was amiss...with my appearance." A
hand touched a tendril of her hair.

"No, nothing is amiss." He took a deep breath,

not knowing how to express what had been going through his mind. "You just looked…very…pretty right then." He cleared his throat. "The way you spoke of these women." His heart was beating so hard he felt it would burst, so afraid he'd offended her by his clumsy compliment.

He looked down at his hands, sure now he had said the wrong thing. "You really think to teach them?" he asked, thinking of the screaming, jeering women in their cells at Newgate. He'd assumed they were all tarts and thieves.

"Why, yes, didn't you hear what I've been telling you?"

"Yes…" He let his eyes roam around the splendid room, every nook and cranny filled with evidence of wealth from the brocade drapes in gold, the plush carpets where a person would want to walk barefoot, to the silks and satins clothing all the people sitting and standing. "I guess I find it hard to take in. I never in all my life imagined I would be sitting in a room such as this, dressed in such finery," he said with a brief nod at his own splendid evening clothes, "as an equal among those I've always considered my betters."

"You look as good as anyone present this evening," she said immediately.

Their gazes locked and her cheeks colored again.

"They are neither your betters nor your inferiors if you are both children of the King."

"Children of the King," he repeated.

"Yes, children of the most high God, partakers of His righteousness through His son, Jesus Christ."

He nodded. Of course, she would mean that. That explained her indifference to her surroundings. "You know what amazes me more than all that?"

Her expression was puzzled. "No, what?"

"You are more excited over a few shillings the duke will throw your way to cover the cost of a few paltry items. He probably has gambled away twice as much this evening. Yet, to you, the wealth found here tonight is just a means to an end, isn't it?"

She pursed her lips. "I neither despise these people, as the Jacobins would have us do, nor do I esteem them more highly than myself. Some of them have been blessed with an inordinate amount of wealth. I see my job—as well as my brother's—as pointing out to them some of their responsibilities with that wealth."

Jonah returned home that night with much on his mind. It was the first time, for one thing, he'd uttered a prayer. He lifted his eyes upward, as if conscious of another presence with him. *Are You there, Lord? Could it really be You'd be listening to some words o' mine?*

He shook his head. The Hathaways' piety must be rubbing off on him. In truth, he had much to be grateful for to his Maker since that fateful day he'd grabbed Miss Hathaway in the crowd. Could it have been destiny? A divine encounter? Could the Lord have cared enough for Jonah Quinn to put him in the Hathaways' path?

As he set down his candle in his room and prepared to remove his jacket, he caught sight of his plum jacket hanging in his wardrobe. He walked slowly toward it. All signs of dirt and dust from the day of the fight had been removed from it. He lifted a sleeve to examine it more closely.

Had Betsy or Mrs. Nichols cleaned and pressed it for him…or had Miss Hathaway?

And why was it important that he know?

Florence found it very hard to settle down to sleep that night. Too many images swirled in her mind of the Duke of Winchester's sumptuous residence and all his illustrious dinner guests and his promise to help with the prison ministry.

Foremost in her mind, however, was the sight of Quinn in his evening clothes, looking more handsome than any man present, sitting beside her, telling her how pretty she looked.

She fingered the collar of her nightgown as she stared upward in the dark. Had he meant that?

He'd said how pretty she looked *at that moment.* Was it only the result of the chandeliers and the effects of the rich food and wine he'd consumed at table that had prompted the compliment? How would he see her in the plain light of day, in her usual morning gown?

Then she remembered the Duke of Winchester's

words, *I've seen you before.* In the darkness of the hours after midnight, they took on an ominous tone. Florence clutched her neck, terror overwhelming her. What if he *had* seen Quinn before?

She found it impossible to cast down all the terrible possibilities that could befall Quinn. She began to pray, and finally fell into an exhausted sleep.

The next morning, Florence knocked on her brother's study, where she knew she would find him giving a lesson to Quinn.

"Come in," he called out.

"Good morning," she greeted the two men seated at Damien's desk. Florence had not seen either one at breakfast since she had slept late and only had had a cup of tea in the kitchen. Now, she hardly dared glance at Quinn. Would she read disappointment in his eyes at how she looked?

She had been tempted to wear one of her prettier gowns, one she knew flattered her, but then rebuking her vanity, she'd deliberately chosen a drabber one, this one a faded mint-green from numerous launderings. Her mirror had told her it only served to make her complexion more washed-out than ever.

Damien put down his book. "Good morning, Florence. We were just finishing up here. What can I do for you?"

She stood with her hands folded in front of her, unsure how to begin. Was she making too much out of a chance remark?

She moistened her lips, and risked a quick peek at Quinn. He was looking at her, but she could read nothing out of the ordinary in his green eyes, since he always seemed to be watching her these days.

"What's wrong, Flo?"

She turned back to her brother. He usually sensed when something was troubling her. "Did you happen to notice any unusual interest on the duke's part toward Mr.…Kendall?" she asked.

Damien took a moment to answer, his slim fingers toying with a pencil. "I'd like to say no, but in truth, I am somewhat concerned. William told me what the duke said to him."

Quinn stood and began pacing the narrow confines of the room. "I don't like it. Every time he looked at me last night, it was as if he knew exactly who I was."

"I find it highly unlikely he could equate you to the man on the gallows," Florence said, wishing she could reassure herself as much.

Jonah stopped and stared hard at them both. "Could it be possible?"

Again Damien didn't answer right away. "It is…possible, but hardly likely. There is sometimes a member or two of the ton present at an execution, depending on how notorious the criminal, but the duke doesn't strike me as the kind to want to see a man agonize on the gallows."

Jonah resumed his pacing.

"What should we do?" Florence asked her brother.

"There isn't much we can do but go on as we have been. Mr. Kendall is rarely seen in public, except at church services." He fell silent and Florence knew he was thinking. She turned back to Quinn.

He continued walking the length of the room. Florence bit her lip, realizing how much she loved watching his strong, fluid movements. His jacket stretched taut across his broad shoulders and tapered down to his slim waist. His strong hands were folded at the small of his back and she remembered their unyielding power when he had grabbed her that night—

She started when she heard her brother speak once again.

"What I would suggest we do is put in place a plan in case it ever becomes…necessary for William to leave here quickly."

Quinn stopped at once. "You mean escape?"

Damien nodded. "We don't know what can happen. We've probably grown a bit lax, assuming you are perfectly safe here. Perhaps this is merely a warning to alert us. I suggest we have a satchel packed with a few necessary items, a change of clothes, some biscuits—nonperishable food—or food that we replenish daily." He glanced at Florence, and she quickly nodded her head in understanding. "Some money…"

"We can leave it by the back door," she suggested. "That way, if it ever became necessary for Kendall to leave in a hurry—" as she said the words, it suddenly occurred to her how difficult such an event might be for her, personally "—he can go out the back and take the satchel. We'll keep his greatcoat there, as well, at all times."

Quinn nodded slowly as if taking it all in.

"If anything should happen," Damien said, directing himself once more to him, "I'd suggest you try to take a ship to Canada. We'll furnish you with enough money to cover your fare and see you a ways…"

Quinn cleared his throat, looking away from her brother. "I can use my twenty guineas. And if it's not enough, I'm willing to do anything to earn the rest."

Damien put his hand on Quinn's arm. "You've done more than enough with all the help you've given Albert. I just pray we'll find a way for you to continue here with us."

Florence's eyes met Quinn's and she realized she'd be willing to do anything to help him escape the hangman's noose.

Without a word, he strode to the window and stood looking out, his back to them, his hands clasped behind him.

Florence felt a bleakness in her spirit at the thought that Quinn might have to leave them. She'd always known the arrangement to hide him was only a temporary one. When had this man's survival ceased being a burden to her and become more precious than her very life?

Chapter Fifteen

A few afternoons after the duke's dinner, Reverend Doyle invited Florence and her brother to take tea at his house.

Florence had found it odd that the invitation had not included Quinn, but when she mentioned it to her brother, he merely said, "The rector is not accustomed to sharing us. Don't fret, he'll soon come to accept Kendall as part of our family."

Florence caught her breath. *Part of our family.* The words came to Damien so naturally. Little did he know the impact they had on her.

Florence was further surprised when, once at the rector's, Doyle invited her outside for a stroll after they'd taken tea.

When she hesitated, he turned to Damien. "You don't mind keeping Mother company a few moments, do you? I wish to show your sister the early blossoms in the garden."

"Of course not." Damien sat back and turned to the elderly Mrs. Doyle and began asking about her latest arthritic complaint.

The rector offered Florence his arm when the two emerged onto the back terrace. The vicarage overlooked the fields of Marylebone Park. Beds of daffodils edged the lawn, bordering the line of elm trees, which separated the grounds from the park.

Florence breathed deeply of the spring air. It had rained that morning, and the scent of damp earth calmed her. Although they'd made all the preparations for Quinn's hasty departure should it become necessary, she had not reconciled herself to the idea, and the fear was never far from her thoughts. "It's a beautiful day."

"Yes, that is why I wanted to bring you out here. You spend so much of your time with your good works at the prison, workhouse and orphanage. You need to take some time and enjoy the fine spring weather we've been having."

Florence looked at him gratefully. Her everpresent worry over Quinn eased. How she wished sometimes that she and Damien could confide their secret to the rector. She was sure it would ease their burden to share it with such a dear, trusted friend and mentor. "You are right."

The rector swung his gold-headed walking stick in front of him. "The duke is most impressed with your work. He has told me so himself. Your brother could do worse than attract the patronage of such a man. You know he has his own chapel at Portman Square. Do not be surprised if he invites Damien to preach there some Sunday."

Florence stopped in the path and looked at him. "That would be wonderful!"

He smiled in understanding. "You care very much for Damien."

"Of course."

He patted her hand, which lay in the crook of his arm. "If his future is secure, you would be free to look after your own."

She drew her eyebrows together. "My future is tied to his."

"Only so long as he needs you, my dear. But you have many fine qualities yourself. It would be a pity if…" His words trailed off as he continued gazing at her.

She wondered at the words left unsaid. They sounded almost like a warning. "What do you mean?"

He sighed as if pained to have to go on. "I mean I would hate to see all your talents wasted."

Her eyes widened and she couldn't help an incredulous laugh. "Wasted?"

He didn't share her humor. "Yes, wasted."

She sobered. "How do you mean?"

"I mean wasted if you are never able to be the mistress of your own home."

She was more puzzled than ever. "But I am. I mean Damien gives me free rein…"

"But you are only his sister keeping house for

him," he explained in a patient tone as if she were too simple to understand. "I am talking of having a husband of your own and setting up your own household."

She looked down, away from his close observation, unsure why she felt uncomfortable with the turn in the conversation. Was it because it paralleled too closely her own yearnings of late? "I feel perfectly at home with my brother."

He patted her hand once again. "Of course you do, my dear." They continued on some minutes without speaking. A squirrel scurried across their path and hurried up an oak tree. Florence was beginning to feel relief that the topic was at an end.

"The ground is not too wet for you?" the rector asked.

He was always so solicitous. "No, the path is perfectly dry."

"I have been wanting to talk to you for some months now about your own future," he said.

She heart sank when he took up the topic again. What could he possibly be referring to? There had never been any discussion about a future for her, only for Damien.

"You would make an excellent clergyman's wife."

Her mouth fell open. The image was so contrary to her own thoughts of…Quinn. No! She wouldn't give voice to them. She stumbled.

The rector tightened his hold on her arm. "Miss Hathaway, are you all right?"

She shook her head with a nervous laugh. "I'm fine. It's just…I…I'd never considered…such a position. I sometimes feel like a clergyman's wife already, with the work I do at the parish."

"That is natural. You have had all the training to take up the reins. All you lack is a…husband."

He was looking at her so strangely that Florence took an inadvertent step back only to discover he still held her quite securely by the arm. "I don't think that is…is likely to change anytime soon."

"My dear, I have watched you since you were a young girl. Your mother taught you well. And since you've taken over the running of the parsonage, you have performed far above what most young ladies of so tender an age as you were when you lost your parents could have done. You have gained the respect of the congregation. You have taken on all the additional chores of caring for the poor. You have proved courageous in venturing into the darkness of the prison. My dear, I cannot praise you enough."

She felt herself blushing under such high accolades from the man whose good opinion she most valued.

He continued down the path, his walking stick tapping the gravel before them. "You know I lost my dear Phoebe over a year ago."

"She was a precious woman," Florence murmured. "I remember her dearly. If anyone taught me to be a good mistress of my brother's parsonage, it was she." Briefly, she thought of the soft-spoken woman who'd always been kind to her as an awkward young girl.

"She was a good wife and helpmate. You know a man in my position has many responsibilities."

"Yes. Your life seems very busy."

"You know only the half of it," he said with a sigh.

They had reached the end of the parkland, and he motioned to a stone bench beneath the bare trees. She took a seat.

"It is not too chilly for you? April weather can be deceiving."

"No, it is fine here. I have a warm cloak." She hugged it to herself.

He took a seat beside her and rested the cane between his legs. "I have need of a helpmate." The words were quietly and simply spoken.

Florence caught her breath. Understanding flooded in. The true reason for the rector's invitation this afternoon hit home. But if he wanted to consult with someone, why hadn't he asked Damien? Maybe he needed a woman's perspective. Compassion filled her.

As she studied the rector's aristocratic profile, she began to realize he spoke the truth. His life demanded the help of a steady partner.

He turned his face to her. "I have for some time now been thinking you might fill the empty place left by my dear wife's departure."

The seconds seemed to slow as Florence stared at him, the meaning of his words only gradually penetrating. Her cheeks grew warm. She'd never...

oh, no, goodness, he was old enough to be her father—well, if not exactly, then in her mind he'd always been a father figure—

As if reading her thoughts, his thin lips turned upward in a gentle smile. "I know this may come as a shock. You've known me most of your life, and perhaps seen me as an older man, a mentor, and not as a…husband."

She swallowed, speechless. She must say something, express some kind of gratitude, but she felt too stunned.

"Say I haven't displeased you with my words. I hope you don't view me now with distaste."

She shook her head, still mute. "No, never that." But in truth, she could not see him as a husband, no matter how much she respected him as a gentleman and minister.

He took her two hands in his. She resisted the impulse to pull away, letting them rest passively in his, although every fiber of her being longed to be free of his touch.

"I greatly admire you, my dear Florence." His eyes probed hers beneath his dark brows. "May I call you 'Florence'?"

She nodded, though reluctantly.

He squeezed her hands. "I know your brother would approve our union. As Mrs. Doyle, you would have much respect in the parish. You could do a great deal more to advance your brother's career, which already shows much promise."

"He has come a long way on his own talents and merits," she began, her lips feeling stiff.

"Think how much further he'd go with the backing of influential people in his life. You know our society is run by power and influence. Look at the Duke of Winchester. He has already taken a liking to you. You could use your influence to the good."

She looked down at the grass at their feet. All that he said was true. Why then did she feel only a sense of…aversion? "You know I can't leave Damien. He needs me."

"I understand your care and concern for your dear brother. I have watched him grow from an unsure youth into a young man who wields God's Word with authority and confidence. He is a man destined for greatness, and I feel privileged that I have been able to help him along the road."

"Oh, yes, Reverend Doyle. Without you, I don't know where we would be today. We owe you so much. You've nurtured Damien, and made it possible for him to go to university."

"Please, my dear, won't you call me Alistair?" He was looking into her eyes so kindly. She could feel her face growing warmer.

"I'm sorry," she faltered. "It would not be seemly."

"I understand, my dear. You are all that is proper and upright in a woman. I admire you for that." He let her hands go. "You look chilled. Shall we return to the house?"

She got up at once. "Yes."

Once again he offered her his arm and the two resumed their walk, although Florence now only looked forward to bidding Mrs. Doyle farewell and putting some distance between the rector and herself.

The rector continued speaking, as if unaware of the turmoil he had caused her. "As to Damien, I admire you for sticking by his side all these years. I know it has not been easy…with his infirmity. I feel the same about my own dear mother."

Florence felt taken aback that he should compare her young, very active brother to old Mrs. Doyle.

"I feel that with a competent housekeeper, Damien will do well enough now that he has achieved respect in his parish."

"I don't like to think of him alone…" she began.

"What I meant was that a good housekeeper would do until he marries. Of course, he would always be welcome at our house," the rector hastened to add. "He can take his meals with us, and if that doesn't satisfy you, he can live with us until he is wed." He pursed his lips. "I've been meaning to speak more to you upon that subject. It is time to begin looking out for a suitable young lady for him. With the duke's connections, I'm sure in no time at all, we'll have a few candidates lined up for Damien."

"I don't know…." It sounded so efficient…like a firing squad shooting down one impediment after another. Was a proposal of marriage supposed to feel this way? She turned troubled eyes on the rector. "Can we find a young lady who will love

Damien for his fine mind and zeal for the Lord, and overlook his…impediment?" Now it was her turn to hate herself for having to point out the only defect in her brother.

"My dear, there are plenty of younger sisters, whose mothers would love nothing better than a clergyman for their daughters, a man of upright character and steady in his ways like our Damien, and one who has such a good living at such a young age. Never fear, we will find a woman to satisfy even your high standards."

His words, though warmly spoken, made Florence feel she was the stumbling block in Damien's way, when it wasn't that way at all. All she wanted was the assurance that it was the right woman for Damien—God's perfect choice for him—a woman who would look past not only the cripple, but also past the handsome face, and see the beautiful soul within him.

"Think about my proposal, my dear. You can take all the time you need. I know this must be a surprise to you. But know that I esteem you greatly."

She felt herself blushing again. "I…thank you," she whispered. "Have—have you said anything yet to Damien?"

"No, I haven't. I thought I'd wait and speak my heart to you first."

"You did right, thank you," she managed.

"Think nothing of it. Your sensibilities are all that concern me. Just know I await the least encouragement with anticipation. Indeed, you make me feel like an eager young swain." Again, he squeezed her hand. "I don't expect your immediate reply. Just know how much I esteem and admire you."

Instead of flattering her, his words filled her with more dismay. She couldn't bear to hurt this man who had always been such a good friend. He had helped Damien to become who he was.

"Thank you," she whispered and quickened her step at the sight of the house ahead.

On the carriage ride home Florence was quiet.

"Are you tired, Flo?" Damien asked when they were only a few blocks from the rector's house.

"What? Oh, no, nothing to speak of." She turned from the window and focused on her brother with an effort. "Did you have a nice visit with Mrs. Doyle?"

"Pleasant enough. How about you? What did the rector want to speak to you about? Nothing more than show you his latest bulbs?"

She laughed, the sound nervous. "Yes. His daffodils. Some new variety from the Lowlands."

Damien looked past her and out the window. "Oh, there's the workhouse. I wanted to stop and see a gentleman who is doing quite poorly. Do you mind if I get off here?"

She shook her head, relieved to have some time to herself. "Not at all."

He tapped on the roof.

As soon as he'd left her, Florence went over the

rector's words. She could still scarcely believe he had proposed to her. Had she misinterpreted his meaning?

But, no, he'd made it very clear that he had chosen her to be the next Mrs. Doyle.

She rested her chin on her fist, wondering why his proposal filled her with dismay when it should bring her gratitude.

After Damien, the rector was the man she most admired in the world. She'd listened to his preaching from the pulpit since she was a girl and loved the way his rich voice read the Scriptures.

But she'd always equated him with his wife. The Reverend and Mrs. Doyle were one in her eyes. How could she have dreamed he would look at her as a possible replacement to his dear wife?

It was too high an honor for her. She could never fill Mrs. Doyle's shoes. The reverend was too lofty a gentleman for her. How could he even look her way? Florence didn't consider herself anywhere near his equal.

Another thought keep niggling at her as she listed all the reasons she should be honored by the rector's proposal. He had said he "esteemed and admired" her. But he'd never used the word *love*. Was it a foolish fancy of hers to desire a man's love?

Her thoughts were no nearer a solution when she arrived home. She pulled open the door to the quiet entry hall.

She stopped short at the sight of Quinn.

"You're back," he said, not moving.

"Yes." The door closed on a gust of wind and she jumped. She leaned against the solid wood, feeling her heartbeat increase to a loud thud. "Are you going out?"

"No." He shifted his feet, as if awkward with her question. "Where's your brother?" Had he been on the lookout for her?

"He had another stop." She took a step forward and reached to untie her cloak, chiding herself for feeling so edgy. Her movement seemed to awaken Quinn. He took a step toward her and before she could stop herself, she took one back. He stopped immediately.

"May I help you with your cloak?"

"Oh—yes, thank you." She was being silly. He hadn't touched her since…that night. She fumbled with the tie and finally managed to loosen it. She felt his large hands on her shoulders removing it. "Thank you," she said, breathless.

"Would you like a cup of tea?" he asked.

She turned to find him standing too close to her. There didn't seem to be enough air in the room. "No, thank you. That is, I've just come from having tea…with Reverend Doyle. And his mother," she quickly added, feeling her face flush.

"How's the old windbag?"

She blinked. "What did you call him?"

"Just what he appears to me." Quinn hung up her cloak then turned back to her with a smile. Florence drew in her breath. His white teeth shone in the dim hallway against his swarthy complexion, his beard already shadowing his jawline.

Her hand came up as if to fend him off, when she realized with a sudden clarity that he wasn't the threat. It was her own overwhelming attraction for him. The thought brought her up short. It wasn't fear of him that consumed her every time he approached her since the night he'd kissed her. It was fear of how much *she* was drawn to him.

The discovery left her short of breath. "The rector is a fine gentleman," she managed to say. "I've known him all my life and he is well mannered." The contrast between Quinn and the rector was so stark to be almost laughable. The one so dignified and refined, and Quinn, whose presence exuded a raw energy that made the very air between them crackle. How could she honor and respect the one so highly while being drawn so powerfully to the other?

"Around you, perhaps." Quinn stood before her now, his stance belligerent with feet planted apart, thumbs hooked in his waistcoat pockets, his shrewd eyes fixed on her…seeing too much.

Her hand went to her cheek. "What is that supposed to mean?" Did he know? How could he have guessed?

"That he wants to impress you." He gave a derisive laugh. "A man knows when another man is at pains to impress a woman."

"That's nonsense." He'd said "woman" and not

"lady." Did that mean he saw her as a flesh-and-blood woman? She untied her bonnet and, before she could hang it on the peg on top of her cloak, Quinn took it from her and did the task for her.

Another defense of the rector came to her lips, but she let it die. Her propensity to fight with Quinn was just another symptom of her attraction to him, she now understood. The heat of anger had simply been a defense to keep him at arm's length.

When he turned back to her, his expression seemed to soften. "What's the matter? You look like you've seen a ghost. Sure I can't fix you that cup o' tea?"

Why was he being so attentive? It had been easier when he was behaving outrageously. She dropped her hand to her side. "I'm fine. I was just thinking of finishing a few letters before going to the prison."

"You're not going there alone at this hour, are you?"

"The days are growing longer. I will not be there after dark."

"I'll take you there."

"No. You mustn't be seen there. I'll hail a hackney on Oxford Street." Why was he being so solicitous?

"Then I'll bring you home."

"It's too risky. Albert comes for me when it gets late." Why this insistence on his part?

Before she could puzzle it out, he asked her with a grin that flustered her anew. "May I show you something?"

Feeling strangely weak in the knees at his smile, she said, "Yes, certainly."

She followed him to Damien's workroom. Quinn walked over to the worktable that was strewn with several clocks in various states of dismantlement. He pointed to an ormolu clock. "My first repair."

She listened to the steady ticking. "That's wonderful."

"It wasn't running steadily. Your brother showed me how to take it apart and clean all the pieces. I had to replace a spring, then put it back together." He shoved his hands in his breeches pockets and stepped back with a shrug. "At least it's a trade that might earn me a few shillings if I need to leave all of a sudden-like. I don't know enough to set up a shop, but it might buy me a meal or two on the road."

If he had to leave all of a sudden. Would it come to that? She didn't want to think about it. "Have… you thought much about where you'd…go…if you had to leave?"

He fiddled with a small spring on the table. "Like your brother said, I'd best head for Canada or America. I've heard a person has a good chance there to earn some gold, get a piece o' land to call his own."

She bit her lip. "I've heard it's a dangerous, wild place." Her heart felt suddenly bleak at the thought of him so far away.

"A man on the run has little choice. It's the land o' the free I've been told," he added, his own lips twisted in an attempt at a smile.

"Whom the Lord sets free is free indeed," she replied, the Scripture coming to her lips automatically.

"Well, it seems He hasn't set me free yet. I'm still living with the threat of the noose around me neck."

She shivered. It couldn't come to that. She wouldn't *let* it.

About an hour later, Jonah heard the front door open. He pushed away from the brick wall he'd been leaning against and waiting for the past quarter of an hour, hoping he wouldn't miss Miss Hathaway's departure, not liking the thought of her alone on the streets of London.

"Are you ready to leave?" he asked her as she was stepping down the front steps, her hands holding two heavy-looking satchels.

She looked at him in surprise and nodded, stopping.

He reached for the bags, looking away from her direct, inquiring gaze. "I'll walk you to Oxford Street like I said." Why shouldn't he? A lady shouldn't be abroad alone at this late hour of the day.

She didn't relinquish the bags to him. "I told you, it's not necessary."

He began to tug harder at the handles then suddenly stepped back with a shrug when he realized it was futile to fight with such a stubborn woman. "I need a breath o' fresh air, anyway," he said, walking ahead of her to open the gate.

Thankfully, she argued no more and followed

him. When he closed the gate behind them, he was glad to see she waited for him. He again offered to take the bags, and this time she offered no resistance. He scanned her face, but she wasn't looking at him. He hoped she didn't still fear him. Since the night he'd…kissed her…he'd done everything possible to show her he could behave like a gentleman. So many times he'd regretted his action. If only he could show her how he'd like to kiss her— but, no, he stopped the direction of his thoughts every time they went that way.

Together, they headed down Edgware Road to the busier corner of Uxbridge and Oxford.

A man lounging against a thick elm at Hyde Park nodded and touched his hand to the edge of his cap as they passed.

"You mustn't be seen out of doors," she whispered as they walked farther on.

He glanced over his shoulder at the man and noticed he'd turned to look at him. Jonah's gut clenched.

When he'd made sure Miss Hathaway was safely in a hackney cab, he returned to the parish, his eyes on the lookout for the same man, but he didn't see him anywhere. No doubt just a vagrant. The city was full of them.

Hours later, long after Florence had returned from her visit to Newgate, she paced the confines of her small bedroom, clasping and unclasping her hands. She didn't know what to do. The Reverend Doyle's unexpected proposal kept ringing in her ears, side by side with the revelation of her feelings for Jonah Quinn.

How could she be feeling what she felt for a convict on the run, a tenant farmer, a man from the lowest strata of the London streets? What had happened to her in the space of a few months? She, who'd worked with the dregs of society in the prison and workhouse, had never experienced what she was feeling now for this man living under their roof. Was she so shallow that she'd be attracted to a man merely because he was now cleaned up and wore a gentleman's clothes?

When she was in his presence why did she feel more alive than she'd ever felt? Why did the tone of his voice ignite every nerve ending? And the keen look in his green eyes feel like a caress against her skin?

Her feelings were hopeless, that much she knew. Quinn had no future in England, for one thing. What was to become of him? No answers were forthcoming.

She mustn't forget her primary obligation was to her brother and his well-being, the way she'd told the rector.

Her thoughts turned with reluctance to the proposal of marriage. As the rector had pointed out to her, a union with him would help her brother immeasurably. Why did the notion fill her with a sense of duty rather than joy?

She sank to her knees and buried her head in her hands. *Dear God, show me what I must do. Grant me Thy grace to do what is right. If You want me to accept Reverend Doyle, who has been such a friend to this family over the years, and who would do all in his power to help Damien, grant me Thy grace to accept his proposal and be the wife I should be to him. Help me to assuage his loneliness and be the helpmate and companion he deserves.*

By the time she ended her prayer, her cheeks were damp. She wiped away the tears with the back of her hand.

An overwhelming sadness enveloped her. She remembered her youth, a time when the young gentleman, Eugene Littleton, had begun calling and paying a marked attention to her. But then her parents had fallen ill, and she'd had to nurse them. She hadn't thought of Eugene in years and could scarcely have remembered what he looked like a few moments ago, but now a sudden image of him appeared before her. She had a clear impression of his ruddy cheeks, his brown eyes and dark blond hair, already thinning a little at the temples.

When she had asked Mr. Littleton to wait, he'd been sorry, but he'd told her he couldn't wait. He needed a wife then.

He'd soon begun courting another girl in the congregation. A few months later, Florence had attended their wedding, smiling and offering her congratulations as if nothing were the matter. Mr.

Littleton and she had never been betrothed. No one had really known they were forming an understanding, so few, outside of her parents and brother, had realized how serious their friendship had been.

No one had been the wiser. And because she'd carried it off so well, she doubted even Damien had suspected how deeply she'd been hurt to see her dreams die an irrevocable death as Eugene and his new wife exchanged their vows at the altar, Reverend Doyle blessing their union.

Thankfully, they'd moved out of the parish, and she hadn't had to continue the friendship much longer after the wedding. By the time they'd left, she'd almost managed to convince even herself that her heart was mended. She wasn't made for marriage. Her duty lay with her brother and the Lord's work with the poor and destitute of the city.

And such tasks had filled her up to now.

Now she found herself weeping for that naive young woman, her past, her womanhood, her youth… Were they all irrevocably gone?

It was clear even a lowborn creature like Quinn didn't find her attractive. He'd kissed her out of pure rage. The more she thought on it, the more convinced she was that the memory of their kiss repulsed him now. That's why he was at pains to act like a gentleman, so that she wouldn't read anything into the kiss but his disdain.

She rose and swiped angrily at her eyes. What did she care if a crude, coarse man like Quinn, who until a short while ago stank like pig, didn't find her attractive? She'd long ago accepted she was not going to marry, not going to have that special partner in life. Neither she nor Damien. Their calling was another. She reminded herself of the Apostle Paul's words, "…to the unmarried and widows, it is good for them if they abide even as I." Celibate. She should be honored and satisfied with her calling.

Why then did the memory of Quinn's lips pressed against hers refuse to go away?

She shook it off. She would accept the Reverend Doyle's proposal. It was the only solution. She would put away childish dreams and realize the Lord was bestowing on her an incredible opportunity. It was clear there was no great passion on his side, either. He merely wanted—needed—a wife and helpmate. He was a kindly man, and he would be kind to her.

That's all she required.

Never mind these stirrings in her heart. She would bury them once again.

Betsy crossed the street in front of the parsonage and headed toward Oxford Street. She needed to reach the shops with the list of commissions or her mother would scold her for tarrying.

How she loved to escape the drudgery of the kitchen and wander the street, looking in the shop windows, and pretend she was a great lady who could afford a new bonnet or piece of ribbon to dress an old one, or admire a bolt of cloth she knew would look perfect against her complexion. She stopped in front of the first window she came to and admired her reflection. She knew she had a good complexion, peaches and cream both in texture and coloring. At least she'd never be an old maid like poor Miss Hathaway. She felt sorry for her mistress, even though she was a little scared of her most of the time. She was so exacting.

She turned to continue on. How she loved the neighborhood of Mayfair. From the edges of London, which seemed more like living in the country, to its great squares, with their carriages drawn up at the curb and liveried footmen looking so dignified, was to be transported to another world. If she was lucky, she'd catch sight of a grand lady riding within. The streets and squares were swept clean, the gardens tidy. Oxford Street by contrast was always busy with traffic.

Slowing her steps, she glanced into each shop window she passed.

"That would look pretty on you," a male voice beside her said. She glanced up, not thinking the person was addressing her. But the man was smiling down at her.

La, but he was a handsome gent. Twinkling, light-colored eyes and dark hair beneath a tall beaver hat. She glanced down at his clothing. Not quite a gentleman's, though certainly respectable enough. Maybe he was a shopkeeper. But her mother wouldn't want her speaking to strange men, so she kept silent.

"What's the matter, cat got your tongue?"

She turned back to the window with a sniff, though in truth she wasn't offended in the least. On the contrary, she felt a twinge of excitement.

"Now, if I had a sweetheart or wife, I'd buy her a square of cloth exactly that color," he continued, pointing to a bolt of creamy muslin.

Betsy gazed longingly at the fabric, which was striped in cerise, with a tiny flower print of the same color running between the stripes. He certainly had good taste. But he was still a stranger. "Well, if you don't have neither a wife nor sweetheart," she replied, turning around abruptly and continuing her walk, "then you are out o' luck, aren't you?"

He caught up in a few strides. "I most certainly am." He continued strolling beside her. "What's your name?" he asked after a bit.

"Gentlemen don't ask such questions."

"Maybe I ain't a gent, just an honest tradesman."

She glanced up at him beneath the rim of her bonnet. She'd been right, proud of her ability to size up a person. Thankfully, she'd worn her new chip bonnet with the yellow ribbon. She knew it looked fetching against her dark curls.

"My name is Bartholomew Smith," he said when she didn't answer him. "At your service." He nodded to her basket. "I could carry that for you if you wish."

She laughed. "Why, if it's empty?" She showed it to him.

"Perhaps when it gets heavy," he replied with a wink, unfazed by her attitude.

"Perhaps," she said, tossing her curls and continuing to the shop her mother had sent her to. How nice it might be to at last have a beau. She could share the news with her friends, who all bragged about their sweethearts.

Mr. Smith stayed with her during her shopping expedition, standing quietly by her side as she made her purchases and, indeed, carrying her basket when it began to feel heavy on her arm.

He was most gentlemanly, making polite conversation about the shops they entered and the fine spring weather. Small talk, Miss Hathaway would call it—the kind of things the visitors to her nice parlor indulged in, never making the least direction toward "flirting" as her friends said of their gentlemen friends.

"Here, I've got that for you," he said, taking the parcel from her, after she'd stopped at the cheesemonger's for the pound of Wiltshire her mother had told her to pick up.

He placed it among the other products in her basket, careful not to have them crushed against the heavier objects.

"You live in Mayfair?"

She laughed. "Oh, no, I live in Marylebone, just beyond really, at the parsonage of St. George's

Chapel. It's nothing like Mayfair," she said, with a wistful glance at the busy thoroughfare they were leaving.

"Ah, toward Paddington. It's a village out yonder," he said.

"You know it?" she asked, brightening. Maybe he lived nearby.

"I have an aunt who lives out that way." He gave her a sidelong look. "It brings me round frequently. Maybe I'll run into you again on your way to market."

"Maybe," she said, giving him an encouraging smile.

"Your parson, he's a young gent, isn't he?"

Her eyes grew wide. He really did frequent the area. "Yes, Reverend Hathaway. Do you know him?"

"I've heard of him. Heard he's a fine preacher."

She nodded. "Yes, that's him."

"So, you live in his household?" He shifted the basket from one hand to the other.

"Yes, with me mum and dad. They work for the Hathaways. We have our own little cottage right near the parsonage, though, on the church grounds."

"Just the three o' you?" He was looking ahead of him, focused on an approaching horse and chaise.

"Yes, that is until Mr. Kendall came to stay with us—with the Hathaways, that is. He helps my da around the parsonage."

"Mr. Kendall, eh?" He gave her a sidelong look. "He wouldn't happen to be a handsome young gent?"

"No!" She laughed. Was he now beginning to

flirt with her? "He's older. Not so old as my da, but older than Mr. Hathaway."

"I bet he finds you a pretty companion."

She turned away from him, deciding to play along. "Maybe he does. I wouldn't know."

"I bet it hasn't taken him long to discover what a charming young lady you are. How long has he been with you at the parsonage?"

"Oh, not so long…let's see…" She began counting on her fingers. "He came to us in February, during an awful icy rainstorm. He was sick about a fortnight. Then another week or so recuperating. We had to nurse him through an awful fever. Oh, it was so funny. Miss Hathaway had to shave his skull because o' the vermin in his hair and beard. He came to us looking ever so awful, black hair and long beard. He would've scared me if I'd seen him, but I was asleep. I only heard me mum and da talking about it that night when they came in. The next time I saw him, he was as cleanly shaven as a newborn babe—and sleeping like one, too." She brought her hand up to her mouth to hide her giggle. "I don't think he was too happy with Miss Hathaway, my mistress, then. But he looks awfully proper now, a real gentleman, he does. Ever so nice, too."

"You're making me jealous."

She gave him a saucy look. "Why should you be jealous? You don't know me."

"But I do know you are a pretty young lady any man would be proud to be seen walking beside."

A lady. She could feel herself blushing. Wait until she told her mum about meeting Mr. Smith. Maybe she'd do better not to say anything to her. Her mum could be so strict about young gentlemen. She suddenly felt uncomfortable. Perhaps her mum would scold her about talking so much. She was always cautioning her against gossip. But it hadn't been gossip about Mr. Kendall.

Her steps slowed. She really didn't want to get home so quickly. What if she didn't see Mr. Smith again?

When they reached the gate of the parsonage, Mr. Smith smiled and handed her the basket. "I won't walk you all the way to your door, since I haven't been properly introduced, but perhaps I'll see you at the shops the next time, eh?"

"Perhaps."

"What days do you usually frequent the shops?"

She shrugged, looking over one shoulder, as if indifferent, though in truth, her heart was beating a hurried pattern against her chest. "I go whenever my ma sends me. P'raps even as soon as tomorrow or the next day."

"Well, I shall have to keep a lookout then, shan't I?" With another wink, he tipped his hat and turned back toward town.

Chapter Sixteen

Her brother stared at Florence after she'd told him about the rector's proposal. "You're joking."

She sat back with a frown. After debating it with herself for several days, she had decided to confide in Damien. Of course, she'd expected his surprise, but she'd not thought he'd treat it as a jest. "Does it seem so comical to you that he'd want me as a wife?"

His smile faded. "No, of course not. I wouldn't be surprised if the duke himself would want you as his wife. What surprises me is that you'd be considering his proposal seriously."

"Why should that surprise you?" Didn't he see the honor being bestowed on her?

Damien touched her lightly on her hand, his eyes looking deeply into hers. "Do you love him, Flo?"

The question took her by surprise and she found she couldn't quite meet his gaze. She studied the pattern of violets running the length of her muslin gown. She and Damien had never talked about "love" in that sense, but she couldn't pretend not to know what he meant. "Not in the way you imply, perhaps, but I know I would make him a good wife."

"Of that I am certain." He squeezed her hand. "But would that be enough for you, Florrie?"

She gave him a sad smile. "How can it not be? I doubt if any other proposal is going to come along and I don't mind that, truly," she hastened to add.

"Are you sure there is no one to elicit that kind of love from you?"

His eyes were filled with such understanding that for a few seconds she feared he saw right through to the traitorous emotions of her heart. No, he could know nothing of those! "I'm not a young girl given to infatuation." She sighed and straightened as if bringing the topic to its conclusion. "Besides, I am perfectly content living here with you, and I've told the rector as much…although he has said you would be welcome to live with us."

He gave a rueful smile. "I appreciate the offer, but you know I couldn't do that. I, too, am content living here, even if I'd miss your company."

She returned his smile. "I thought as much. Which is why, if I refused him, that would be the main reason."

Damien frowned. "I don't want you to refuse him on my account. You know what an independent fellow I am. I hardly know who is around me once I shut myself off in my study or workroom."

"I know. I wouldn't even consider the rector's offer unless I knew we'd continue to see each other frequently and you'd promise to take your meals with us. And of course, we would continue our parish work together."

"Of course. I'm very happy for you, Florence." Again, his blue eyes searched hers. "As long as you are sure."

She nodded, but looked away from him first. There really wasn't any choice to consider. It was for the best of everyone.

Jonah sat on the milking stool, his fingers working a steady rhythm on the cow's udder, the only sound the quiet squirt of milk into the bucket at his feet.

This was one of his favorite times of day, before breakfast, when he could allow his thoughts free rein. What might keep him up nights took on a more benign appearance in the light of dawn. The smells of hay, leather and animal were reassuring and familiar, bringing back his old life, when each day had a comforting sameness.

He'd had a lot on his mind lately. He couldn't shake the sense of disquiet since he'd noticed that man looking at him on the road. Jonah had kept pretty much to the house and fields since then, but still, he was always checking over his shoulder.

More than that worry, though, were his thoughts of Miss Hathaway. He knew it wasn't proper to be thinking so much of a lady. He'd lie awake at night remembering something she'd said to him in the course of the day…or trying to figure out what a certain look in her gray eyes meant, when he'd caught her observing him. She'd always look away, and he'd be left feeling abandoned. Worse than anything was how much he found himself looking at her lips and remembering…

But of course, a lady like Miss Hathaway wouldn't be having the same kinds of thoughts as he was. No, sir.

He got up from his stool and put it aside. "I'm looking forward to a warm bowl of Mrs. Nichols's porridge now with some fresh cream," he told Albert as the two left the barn.

"Aye. Nothing more filling," the other man replied.

"What d'you have planned for this fine morning?" he asked Albert. The older man didn't answer him. When Jonah turned to him, thinking he hadn't heard, he noticed Albert looking beyond him to the road.

Suddenly the older man gripped Jonah's arm. "Look."

Jonah followed his gaze past the hedgerows. Half-a-dozen redcoats rode along Edgware Road at a slow pace.

"They're slowing down, as if they mean to turn in here," Albert whispered. "Wonder what they'd want here."

"I don't know." Jonah quickened his pace,

thinking it better to be out of sight. "But I don't aim to find out."

Albert followed right behind him as the two entered the back door into the kitchen.

Miss Hathaway stood next to Mrs. Nichols at the table. They both looked up as the men entered the kitchen.

"Some redcoats are headed up the road," Albert said.

Miss Hathaway dropped the kitchen towel she'd been holding, her eyes going immediately to Jonah's. "Are…are they coming this way?"

"They're slowing down," Albert answered. "They seem to be looking all around them pretty carefully."

She left what she was doing and came up to Jonah. "We mustn't take any chances." Her eyes scanned his, worry uppermost in their gray depths.

Albert turned to Jonah. "Do you think they know who you are?"

Jonah stared at him. "You know who I am?"

Albert nodded toward his wife. "Aye. Elizabeth and I both. We've known for a time. Don't worry, your secret's safe with us—"

The clatter of horses' hooves sounded on the drive.

Miss Hathaway clutched his arm. "You must go. Quickly, before they come to the back."

Jonah's glance went immediately to the satchel he had hanging on a hook. He'd never really thought this day would arrive.

Albert threw Jonah's greatcoat over his shoulders while Mrs. Nichols thrust some freshly baked scones into his satchel. Just then, Betsy entered from the larder, a crock of butter in her hands. "What's going on?"

Loud banging on the front door echoed all the way to the kitchen. "Open the door in the name of the king!" a sharp voice called out.

Albert shoved at Jonah when he still didn't move. "Go! I'll help Mr. Hathaway hold them off to give you time."

The next round of bangs on the door sparked Jonah to action. He turned to the door and grabbed the knob.

Suddenly, Miss Hathaway stood before him. The two stared at each other while the banging on the door reverberated through the kitchen.

Jonah realized he would never see her again— unless it was at the foot of the gallows.

"Goodbye," he began before his throat tightened up. If not for this woman, he wouldn't be alive now. How did one thank someone for one's life?

Her bottom lip trembled. That soft, sweet lip he'd hurt. "You'd better go," she said, her voice a hoarse whisper.

Still, he hesitated. "If…if they should catch me…and hang me—"

"Yes?" Her voice sounded breathless.

"Will you…be there?"

She swallowed. "If…if you should want me there."

"Aye. Promise me."

She nodded. "I promise."

* * *

Florence's glance fell from Jonah's eyes to his lips. How she wished that he would kiss her goodbye. To feel his mouth against hers once again, this time with tenderness and not in scorn, what wouldn't she give? She would never know. She would never see him again, never even know if he had gotten away safely. The realization tore at her heart.

Like a distant echo, she heard Albert's footsteps down the hall and Betsy's questions to her mother.

She swallowed, needing to be able to get the words out. "Will…if…you can ever…get us…word that you arrived somewhere safely…wherever you end up…will you let us know…" Her voice broke then and she couldn't finish.

Quinn took one of her hands and she felt the rough texture of the pads of his fingertips against the top of her hand as he rubbed it. "I will." They looked at each other one long second more, and Florence thought she read there everything she wanted to see: care, respect, admiration, gratitude…

And then he squeezed her hand and let it go. The next moment the kitchen door closed quietly behind her. She peered through the gauze curtains, as Jonah headed for the wall at the end of the garden. A second later, he disappeared over the top.

She knew he'd probably escape through the orchard and across Edgware Road until he could disappear down an alley, from where he could lose himself in the streets of London.

But where would he go from there?

Would he stow aboard a brig bound across the Atlantic? Would he head for the coast and pay a smuggler to take him across the Channel into France?

Her mind went over the supplies they'd put in his satchel. Thankfully, it had sufficient gold to get him a long ways away.

A few moments later, she heard soldiers enter the kitchen behind her.

"We have orders to search this parsonage."

Florence turned and stared at the three soldiers standing in her kitchen. They looked little older than boys. "Orders by whom?" she asked, her voice cold as granite.

The tallest one looked away, his ruddy cheeks reddening even more. "Orders from the warden of Newgate. There's been a report that the escaped prisoner, Jonah Quinn, was last seen here."

Florence drew herself up straighter. "That's ridiculous. What would he be doing at a parsonage?"

The soldier shrugged again. "Nevertheless, them's our orders. You haven't seen the prisoner Jonah Quinn?" he asked, unrolling a wanted poster.

Florence stared at the crude drawing of the man who had stood at the gallows those months ago, black haired and black bearded, eyes fierce and defiant. She pretended to examine the picture. "No, I have not," she answered, even as her conscience smote her for lying. But she knew she would do everything in her power to save Jonah's life.

The redcoat turned to Mrs. Nichols. "Have you seen this escaped prisoner?"

Mrs. Nichols shook her head. Betsy clutched her mother's arm and shook her head, looking terrified.

The soldier rolled up the poster then hoisted his musket farther on his shoulder. "All right, men, search the premises." Florence remained standing, motionless as they moved through the kitchen and into the buttery and scullery.

Finally, she heard the back door slam as they went into the garden. She turned then and looked out the door. The soldiers, joined by more from the street, swarmed over the yard like invading ants. They trampled the kitchen garden that Quinn had helped plant only a few weeks ago, leaving their boot prints in the soft mud. They entered the barn and other outbuildings and spread out into the orchard, now in full bloom.

Only when it was clear they had found no trace of Quinn did Florence unclench her fists and bring a hand to her cheek. Only then did she notice how wet it was.

When the soldiers finally departed, Florence turned to Mrs. Nichols, who was comforting her weeping daughter. "Mama, what did they mean about Jonah Quinn?"

"Nothing, dear. You were right to say you'd never seen him."

The normally tidy kitchen looked as if a storm

had been unleashed in it. Chairs were knocked over and cutlery upset.

"I'm sorry, Mrs. Nichols, about this," Florence began. "I didn't mean for you to be drawn into this…to…" She wanted to say "lie" but hesitated to speak too openly in front of Betsy. The girl knew nothing.

"That's quite all right, Miss Hathaway. Now, why don't you go in search of the reverend, make sure he's all right, and I'll begin clearing up here. I think what we all need is a bracing cup of tea."

Before she could take Mrs. Nichols's advice, Damien entered the kitchen, followed by Albert.

Florence went immediately to her brother's side. "Are you all right? What did they ask you?"

He nodded. "I'm fine. They only demanded to know if we were housing Jonah Quinn. When I said no, they showed me an order to search the premises." He looked at the others in the kitchen. "I think I owe you all an explanation. Please, have a seat." He nodded to Betsy as well. "All of you."

They busied themselves righting the chairs and bringing them to the table. Mrs. Nichols poured hot water into the teapot and told Betsy to bring them all cups.

When they finally sat down, they looked toward Damien. He pulled out a chair for Florence, but she gave a small shake of her head, feeling too nervous to sit still.

He folded his hands on the tabletop. "There is

something Miss Hathaway and I should have told you when Mr. Kendall first arrived here." He paused. "Kendall is not really the man's name. It is Jonah Quinn."

Betsy's hands flew to her mouth. "So, it's true what the man said."

Damien nodded. "Yes, it's true what the soldier said."

The girl's pink cheeks turned a deeper shade as she looked down at her clasped hands. "No, I mean...the other gent."

"Who are you talking about?" Florence asked sharply.

Betsy bit her lip, looking down at her teacup.

"What man's been talking to you?" her mother prodded, her gray brows furrowing. "Why didn't you tell me about this?"

Betsy refused to look up. "He was a nice man, almost a gent." Her thumbnail dug into the table-cloth. "He...spoke to me...the day I...went to the shops for you."

"You know better than to be talking to strange men."

"Mrs. Nichols," Damien interrupted softly, "perhaps we'd better hear Betsy out. It could be important." He turned to the young woman. "You said a gentleman spoke to you. Did he speak to you about Mr. Kendall?"

"Not right away. But he asked me about who else lived here with us." Betsy's glance slid away from them and fixed itself at a point on the tabletop. "The other day he…he showed me one of those posters…of wanted men, like the soldier had today." Her voice ended in a horrified whisper. "The man in it…it looked just like Mr. Kendall, the way you said he looked, Mum—" she turned to Mrs. Nichols "—when he arrived here that night." She folded her hands together tightly.

Florence took a step toward Betsy. "What did you tell the man?"

Betsy glanced up at her and her eyes widened in fright. "I…I couldn't help it." Tears started up in the young woman's eyes. "Honestly, I couldn't help it."

Her voice rose. "What did you tell him?"

Betsy began to sob. "I…I s…said i…it looked just like M…Mr. K…K…Kendall. He had the same eyes and looked so funny with a long beard and hair!" She hiccupped, the tears thickening her speech. "But I didn't say it were him…j…just th…that it…it looked like him."

"You silly, foolish girl!" Florence raised a hand, wanting to slap the girl for her loose tongue. Would the admission cost Quinn his life?

Betsy raised her arms and covered her head.

"Florence." Damien's voice held warning.

She lowered her hand, shaking with fear and rage. Pressing her lips together, she turned her back on Betsy, afraid of what she might do to the ignorant girl.

Damien spoke to Mr. and Mrs. Nichols. "I'm sorry we didn't let you into our confidence sooner.

We didn't want you to be in any way to blame if Quinn were ever discovered."

Albert cleared his throat. "We—that is Elizabeth and I—kind of figured out who Kendall—Quinn—was when he arrived. We thought you were just offering him shelter the way you have so many times to a soul in need."

"Thank you for your trust."

Betsy let out a wail. "Why didn't anyone tell me? I never would'a…" Her words were muffled by her tears as she put her head down on her arms and began to weep. "I'm sorry. I didn't mean no harm to W…William!"

Her mother put an arm around her shoulders. "There…there, we know you didn't mean no harm. You just don't know how to hold your tongue. That's why no one told you anything."

"I'm afraid the situation is very grave," Damien told them. "We'd begun to hope…with his trans-formation into a gentleman that perhaps Quinn was safe." He frowned. "Even though he has escaped for the moment, we don't know how long he'll be able to elude the authorities. We had packed a sack of provisions for him, including suf-ficient money to see him a ways." He paused. "We need to pray."

Florence joined them around the table where they joined hands. "Dear Lord," began Damien, his head bowed, his eyes closed. "'O Thou that hearest prayer, unto Thee shall all flesh come,'" he began, quoting the verse from a psalm. "We ask for Your mercy and grace in our time of need…"

Florence felt her faith strengthened as she listened to her brother's words. Surely the Lord would make a way of escape for Quinn.

Oh, dear God, she continued silently, when Damien had finished his prayer and yet they all remained seated, *show him a way out. Have mercy on his soul. He doesn't deserve to die. Please don't take his life, not like this…* She could feel the tears squeezing from her tightly closed lids and rolling down her cheeks. *Please, Lord, protect him…even if I never see him again…take him away somewhere safe….*

Florence spent the next hour alternately pacing her room and praying and looking out the window down to the yard, remembering her last sight of Quinn.

She was worried about both Quinn and her brother. Shortly after the guards had left the parsonage, an official summons had come for Damien from the warden at Newgate and he had left immediately.

Would he be held responsible? What would he say?

Finally, she could stand it no longer. She would go herself to find out what had happened to Damien. Just as she reached the ground floor, Damien himself returned.

She fairly flew to him. "What happened?"

"It's all right." Before he could say anything more, they both turned at the sound of horses' hooves and coach wheels on the drive. She looked at Damien. Had the soldiers returned?

She let out a breath of relief when she saw it was the rector's coach.

"Perhaps he's heard something," Damien murmured.

"Maybe he'll be able to help us," whispered Florence, already thinking ahead. If Damien were to be charged, they would need the rector's influence.

"Come," Damien said when he'd removed his coat, "let us wait for him in the drawing room."

"Yes, you are right."

A few minutes after they were seated themselves, the rector was shown in by Betsy.

He nodded to them both. It was only after he had taken a seat, his slim hands folded over his walking stick, that he spoke. "I received the most extraordinary news today. I confess I would not have countenanced such nonsense except that it came from a most reliable source."

Florence's glance darted to Damien. What could he be referring to?

"What news was that?" Damien asked gently.

The rector's dark brows drew together. "I was informed that the convict, Quinn, has been hiding here."

Florence felt both dread and relief. She had not liked keeping a secret from their friend and mentor. Was he angry? Would he help them? She glanced at Damien.

As always, he remained calm under pressure. "May I ask how you came to be informed?"

"The Duke of Winchester sent me a note."

Florence gasped then endeavored to compose her features when the rector's eyes turned to her.

"Shocked would not begin to describe what went through my mind when I was told." The mantel clock ticked loudly in the still room as the rector's stern look included them both.

"I can understand your alarm." Damien's tone remained calm. "Perhaps we need to explain things fully."

"Indeed." The rector leaned forward on his walking stick.

Florence's attention went back and forth between the two men. The rector, thankfully, did not look her way again.

When Damien said nothing right away, Rector Doyle cleared his throat. "When the duke informed me you were sheltering a fugitive, I dismissed the notion immediately." He paused and continued looking steadily at Damien, whose face radiated the serenity of a person whose conscience is clear. "However, what he told me is very difficult to ignore."

"Why would the duke know anything of this matter?" Damien asked.

"The duke said there was something he found familiar about Kendall from the first moment he saw him. He couldn't rest until he got to the bottom of it. He hired someone to follow your houseguest and see if he could discover anything more of his identity. The man showed someone in this household a poster of the convicted man—a man sentenced to be hanged." Here, the rector's eyes turned Florence's way.

"The same man who abducted you." Florence pressed her lips together, afraid of saying anything to further risk either Quinn's or her brother's safety.

"It was this last piece of information that pained me the most," the rector continued softly. His eyes remained pinned on her. "I assured him I hardly thought you would harbor a dangerous fugitive in your midst."

"How…how was Kendall identified?" she asked, her voice sounding faint to her ears.

"As I said, this Bow Street Runner showed a member of your household a wanted poster with the man's picture. It was confirmed that Kendall's appearance when he first arrived on your doorstep was that of the man in the poster."

"Bu-but that poster shows only a black-bearded man—he could resemble any number of people," she faltered. "It is true that Mr. Kendall arrived to us in a bit of a dirty, disheveled state, but that doesn't mean he is a convicted criminal."

"Florence," her brother said gently. She turned her eyes to him, unable to believe he wouldn't continue to protect Quinn's identity. His next words confirmed her worst fears. "I believe we must be truthful to our brother in Christ, Reverend Doyle."

What was he saying? She turned to the rector. Would he understand? He *must.*

Damien was addressing Doyle. "Kendall is indeed the man you speak of." He held up a hand to forestall the rector's words. "Before you jump to any conclusions, I beg you would hear me out. I do not pretend to defend my conduct, but to explain the circumstances we found ourselves in."

The rector sat back in his seat. "Of course, dear boy. I have all confidence in both of you." His glance encompassed Florence, and she began to feel a measure of ease. Perhaps he would help Quinn. "I told the duke as much."

Damien began to speak, in the same measured way he addressed the congregation on a Sunday. Florence was sure his words would move the rector.

"So, you see, Reverend Doyle," he summed up, "why I decided to give Quinn refuge here in our parish. I believe the Lord sent him to us. Moreover, I believe he is innocent of the crime he was accused of. I believe with all my heart that the Lord is doing a good work in the man, for the saving of his soul. Moreover, Mr. Quinn's behavior while he has been under our roof has been exemplary."

The rector contemplated his folded hands on the walking stick. When he looked up at them, she couldn't read whether Damien's words had moved him or not. His expression remained as solemn as when he'd first come in. "I must confess I am disturbed, deeply disturbed, by this story you have related to me."

Damien gave a slight nod of his head. "I understand your disquiet."

"To begin with," he continued, without seeming to hear Damien's words, "that you should make such a weighty decision without consulting me. I am deeply hurt. I have nurtured you, mentored you in your Christian faith. To take it upon yourself to use deceit, nay, to lie to your congregation, to me, to all those who see your clerical collar." The rector shuddered slightly and shook his head. "No, dear boy, it is no light thing you have chosen to do."

Damien rubbed his hand over his jaw, the only sign of agitation he gave. "All I ask is that you give the man a chance. If the authorities apprehend him, he will surely be hanged."

"The man was tried in the highest court in the land and was found guilty as charged."

"You know what a trial like that means. He had no legal counsel. His accuser, a shady character, and one witness alone, were brought forward. The case was decided in under a quarter of an hour. It was a miscarriage of justice at best, a farce at worst—"

"It was a trial at the Old Bailey with a respected judge presiding. The accused is one of the scum that is the scourge of our fine city." The rector stood, his argument growing more heated. "If we don't stop their outrages by using one as an example, the city will be overrun by counterfeiters and extortionists.

I could see from his uncouth behavior the moment you introduced me to him that there was a criminal element in him."

Florence opened her mouth to protest this last accusation but a quick look from her brother stilled her.

Doyle shook his head grimly. "So, this Quinn once again has eluded the law."

Damien stood to face the older man. "Reverend Doyle, I beg you to consider a man's life, a man whom I truly believe did not commit the crime he was accused of. And if perchance he is guilty, weigh the crime against the sentence. Does he deserve death?"

"Damien, I am appalled and deeply disappointed at the stand you are taking in this affair. This country's very future is at stake. Do you not understand what has happened across the Channel barely two decades ago? Do you not see how close our own nation has been to falling to the radical voices of revolution? When citizens take the law into their hands—" His knuckles were white against the head of his cane. "No, I cannot permit such a thing to happen here."

Florence stood and advanced toward the reverend. "We are commanded by Holy Scripture to help the prisoner." She reached the rector and placed a hand on his arm, lowering her voice. "Please, Reverend Doyle, have mercy on this man's life." Dismayed by the emotion that made her voice shake, she stepped back.

The reverend stopped her with his hand over

hers. "My dear, calm yourself. Surely, you can see my position. I expected you to help me reason with your brother. I am sure you were abducted and very likely terrified by your experience. The man—the brute—ought to be hanged for this crime alone, taking a helpless young lady as a hostage."

"It wa…wasn't exactly like that," she began.

"I know your sympathetic nature. Very likely, you've convinced yourself of the man's story. You do your brother no favors by harboring and protecting a criminal. Believe me, I will do all in my power, as well as beg the duke's influence, so that your brother will not be accused of breaking the laws of this land."

She drew in her breath. "Please, Reverend Doyle, my brother did nothing wrong. It was I who brought this man to our house, and if Damien is guilty of anything it is of obeying his conscience."

"I know, my dear, which is why as rector of this parish I will be indulgent with him as a first-time offender." He turned his attention to Damien, his tone hardening. "That is why we must act swiftly to bring Quinn to justice. The court must see that you two have in fact been held hostage by this criminal—"

Panic flooded her veins like a raging river. "Haven't you heard what my brother has said? A man's very life is at stake."

Doyle brought his unyielding focus back to her. "I am saddened by your behavior as well. I always considered you a steady, levelheaded lady, not given to hysterics or excesses of emotional outbursts."

She stepped back, her hands clenched at her sides. "Perhaps you haven't known me."

"I trust that I have. I have known you since you were a young girl. The quiet, well-behaved, God-fearing woman whose hand I asked in marriage is the one I trust is the real Florence Hathaway."

In that instant, Florence felt as if her heart, which had been encased for so long, was finally breaking free. "The real Florence Hathaway is a woman who hates injustice and who has given her life to fight it wherever she finds it."

"Fighting injustice is a noble undertaking, but to break the laws of the land is quite another thing altogether. I cannot condone such behavior in the future Mrs. Doyle. I seek a wife who is 'discreet, chaste, a keeper at home, good,' and above all, 'obedient to their own husbands, that the word of God be not blasphemed,' as St. Paul exhorts."

"She also 'stretcheth out her hand to the poor; yea, she reacheth forth her hands to the needy.'" Florence found herself quoting back to him from the Book of Proverbs.

"The devil will quote Scripture to his own use," he said, his voice growing stern.

She fell back. How could she have contemplated giving herself—her autonomy—to this man? Suddenly, she could see what her life would have been like. She would have had no voice except what the reverend said. She would have been merely his mouthpiece for what he allowed her to speak.

"Perhaps you need to take back your proposal of marriage," she said in a composed tone.

"Florence!" Damien's eyes were wide with a touch of warning.

"My dear Florence, you are overwrought," the rector's voice had taken on a soothing tone once again. "My offer of marriage still stands as long as I can have your assurance that you will repent of this ungodly step you've taken and follow to the utmost the letter of the law."

"I will not betray a man who has sought mercy of my brother and me." Her voice now sounded cold and hard even to her own ears. Why was she risking all for a man she had up to now fought against so? She wasn't sure yet, but she felt a certainty of conviction that didn't allow her to back down.

"You don't know what you are saying." The rector held her gaze.

She didn't falter under it. "I only know it is right."

"Then, my dear, you leave me no choice but to withdraw my offer of marriage." He took a step back and bowed his head as if with great sorrow.

"Florence." Damien came to her and put a hand on her shoulder. "You don't have to do this for me. I can very well champion Mr. Quinn's cause. Don't throw away your future happiness."

She squeezed his hand. "Don't worry, I'm not." She gave him a tentative smile, not sure of anything right now except her desire to protect Quinn, whatever it cost her.

Damien turned to the rector. "Reverend Doyle, all we ask is that Jonah Quinn be given a chance to escape."

The rector sighed and shook his head, as if deeply disappointed. "I promised the duke I would report my findings to him, and he awaits me now. I cannot but be truthful to him, however much it grieves my heart to implicate my two dearest disciples." He bowed his head and turned away from them.

When he'd gone, Florence's legs threatened to collapse beneath her. She looked at Damien. "What will happen now?"

He took out a handkerchief and wiped the perspiration from his brow. "I don't know. I…must admit…" His blue eyes held pain. "I was…disappointed in the rector's response to our plea."

Florence reached for his hand. "Will you be in much trouble? It's my fault for bringing you into this."

He gave her a crooked smile. "Oh, Flo, how could you not offer Quinn a place when he needed it? You were only following the dictates of your heart." He gave her hand a squeeze before letting it go. "Don't worry about me. They questioned me thoroughly down at Newgate, and I was truthful. They let me go, I think mainly because I'm a clergyman. It gives me some sort of immunity, although they've made it plain they might call me in again for further questioning.

"It is Quinn who should concern us now. We can do nothing more than pray for his safety, but that is not a little thing."

She nodded. Yes, she would pray for the man who'd grown to mean more than her reputation…more than life itself in the short time she'd known him.

She would give all of herself to prayer now.

Chapter Seventeen

Jonah shifted on the damp riverbed, easing the kinks in his legs. He'd been squatting there some time, his fishing line floating in the small stream. The water, stained red from the nearby tanneries, hardly yielded any fish, but he dared not venture far from his hiding place, and then only after dark.

He had little choice. Buying provisions was out of the question. Wanted posters for him were up everywhere, this time offering a handsome reward of twenty guineas for his capture. The irony of the sum wasn't lost on him. The prize money still rested in its leather pouch at the bottom of his satchel.

He had the blunt but dared not spend it. He rubbed his hand over his chin, feeling its smoothness. He'd been shaving every night in the same river water, with the bar of soap Miss Hathaway had so thoughtfully packed for him, so he was hopeful he still didn't resemble that frightful figure on the wanted posters.

He scratched his still short hair. It was beginning to curl now, making him look more like the face on the wanted posters, but he wouldn't be able to cut it as it grew out. Not unless he was far from England.

America. Once again he thought of that distant land, of which he knew almost nothing. Tobacco and savages were the only images that came to mind. And if war broke out, the way Damien had warned, would it even be possible to head there?

He'd have to select a ship soon and attempt to stow away. He'd been watching the docks and had his eye on a brig, the *Sea Queen,* a vessel preparing to head across the Atlantic. It was filling with cargo and would soon push out to sea with the tide. The quay was also lined with East Indiamen, merchantmen armed to the teeth, so he had to tread very carefully.

He felt a tug on his line and pulled it in. A small fish struggled on his hook. Jonah hauled it in easily and smothered a sigh of disgust. A baby chub, hardly worth building up a fire for, more bones than flesh.

But it would still the gnawing in his gut for a while at any rate, at least until he could get to sleep. The orchards around him were only just budding and the fields just planted, so there was no food to be had there. Instead, he'd managed to filch a few things from the wharves lining the south side of the Thames.

Again, he shook his head over the fact that his

purse was full yet he dared not show his face to any shopkeeper to purchase food for himself.

He scrabbled over the muddy embankment to reach the land above the river. He skirted the open, freshly tilled fields until he arrived at his hideaway, a broken-down, abandoned barn.

After a bit, he managed to light a small fire, and he sat back, the small fish on a green twig. As he held it aloft, he assessed his situation.

It had only been four days since he'd left the Hathaways, yet it felt like four years. He glanced down at the torn knee of one trouser. That had occurred two days ago when he'd slipped down the last several feet climbing out of a warehouse at St. Katharine's Docks across the Thames.

That had been a close one, when a watchman had heard him and came his way with a lantern. His knee still hurt from the impact on the slippery stone, and all his foray had yielded was a sack of rice, which he had no idea how to cook. He'd tried to chew it but it was harder than the biscuits given him at Newgate. He'd tried boiling it in a cup of water, but it hadn't softened much and scorched on the bottom.

The smell of burning startled him out of his thoughts, and he stifled the curse at the blackened fish. Probably still raw inside. Well, no matter, he was hungry and would have it now before it charred away to nothing.

Bringing it gingerly to his lips, he began to bite

into it and cursed again when it burned the tip of his tongue. He set it down on a broken barrel stave and began to smother the fire with the ashes from a previous fire. He'd rather brave the cool nights than risk someone coming to investigate.

He snuffed the last tiny coals with the toe of his boot—not his good boots, thank goodness, then stopped in midthought. What did it matter now, preserving his good clothes and shoes for those occasions when he must appear the gentleman among folks?

He folded his arms on his drawn-up knees and bowed his head on them, weariness engulfing him.

…Whither wilt thou go?

It was a fragment of a Scripture Damien had read to him recently. He heard the words as if Damien were sitting there reading to him once again in his study, the fire glowing on the hearth.

Did he really think to run away and start a new life somewhere? His shoulders slumped with the weight of despair. Who was he and what did he matter in this universe, its inky black expanse above him each night showing him his insignificance.

Whence camest thou? The Angel of the Lord had asked the woman, Hagar. *And whither wilt thou go?*

Jonah raised his head slowly. Where did he come from and where was he going? He didn't know. He felt like Cain, a tiller of the ground. He remembered other Bible readings of Damien's. *And the Lord God formed man of the dust of the ground…*

That's exactly what he felt like now, dust of the

ground. He contemplated his fingers, soot from the recent fire blackening the skin, dirt filling each nail. Where had the fine gentleman gone? He let out a disgusted breath. So much work on Miss Hathaway's part to make him into a fine gentleman. In vain. She had been right to chastise him for his uncouth and ungainly ways. She should have given up on him from the first. Who knew what trouble he had brought now to her and her brother.

He fretted each night as he lay on the hard ground, wondering what charges they might face. Conspiring with a criminal against the Crown? Treason?

He shuddered thinking of the possible consequences of their unselfish acts.

For what? He was nothing but dust of the ground.

And whither wilt thou go? The question kept coming back to him, giving him no peace, as if God were looking down on him, probing him to the core. He looked up at the rafters of the high roof, gaping holes revealing the sky. *You know as well as I do, Lord, I've nowhere to go.*

"Who am I, Lord?" he whispered. *Am I nothing but dust?*

So God created man in His own image, in the image of God He created him...

Miss Hathaway's words came back to him. *You have been made a temple of God.* He remembered the way her eyes had shone that day, as she'd striven to impart something precious to him.

A temple of God. Was that what he was? "All

right, Lord," Jonah spoke into the still night. "I am Yours to do with what You will if You receive me."

What had the Angel of the Lord told Hagar? To return and submit.

Return? If he returned now, he'd be hanged. There would be no second chance for him.

He tried to shut out the idea, but all night long it kept recurring until finally in the dawn, fog hanging heavy on the Thames, he knew what the Lord required.

In the evening Florence was darning socks in her brother's study, waiting up for him. Damien was once again meeting with the rector. Ever since Quinn's escape, the rector had been doing his best to protect Damien from any disciplinary action for his part in hiding Quinn. What both she and Damien both feared was that it would be at the expense of Quinn's reputation. The rector was telling everyone that Quinn had held them hostage.

Florence cocked her ear, thinking for a second she had heard something. She was too jumpy these days. It was merely a tree branch scratching against the windowpane, she decided.

There it was again. This time there was no mistaking the insistent tapping against the glass. Her heart thudding, Florence set down her mending and hurried to the window. Her immediate thought was that it was Jonah. Of course not. He was aboard a ship by now, or on foreign soil. As these thoughts rushed through her mind, she strained to see through the dark panes.

She almost fainted when she made out his broad outline.

What was he doing coming back? Even as joy at the sight of him flooded her senses, terror immobilized her. He wouldn't be able to escape a second time. Guards had been posted on their street since the day Quinn had escaped. He must have sneaked in through the orchards at the back.

Not wasting another second, Florence hiked up her skirts and ran to the back door. The Nicholses had already left for the evening so she had to unbolt the door.

She was almost weeping in frustration as her fingers fumbled with the bolt and then the lock. By the time she opened the door, Quinn waited on the stoop.

She reached out and pulled him inside. "There are guards everywhere!"

"I know," he said, humor underscoring his words. "Those blind oafs wouldn't have seen me if I'd a crossed right in front of them. They're too interested in the bottle they're passing around."

She shut and bolted the door as soon as he crossed the threshold then leaned her back against it as if she could hold off the guards single-handedly. "Are you mad?"

He said nothing, just stood there looking at her.

As the minutes drew out, she became conscious

of how she looked in her old gown. Her hand stole up to one of the ties of her lace cap, which had come undone.

She bit her lip, feeling her lips begin to tremble. She'd thought never to see him again. And now, here he was, standing in the same place she'd bidden him that hurried goodbye. He looked awful. His coat and breeches were muddy, his hair disheveled, his jaw shadowed with several days' growth of beard. Yet, instead of the distaste she used to feel, all she wanted to do now was run to him and throw herself into his arms. She clenched her hands at her sides.

"What are you doing here?" she whispered. "Don't you know how dangerous it?"

He tunneled his fingers through his hair, leaving it in short standing tufts and smiled, a tired effort. "Aren't you happy to see me? I came back because of you."

Her heart started hammering in her chest so she could hardly hear him. "Me?"

"I was recollecting the story of Hagar. The Lord told her to come back and submit to her mistress." His lips turned up at one corner. "So, here I am, submitting to my taskmaster."

"I'm not your taskmaster!" Was that the only way he saw her? How else must he see her, she who had done nothing but badger and browbeat him into conforming to her way of behaving?

"Of course you are. Without you, I would never have turned into any kind of gentleman." He gave a look downward at himself. "Not that I make much of one now."

"You make a fine gentleman."

He looked at her and, once again, the very air between them was laden with unsaid words.

"I came back—" He stopped and cleared his throat. "I came back because I couldn't leave my friends to face things alone, now could I?"

"But they'll—" She couldn't say it. She covered her mouth to prevent the sob that threatened. "You must go."

"Nay, there's no more running for me. I've thrown my lot in with the Lord's. Let Him do to me what He will."

His words filled her with amazement. He was demonstrating more trust than she in the Lord's goodness. Yet she couldn't prevent the tears filling her lids. She must be strong in the face of his courage, she told herself, digging her nails into her palms to keep from running to him.

He took a step toward her and covered one of her hands. "Don't fret for someone like me. I wouldn't want ye to worry over my worthless hide."

Her lips trembled. "I'm scared for you." A tear ran down her cheek.

His forefinger came up and wiped it away. "There now, there's nothing to be frightened about."

"Th-they'll kill you."

"Don't fret yourself for my sake, lass," he repeated, his voice low and warm.

He'd never called her that. "I'm not a lass…not like Betsy…"

She searched his eyes. All she could read in their green depths was tenderness. "Nay, not like Betsy, but a lass nonetheless. One who's always strong for everyone else…and never lets anyone see any fear or weakness." His forefinger trailed down to her jaw. "Mayhap once in a while she needs someone to be strong for her."

And then somehow she found herself wrapped in his embrace.

It was all she could have dreamed. Power held in check. Tenderness with the promise of passion. His arms enfolded her and for a moment she felt safe, hidden in a secret place where she could be the woman she had never let anyone see.

He didn't hold her tightly, just enough for her to feel the comfort of his presence. "My Judy used to tell our wee ones when they came crying that sometimes only a hug would do."

She heard his voice a soft burr above her head, her cheek pressed against his broad, hard chest. She breathed deeply of the scent of him—sweat, smoke and the lingering lavender of the soap she'd given him. "Your Judy sounds like a very wise woman," she stammered, pushing her hand gently against his torso at the mention of his wife.

He let her go immediately. She moved away, blindly pulling out her handkerchief and dabbing at her eyes.

"The wisest."

She nodded, not quite looking at him.

"She was a simple one, not complicated at all." He continued looking at her, a curious expression in his eyes. "Not complicated at all."

She cleared her throat and moved farther away from him, her fear returning. "We…we must tell Damien when he comes in. I'm not sure what else must be done. Are you sure about this?"

He nodded wearily. "Aye. There's no more running for me, lass."

She swallowed, hardly able to bear the tenderness in the endearment. Was she to hear it only once before he was taken away from her forever?

The silence between them stretched out.

Jonah shuffled his feet as if suddenly embarrassed. "I would beg one favor of you."

"Anything." She'd do anything for him.

He looked at her a few seconds and she could feel her face warm. Then he broke the connection and cleared his throat. "I'd like to have a bath and change of clothes, if that's all right." He ran a hand along his jaw. "I'd like to present myself at Newgate…as a gentleman this time."

"Of course." She nodded. "Of course," she repeated, her voice firmer. "I'll put some water to heat and fetch some towels."

"I can take care of the water. I know where to find everything. I feel like I've come home, even if it's only for a short spell."

She nodded, her throat too constricted to say anything more. This was his home. Was it to be too late?

Jonah entered his bedroom while the water heated on the stove. He went to the chest of drawers and took out some clean linens. Everything was folded into neat stacks. He pressed a clean shirt to his nostrils, welcoming the scent of dried lavender. Then he went to the oak wardrobe and looked at the row of his coats hung there.

He pulled out the plum-colored one. He examined it now, touching the soft velvet with his hand. It appeared as clean as when Mr. Bourke had first delivered it. The rip at the shoulder was no longer visible, as if it had never been. He scrutinized it and could find no evidence of it. The dust and streak of dirt were gone. He sniffed it; it smelled like lavender and not of the dirt and sweat of the boxing ring.

He pulled it out and carried it down with the rest of his clean garments to the kitchen.

When they took him away, he would leave with the dignity of a duke.

A couple of hours later, Florence stood at the front door with Jonah, Damien and the rest of the household. They'd all been apprised of Jonah's intention to turn himself in.

"How did you get past our guards?" Damien

asked, with a nod toward the two sentries who had been stationed at the end of the front walkway since the day Jonah had been discovered.

Jonah shrugged. "Those fools couldn't spot a fugitive if he went up and tapped them on the shoulder."

Albert and Damien chuckled, but Florence couldn't summon even a smile. She looked at Jonah now, trying to memorize his every feature with the thoroughness she hadn't had the opportunity to do the day he'd had to escape so quickly.

He'd never looked so handsome. He wore the velvet plum-colored coat she'd repaired and sponged off and an ivory satin waistcoat embroidered in shades of green. His white neckcloth was perfectly tied in an Oriental. His tight-fitting black pantaloons were tucked into the calf-length tasseled Hessians she'd polished for him herself after he'd left.

Before she could reach for her cloak, Jonah turned to her and stayed her hand. "I wouldn't have you accompany me."

She curled her hand under his, wishing she could turn it palm up and have it enfolded by his larger one. "Why ever not?" Even before she ended the words she knew by the expression in his somber green eyes.

His eyelids flickered downward. "I don't want you to witness…it."

Damien cleared his throat. "Let us go then." They had already prayed as a group. Jonah shook each one's hand in turn. Mrs. Nichols reached over and gave him a hug. He patted Betsy's shoulder in an awkward gesture. "None o' that now," he said softly at the tears on her cheeks.

When he reached Florence, she didn't know what to do. Every fiber of her being wanted to fling herself on him and never let go. Yet, though he'd embraced her earlier, now it no longer seemed appropriate. So she stuck out her hand, and he grasped it after a second. He held it firmly, looking into her eyes.

"It takes a real gentleman to come back the way you've done and face whatever he must face," she whispered.

His square jaw worked as if he wanted to say something, but he remained silent.

"Godspeed."

"Thank you," he said, his own voice low, pressing her hand a final time before letting it go.

Damien clasped him on the shoulder and led him to the door. Quinn looked back once more, seeking Florence. She tried to smile.

And then he was gone. Florence peered through the lace curtain at the long window beside the door, Betsy and Mrs. Nichols on the other side.

It was worse than she'd imagined.

When the two men reached the guards and Damien began to explain to them, they turned their attention to Jonah, their expressions becoming menacing. Suddenly one of them pointed his musket at Jonah, touching his coat with the tip of his bayonet.

Florence gasped and felt Mrs. Nichols's hand on her arm. Although Jonah remained standing, the two soldiers grabbed his two arms in a rough grip as if he were attempting to escape. Damien stepped forward, but they shoved him aside.

Florence stifled a cry as Damien stumbled backward. "I must go to them." She stepped toward the door, but Albert held her back.

"It's best you not go out," the old man said in a kind voice. "I'll see to him." He grabbed his cap and exited.

As Albert helped Damien to his feet, the guards were already placing leg irons on Jonah's legs and manacles on his wrists.

Florence pressed her fist to her mouth, unable to bear watching and helpless to move away.

When Jonah had trouble climbing aboard the wagon, one guard butted him with his rifle. The others laughed and reviled him. Their muffled shouts came to her through the windowpane.

Dear God, grant him Your grace to endure, she prayed. *Grace to endure to the end. May he see Your glory.*

Even as she prayed, her mind was working furiously at what she could do now to help set him at liberty. First, she must see the rector. She had to convince him to help Quinn. They must request an audience with the lord chancellor. Perhaps if he could be made to understand Jonah's innocence, he would rescind the execution order and recommend transportation. That would be preferable to execution even if it meant she'd never see him again until glory. If that didn't work, she would go all the way to the home secretary, doing whatever she had to to be heard.

Whether she had to beg, cajole, plead, admonish—whatever it took—she would see justice done in Jonah Quinn's case.

Jonah sat hunched in his cell, a guard whistling off-key just outside the thick door.

One side of the dark cell was slightly more than the length of him, a few feet longer on the other side. A stone ceiling arched above him, with a small, double-grated window on the wall too far up to see out of. A board on the stone floor served as a pallet.

When he'd first entered the prison corridor, he'd been overpowered by the stench. In the months since his freedom, he'd forgotten just how foul it was.

He'd expected rough treatment since turning himself in, but he hadn't expected the rage that greeted him from both the prison guards, who considered themselves personally offended by his escape, and the other prisoners, who jeered at him as news of his recapture traveled through the men's large cell.

By their angry shouts, he'd realized they considered they'd had to pay the price for his escape, with harsher treatment and more vigilance.

"Flog him! He deserves a flogging! Hang him! Traitor!"

Finally, the clamor had died down. He'd been

sitting now in the semidarkness of the solitary confinement reserved for the condemned. He'd lost track of the time. He knew from his prior experience that hours, days, weeks blended into one another, but he also realized they would probably hang him sooner than later this time around.

Worse than anything was the inactivity. There was nothing to be done in solitary confinement but wait. A man could go mad in here. Jonah clutched his head in his hands, the shackles around his wrists and ankles clanking with each movement. He remembered Miss Hathaway's first visits to him. Back then, he'd been anxious to see her leave. Now, he'd have given anything to see her face through the tiny grate in the door, to hear Scriptures from her soft lips…

Lord, did I hear You aright? Have You brought me to this place? D'You mean for me to face the noose once again?

It would no doubt come quickly. The prison officials would want to exact a just retribution upon him and make a public example of him.

He prayed for the courage to face it once again.

Forgive me, Lord. You gave me a new chance at life, and all I did was chafe at the bit. I didn't deserve it. I'm nothing but scum o' the Earth.

A verse came into him with such clarity it stunned him.

"Fear not: for I have redeemed thee, I have called thee by thy name; thou art mine."

What was his name? Jonah. He remembered the

day Damien had taught him about his namesake. He had chuckled about the prophet Jonah caught inside the whale's belly three days. Now, he no longer smiled as he remembered how Jonah had compared his time in the seas with being in the depths of despair. He had cried out to the Lord then and it was then, only then, that the whale expelled Jonah onto the dry land.

Damien had explained how the story illustrated the redemption a person had in the Lord Jesus.

Once again he heard the words, *I have redeemed you and called you by name.*

What did it mean? It was almost as if the Lord were holding out to him the chance at a new life. But that was impossible. They would never let him out now. He had made a mockery of the system and they would make him pay for it.

Perhaps the Lord was holding out to him the promise of eternity.

He'd see Judy and the babes once again. He tried to comfort himself with that thought.

Instead his mind pictured Florence Hathaway and the way she'd looked at him when they'd said goodbye. She'd looked at him…as if in admiration. How could a lady as noble as she look at someone like him in admiration?

He remembered the feel of her slim figure in his arms, her face pressed to his chest. He'd felt like her protector then, like a man worthy of being a knight to a fine lady.

It was nonsense. But perhaps the memory would help him get through the last moments he had on Earth.

Would he see her face once more at the front of the crowd at the hanging? Or would she and her brother be locked away for their part in hiding him?

He prayed for them both, asking for the Lord's protection and mercy over them. *They did nothing wrong, only helping a dog like me. Forgive them, Lord.*

Florence sat on the edge of the velvet upholstered chair in the rector's private sitting room, her hands on her lap, clutching her reticule. "I've come here today, Reverend Doyle, to ask for your help in securing Jonah Quinn's release."

She faced the elegant man sitting in front of her as the spiritual leader she had looked up to all her life. She hoped and prayed he harbored no ill will toward her for her refusing to marry him, reminding herself it was he who had taken back his proposal.

The rector raised a dark eyebrow, which contrasted with his gray hair. "My dear Florence, you are overwrought, or you would not ask—nay, think—such a preposterous thing."

Florence moistened her lips, bringing her thoughts into submission. She must remain calm and plead Jonah's case in a logical, reasonable way. "Reverend Doyle, you do not understand all the circumstances."

He held up his hand. "My dear, Damien has explained the whole history of the infamous Quinn quite clearly and fully to me over and over. I'm just relieved the man saw fit to turn himself in. The mere thought that you had him under your roof all those months. I shudder to think of the danger you were in."

"But, Reverend, you know how sound Damien's judgment is. If he determined Mr. Quinn was a man worthy of his help, surely that deserves a second look by you."

"I know the criminal mind can deceive even the most astute person, and one as sensitive and kind-hearted as your brother has little chance against someone as cunning as Quinn."

She gripped her reticule more tightly. "Reverend Doyle, I am begging you to help me. I need to secure an audience with the home secretary. I need to know that the rector of my brother's parish—our friend and advisor—is fully behind my plea."

He shook his head, his regard full of pity. "My dear Florence, even my help wouldn't do any good. The home secretary will do nothing on the man's behalf. Quinn flaunted the entire judicial system. What kind of example would be set, letting a man like that go free? What kind of message would it send to other prisoners or criminals still at large? The Tory government wouldn't hear of it. There is too much unrest in the city as it is. Crime is on the rise."

She stood, a despair so profound filling her she could scarcely breathe. "I'm sorry you see it this way."

"Don't go so quickly, my dear." He stood and took her hand. "I feel you are taking this to heart too severely. I would not want it to come between us. Ours is a friendship of years. How long have you known this criminal?"

Hope rekindled in her. "It is precisely because of our friendship that I have appealed to you. You are a man of God. You know that our Lord commanded us to help the prisoner."

"Don't twist Scripture for your own ends. He never said to help a convict escape."

"But where a man has been wrongfully accused?"

"You have no proof of that, only a convict's word. And what is his word worth? How stellar has his conduct been? A man doesn't change his ways overnight."

She released her hand. "All I know is Mr. Quinn has been a gentleman in the time he has been in our household. Moreover, he came back of his own free will. He turned himself in at the urging of his conscience."

"That is a sign of guilt."

"No, it is a sign that the Lord touched him, and that he trusts his Lord and Savior enough to put himself into His hands."

The rector continued looking unconvinced. Florence felt a profound disappointment in the man she'd admired all her life. "I call that an act of a true gentleman."

"A true gentleman is one by birth and not by a superficial acquisition of some manners."

She stepped back. "Then neither is Damien a

true gentleman nor am I a lady. Perhaps you should rethink your friendship with us both."

"My dear, yours is not a mere veneer of polish but a lifetime's acquisition of manners, education and moral uprightness."

She lifted her chin. "But it is not by birth."

He cleared his throat. "Well, perhaps I was a bit hasty in using that qualification."

"Yet, it is nevertheless true, is it not? In the eyes of society, there are rigid definitions to what constitutes a lady and gentleman."

"In your case, my dear, I overlook any—er—inferiority of birth in light of your superiority of spirit and mind."

She bowed her head. "I thank you for your condescension, but I am afraid our views on the subject are too far removed to ever be reconciled. Good day, Reverend Doyle."

She left without giving him a chance to say anything more. The friend and advisor she had counted on since the death of her parents was not the man she had supposed him to be.

Chapter Eighteen

She and her brother talked things over that evening and decided to procure the services of a lawyer. The next day Damien consulted with an acquaintance in the city, who gave him the name of one of the most distinguished barristers for criminal cases.

A few days later they sat in his office at Gray's Inn.

"I'm afraid your chances are as good as nil." The imposing middle-aged lawyer steepled long fingers in front of him. He had heard them out, giving nothing away, raising Florence's hopes as he listened to them in silence.

Now, she felt herself deflate at the words said almost indifferently. "The court will show no leniency to an escaped convict. Not in this year of food riots, equipment smashing and general unrest among all the unemployed." He shook his head and shuffled the papers in front of him, giving the impression he was ready to move on to the next case.

"I'm sorry to crush your hopes. I would feel dishonest in taking your money."

Florence refused to give up. "Can we not appeal to the home secretary?"

"I doubt he would give you an audience." At the look on her face, he added, "I can try. I have a few favors to call in from an undersecretary. I shall see what I can do."

Florence stood up and held out her hand. "Thank you, sir. We shall await your summons then."

She and Damien spent the next few days trying their best to secure news of Jonah, but they were not permitted inside the prison. They tried to get money for him to buy food and were finally able to find a turnkey who'd always been friendly to them.

He told them that Mr. Quinn seemed to be doing well in his solitary confinement. "As well as the condemned do in their cells," he added with a shrug.

Finally, they received a message from the lawyer. "What does he say?" she asked, watching Damien break open the red seal.

He scanned the contents then looked at her. "We have an audience tomorrow afternoon at two with Secretary Ryder."

She let out a breath of relief. "Thank God." She turned to her brother. "Let us pray for God's favor."

Jonah spent the hours fretting over Miss Hathaway. Had she been to the prison? He hoped neither she nor her brother would do anything to put themselves at further risk. Knowing her spirit, though, he knew she was probably doing something on his behalf, no matter how hopeless. She was a fighter, she was.

His grin widened, remembering the time she'd grabbed the soapy washcloth and scrubbed out his mouth. Would he ever have let anyone else treat him so? Would anyone else have dared? He tried to imagine his Judy doing such a thing and sobered. It wasn't possible.

Oh, Judy love, would you ever have thought your Jonah could have these thoughts about such a fine lady?

She would have laughed in his face and made some coarse remark about his getting too far above his station.

He wasn't bothered by the fact of thinking about another woman. Judy was gone and would have expected him to find another wife, just as if it had been Judy who'd survived him, he'd have fully expected her to marry and have someone to take care of her and the babes.

But they were gone, and so, too, would he soon be, so why was he thinking such foolish thoughts as taking Miss Hathaway for a wife?

The moment the word popped into his thoughts, he froze.

Miss Hathaway for a wife. Suddenly, other images crowded his mind, a host of them—waking to her each morning, dining at her table each day, walking with her, assisting her in her prison work, working her land (what a tidy farm that would be), protecting her—so many of the things he'd already been doing, but with the difference of now being her equal and helpmate. It was impossible to conceive of it.

Nevertheless, once the thought had expressed itself, he couldn't help his imagination roaming further. At least it kept the gloom surrounding him at bay. He pictured Miss Hathaway. Everything about her was fine, from her slim ankles, which he'd noticed more than once, to her pale hands, always so clean and soft-looking, not red and chapped like all the women's of his class, to her small waist, which he could imagine spanning with his broad hands... He remembered her graceful neck rising above her neckerchief...her pale cheeks except when those two spots of color appeared on them, whenever she was annoyed beyond measure.

A frown clouded his brow when he thought of that lily-livered man, the rector. If ever a bee was after pollen, it was that old hypocrite. That man loved his food and drink and place in society more than any spiritual matters. Jonah would have put money on it. Yes, sir. He nodded in the dark.

He sighed. He'd never know now if Miss Hathaway would be fooled by the rector's soft words. Would the two end up wed? He hated to think of Miss Hathaway under the rector's thumb. He'd seen men like that before, all sweetness while they wooed a woman, then the moment they'd snagged her, they became tyrants. The women usually grew more silent with the passing days, humbly scurrying to do their husbands' bidding. Bullies these men were. Wolves in sheep's clothing.

Jonah couldn't imagine Miss Hathaway's fire snuffed out like that, by an old windbag, but it worried him to see her so meek around the rector, just because of his rank in the church. Bah! He almost spit in the dark and refrained himself just in time.

Why stop now? Who would see him and scold him now? But he refrained, nonetheless, swallowing the saliva in his mouth. If he were to die tomorrow or the next day, he'd do it as a gentleman…to honor Miss Hathaway and her brother. His focus traveled upward into the dark recesses of his cell…and to honor his Maker, Who'd brought those two individuals into his life.

"There shall no clemency be shown to a man who has made a mockery of the laws of this land," the home secretary pronounced from behind his large desk. Without letting either Florence or Damien address another word, he turned to his assistant, a young gentleman hovering in the background in the book-lined chamber of the Houses of Parliament. "I do not understand why you have wasted my time on such petitions, which are clearly not in the interest of our government."

"I beg your pardon, sir," the man stammered.

The home secretary turned back to them and

addressed Florence directly for the first time. "I have heard of your good work at Newgate. For this I commend you. But you must not take it upon yourself to aid and abet one who has so egregiously broken the law. Now, good day to you both."

Florence strode ahead of her brother and the barrister, her lips pressed down in anger and frustration. Once on the street, she whirled around to them. "This is not right."

A spring shower dampened their cloaks with its fine mist as they stood on the curb.

"I'm sorry, but I'm afraid you have had your answer," the lawyer said.

She refused to accept the fact that they had exhausted all avenues, appealing first to the lord chancellor and now to the home secretary. But as the distinguished barrister continued looking at her, her hope diminished. Her shoulders slumped.

"All but one," said Damien in his quiet tone. Both Florence and the lawyer stopped.

He looked at each one in turn. "The prince regent himself."

The barrister shook his head. "As I explained to you, the home secretary exercises the royal prerogative of mercy on behalf of the monarch. His refusal to look further into Quinn's case means we cannot go any further."

"And if we appeal directly to the regent?"

The lawyer smiled sadly, as if trying to explain

something to someone too naive to understand the basics of English law. "I'm afraid that is impossible. Unless the home secretary grants you his recommendation, the regent will not hear the case."

Florence turned away from his pitying face and gazed across the busy street. They would need a miracle to obtain an audience with the regent, who had so recently acquired full powers of the monarchy since old King George had fallen irrevocably into madness more than a year ago. She thought of Queen Esther obtaining favor from the king.

But Florence was no queen to request an audience with the monarch. *Lord, what would You have me do?*

At that moment, she thought of the man who had been responsible for Quinn's capture. The Duke of Winchester. Apart from having hired a detective to discover Quinn's identity, the duke had always struck Florence as a reasonable man. Perhaps he could procure them an audience with the regent.

She turned to the barrister. "I thank you for all you've done on Mr. Quinn's behalf. I'm sorry your time proved fruitless."

"I have been well compensated for my time. It is I who am sorry to yield so little results for my fee."

It had cost them dearly to engage the services of a highly recommended lawyer. "'A workman is worthy of his wages,'" she replied before turning to her brother. "Come, Damien, we still have work to do."

The lawyer raised an eyebrow. "You mean to pursue other avenues?"

"We mean to seek favor with the king."

When she explained her plan to Damien, he thought it an excellent one. He helped her draft a note to the duke as soon as they returned to the parsonage.

Since her last interview with the rector she had avoided Doyle. He'd called twice and each time she had remained in her room. He'd kept his visits short. Damien told her he had asked for her. "He also asked me what we are doing about Quinn."

"A lot he cares about the poor man's fate."

"I suppose we can't expect him to understand our interest in Jonah. He never really got to know the man."

"He never was interested in getting to know him," she said with a sniff.

"I hope this doesn't make you bitter concerning the rector. He cares very much for your good opinion," Damien said softly.

"Does it matter much to you what my opinion of him is?" she asked. "I know he is your superior in the church, and I have always tried to respect that."

"I just want you to 'be at peace with all men,'" Damien replied with a smile.

"Let us pray for favor with the duke."

"Indeed."

The next day, Florence sat in the anteroom of the duke's palace. He had replied to their note the same day, agreeing to receive her.

She was not kept waiting long. The frosty-looking

footman, who had shown her in, returned and bowed. "If you please, follow me."

She and Damien had decided that she should see the duke on her own. "He was very admiring of your prison work. Perhaps he will be more sympathetic to a female plea of mercy," Damien had said.

The duke was seated at a small writing desk and looked up as soon as the footman announced her at the doorway to a richly appointed office. "Good morning, Miss Hathaway," he said in a pleasant voice. He rose from his gilt chair as she entered.

When she hesitated on the threshold, he advanced toward her. He was dressed in a sky-blue coat and ivory-colored waistcoat and pantaloons.

What could she say to this august personality whom she'd only spoken to for a few minutes at his dinner some weeks ago? He might have shown an interest in her work at the prison, but he had also been responsible for Quinn's discovery.

Her knees trembling, she managed a curtsy before him. Her mouth felt so dry she could hardly formulate a greeting. "Thank you…for taking the time to see me on such short notice."

"I gladly make time to see such a worthy lady," he said, bowing over her hand then indicating a chair with a slight wave of his hand. "Would you care for any refreshment?" he asked her when she'd seated herself.

"No, thank you," she said, crossing her legs at the ankles and folding her hands over the reticule she

held on her lap. She hadn't removed her hat or
pelisse.

Winchester dismissed his footman with the
barest nod then took his seat. He sat back, crossing
his long legs at the knee, his fingers toying with a
fob on his watch chain. "Now, what may I do for
you, my dear lady?"

Florence moistened her lips. "I have come about
Jonah Quinn." Her voice sounded too quiet to her
ears, lacking its usual forcefulness. She straightened,
reminding herself this was a man, like any other.
"The man *you* turned in." She placed only a slight
emphasis on the pronoun and remained focused on
the duke although her insides were quaking.

He examined his fingernails. "Ah, yes, the notorious Jonah Quinn, the man who slipped through the
fingers of the hangman and has made a laughing-
stock of the prison officials who have hunted for
him high and low with no success." He looked at
her, a slight smile on his lips. "And where should
he be hiding but in plain sight, befriended by an
honest clergyman and his spinster sister?" He shook
his head. "My compliments to you, Miss Hathaway.
My admiration for you grows daily."

She did not return his smile. "Why did you
expose his whereabouts, if you were filled with such
admiration?"

He lifted an eyebrow as if surprised by her
question. "Why, to see justice done, of course."

"And what of mercy?"

"Ah…mercy. 'It droppeth as the gentle rain from heaven…'" he quoted softly.

"A quality you have not seen fit to demonstrate."

"I was not aware this case warranted mercy."

Her fingers gripped her reticule, and she wondered if she was making any headway with this man who seemed to treat everything lightly. "Perhaps if you understood all the particulars."

"Perhaps."

"You didn't care enough to inquire about them when you exposed Mr. Quinn's whereabouts."

He narrowed his eyes a fraction. "I confess, you arouse my curiosity."

"I was hoping to." She took a deep breath. "Tell me, Your Grace, how did you recognize Mr. Quinn?"

He waved a hand in the air. "I was at the execution. I came out of curiosity. I don't usually attend such gruesome spectacles, but the case interested me. You see, we have spent a good deal of time in the House of Lords debating the issues of enclosures. This man Quinn was a supposed victim of the laws of enclosures. He'd lost his land and had turned to a life of crime in retaliation."

She leaned forward, hope beginning to grow in her. "Or, he tried desperately to seek work—any work from digging ditches to competing as an unskilled laborer in a world of skilled workers—and fell by chance into the hands of a corrupt individual who used him as a hapless pawn in his game of deceit."

The duke straightened in his chair, his look intent. "Go on. Perhaps I was ignorant of the full story."

She cleared her throat. "Your Grace, a man's life is at stake. A man whose life has shown a remarkable transformation from a coarse laborer barely able to read to a…a…gentleman who sat at your own table." Her voice rose as she spoke.

At his nod, she continued. "Jonah Quinn was rescued from the gallows by a band of men he didn't even know and still doesn't know. An escape that was not his doing, and for which he should not be held to blame. I ask you, wouldn't you grasp the chance for freedom if it were suddenly held out to you and you knew you had been unjustly accused?"

"I confess I would."

Once again Florence related the story she had come to memorize. But she had not grown weary with the telling. Instead her voice resonated with emotion, surprising even herself with her impassioned plea. She tried to read the duke's expression, but could detect nothing from his calm demeanor and steady observation except that he seemed to be listening.

Several minutes later, when Florence ended her narrative, she heard a clock strike the hour above the mantelpiece. "I'm sorry to have taken up so much of your time, Your Grace," she began, drawing herself up.

He waved her back down. "Have no thought for that. I thank you for coming to inform me fully of the circumstances concerning your Mr. Quinn."

Your Mr. Quinn. Perhaps once he'd been so. Her Mr. Quinn, to reform and teach, but no longer. Would she ever see Jonah again this side of eternity?

The duke sat silent long moments, and she didn't know what to do. He seemed deep in thought and she didn't dare say a word for fear of distracting him. What *could* he do, after all? He might hold a high title, but he was only one man—a man from the party that despised those like Jonah Quinn and had spent their lives fighting them.

She started when he spoke. "There's only one thing to be done."

"What…is that?"

"We must secure you an audience with the regent."

The prince regent. The only one able to grant a pardon.

The duke uncrossed his legs and sat forward, a light touching his eyes, giving them an intensity that was lacking before. "You spoke of mercy. We shall petition the Crown for a royal prerogative of mercy. If the regent hears Quinn's story the way you have related it to me, he is sure to be moved to pardon the man."

She swallowed her sense of disappointment. "But we have already petitioned for such a pardon through the home secretary's office."

He waved away her words. "Of course, the official channels. But Ryder cannot be expected to view such a case in human terms. The man is an official, a hardened Tory. To him, Quinn represents every radical, criminal element among the poor."

"And the prince would view Quinn's case differently?"

He made a motion of disdain with his hand. "The prince is a man moved by whatever emotion grabs his attention at the moment."

"I see." Her lips turned downward. "Unfortunately, some would say I am a woman of hard and fast principles, not a woman to move a man to emotions." A fleeting memory of Quinn's kiss flashed before her. She might move a man to anger, but not to sublime emotion.

He chuckled. "On the contrary, my dear Miss Hathaway, I would say you are quite adept at moving a man to great emotion." He rubbed his hands together and turned toward his desk. "Now then, you may leave things to me. As soon as I have secured you an audience with Prinnie, I will send word to you."

She swallowed. "You would do this for him?"

"I got your gentleman into this mess. I feel called upon to help get him out."

She stood, hope beating in her breast. "Ca-can you do it before they execute Mr. Quinn?"

A ghost of a smile crossed his lips. "I shall endeavor my utmost."

Minutes dragged by into hours, night turning into day and back into night through his small window as Jonah alternated pacing the tiny confines of his cell with sitting or lying on his wooden pallet. How much longer did he have?

When he heard the squeaky wheels below in the street and the shouts of the crowds gathering, he knew the time was drawing near. The gallows had once more been brought to the front of the prison.

When the guard gave him the tray of stale bread and cup of water, he leered at him through the small grating, his bushy gray eyebrows twitching. "You've the honor of hanging tomorrow. You've the gallows all to yourself once again. There must be something special about such a fellow." He scratched the scraggly gray beard on his thin cheeks and cackled. "Mebbe you were marked at birth!" He turned away and walked back down the stone corridor, the keys jingling at his side.

Jonah strained toward the small window on the opposite side of his cell but to no avail. He could see nothing but a small patch of sky. It was overcast but not with heavy clouds that portended rain, only high, pale gray ones that shut out the sun.

He turned away in disgust and threw himself back down on the hard pallet, ignoring the pain to his shoulder blades. He played with one of the brass buttons on his coat. The thread was loosening, soon it would come off if he didn't stop his fiddling. What did it matter, as long as it lasted until the morrow? He glanced down at himself. So much for appearing a gentleman on the gallows.

He was once again filthy from top to toe. The time spent bathing and dressing in fine clothes in the Hathaway household hadn't made any difference. A week in this cell, and he was no different from the man who'd first appeared on Miss Hathaway's doorstep. Resembling more beast than man. He stroked the sharp stubble covering his face and ran his fingers through his matted curls. His scalp had begun itching again. Soon, he'd probably be covered with vermin. His stockings and clothing had protected him from the worst of flea bites, but he'd already scratched at a few on his wrists.

He smoothed down the nap of the plum-colored velvet coat. It was stained and dusty beyond repair this time. He remembered how Miss Hathaway had made it look as good as new the last time he'd broken her rules and gone back to his old way of life. He shook his head at his silly pride in presenting her with his winning purse. "Filthy lucre!" she'd rapped back.

No, he was no gentleman. What had he been thinking to presume to think of her as someone to cherish and share a life with?

She was well rid of him.

She'd only managed to change him on the outside. This week in Newgate proved how little an outward change made to a man. It took but a few days for the effects to be obliterated. He studied his crossed feet, the toes of his boots dusty and scuffed.

I have redeemed you and called you by name.

He remembered Miss Hathaway's belief that a gentleman was not determined by his outward appearance but by his heart.

He sat up, the words coming alive for him. With God's grace he would prove it. If he had to die on the gallows, he would do so as the gentleman Miss Hathaway had taught him to be, *a man of principle, of honor, of chivalry.* Her words reverberated in his memory.

Jonah Quinn, gentleman if not by birth, then by the redemptive blood of Jesus Christ.

Chapter Nineteen

The duke's missive came two days before Jonah was set to be executed for the second time. There had been numerous delays to the execution. First, there had been the unrest in the city since the day it was known Jonah had been recaptured. The officials, fearing mass protests, had sent in the horse guards to patrol the streets. The sight of so many redcoats had brought about further unrest. The memory of the food riots during the hard winter months was on everyone's minds.

Then the gallows had lost a wheel on its way to Newgate. The warden had feared a deliberate sabotage, but on further investigation, it was found it was merely the result of running into too deep a gully after the recent rains.

That had delayed the execution another day, which had caused Florence no end of relief, since she had heard nothing from the duke.

The day she finally received his message, it had been brief and to the point. He would send his carriage to take her and her brother to Carlton House for an interview with the prince regent. He had agreed to a brief audience, finding himself "curious as to the hubbub concerning Mr. Quinn," as he'd expressed to the duke.

Florence and Damien spent the intervening time in prayer. When the morning of the interview dawned, the day before the final scheduled execution, Florence opened her curtains to find an overcast day greeting her. Undaunted, the birds made a riot of sound outside her window.

After reading her Bible and praying, she went to her wardrobe to select her gown. What did one wear to see the future monarch? She had no court dress, nor had the duke instructed them on what attire to wear.

She finally decided on a simple gown of light blue with ivory embroidered along the neckline and sash. She tucked a thin muslin scarf into the neckline and dressed her hair in its usual simple knot. The image that looked back at her from the mirror inspired no confidence that she could do or say anything to move a monarch.

She turned away from the glass, impatient with herself. She was the way God had made her and that was enough for her. If she made any good impression with the regent, it would be due to God's favor, and not to any attractive qualities of her person.

She grabbed up her reticule and bonnet and headed downstairs to await the duke's coach.

She and her brother rode in silence. The coach was more magnificent than any she'd ever ridden in. Its roomy interior could easily have seated a half-dozen occupants. Its rich leather upholstery was as smooth as satin, its interior walls damask.

It rumbled at a dignified pace toward its destination at the opposite end of Mayfair, an area Florence rarely ventured to. They made their way down the elegant Pall Mall, past St. James's Palace, the official palace of the regent, but continued down the wide avenue until arriving at his residence, the relatively new Carlton House. She peered through the window at the mansion she'd heard so many stories about, from the countless decorating projects the prince had carried out on it, spending a fortune on each, to the stories of the decadent parties held within its walls. It was a long building, built on classical lines, an endless row of columns stretching almost the length of it, with an arch at either end.

The liveried footman opened the door of the coach as soon as it had stopped in front of the mansion, and lowered the steps of the coach. Damien handed her out and followed behind her.

Dozens of footmen lined the columned portico and foyer. One of them escorted her and Damien up the curved staircase to the receiving room.

There seemed to be people everywhere, all elegantly dressed even though it was not evening. Florence felt dowdy by contrast and her confidence dwindled with every step forward down the red-carpeted corridor.

"You will wait here until you are summoned," the footman instructed them, leaving them in a crowded anteroom. A few minutes later gold-liveried servants came and laid down a scarlet runner.

Several more minutes passed, when someone announced, "The prince is coming!"

More gold-liveried footmen opened double doors at one end and a procession began to file in.

"The Bishop of Gloucester," she heard Damien say under his breath, indicating a man in robes and miter. He was followed by a great lady in full court dress and several gentlemen in dark suits.

Then came some of the royal dukes, brothers of the crown prince, and a host of official personages, including the lord mayor.

The bishop came up to Florence and offered her his arm. "I am instructed to escort you to the prince regent." He inclined his head toward Damien. "You are to follow me."

Everyone clapped when, at the end, the prince himself entered the room. Florence stared at him, her nerves momentarily forgotten as she studied the man who in so short a time had become so unpopular with the common people. A man who lived isolated among his select circle of wealthy friends, politicians, artists and writers.

He was a large man, both in height and build. He wore a sumptuous suit of black velvet with gold facings. His neck was swathed up to his ears in a white neckcloth with his shirt points barely peeking through at either end against his jaw. His dark hair was swept around his head in studied carelessness, brushed forward to form curls along his temples and forehead. He had prominent eyes, which he now focused on her.

The bishop urged her forward by a slight pressure on her arm.

She dropped into a deep curtsy before the prince.

When she rose, he lounged in his large gilt thronelike chair, his chin resting on his fingers. "We have been told you are responsible for the escaped prisoner's long evasion of the authorities."

"Yes, Your Royal Highness, my brother and I—" she made a gesture behind her to include Damien, "—felt led by the Lord to offer Mr. Jonah Quinn aid and succor in his flight from an unjust sentence laid upon him."

"Unjust?" He turned toward one of the individuals standing at his side. "Did you hear that, my lord chancellor, this lady says the sentence passed by the Recorder of London was unjust." He gave her his attention once more. "Do explain."

Once more she began to relate the story as she'd told it to the duke, of the unfortunate circumstances that had befallen Jonah since he had come to London after losing his small holding. She tried to keep strictly to the facts as she knew them and the narrative as brief as possible, knowing it was probably only a whim that had brought her to the regent's attention. If she went on too long, he'd likely become bored and have her dismissed.

"So, you see, Your Royal Highness," she ended, "how he was betrayed by his employer into carrying that forged note to the man's competitor."

She could read little from the regent's attentive expression. He seemed to offer goodwill, but she knew from all the stories what a capricious man he was. He and his father, old King George, had continually been at loggerheads, the old king railing at his son's extravagant ways. He was continually petitioning the House for funds to pay his exorbitant debts.

She could already see the effects of the dissipated lifestyle in the fleshy jaw and wide girth. She felt a pang of pity for the man who had been given so many talents and seemed to be squandering them on worldly pursuits.

"While he has been under the tutelage of my brother, the Reverend Damien Hathaway, Jonah Quinn has been transformed from a man brutalized by his circumstances into a man noble and true, living his life according to the dictates of God's Word. The proof of this is that even when he was rediscovered in our parish and managed to escape a second time, he came back of his own accord and gave himself up to the authorities, not because he admits any guilt in breaking the law, but because he felt the Lord's leading to turn himself in and throw himself on the mercy of the courts and prove himself an upright and law-abiding citizen."

The prince stroked his jaw as if considering. "What say you to this, my lord chancellor?" he asked abruptly, turning away from Florence.

"The prisoner has mocked the courts and must be made to hang. He is not only a criminal, but a revolutionary, and will cause further unrest among the populace if he is let off free. He must hang!"

The prince turned back to Florence, his protruding eyes showing a hint of sadness. "You see, my dear lady, we must abide by the original order, or chaos would ensue. We would not follow the fate of our counterpart across the Channel."

"Mr. Quinn is no revolutionary, Your Royal Highness."

He continued looking at her for a moment more, in which time she prayed that the Lord would move him.

Suddenly, he spoke. "No. We cannot have it. The man must hang. He has made a fool of us!"

She felt crushed and could hardly support herself. This couldn't be it. No, no, no!

The prince rose, and all around the room Florence heard people coming to attention. She felt a wave of panic rise in her. Damien, as if sensing her despair, came to stand behind her and gripped her arm.

Before the prince had a chance to move, Florence took a step forward, not knowing what she would do, only sure she couldn't let him leave like this. He didn't understand the finality of his pronouncement. "Please, Your Highness." Without another word, she dropped to her knees before him.

The regent's round eyes widened in surprise.

"Now, see here!" She heard the bishop behind her. His fingers dug into her arm as if to pull her up and away. She ignored him and fixed her eyes on the prince alone. "Your Royal Highness, please…" Her voice broke on the whispered plea. "I beg your mercy for this man."

She could no longer see the prince. She was looking down at the red carpet before her knees, and her eyes were blurry with tears.

The prince took a step toward her and paused. "My dear lady, you mustn't weep. Does this prisoner mean so much to you?" His tone was indulgent.

She nodded, hardly able to speak.

"You would have us pardon him?"

"Yes, Your Highness…yes, I would," she finally managed to whisper.

"Tell me, why should we grant a man mercy who has not only broken the law but flaunted it?"

Slowly she raised her head to meet his eyes, unmindful of the tears streaking down her cheeks. The prince seemed genuinely curious. In that instant, she felt her heart fill to overflowing, wanting with every particle of her being to save Jonah. It was as if a floodgate inside her had opened, and she could no longer contain it. "Because…I love him."

When he said nothing but continued to regard

her, his face showing an animation and interest it hadn't before, she continued. "This man has proved I still have a heart and it would be irreparably broken if I could never look upon his face in this lifetime."

She heard the ripple of reaction behind her as people gasped and began to murmur. She could hardly believe the words that had come out of her mouth. When had she realized she loved Jonah Quinn?

The prince's lips curved upward in a smile. "You have touched a kindred spirit. I, too, have known what it is to love and lose." He rose and came toward her, offering her his hand. She rose to her feet, feeling as if she were in some sort of dream. The prince was smiling down at her, a benign look on his face.

"This woman shall have what she has asked. Free the prisoner. Commute his sentence and set him free!" He turned to his ministers. "We grant a royal pardon."

The murmurs became loud exclamations of outrage as well as applause. "Hear! Hear!" drowned out the sounds of dismay.

Florence didn't know how she made it out of the hall. She was only vaguely aware of Damien's arm around her, leading her down the red carpet. All around her, she heard murmurs and felt the stares of the people, some outraged, others approving.

Once outside Carlton House and in the coach, Damien took her hands in his and smiled into her eyes. "Well done, big sister. God was on our side, eh?"

She tried to smile but her lips felt numb. "Was the pardon real?" she managed. That's all that mattered.

He pressed her hands. "Yes. No doubt there'll be a hue and cry from the Tories, but they can't rescind the king's prerogative. As regent, his word is as good as the king's."

Florence breathed a sigh of relief and sat back against the squabs. She closed her eyes, wishing it were as easy to shut out her thoughts. *What had she done?* reverberated to the jostle and sway of the coach over the cobblestones beneath them.

"Did you mean it?" Damien's voice was quiet, but she knew exactly what he referred to.

She didn't open her eyes. "Pray, do not ask me that."

He said no more, for which she was grateful. She could not lie to her brother.

Truly, she didn't know the answer to his question. What had possessed her to kneel before her future monarch and plead—nay, beg—for a man's life using a sentiment of the heart? *Because I love him.* The words resonated in her mind. What had she said? She cringed in shame. Parading her deepest secrets for all the world to see.

All that mattered was that Jonah would soon be free, she told herself. He could go where he would, a free man.

What would she say when she saw him? Would it be possible to keep her revelation from him? She could trust her brother, but all the world would soon know what she had confessed to the prince. Would the scandal sheets have a field day?

She clutched a hand to her mouth, wanting to moan with the humiliation of it. She could imagine it now. Spinster on Her Knees Pleading for Life of Convict.

When they arrived home, Damien handed her down from the carriage. Instead of going in with her, he turned back to the coach.

"Where are you going?"

"I promised to meet our lawyer at Newgate. We aren't wasting any time demanding Jonah's immediate release."

Her heart leaped in an instant and she made a move as if to follow him, but then stopped. How could she face Quinn now? Her glance skittered away from her brother's. "W-will you bring him here?"

"Of course." He gave her shoulder a quick squeeze. Was that sympathy she read in his eyes? "He has nowhere else to go, Florence."

"Yes, of course."

She walked up the flagstone path like an aged woman. What would she say to him when she saw him?

Mr. and Mrs. Nichols were waiting at the door as soon as she entered, with Betsy hovering behind them. Her eyes went from one eager face to the other and she couldn't bear to diminish their joy. She nodded at each one. "Bless God, the regent granted a pardon."

She'd hardly finished the sentence when there was whooping and hollering and hugging all around her.

She shared their joy. Even if her character was another sort, which couldn't express itself with such exuberance, she felt the joy and relief equally—if not more so. It was there, deep down, reserved in a place, awaiting a moment when she would be alone to fall on her face before God and pour out her thanksgiving.

She extricated herself from Mrs. Nichols's embrace and began to untie the ribbons of her bonnet. "Well, the Lord has been gracious."

"But, Miss Hathaway, what did you do, what did you say that the prince showed you such favor?"

Their questions came hard and fast, and Florence braced herself. "It was the Lord's favor, is all I can say. I stated Mr. Quinn's case as plainly and simply as I could, and…the prince regent was…moved to grant the pardon." She hurried on. "Mr. Hathaway believes there'll be a protest by some members of the government, but he assured me they cannot take back the regent's decision."

As they made their way down the hallway, the others continued to argue the possibility of this. Suddenly, Mrs. Nichols took one look at Florence and stated, "I think you could do with a good, strong cup of tea."

She smiled wanly. "Yes, that would help me immeasurably. Could you please bring it to me in the study?" All she wanted now was to be alone.

"Of course, dear. You just go in and sit yourself down. You look awfully peaked." Mrs. Nichols patted her hand and shooed her into the study.

Florence closed the door softly behind her. After the noise of the regent's court and the hubbub of the streets, quiet enveloped her. She walked to the window and stood staring, but she didn't see the peaceful springtime scene of budding flowers and tender green shoots of grass. She saw only Jonah's face the day he'd said goodbye to her and felt his arms around her as he had held her so gently, his voice soothing her. Why had she broken away from his embrace so quickly? The reminder of his wife had spurred her, of course. The fact of his already having loved someone didn't bother her in itself. She honored the memory of his wife, and remembered how he had told her he'd been faithful to her.

No, the mention of Judy had served to bring her back to reality. Jonah Quinn could never love someone like herself. No man had ever loved her like that. Eugene's affection had been tepid at best. The Reverend Doyle's regard was only that: respect and estimation for someone he perceived would make him a good helpmate.

Oh, how she longed to be someone's helpmate. But just as strongly, she yearned for something more. How she longed to offer a man all the passion she'd felt building within her since the day she'd met Jonah. This was a woman she hardly knew but whom she no longer wished to deny.

Her thoughts returned to Jonah.

Where would he go? He had his prize money. She knew Damien would not take back any of the additional money he'd given to him.

Would he still go to America, or Canada? He could probably do very well in a land like that. She shuddered at the dangers of crossing the Atlantic during this time of blockades.

Finally she sank down on her knees and gave the Lord thanks for sparing Jonah's life on this day. That was all that was important.

Jonah heard the clank of the key in the lock on his door. He immediately stood. What could it mean? The hanging wasn't until tomorrow morning. He wasn't ready. Panic rose in him, threatening to cut off his breath.

"I will fear no evil," he murmured, his thoughts clutching the remnant of the psalm Damien had taught him.

The heavy, studded door opened, admitting the turnkey. The man was grinning in his usual sly way. Was he here to gloat?

"Well, I don't know what kind o' power you have with your betters, but I'm here to take you out."

"What are you talking about?" Was he to be hanged early?

"Free as a bird you are," the man cackled.

"Free?" What could he be saying?

"Prince George has pardoned ye. Come on, move

along. I haven't got all day." He laughed again, as if that was the biggest joke of all.

The door stood open and the turnkey gestured him out. Jonah didn't take any chances that it would prove a mistake. He stepped through the door, not bothering to look back. He had left nothing there. He went out wearing only the suit of clothes he'd come in with.

He was led past the large, common cells, filled with men awaiting transport or sitting there until their debts were paid. When they saw Jonah, the men hung on the bars and shouted at him.

"He got his freedom!" "Quinn's got the royal pardon!" They banged their cups or spoons against the iron bars, making a maddening commotion. They hooted and hollered, stretching out their hands to touch him, pat him on the back, tug at his coat. It seemed he was a hero again.

"Don't forget me when you get out!" came the calls.

He walked as if in a fog, still not understanding any of it. Could it have been something the Reverend Hathaway had done for him? He had heard of something called the "benefit of the clergy," in contesting a death sentence but knew it wouldn't apply in his case. And it would only mean transportation to the colony. No, he'd escaped a hanging once. There would be no mercy shown him a second time.

Down the dark stone stairs and along another

corridor and finally into the daylight of the press yard. Just like the last time, the turnkey bent down and unlocked the fetters from his ankles then straightened and proceeded to do the same with those around his wrists. The chains fell with a sharp clank against the stones.

This time instead of having his arms tied at his sides prior to being led up onto the gallows, they were left hanging free.

"Come along with ye then." The turnkey gestured with his chin.

Jonah stumbled on a cobblestone. He'd never thought to see the outside, not until tomorrow morning when he'd have been led once more to the gallows. He followed the man to the lodge, where the prison warden lived. He halted in the dim passageway, making out the silhouette of a man standing there. The bright light from the archway blinded Jonah to his face, but the wooden leg identified him immediately as Hathaway.

"Damien! Reverend Hathaway," he shouted, his voice hoarse, as he hurried toward the curate.

Damien met him halfway along the stone passageway, his wooden leg thumping against the cobblestones. He clasped Jonah by the shoulders, his face beaming. "You're free. God be praised, you are a free man!"

Jonah could only stare at him. It was finally beginning to seem real.

The next moment Damien embraced him, laughing.

"You look as if you don't understand a word I'm telling you. Man, you're free! Believe it!"

"How…?" he began, then suddenly he hugged Damien back, laughing, no longer caring if this was a dream or true. Whatever it was, he'd enjoy the moment before waking up.

"All right, clear out o' my prison," the warden's sour tones interrupted their joyful reunion.

"I'm a stinking mess," Jonah said, pulling away from Damien, embarrassed by the emotion he felt.

Another man stood near them. Damien immediately introduced him as his lawyer.

Jonah held out his hand when he saw the other man's hand extended. "Pleased to meet you. Are…are you responsible for my…freedom?"

The man smiled but shook his head. "I wish I could take the credit, but, no. You have the Hathaways to thank—Miss Hathaway, to be precise. I feel I'm robbing them to collect a fee."

Jonah looked from one man to the other. Miss Hathaway? What did the man mean? Had she engaged the lawyer for him? After all the things they'd given him to escape? How much he owed them…

Damien broke the silence. "Come along. It's time to go home."

Home.

He followed Damien out into freedom.

Chapter Twenty

By the time their carriage—a very posh one by Jonah's estimation—had wended its way only halfway down the Old Bailey Lane, crowds began to gather.

"What's all the commotion about?" he asked, peering through the curtain.

"You, I expect. I think word has begun to spread on the regent's pardon."

He leaned toward Damien. "The regent's pardon? Tell me how all this came about. I can scarce believe I'm out o' that stinkin' hole."

He listened, his astonishment growing as Damien recounted what he and his sister had been busy with since the moment Jonah had been arrested.

"Florence didn't rest, trying to see anyone who might be of influence. But she met nothing but stumbling blocks." His face clouded briefly. "No one wanted to have anything to do with you. Your

escape and the Crown's inability to apprehend you
were a major embarrassment for prison officials.
It wasn't until she hit upon the scheme of going
to see the Duke of Winchester that she achieved
any success."

"The duke? Isn't he the one who was suspi-
cious of me?"

He smiled. "The very one. In fact, it's because
of him that you were eventually discovered. The
irony is wonderful. Florence went to see the very
man responsible for your being in Newgate the
second time."

"But what could he do for me?" He still couldn't
begin to grasp it all. Uppermost in his thoughts was
the efforts these two had gone to on his behalf. Miss
Hathaway's name seemed to crop up the most in Mr.
Hathaway's speech. Was he just being his usual
modest self, not wanting to take any credit, or was
he telling Jonah what really happened?

"Florence wanted me to go with her, but I
thought she should brave the duke alone since he
had seemed so admiring of her work at Newgate. He
proved a most sympathetic man. He listened to the
full tale of your plight and immediately decided
Florence must be given an audience with the prince
regent himself." His voice quieted. "At this point,
the regent was your only hope. Only he could issue
a full pardon."

Jonah continued listening, his astonishment
growing. That the crown prince should be inter-

ested in one Jonah Quinn, a common laborer, a nobody, was beyond his ken.

Damien leaned forward and tapped the back of his hand. "Jonah, we serve a mighty God. He made a way for my sister to be presented to the highest authority in the land, just as he did for Queen Esther so many centuries ago. He gave Florence favor with the future king, who listened to your woeful tale and took pity on you."

Jonah shook his head, more intrigued than ever. "What did she tell him? That I was a miserable, hardheaded pupil?"

Damien chuckled a bit nervously, it seemed to Jonah. "Well, she was most eloquent in your defense. The prince couldn't help but be moved. There was a crowd assembled—members of Parliament and various other dignitaries, members of the royal family, and a host of other important people. I felt quite overwhelmed in such august company. I'm glad I didn't have to do the speaking."

Jonah sat back, enjoying the scene. "Oh, come, Reverend Hathaway, I don't think you would have been overcome by such a company."

He grinned. "But the Lord chose to use Florence. She had…a way with words that I could not possibly have equaled on this occasion, trust me."

Before he could ask for the particulars, Jonah was distracted by the shouts around the carriage. He lowered the window and craned his neck out. The moment the people around it saw his face, they began chanting. "Jonah Quinn! Jonah Quinn innocent!" Others pushed their way near him. "Saved from the noose twice! A miracle! You're blessed by God!" They held out their hands to him, trying to touch him. He shook as many hands as he could, but when he saw it was never ending, he pulled himself back into the coach.

Before he could shut the window, a voice above the crowd made itself heard. "Woman saves condemned man!" The man's strong shout cut through the rest. "Love of woman moves prince!"

It was one of those hawkers, like the ones who'd sold broadsheets of his supposed last confessions on the morning of his hanging. Jonah leaned out again, ignoring the hands clasping his, and strained to hear the words.

"Woman kneels before regent! Pleads for condemned man!"

He turned to Damien. "What do they mean, 'woman pleads for condemned man'?"

Damien seemed to blush a bit and looked away. "Perhaps you should ask her yourself."

He frowned, unable to picture Miss Hathaway as the woman being described. Suddenly, he had to know. Seeing he would get no more from her brother, he gestured out the window. "I want to read one of those papers."

"They may very well exaggerate things."

"If I can't get anything out o' you, I'll get it from the press."

Damien considered. "Very well." He leaned across Jonah and signaled to the man. "Give me a paper." He fished out a tuppence and held it aloft.

The broadsheet was handed to someone in the crowd and passed along until it reached the coach and Damien handed back the coin. He ducked his head back into the coach, pulled up the window and drew the curtain. He scanned the front page before handing it to Jonah. "Here, the full story, hot off the press."

Jonah took the limp, damp sheets from his hands, suddenly afraid of what he would read. Would he be *able* to read it? The smell of wet ink reached his nostrils as he looked at the headlines. He didn't have to go far. A caricature showed a skinny woman kneeling, her hands folded in a begging gesture, a corpulent prince seated on a throne before her. "Please, Your Royal Highness, Save my Lover."

He swallowed an oath and peered at the smaller print beneath. He breathed a sigh of relief when he was able to read it without too much difficulty.

The caption read "Woman in Love Saves Prisoner's Life."

After exhausting all pleas, Miss Florence Hathaway, spinster, got on her knees in a passionate plea before the prince regent, proclaiming that she loved the convicted forgerer, Jonah Quinn. She begged for a royal pardon, claiming she would die of a broken heart if the regent did not grant her request.

The prince, moved by the woman's sincerity, issued a royal pardon, declaring he was a sentimental fool when it came to matters of the heart.

The story went on to describe Jonah's escape from the hangman. Jonah laid the paper on his knees and stared at Damien.

"Is—" His voice came out a croak and he had to begin anew. "Is this true what she did?"

Damien met his eyes across the coach. "In essence."

Jonah looked away from him. He swallowed. "Does…she…love me like it says?"

"She loves you as her brother in Christ, I can certainly attest to that."

Did he feel a twinge of disappointment at the reply? "But, the words…make it sound like she loves me…as a…man." He felt his own face grow warm. The sheer presumption of even voicing the words made him squirm. Damien would have a right to call him out.

"I don't know what my sister's feelings in that regard are toward you. You shall have to ask her yourself." The words were gentle.

Jonah dared to look at Damien. Could they be words of encouragement? "That wouldn't displease you?"

"You are a man after God's heart. You have proved yourself stalwart and true. No…it wouldn't displease me if I found you cared for Florence as deeply as this story makes her seem to care for you."

Jonah could only nod his head and look away again, his throat too full to speak.

Could it be possible Miss Hathaway loved him?

Florence knew exactly when they were back. She heard the commotion at the front door as the Nicholses greeted the returning hero. She gave a grim smile, knowing she would soon have to exit the sanctuary of the study and face him, offering him her congratulations and welcoming him back as if nothing more had happened but the miracle of his release.

She glanced down at the bits of tea leaves floating at the bottom of her cup. With hands that trembled, she set down the cup and saucer.

She heard their voices, her own name mentioned once, as if they wondered where she was. Finally, the voices quieted and footsteps trooped by her door and on down the corridor. She could imagine how Mrs. Nichols would set a cup of tea before Jonah, inviting him to sit at the place of honor at the kitchen table and have him recount all that had happened to him, and tell him, in turn, all that had occurred to get his pardon.

She clutched her hands together, feeling frozen to her chair. She knew she must rise and make her way there. The first moments would be the hardest, and each successive one easier, as they once again took up the threads of their lives the way they had left off before Jonah had turned himself in.

She started when she heard the door handle move. Relief that it must be Damien quickly evaporated when she glimpsed Jonah's broad shoulders first, then his entire person, standing there, alone.

She could hardly breathe. Her hand to her throat, she could only stare.

What was she to do? She couldn't hide anywhere. She couldn't run. Slowly, she rose.

She felt a wave of dizziness pass over her so she thought she would faint. Her hand crept to her mouth, stifling the cry she wanted to give.

"May I come in?" His voice was low, diffident.

She could only nod. There was nowhere to retreat. She stood by her chair, her hammering heart drowning out all other sounds.

He closed the door softly behind him and stood a moment looking at her.

She couldn't for the life of her look away. What was she telling him with her eyes?

He began to walk toward her, his steps hesitant. When he stood only a few feet from her, he gestured with his hand at himself and said with a shaky laugh. "I don't think you can do anything to repair my coat this time."

Her gaze traveled downward, over his now gray and crumpled cravat and to the plum-colored coat, filthy and stained.

"Soap and water won't be enough to ever get the dirt out of it," he said, when she said nothing.

Her eyes traveled back up to his face. Dark stubble covered his jaw. His black hair was tousled and his clothes were rumpled, the same ones he had left in, so neat and polished that day.

"It…" She tried to say, *it doesn't matter,* but her mouth refused to form the words. Her lips began to tremble and to her dismay, her eyes began to fill with tears. She could cover her mouth, but she couldn't stop the tears from flowing.

He looked worried. "There now, don't cry for me. I'm a free man now, thanks to you."

She could only shake her head and try to swallow back the sobs, but to no avail. She sniffed and that led to a sob escaping her. She turned away, but he was there at her side. There was nowhere to hide.

"I'd offer you a hankie, but I'm afraid mine's too filthy," he said with a nervous laugh.

"I—I—thought to ne-ne-ver see you again—not on this Earth," she stuttered between sobs. What was the matter with her? She felt her heart would burst. She felt more nervous than she had before the crowd in the prince's palace. She swiped at her eyes. "I—I—I'm sorry!" She bowed her head but her shoulders shook and she couldn't stop the tears. She groped for her handkerchief.

He took hold of her arms and turned her around to face him. She fought him at first, trying to evade him, but he only stepped closer, his body large and solid, planted square in front of her. Then he drew her to him and she found herself unable to resist sinking against his broad chest. "There, now, you'd best have your cry." He held her so gently, his hand patting the back of her head, the way Damien would. She should be happy with that.

She clutched the lapels of his coat as the tears continued to roll down her cheeks. Relief flooded her in a way that she'd never anticipated. She'd known she would rejoice in his liberty and ability to make a new life for himself. But she'd never imagined the reality of seeing him again in the flesh.

"I'm…I'm s…so sorry for the w…ways I've treated you. I…I w…was an awful example to you of what a Christian should be, always harping on your manners and criticizing you—"

"Now, none o' that. You did what you had to. No one ever cared enough for me to push me to do better. You were like steel sharpening me." His arms closed around her, warm and firm…and, oh, so real.

As her crying abated, a sense of peace and contentment began to replace the distress and remorse she'd felt at seeing him again. His arms tightened their hold. She breathed in the smell of him—the sweat, the sheer presence of him. She loved him, all of him, and didn't want to change anything.

"You'll probably have to burn this coat."

She shook her head, weak laughter now mixed with her tears. "No, no!"

"And probably shave my scalp again."

She glanced up in horror. Not his beautiful hair, which curled around his head. "No, absolutely not!" Unwittingly, she raised her eyes to his and found herself caught by those green eyes fringed by the thick black lashes. They held humor and joy in them.

She could sense the moment his look changed. "Did you mean what you said to the prince?" he asked, his voice a soft burr above her.

She dabbed at her eyes with her handkerchief. How much did he know? Had Damien told him all? "I said...a lot of things."

"Did you mean them all?" His look allowed her no concealment.

"I can't remember all I said." She lowered her eyes, feeling her face begin to heat as she pictured herself once more kneeling before the prince, shedding all pride, all dignity, as she confessed her secret love for Jonah. She began to back out of his embrace.

His arms tightened around her like iron bands. "Not so fast."

Her eyes flew to his. *He knew.* "What are you doing?"

"You're going nowhere till you tell me all."

She swallowed. Was he going to use his knowledge to lord it over her? "I told you I can't remember everything."

"Liar." His fingertip came up and lifted her chin. "You're not a coward, Florence."

How could she tell him the truth? Surely, he would laugh.

"You told him you loved me."

Could she trust him with her heart? With the
depth of her feeling for him? Could she lay herself
bare to him the way she had done to the regent? All
these questions rushed through her mind as she
scanned his eyes. But she could read no mockery in
their green depths. He looked as serious as she did.
She lowered her head and spoke against his chest.
"I don't make a habit of lying." She tried making
her voice as pert as usual. Instead it came out
sounding strained.

"Did you mean it as…a sister…or as a…woman?"

Her gaze returned to his and once more, she was
lost in it. Before she could answer, he said, "Could
you ever love someone like me? I'm nothing…and
you…you're a lady."

She tightened her hold on the lapels of his coat.
"You sell yourself short. A lot of women could love
a man like you."

"But could *you?*"

She knew in that moment she could never take
back the words she'd said to the prince. "There was
a whole roomful of persons who heard me say the
words." There was a trace of defiance in her voice.

He reached up a hand to cup her cheek but
stopped short of touching it though she yearned for
the contact. "Oh, Florence." It finally registered that
this was the second time he'd called her by her
Christian name. His voice was filled with awe.

"You are truly a fine man, Jonah Quinn," she whispered. "Any woman would be proud to love you."

His eyes gazed into hers warmly. "But I want only the love and regard of *one* woman."

They looked at each other a moment longer. Then, slowly he bent his head and closed the space between them. His lips touched hers and she felt herself suspended in a place where there was no safe retreat, no firm ground on which to stand, only a need she could no longer deny.

His kiss was as tender as she could have desired. She leaned into him. How long she'd dreamed of this moment.

She brought her arms up to wrap around his neck, seeking to draw him closer to her. He seemed almost afraid of touching her. He suddenly drew back and she almost cried out. Had he changed his mind? Had her kiss disappointed him? All her old fears rose up. How could she have thought to please him? He couldn't want a woman like her.

But he only gazed at her, concern in his eyes. "I hurt you before. Forgive me, my love."

My love. Her heart thrilled at the sound of the endearment on his lips. His eyes reflected the sentiment of the word. Slowly, she shook her head. "You didn't hurt me." She remembered that night, the taste of the blood on his lip. She touched the corner of his mouth where only a tiny scar remained. "I think I hurt you, though."

He grinned. "I thoroughly deserved any pain you caused me." His expression became troubled again.

"I meant to hurt you...to punish you, and that's not how it's meant to be between a man and a woman."

She searched his face. "Show me...how...it's... supposed to be..."

"Are you sure, love?"

At her tentative nod, his hands came up to frame her face. "I shouldn't...not until I've washed and shaved..."

As he continued to hesitate, she leaned forward. "No. I've waited too long...and died a thousand deaths in the last week."

His eyes looked into hers. "You..." His voice thickened. "No one has ever...done so much for me as you have...since the day you met me." His eyelids closed over his eyes and his voice broke.

"I would have done more if it meant your freedom...even if it meant having to give you up..." Her own eyes filled with tears.

"Oh, Florence. I only hope I can be worthy of your love."

Her fingertips touched his lips. "Shh." And then, with a boldness brought on by her wish to reassure him, she brought his face down to hers and touched her lips to his.

He needed no more encouragement. After a moment, a chuckle erupted deep in his throat. "You're doing just fine," he murmured.

"I'm not—"

But he didn't let her say anything more as he deepened the kiss. His mouth began to explore hers, and Florence marveled as the mystery of the love between a man and a woman began to be revealed to her.

She touched his rough jaw and fingered the cleft in his chin. Could this man really want her as she wanted him? Could he be feeling what she was feeling? Her fingers traveled up into his thick hair and pulled him closer.

As if her touch was all the prompting he needed, suddenly she was being caressed in a way that left her in no doubt what he felt for her.

Breathless, they broke apart a fraction. She sniffed and tried to wipe her eyes, realizing how wet her face still was from crying. "I'm a mess," she protested. She brought her handkerchief to her nose as he loosened his hold enough for her to manage.

She half turned from him and blew her nose and wiped her eyes. Suddenly, she was so afraid of what he'd see. Her hair was mussed, her eyes and nose red.

As if understanding her fears, he touched her chin and turned her around to face him again. "You're a beautiful woman, Florence Hathaway." He reached out and smoothed the loosened hair around her temple before drawing her back to him. When he held her once more captive within his embrace, he looked down at her and shook his head, a humorous glint in his green eyes. "I still cannot fathom how a lady like yourself can even look at the likes o' someone like me, but I pray to the good Lord that He'll keep you blinded for the rest of your days."

She returned his smile tentatively, her eyes tearing again.

"I've received your brother's blessing to, well…" Again his skin took on a ruddy look. "To ask for your hand…if, that is, you'll have a lout like me."

She swatted at his arm. "I'll not have you calling yourself such names."

His grin widened. "I suppose you'll be bossing me around unmercifully and I'll do your bidding like a meek slave."

Her smile disappeared. "I'm probably too independent to make you a good wife. I shall have trouble being fully submissive." She pursed her lips in mock annoyance. "Although, I've come to admire and respect you so much, I'll probably defer to you in everything and you will lord your authority over me."

He touched her cheek with infinite tenderness. "I suggest we meet halfway and be true partners, deferring and consulting with each other in all things."

She returned his smile. "I submit to your wisdom."

He drew her to him again and, with a shout of laughter, picked her up and whirled her around. "God be praised! He has saved me from the noose and given me the best woman on Earth!"

Florence joined in his laughter, tightening her hold around his neck, and thanking God for His infinite mercy and grace.

* * * * *

QUESTIONS FOR DISCUSSION

1. What does the title of this book mean in a literal sense? In a metaphorical sense? When Florence attempts to train Jonah to resemble a gentleman, what kind of transformation is she really seeking, even when she doesn't realize it yet herself?

2. Although Florence is a compassionate woman who is deeply committed to helping the inmates of Newgate, why does she find herself so intolerant of Jonah Quinn?

3. There were three very distinct classes in British society in regency times: the lower class, an emerging middle class and an upper class. To which do Florence and her brother belong? Jonah? The rector and the duke? How do these levels influence Florence's view of each of these individuals?

4. How does Florence's view of her own place in society affect her view of Quinn and her emerging feelings for him? How is this view at odds with her Christian view?

5. How does Florence's relationship with the Reverend Doyle aggravate this sense of class distinction?

6. What are some of the biggest hurdles Quinn faces in transforming himself into a gentleman?

7. In drawing a parallel with the experience of a person when he/she first comes to Christ (being born again), what are some of the challenges new Christians find in changing some of their behaviors or breaking old habits? And how are they sometimes viewed by their new Christian community? Do more seasoned Christians occasionally make the mistake of measuring a new Christian's progress by outward benchmarks?

8. How does Damien's Christian witness differ from Florence's? Why does it seem easier for him to accept Quinn and his shortcomings?

9. Why is entering the boxing match and winning it so important for Jonah? What kind of approbation do we Christians seek from the world and how does the Lord deal with this need in us?

10. Jesus told his disciples in Matthew 16:25, "For whosoever will save his life shall lose it: and whosoever will lose his life for my sake shall find it." How is this literally applied in Jonah's case?

11. How does having to come full circle in his life (from the hangman's noose to the hangman's noose) serve to prove God's love to Jonah?

12. Why is it necessary for Florence to have to confess her emotions before a whole crowd, including the prince regent? How is this a liberating experience?

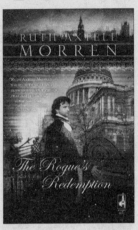

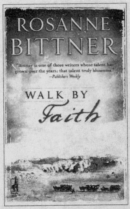

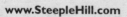

Deborah Raney

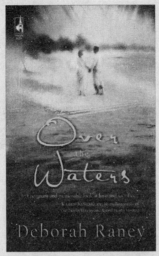

In the Chicago suburbs Dr. Max Jordan has a lucrative business giving Botox injections to wealthy women while fuming over his son Joshua's "wasted" charity work in Haiti with orphans. After Joshua's death, Max flies to Haiti to try to understand why his son chose to work there. While volunteering at the orphanage, Max meets Valerie Austin, whose broken engagement and frustrated longing for children led her to Haiti, too. Sparks fly, and soon Max is reexamining his life's work and his interest in his son's Christian faith.

Steeple Hill®

Available wherever books are sold!

REQUEST YOUR FREE BOOKS!

2 FREE INSPIRATIONAL NOVELS
PLUS 2
FREE
MYSTERY GIFTS

Love Inspired.
HISTORICAL
INSPIRATIONAL HISTORICAL ROMANCE

YES! Please send me 2 FREE Love Inspired® Historical novels and my 2 FREE mystery gifts (gifts are worth about $10). After receiving them, if I don't wish to receive any more books, I can return the shipping statement marked "cancel". If I don't cancel, I will receive 4 brand-new novels every other month and be billed just $4.24 per book in the U.S. or $4.74 per book in Canada, plus 25¢ shipping and handling per book and applicable taxes, if any*. That's a savings of over 20% off the cover price! I understand that accepting the 2 free books and gifts places me under no obligation to buy anything. I can always return a shipment and cancel at any time. Even if I never buy another book, the two free books and gifts are mine to keep forever. 102 IDN ERYA 302 IDN ERYM

Name	(PLEASE PRINT)
Address	Apt. #
City	State/Prov.	Zip/Postal Code

Signature (if under 18, a parent or guardian must sign)

Mail to Steeple Hill Reader Service:
IN U.S.A.: P.O. Box 1867, Buffalo, NY 14240-1867
IN CANADA: P.O. Box 609, Fort Erie, Ontario L2A 5X3

Not valid to current subscribers of Love Inspired Historical books.

Want to try two free books from another series?
Call 1-800-873-8635 or visit www.morefreebooks.com

* Terms and prices subject to change without notice. N.Y. residents add applicable sales tax. Canadian residents will be charged applicable provincial taxes and GST. Offer not valid in Quebec. This offer is limited to one order per household. All orders subject to approval. Credit or debit balances in a customer's account(s) may be offset by any other outstanding balance owed by or to the customer. Please allow 4 to 6 weeks for delivery. Offer available while quantities last.

Your Privacy: Steeple Hill Books is committed to protecting your privacy. Our Privacy Policy is available online at www.SteepleHill.com or upon request from the Reader Service. From time to time we make our lists of customers available to reputable third parties who may have a product or service of interest to you. If you would prefer we not share your name and address, please check here. ☐

LIH08R